co-WRECKER

MEGHAN QUINN

Published by Hot-Lanta Publishing
Copyright 2017
Cover design by Meghan Quinn
Photo credit Lauren Perry
Formatting CP Smith

This ebook is licensed for your personal enjoyment only. This ebook may not be re-sold or given away to other people. If you would like to share this book with another person, please purchase an additional copy for each person. If you're reading this book and did not purchase it, or it was not purchased for your use only, then please return it and purchase your own copy. Thank you for respecting the hard work of this author. To obtain permission to excerpt portions of the text, please contact the author at meghan.quinn.author@gmail.com

This book is licensed for your personal enjoyment only.

All characters in this book are fiction and figments of the author's imagination.

www.authormeghanquinn.com

Copyright © 2017 Meghan Quinn
All rights reserved.

DEDICATION

To all of the Whitney Pointers in my life. Thank you for teaching me what true friendship is all about. I love you all.

co-WRECKER

CHAPTER ONE

ANDREW

"Why do you have a box labeled calculators?" Jimmy asks, setting my precious box on the stripped twin mattress in the middle of my tiny room.

Kicking the mattress to the side, I say, "Did I ask you to look at the boxes? Just move them."

"Please tell me when you wrote calculators on this box, it's actually code for porn. There's porn in this box, right, Andrew? If I were to open it up, I would find a smorgasbord of boobs bouncing in barns and miniscule generic football jerseys on altered plastic chests."

Rolling my eyes, I rip the tape off the top of the box, stick my hand inside and pull out my TI-84 EZ Sport graphing calculator, garnering a severely disappointed look from my brother.

"Dude..."

I push my thick-rimmed glasses back on my nose and say, "Who needs a box of porn when everything is practically free on the Internet?"

Exhaling roughly, my brother nods his head. "I'm glad to hear you have some man left in you. For a moment, I was starting to think you were sleeping with your calculators."

Only when I'm doing homework late at night and I'm lonely, but Jimmy doesn't need to know that. Waking up with a SIN COS button imprint on my cheek signifies a fulfilling night.

"I think that about does it," Mae, my brother's quirky girlfriend, says, brushing her hands off on her high-water khaki pants. She's a beautiful girl with long legs and a love for all things Star Trek. How my brother found her—*and keeps her*—I have no idea, but he's a lucky guy. "Do you want me to hang your curtains for you?"

Given the size of my small bedroom in the six-bedroom house, I'm shocked I have two floor-to-ceiling windows. The minute Mae saw them, she bought navy blue curtains to match my life-size Derek Jeter cutout.

That's right, calculators and Derek Jeter. I'm a man of odd interests. But please note, I don't have an infatuation with Derek Jeter. I'm a huge Yankees fan. Born and raised. Ever since my great grandpa got lost in the Yankees locker room, back when kids wandering in ballparks was acceptable, our family has sworn to love and praise the Yankees every year, even during the rough times . . . like the eighties. Such a terrible era for the pinstripes.

"Sure, hang the curtains." Mae gets to work while I try to decide how to situate my room.

"Mom and Dad are on their way," Jimmy says, arms crossed and leaning against the doorway, giving me more space to move my bed, dresser, and desk around, the only pieces of furniture in my room.

Sighing, I answer, "I know."

"They're going to try to convince you to move home."

"I know."

"They're not thrilled about you living two hours away after everything you just went through."

"I know," I snap, not wanting to hear Jimmy repeat what I've been listening to for the past few months. Trying to reassure my brother, I look him in the eyes and say, "I'm not changing my mind."

"Are you sure?"

"Yes."

"Hello?" My dad's voice travels up the staircase, causing me to cringe.

Jimmy grips my shoulder. "Be strong." Then he calls down the stairs, "Up here, Dad."

From the other side of my thin wall, the stairs creak, indicating my parents' approach. I've been dreading this moment for quite some time, ever since I made the executive decision to go against my parents' wishes and jump right back into school after "the ordeal." Transferring to Binghamton University was easy given my GPA and the honors I'd earned, but getting my parents on board was another story. Being the youngest man in my family and the one with a "sensitive brain," my parents wanted me to take a semester off, live at home, and recoup. But I had different plans. I didn't want to hide away. I wanted to continue to move forward with my education. That's why I transferred to Binghamton, the beautiful armpit of New York, enrolled in the engineering school at Binghamton University, and found a job for the summer until classes started.

"Oh these stairs are deathly," my dad complains, making his way to the top where he grips the doorway, pushing Jimmy to the side. His eyes scan my room, which takes about two seconds given its size. Tsking, he mutters, "This most definitely won't do. Where are your housemates? You're switching rooms."

"Dad, I can't switch rooms. This is what was given to me."

My mom joins the party and takes a look around as well. "Nice molding," she grunts, putting her hands in her pockets.

Sounds about right coming from her. She doesn't say much, but the woman knows fine craftsmanship when it's in front of her.

"You're just going to take what was given to you? How is that fair?" Before I can stop him, my dad stomps around the second-floor landing where three other doors are connected and starts throwing them open, revealing much larger rooms. "This is preposterous. Look at the size of these rooms." Turning on a dime, his hands at his waist, he asks, "Are you paying the same amount of rent as everyone else?"

"Yes, Dad," I sigh, knowing this conversation isn't coming to an end anytime soon. "I don't just pay for my room, I pay for the common areas as well. It was the only place I could find with such short notice. And the girls are really nice," I add.

"Girls?" My dad's eyebrow lifts.

Uh yeah, did I forget to mention that part? From the look on my dad's face, as well as Jimmy's—and Mae's for that matter—I guess I did. My mom on the other hand is less than fazed. She's more interested in the smooth texture of the 1920s solid-wood molding than my little announcement of shacking up with five women.

Yes, five.

And I know what you're wondering, how many bathrooms. Rest assured, there are two . . .

Two . . .

Oh shit, I'm fucked.

Visions of clogged drains with rat-nest hair plugs start dancing in my head. The horror.

Swallowing hard, I nod, "Yeah, Dad, girls."

"What kind of girls? Is this a sorority?" Jimmy starts chuckling, which garners a slap to the back of the head from Dad.

"It's not a sorority, Dad."

"Then what is it?" he asks, arms crossed over his conservative button-up shirt.

I know what you're thinking: I'm hiding out in a sorority. I'm the guy that goes through an "ordeal" and decides to hide within the labyrinth of females and their hair nests, perfume-soaked carpets, and beastly hormones that are bound to calculate together for a monthly tirade only the wrath of the devil serpent himself can compete with.

That couldn't be further from the truth.

The reason I'm living with a bunch of women is because it really was the last option in housing. My choices were either live with five women, which would be against my father's conservative ways of seeing the world (men and women live together when they're married . . . cue the eye-roll), or spend the next year shacking up with who I can only describe as Gollum's drunk, pinball-playing uncle. Graduating with honors is important to me, and Uncle Gollum didn't seem like the kind of guy who would leave me alone, especially given the entire time he was giving me a tour of his dwellings, he couldn't stop circling his bellybutton with his middle finger. Five girls would be less of a distraction.

At least I hope so.

"Well?" my dad asks, pushing for an answer.

Sighing, I say, "It's not a sorority. It's the starting lineup for the women's basketball team at Binghamton."

I'm a tall man at six foot, but these girls either match my height or are slightly taller than me. When I first met them, I was intimidated, and then they started talking with heavy European accents and I was intrigued. Two girls from Finland, one girl from Latvia, and one from France. The fifth girl, the only other American in the house, she said they were looking for another American to take up the sixth room because the girls wanted to improve their English.

My dad's eyebrows test the limits of his forehead. "Basketball." He leans back on his heels and thinks about his next sentence carefully, hands in his pockets now. "Basketball," he repeats and then leans forward. "Do you think they could get us free tickets to games?"

Rolling my eyes, I get back to unpacking my boxes. "Games are free anyway, Dad, but glad to know where your head's at."

"You're not romantically involved with any of these girls, are you?"

"No," I answer quickly, avoiding eye contact with him. I don't want to see that look on his face, the *You shouldn't be dating anyone right now* look.

"Because if you were—"

"I'm going to stop you right there," I say, gripping my brand-new spiral notebooks purchased for the fall semester. "I came to Binghamton for one reason: to finish my degree and pursue my master's in computer engineering. I have no intention of frolicking around with the Amazons of Binghamton's sports world."

"I didn't ask about frolicking, son. I asked if you planned to have sex with them."

Holding up his finger, Jimmy interjects, "Technically you asked if he was romantically involved with any of them. Sex was never part of the equation, but now that you've thrown it out there, are you going to bone them, Andrew?"

Another slap to the back of Jimmy's head.

"Don't say bone," Mae says while fluffing my newly hung curtains. "Andrew is clearly not the boning type." A smirk peeks past her mouth.

"I've boned!"

Although, my boning is limited. Very limited. Boning lately has been with my hand, and it just doesn't feel like boning—feels more like self-mutilation, especially when you lack lotion.

And let's be honest, spitting on your hand really doesn't do the trick. It might for some people, but I just don't have excess saliva to provide sufficient lubrication to avoid chafing.

"Who have you boned?" my dad asks. My mom is now on the ground, checking out the original hardwood floors. Did I mention she's into wood? And I know where your head went just now, wood equals penis. Ha ha, my mom likes dick.

"I'm not going to talk about my sex life with my family. Can we just unpack boxes and then get some Nirchis Pizza?"

"I'm ready for pizza." My mom stands and brushes off her hands, looking around to see who's with her.

Yes, wood and pizza. My mother's interests are wide and varied.

Shaking his head, my dad opens a box, starts unpacking my clothes, and then places them in drawers. "I just don't understand why you needed to come down here so early. You could have spent the summer with us in Middleburgh and helped at the shop. We would have paid you."

"Paying people in fudge is not paying people, Dad," I deadpan.

"I said I would pay you in fudge and hugs."

"Oh hell." Jimmy steps up and raises his hand. "I didn't know hugs were involved. Shit, sign me up. Forget Sears, I'm in."

"Don't be a smartass." My dad goes for another smack to the back of Jimmy's head but he ducks out of the way and loops his arms around Mae for protection.

Jimmy has been working at Sears and paying his way through college ever since his freshman year. It's taken him some time to earn his education, and he scrimps every penny he has, but he's determined to graduate debt free. He's in his last year of earning his master's in Special Education. *He* can see the end. I'm glad I can spend one year with him in the same town before he graduates.

"Did you hear back about the job?" Mae asks, changing the topic.

"I did. I got it." I puff my chest a little. My first job.

That's right, I'm going to be a junior in college and finally have my first job. Don't judge. Did you hear the part about being paid in fudge? Ever since I can remember, I've worked at my parents' shop—sans *bankable* pay. It was time I ventured out into the real world and learned about the work force. When I heard from Stuart, the manager at Friendly's, that they wanted me full-time for the summer as their fountain boy, I jumped on it.

This kid would be earning a paycheck that didn't consist of butter, sugar, and "fun" flavors.

"That's great." Mae cheers and claps. My dad huffs, and my mom returns to the floor examining the baseboards, realizing pizza time isn't in the near future.

"Oak," she mutters, knocking on the wood with her middle finger. "Nice."

"You got the job, huh?" my dad asks. One thing you need to know about my dad, he loves repeating sentences . . . and clearing his throat. Lord Jesus, if I ever clear my throat as much as my father, please strike me with one of your electric bolts right then and there.

"Yes, Dad, I got the job." Hear the annoyance in my voice?

"Hmm." *Clears throat* My teeth grind together and I'm almost sure a faint growl pops out of me. I'm about to explode. "What will you be doing there? Working the grill?"

"Scooping ice cream. As I said, I will be working the fountain," I answer, pulling out the rest of my school supplies then placing them in perfect order inside my desk.

"You're a . . . *fountain girl?*" The level of disgust in my dad's voice is borderline offensive.

"Fountain boy, Dad. Fountain *boy*. I have a dick; remember the whole boning conversation?"

"Are you going to have to wear one of those candy-striped frilly aprons?"

Jesus.

"No." Do not lash out at your father. I repeat, do not lash out at him. "Times have changed, Dad. I have a red shirt, a black no-frill apron to wear, and a baseball cap."

"Baseball cap, huh?" Once again, he rocks on his heels, puts his hands in his pockets, and pauses before he asks, "Think we can get free ice cream from you?"

Exhaling heavily, I look up to the ceiling and beg for patience.

Can you tell my dad is a cheap bastard?

"Oh, good question." Jimmy turns to me. "Can we get free ice cream?"

Giving up on unpacking, I step past my boxes and say, "Okay, pizza time, then you can all leave."

I can finish unpacking in silence. Well, maybe not in silence, as I might watch the game while I unpack. The Amazons won't be moving back into the house until August, so I'll have the house to myself for the summer, the perfect excuse for cranking up the game and strutting around in nothing but shorts.

My dad, Jimmy, and Mae argue but I don't listen to them and instead wrap my arm around my mom's shoulders and guide her down the stairs.

"Real nice place, Andrew dear. A stable foundation for you to start a new life." My mom gets it. She gets *me*. "I couldn't ask for a better set of baseboards for my son."

Or maybe she doesn't.

CHAPTER TWO

SADIE

I put the car in park in my usual parking spot, and rest my head against the steering wheel. Four years. Four *long* years at this hellhole and Stuart still has me training the newbies in the fountain area. You would think after four years of working for him, and the fact that my uncle is his best friend, Stuart would NEVER put me in the fountain; he should also understand my hatred for training.

Nope. He likes to torture me.

"You can do this; it's just for today and then you'll be back on the main floor racking up tips." I mentally prep myself, but dread still looms in my stomach.

Trainees. God, they are the worst.

Throwing on my aviators, I snag my keys from the ignition, toss them in my patchwork Yankee purse Smilly made me, and start to get out of my car when my phone rings.

Speak of the devil.

"What's up?" I answer, twiddling the fabric straps with my fingers. I'm not a purse kind of girl, but my best friend made this for me, therefore I use it.

"Hey, Maaaaaaaaaaaa," she yells into the phone. Yup, she

calls me Ma. "When do you get off work, again?"

"Eight. You're going to stop by, right?"

"Yeah. I'm stopping at the DG for some Doritos, dropping off your cough syrup, and then Saddlemire will pick you up later."

For those who don't speak Smilly, DG is the Dollar General and Saddlemire is her boyfriend.

"Sasquatch is picking me up? Can't promise I won't be tempted to feel up his man thigh on the drive out to your mom's."

"Hey, you do what you got to—" There is fumbling on the other side of the phone and then all I can hear is Smilly yelling in the background. "Monroe! Don't paw!" Monroe, Smilly's mom's pit bull.

"Smilly, I have to go or I'll be late."

"Okay, Ma. I'll be by later."

I hang up and make my way to the front of the restaurant, ducking my face under the bill of my hat to avoid eye contact with everyone.

Am I unsocial? No, I'm actually a pretty social person, but only with my people. Work people are not my people. Growing up in a small town, I formed a circle, a tight-knit circle of humans that I knew I could rely on. People I can *trust*. Trust being the key word.

Funny thing is when you're young and vulnerable, you *should* have two people you can trust: your parents. They are the people you're supposed to rely on, the people who are supposed to shelter you from the relentless storm we call the world. But when one of them destroys every aspect of your childhood, it's hard to trust anyone else. It's hard to let people in when your heart has been hardened to the outside world. *Why would you? Why would you make yourself so vulnerable again?*

The people who were by my side when I was a little girl, wearing Elmo shirts in middle school—yes, middle school—

sporting a bowl haircut and a black heart, they are the people I've surrounded myself with because they've never left my side, and they've never attempted to screw with my trust.

There are no vacancies in my little circle.

None.

"Catch the game last night, Sadie?" David asks from the grill as I walk by.

Okay, there may be no vacancies open in my little world, but I do put on a good face when I need to. I'm not a horribly wretched bitch.

"Yeah, Yanks blew it in the ninth. The new kids need to get their shit together," I call over my shoulder as I head to the back of the restaurant where I stuff my purse in a locker and put on my full apron just as Denise walks in.

"Fountain today?"

Denise is the mother hen of the waitresses. If I had to say I had one friend at the restaurant it would be Denise because she gets me. There is a little black in her heart too; I can see it in her hardened, stony eyes. She's a lifer at Friendly's, whereas this is a steppingstone for me . . . at least it's supposed to be.

"Yeah. Stuart didn't get the memo." Adjusting my cap, I groan to Denise, "I hate wearing these godforsaken hats. My hair get tangled in the Velcro in the back." I try to adjust my blonde, messy bun but there is no use. I'll be ripping hairs out again today.

Another plus about being a waitress, you get to wear your hair how you please and you have a half apron, instead of a full one.

"It's just for the day. It will be over before you know it." She snaps her order holder and sticks it in the front of her apron. Pointing at me she says, "But if you let the newbie make any of my customer's ice cream, I will kill you."

Laughing while wrapping the apron strings around the front of my waist, I say, "Not going to happen. I don't plan on staying late to clean up the bloodshed if that occurs. I've got your orders, Dennis."

"Don't call me that."

I chuckle to myself as I make my way past the dish-cleaning station and out to the fountain where I start assessing the toppings to see if any need refilling. I lean over the ice cream freezers and look in each topping compartment, mentally taking notes on what I need to restock.

It's routine.

Before I became a waitress, I worked in fountain for a year and even went to the Fountain Olympics where all fountain workers in the tri-state area came together to compete to see who made the best sundaes.

A moment in time I really wish I could block from my memory.

"Hey Sadie," Michelle calls from over the counter that separates the main dining area from the fountain. "Have you seen the new guy? He just arrived and is in the back with Stuart. He's yummy."

Michelle. She was born to gossip about anything that floats in her ears. Even if it's about someone breaking a toenail in the freezer, she needs to tell the story. She's my age, attends Binghamton University during the school year, loves smoking, has fake boobs, *and* she "loves to party." She's said so often, constantly looking for an invitation from me.

She has yet to get one.

"Don't you have customers waiting for you to shove your boobs in their faces?"

Giggling, she rounds the corner and pushes my shoulder. "Oh, Sadie, you're so funny. I only have families right now. I wouldn't dare do that in front of children." Scanning the dining area, she turns back to me and says on a hushed tone, "Anything going down tonight? I'm free if there is."

"Not that I know of," I answer, sealing my lips about the bonfire Smilly is having at her mom's house tonight.

She nods and continues to look around. "Well, you have my number"—I really don't—"so text me if you hear anything. I'm itching to go sans panties tonight."

So many things wrong.

"Will do." I try to hide my wide eyes. Yikes.

I can admit it; I kind of want to congratulate her for being proud of her whorish ways. It's not often you find a person who is a slut and enthusiastically promotes themselves as one too. She's tapped every guy in the restaurant, including the truck driver who brings our supplies every Thursday, and now she's trying to mingle her way into my group of friends. Yeah, no. I'll have none of that.

"Michelle, your tables are asking for you," Stuart's voice booms from behind us.

Turning around, I notice Stuart's tall and broad stature in the fountain entryway. I've known this man for quite some time so his intimidating tactics don't work on me, but Michelle is intimidated, but not to the point that she doesn't forget her slut. Puffing her chest out and flipping her hair to the side, she winks at Stuart and takes off toward her tables. She's impossible.

"Sadie, I would like to introduce you to your trainee for the week."

The week?

Uh, this is news to me.

Maybe Stuart has yet to put out the rest of the schedule. Bastard.

With a bug already up my ass, I clamp my lips shut, trying

not to mouth off to the manager.

A whole of week in fountain? That's going to be a huge hit to my bank account.

Stepping to the side, Stuart holds out his hand and says, "Sadie, this is Andrew. Andrew, meet Sadie, one of our top fountain girls."

"Waitresses." I give Stuart a tight smile and then turn to Andrew who stands taller than me in his red collared shirt and black apron. I can't help it; I give him a little scan, taking in his black tight-fitting pants and his black, worn-in Chuck Taylors. He's not going to be able to wear those for long. Moving my eyes back up, I notice his broad shoulders that seem to have decent definition to them under the hideous shirts we're required to wear, and under the bill of his hat rests black-rimmed glasses, framing a set of hazel eyes.

Hmm . . . maybe he's a little yummy.

"Nice to meet you, Sadie," he says, jumping right in and grabbing my hand that was at my side, shaking it vigorously. "It's a beautiful day out today, isn't it?"

Wow. Invigorated, this one.

"Uh, hey," I say, taking away my hand from the brutal earthquake he shook through me.

Clasping Andrew on the shoulder, Stuart says, "Sadie here is going to show you the ropes. You're in good hands. I'll be in the back if you need anything." Turning to me, he says under his breath, "Be nice."

Before he gets too far, I chase after him and say, "About this week."

Turning, he stops me in my tracks. "Don't start with me, Sadie. You're on fountain all week. You know I need you to train him. Carla is gone for the week, and I don't trust Darleen. She barely knows the difference between chocolate and vanilla ice cream."

"What about Sherry or Blaine? They've all been on fountain," I counter, wracking my brain for any waitstaff with fountain experience.

"They don't train like you do. I think this kid will be good, and I'd like him to stick through the whole summer."

Tapping my foot, my arms crossed, the feel of Andrew's eyes on my back, I say, "You know, I'm not really into nepotism here, but I'm not short of calling my uncle . . ." It's a low blow but I'm desperate here. A whole week on fountain means a significant drop in pay, which will make it difficult to store away much-needed cash this summer.

Patting my head like a dog, Stuart says, "If you call your uncle, remind him it's his turn to bring the queso dip for our billiards night on Thursday. Thanks, sweetheart." With a wink, he walks back to his office.

Well, that didn't go as planned; that didn't go as planned at all. And to hell if I'll be telling my uncle about the queso. Shows him.

Head held high, I turn toward the fountain area where Andrew is standing, shifting on his feet, looking a little too eager for my liking. Why is he so eager to be in a little area surrounded by ice cream cartons?

Sighing, I walk toward him and assess his shoes again. "Didn't Stuart tell you to get non-slip black shoes?"

We both stare down at his shoes as he wiggles his toes in them. "I kind of forgot, but I'm getting them tonight. I guess Walmart has a killer pair that will do just great."

"Sure." I take a deep breath and look around; here goes nothing. "So, we should—"

"Can I just say something?" He's bouncing on his feet; joy exudes him. I'm kind of thrown off. I've never seen someone so happy to be at work before.

"Uh, sure."

Pushing up his glasses again, with a great big smile that knocks me back on my heels—only slightly—he says, "This is my first job, and I'm really excited to be here. I mean, I've worked before, but for my parents in their shop upstate a little, toward Albany. Middleburgh actually. Have you heard of it?" I shake my head, watching his mouth move rapidly with each word fluttering out of it. "Well, anyway, it's a really small town, one stoplight and all. But they have a shop on their property and I've worked there but never really earned anything because my dad is cheap and believes in hugs as payment." That sounds like torture. "Anyway, that's all beside the point. I just wanted to say I'm super excited and ready to learn from the best." Gesturing to me, I hold in the gag beginning in the back of my throat.

Christ.

The guy definitely is cute, but his energized personality isn't going to match well with my tainted mindset.

By the end of the day I'm either going to stuff myself in the freezer with the chicken fingers, or I'm going to stuff him in there. *I'm leaning toward the latter.*

CHAPTER THREE

ANDREW

"And this is where the apples are." Slowly, with the pace of a Commodore 64, Sadie lifts the ladle of the sugared apples and then sets it down, as if it was the most difficult thing she's had to do all day.

Wow.

I kind of want to reach over and dust that chip off her shoulder, knowing that, if there is an actual chip there rather than a metaphorical one, she could turn so fast and swat me in the testicles, and I'd have no time to react.

"And these are the rest of the toppings." She gestures to the other little black bins lined above the ice cream freezers that make our part of the counter. "All directions on how to make the different sundaes are up above." She points, and my eyes follow to a few laminated sheets that are eye level for me, her not so much, with colorful sundaes on them. "Tickets from in-house will come from that printer over there. Line them up here and make them in order. If there is someone at the takeout counter, be sure to take care of them first because all waitstaff should know how to make their own sundaes if need be."

"Okay, that seems a little stressful."

Hand on her hip, a smirk on her face, a beautiful bit of a side smile, she says, "It's making sundaes, Andrew, there is nothing stressful about it." Just as she finishes casually insulting me, the printer where the in-house tickets come from starts printing. "Your first sundae, better start learning now."

Swiping the ticket from the printer she stuffs it in the ticket holding area and then turns to me, hand on the counter. "It's a make-your-own sundae. Have at it."

Uhh, I know I'm a smart kid and can program a computer by using a foreign language, and I once wrote an article about the ten most beautiful mathematical equations, but ice cream is not something I'm familiar with.

Not wanting to show my ineptitude, I put on a brave face and take a look at the slip.

Dble, straw, choc, RPiece, fudge, no cream, cherry, cherry.

Okay, not so bad. I got this. Thinking back to the Friendly's study sessions I conducted every night up until my first day, the order is for a double scoop, one of strawberry, the other of chocolate with a topping of chocolate fudge, Reese's Pieces, no whipped cream, and I'm going to assume two cherries.

Ha!

With swagger in my step, I reach for a sundae glass, throw open the freezer top, grab a scoop from the scoop water trough and scoop up a ball of strawberry. Sadie watches me, a gleam in her eyes.

What's she smirking about? I'm going to nail—

Hmm . . . I look down at my sundae glass and at the ball of strawberry ice cream stuck halfway down. That doesn't seem right.

"You seem to have yourself in a bit of a pickle, don't you?" Sadie asks, now smiling bigger than before.

"Nah." I wave her off. "Just have to convince the ice cream

to work with me." Sticking the ice cream scoop inside, I try to shove it all the way down but the glass narrows at the bottom making it impossible to get the ice cream to the very base of the glass. "Well, that seems good enough," I say, knowing it looks like shit.

I wash off the scoop and reach for the chocolate when Sadie stops me. "You can't serve that. Not only will the customer be upset it looks like you screwed them out of a full sundae, but the waitress is going to be pissed at you because something as simple as what the ice cream looks like effects their tips."

"Oh, okay. Sorry. Umm . . ." Staring at the ice cream, I do the one thing that comes to mind. "Let me fix this." Sticking my glove-covered finger down the middle of the glass, I push the cold cream to the bottom, struggling a little since my hands are wider in the glass than I expected. "There." I hold up the glass, and ice cream is smeared all over the side and distinct finger marks are poked through the sundae. "That's better."

With an emotionless face, Sadie crosses her hands over her chest and says, "You can't serve that."

"Why not? I'm not done yet."

"For one you stuck your fingers in it."

I hold up said fingers and wiggle them. "But they're covered in plastic. Nothing creepy is getting in there."

Leaning forward, she whispers, "You molested that ice cream."

"What? No, I didn't. I massaged it in to place."

"Did it ask for a massage?" She leans back now, questioning me.

Tilting my head to the side, completely confused, I ask, "Um, does the ice cream have feelings? Because if so, I would really like to know which ones are the most sensitive so I don't piss them off."

"Are you trying to be funny?"

"Is it not coming across that way? Have I unintentionally upset the ice cream again?" Whispering back to her, I ask, "Is it the pistachio? Is she the most sensitive?"

Not amused, she points to the ice cream and says, "Dump it."

"Dump it? In the trash?"

"Yes, you have to start over."

"But," I bite my bottom lip, "then it wouldn't fulfill its ice cream duty."

"Oh for fuck's sake," she huffs. Taking the sundae glass from me, she dumps the ice cream back in the carton just as a waitress walks up to the counter.

"Sadie, is my sundae ready yet?"

Looking over her shoulder, she eyes a middle-aged blonde. "Not yet. This kid apparently has some attachment to seeing out the ice cream's destiny."

"What?" the lady asks with a squint in her brow.

Turning toward her, I go to explain. "Ice cream has feelings too and if we just—"

"Andrew," Sadie taps me on the shoulder, "she doesn't need to know about your ice cream issues. Focus." Turning to the waitress, she adds, "Five minutes, Sherry."

Okay, I'm starting to get the impression that Sadie may not like me, which not to flog my own damn log, but that seems a little unlikely. I've never come across a person who doesn't like me. I'm a likeable, funny guy. Yes, I may have a collection of calculators in my small closet right now, and yes, I tend to find computers and robots fascinating, but that isn't a black mark on my personality, more like an *Oh hey, you seem interesting* mark.

Looking Sadie up and down, I can't help but notice her skinny black pants, the way they cling to her legs perfectly, or the fact that the work shirt she's wearing has to be a children's small because it's clinging to her in all the right places. And that hair. I'm just going to admit it; I'm a hair man. Some men like tits—well, all men like tits—but some like them more than others. Some men like to twiddle around the ass, whereas I'm a man who loves hair. And I know what you're thinking: Andrew likes pubes and hairy armpits. And you know what, I do.

Did you just cringe? Did I get you? I hope so. Get your mind out of the gutter. I like a head of hair and from what I can tell, Sadie has some really long blonde locks. I can't tell completely because of the baseball caps we're required—

"Are you paying attention? Were you watching what I just did?"

Oh shit. I peel my eyes away from her blonde bun and focus my attention on the sundae glass in front of her with a perfectly swirled strip of ice cream flowing all the way to the narrow tip of the bottom. How the hell did she do that?

"Uh . . ." Say something smart, something intelligent, say something that's not going to piss her off. "You have nice hair." Her eyes narrow on me and I cringe. Nope, not the right thing to say.

"Were you staring at my hair this entire time?"

"If I said yes, would you take that as a compliment?" I give her my most charming smile with an added push of my glasses up my nose.

"No. I would think you were a creep."

Hmm . . . really not making a good impression here.

"Okay, then, uh, I blacked out for a second."

Setting the sundae glass on the counter, she repeats, "You blacked out for a second."

"Is my sundae ready?" Sherry interrupts.

Not even bothering to look behind her, Sadie holds up her hand and snaps, "Not yet, Sherry."

Leaning forward, I whisper, "I thought we didn't want to piss off the waitresses."

Raising an eyebrow, she asks, "That's what you paid attention to?"

Taking a deep breath, I try to reel this conversation back in. "Listen, I think we got off on the wrong foot. It seems like you're angry at me for some reason."

"Not at you. Mad at life."

Well, that explains things.

Before I can even offer something remotely empathetic, she rolls her eyes and says, "Now pay attention. In order to create a good sundae, you have to flare the ice cream with the scoop to create a corkscrew to fit it down to the bottom, and then you do the ball scoop on top."

For the next two hours, I stick closely to Sadie, watching her flare technique, trying to keep up with the orders, restocking of toppings and ice cream, as well as serving dishes, and ignore the fact that no matter how many jokes I crack, I can't seem to break through the wall she's built up around her.

Tossing a rag on the island in the middle of the fountain area, she says, "There's a bit of a lull right now, why don't you restock the chocolate and then wipe down the counters? I'll man the counter and ticket machine."

"Okay."

Taking her direction, I head back to the freezer where the ice cream is, bypassing the grill and the waitstaff station where side salads are prepared and soup is poured. Sal is at the dishwashing machine, listening to his music while bobbing his head away. As I scoot by, he gives me a head nod, just like all the other times and I return the gesture. I never formally met him, just a nod in passing, but he seems like a nice older man. Apparently he's been working the dishwasher machine for ten years. Doing dishes for ten years, now that's dedication.

The freezer is full of food ready to be fried and ice cream ready to be scooped, not to mention it's cold as balls. Luckily, it's not one of those freezers you see in movies and TV shows where people get stuck. No, there is a handle on both ends, which is reassuring because now I don't have to worry about some creepy initiation of someone locking me in the frigid cube.

Sifting through the boxes of ice cream, I find the chocolate and head back to the fountain area, nodding at Sal and nearly running into Denise, the head waitress, who Sadie specifically told me not to fuck with.

I don't know what she thinks I'm planning, but fucking with people is not on the to-do list while I'm at work.

"Watch out, sweetheart. You don't want to trip and fall on your first day, now do you?" Denise asks, carrying her tray away from me.

Tripping and falling on the slippery floors is also not on my to-do list. Although, I do see why the non-slip grip shoes are required.

Making my way back to the fountain area I find Sadie talking to a customer at the counter. Letting her handle the order, I get to work on replacing the chocolate ice cream, which requires scraping the sides of the old carton, pouring the remnants on the new carton, and changing the boxes out. It doesn't seem like an ordeal, but it is.

In the midst of my scraping, I can't help but overhear Sadie's conversation with the customer who I'm assuming is a friend by the casual chatting and the way Sadie isn't taking her order.

"Thanks for bringing my cough syrup. I need it." Cough syrup? Sadie doesn't seem to be sick. Maybe it's preventative.

"Rough day?" the girl with the short brown hair and eclectic clothing asks.

"Yeah." From the perch of me pretending to mind my own business, I can see Sadie sneak a glance at me and then speak softly, but not softly enough. "I have to train this annoying guy today."

Annoying! When have I been annoying today?

Flashbacks of our few hours spent together float through my mind.

Jokes about sensitive ice cream.

Walrus straw guy.

Fingering the ice cream.

Bumper cars in confined spaces—yeah, she didn't like that one all that much.

Maybe there were some annoying *instances* . . .

"He's cute. What's his name?"

Cute, huh? I would go with hot, handsome most of the time, elegant only when I'm in the shower, and of course sexy when I'm reciting all the elements from the periodic table, but I will cut the girl a break since she doesn't know me yet.

"You have a boyfriend," Sadie whispers.

"I know, but I can still look. What's his name?"

"I don't know. Adam?"

Adam? Now that is insulting. I know her name. I know her favorite ice cream—strawberry—because I asked five times until she told me. And dare I say it? I know what her face looks like if she has to pee because every time she's wandered off to the bathroom, she's scrunched her nose right beforehand. Scrunched face equals Sadie has to pee. I'm observant, I understand this, but she should at least say the right name while talking to her friend.

Knowing I will probably regret this, I lift from the freezer, ice cream scraper in hand, and jerk toward Sadie just in time to slip on some melted ice on the floor shooting me across the fountain and straight into Sadie.

But not just Sadie; straight into her chest—her billowing, womanly chest. It's a satisfyingly soft cushion for my head but from her instant outrage, I'm going to guess she's not keen on me using her breasts as a pillow.

"What the hell are you doing?" she asks, trying to back away, difficult when I've got her pinned against the counter.

Fumbling to get some kind of grasp on my falling body, scraper still in hand, I give her a bit of motor boat—not on purpose—and muffle in her breasts, "I'm sowwy."

"Get off me."

"I'm twying," I say, finally getting a grip on the counter behind her and standing tall. Glasses askew, hat on the floor, and a smothered feeling on my face, I straighten my apron and clear my throat. "My apologies." Her friend is laughing, hand on her stomach, as I push my glasses back on my nose. "Although, I'm grateful for your sturdy bosom for catching my fall. It might have been a twisty straw to the eye, and I'm not sure my glasses would have held up on such an impact."

Sturdy bosom? Shit, Andrew, don't fucking say words like bosom. And for the love of God, don't say a woman has a STURDY bosom. Say words like tits. Tits are more manly.

"Tits," I mutter.

"Excuse me?" Sadie has the look of horror on her face.

Fuck, did I say that out loud?

"I think he said tits, Sadie," her friend cuts in, thumbing through the straw holder. Yup, I said tits out loud.

"I heard him, Smills," Sadie mutters under her breath.

Glaring at me, looking for an answer, I shrug my shoulders, because I have nothing. No way of digging myself out of this one. Funny how your brain can literally stop working the minute you need it the most. Come on, old fella, kick it into high gear.

Come up with something witty, something snarky, something that will put a Band-Aid over this rather raw and embarrassing incident.

But, good fuck. I just had my face in her chest. What man could come back quickly from that?

"Well . . ." Sadie has her arms crossed over her *bosom*, waiting for an answer. *No. Her arms are crossed over her breasts.* Shit. *Shit.*

Nerves crawl up the back of my neck, igniting my ears into lava levels of heat. Crap. Just say anything.

Clearing my throat, I pat her shoulder and say, "Sturdy tits."

And here I thought it couldn't get any worse, at least my hand didn't pat down her breast to see if her nipples were made of steel, or to see if her areolas consist of chain-link mesh. You have to look at the positive.

Leaning forward, Sadie moves in, inches from my face, a slight hint of vodka on her breath—huh? "Plant your head in my 'bosom' again, and I will be sure to use your dick as a straw for a milkshake."

Gulping, I ask, "Can you make it a strawberry milkshake when you do? I tend to favor the pinky flavor." She lets out a long huff of breath and just to make sure I'm securely buried in my grave, I add, "And it seems like your cough syrup is full of alcohol."

"Thanks to you," she mutters, brushing past me, knocking my shoulder in the process.

Real smooth, dickhead.

Silence falls over the fountain area, leaving me with Sadie's friend. Pointing a straw at me and then sticking it in her mouth, she says, "I like you, Adam."

Tossing her purse over her shoulder she heads for the door.

"It's Andrew." To myself, I repeat, "It's Andrew."

Yup, great start to your first day at your first ever job. I'm a real winner.

CHAPTER FOUR

SADIE

"Sturdy tits is here, everyone," Smills calls out from her lawn chair circling the bonfire.

Walking up to her, I plop down on the grass and say, "Don't call me that."

"I don't know; it's really starting to tickle my fancy. Sturdy tits, it fits you."

I let my hair loose from the messy bun I had it in all day and bring my knees to my chest, looking past the flames. What a freaking long day.

"Why are we calling Sadie sturdy tits?" Saddlemire, Smilly's boyfriend asks as he sits next to me, beer in one hand, a tonic in the other for me.

"Oh, she didn't tell you on the drive over here? Why would you deprive him of such a story?"

Sipping down the classic Gatorade and vodka combination, I say, "Maybe because I didn't think it was worth mentioning."

"Anything about tits is worth mentioning," Saddlemire answers.

Rolling my eyes, still looking out into the fire, I say, "The new kid I had to train today slipped and fell into my chest, then proceeded to tell me I had a sturdy bosom."

A burst of laughter pops out of Saddlemire as well as Smilly. Glad I could amuse everyone.

"Oh shit, he really said bosom?"

I nod as Smilly says, "He did. I was there. When you left, Sadie, I told him I liked him. You should have invited him out here tonight. He looks like he could be a good time."

"No," I answer point-blank. "I'm not in the market for new friends."

"Who's talking about friends?" Smilly asks. "He's a looker. He's got that whole hot-nerd vibe going for him. Bet you he's got Clark Kent superpowers under those glasses of his. Never know until you take him to a phone booth and strip him down."

"Not going to happen."

Shoving my shoulder, Saddlemire says, "Look, she's blushing. She likes him."

"I do not," I shoot back.

"Oh my God, you so do. Sadie likes Adam."

"It's Andrew," I correct, causing both Smilly and Saddlemire to open their mouths in surprise and laugh. They exchange knowing glances. Annoying glances.

"You *so* like him."

"They're practically engaged," Saddlemire adds.

"I'm telling you right now, I don't shop registries so don't expect me to get you something from one."

"I do," Saddlemire points out. "Do you want the vacuum cleaner or the gravy boat?" Shrugging, he takes a sip of his beer.

"Hell, I'm going for the bath towels."

"No, get the bed sheets. That way we can take advantage of them when we house-sit for them."

"Smart thinking." Saddlemire winks at Smilly and then they both take a sip of their drinks.

Annoyed, I stand and say, "I'm out."

"Aww, come on, Sadie. We're just teasing." Pausing, Smilly smirks. "I'll make sure Saddlemire gets the gravy boat. I know how important it is to you."

Flipping them off in the least ladylike way, I brush off my butt and head toward the house where I know I'll find Emma straightening up and taking care of all the drunks in the group. Despite drinking my "cough syrup" at work, I have zero buzz. The minute Andrew figured out I was drinking at work, I felt so damn guilty. I stopped. Hence the shitty attitude I have right now.

Andrew.

Ugh, why does he have to be so . . . so . . . *annoyingly* attractive.

Yes, I admit it; it doesn't hurt the eyes to look at him. It's the exact opposite actually. It's that damn smile of his, so innocent, so sweet and caring. No guy should have a sweet and caring smile. They should be devastating, almost cocky, not sweet and caring. And his eyes. They were kind, inquisitive, and interested in every freaking word I had to say. Every word I had to say about making sundaes. MAKING SUNDAES. Who cares that much about ice cream? It was almost like he didn't care about the topic, but rather just enjoyed listening to me, which made me uncomfortable. I don't want someone caring about what I have to say. *I especially don't want someone I can't read in my circle.* Is he actually intelligent beneath the sweetness? Or as dim-witted as I thought on first meeting him?

I have my people. Anyone else in the mix will just throw my life into a tailspin.

You must be thinking, *what a bitch,* right? This girl has a nice guy who has done nothing but act genuine, and yes, he might have motor-boated me a little, gave the balloons a little helium lift, but he didn't mean to. I get it, he's a good guy; it's obvious. But this is what I know . . .

I know the value in relationships, platonic and romantic, and I don't take advantage of them. I don't just walk into them on a whim, pulling in the positive. I can't. Being burned does that to you.

Broken woman, you ask?

You can say that, but I like to say realistic.

I've seen what a relationship can do to a person. I've seen it happen to my dad. I've seen his world get flipped upside down by my mother. I've seen a woman cut ties with all her children for a life never to be talked about. I've seen it firsthand. My dad curled up inside himself, and pushed my sisters and me into therapy. Rather than talking to us. Rather than listening to our thoughts.

I've had the comfort of trust and love ripped right from my hands and heart.

I don't live in the sky, dreaming of all the possibilities this world has to offer me. I'm a realist, someone who sees the world as it is: dull and grey with limited potential.

That's why I keep things to myself. I have my friends. They know my past, they accept me for who I am, and they let me be the realistic, slightly crotchety girl in the corner. No need to change anything about that. It works.

Opening the screen door, I make my way into the house where I call out Emma's name, looking for a ride home. I know she won't mind taking me to my car at work. She usually doesn't stay too long at these parties.

"In the bathroom, Sadie," she calls out. "Might need your help."

Setting my drink down, I head down the narrow hallway and turn the corner to the bathroom where I see our pretty and very smart friend, Amy, naked ass in the air, bent over the tub and drinking from a straw. With a small wave, she says, "Hey Sadie, come on in."

Let me explain. Amy is going to school to become a doctor. She shared the valedictorian title with me in our graduating class. She's incredibly intelligent, very book smart, but give her a drink and she becomes the hot-mess express, selling tickets for everyone to see.

"Amy, what do you have going on there?" I ask, resting my shoulder against the doorway.

Lips quirked to the side in disappointment, she says, "I sat in some poison ivy."

"How did you do that?"

Emma pulls her head from under the sink cabinet and shakes a bottle of calamine lotion. "She saw fireflies and decided to chase them."

Yup, your future MD right there. Frightening, isn't it?

"They're like fairies." There's a mystical awe in her voice.

"They're bugs whose asses light up. Come on, Amy."

Shrugging her shoulders, she continues to sip from her drink, not a worry or care in her right now. She'll regret it tomorrow morning. She always does. It will be the classic Amy Apology. She sends out her group text apology for "acting immaturely" and then begs us not to mention anything to her mom, who would scare the stash off Hitler. It's okay to have a Hitler reference here; she's that scary.

"Do you plan on leaving anytime soon?" I ask Emma, who's doing a very gentle job dabbing at Amy's ass. Why she has poison ivy on her actual butt, I have no clue. I really don't want to know.

"Didn't you just get here?" Emma asks.

"Yeah, but I'm not feeling it tonight. I need a ride back to my car."

"You're leaving?" Amy whines. "We haven't even had s'mores yet."

"Next time." I plaster on a fake smile and then say, "I'll wait for you in the car, Emma."

"Okay, give me a few minutes."

Making my way past plastic cups, bottles of Hawaiian Punch, vodka, and a keg, I navigate toward Emma's red Jetta parked off to the side so no one could block her in. You can always count on Emma for a ride.

"Leaving so soon?" That deep, rough, rustic-filled voice. I stop in my tracks. Of course he would be here. Why wouldn't he? He never misses a get-together with our friends.

Leaning against the base of an oak tree, arms crossed over his chest, a beer in one hand pressing against his strong bicep is Tucker, the one boy I can't seem to shake.

"Not feeling it tonight," I say, still making my way to Emma's car, hoping to avoid any interaction with Tucker, but from the rustling of grass behind me, he's following closely behind.

"Need a lift home?"

"Not from you," I answer, now leaning on Emma's car, giving off serious stay-away vibes.

Rounding the hood of the car, he approaches me with such swagger in his step that I have to look at the overgrown grass to stop myself from staring. Easily, without even trying, he can hypnotize me. He's done it more than once, leading me, once again, into another volatile, toxic relationship. Sometimes two broken souls can heal each other, but in our case, we nearly destroyed one another.

"What's going on in that pretty head of yours?" His broad body stands directly in front of me now, one hand in a pocket, the other dangling at his side, holding his beer. His rough scruff is highlighted under the moonlight, and the loose-knit hat he wears on his head only previews a few strands of his dark hair.

He takes another step closer.

"Just a long day," I answer, now looking at my clasped hands.

He moves in even closer. His body is almost pressing against mine, and a mix of our breaths dance between us. A sharp scent of his signature cologne spices my nose. Reaching out, he runs this thumb along my cheek, and I let him for only a second.

"Don't," I warn, but don't pull away because my will isn't strong. *It never has been. But surely I've learned. Surely I can repel his charms . . .*

Not listening, he steps even closer so our bodies are pressed against each other. "I miss you, Sadie."

"Tucker," I sigh, warning him.

"Come on, Sadie." He leans forward and runs the tip of his nose along my jaw, his scruff occasionally scratching my skin. "Give us another chance."

His voice, so primitive and needy, catches me straight in my heart. We've been through so much together. He knows my past. He knows what haunts me. He knows what buttons to push to turn me into mush. He's addicting, yet fatal in every way. *To me.*

"No, Tucker." With every ounce of strength I have, I place my hands on his chest and put distance between us. In response, he nods his head and sips his beer, looking out toward the bonfire.

"It's not going to be that easy, Sadie, letting go." Tell me about it. "You're my best friend—"

"No, I'm not. Don't say things you don't mean."

"I do mean it," he replies, a little anger in his voice. "Growing up, you sheltered me, you gave me a home. You were my first, and you taught me what love is. You're everything to me, Sadie."

Not the first time I've heard him say those words, and it's not the first time they've dug a deeper hole in my heart.

"We're not good for each other, Tucker. We drag each other down rather than lift each other up."

"It's just because we have history."

"No, it's because we're toxic to each other."

"Are you ready?" Emma calls out, unlocking her car, making it beep a few times, probably trying to scare Tucker away. She's not a fan of us, never has been.

"Yeah," I answer, my eyes still on Tucker.

"We're not done here," he warns, taking another sip of his drink. And hell, I wish that wasn't the truth, but for some reason, it feels like the pull between us will never cease to exist.

Not answering him, I get into the car and buckle up, clutching my bag to my stomach.

Emma, the quasi-older sister, starts clucking out her opinion. "I don't like him for you. He's bad news, Sadie."

"I know," I sigh, looking out the window.

"He's always been bad for you, and you deserve more than that. He just smells of trouble and divorce."

Chuckling, I shake my head. "Are you always thinking about marriage?"

"It's okay to have family goals, you know."

Large trees of the back country pass by as Emma drives down the winding road that I could drive with my eyes closed. "Not everyone is meant to have a family, Emma," I answer her solemnly.

"You don't know that," she counters.

"I do," I answer on a sigh. I know very well actually. "I don't plan on ever having a family. No need to bring children into this fucked-up world."

Emma pauses as the car comes to a halt at a stop sign; turning to me, she places her hand on mine and with kind eyes, she says, "You're not your mom, Sadie. You know that, right? You would never do to your family what she did to yours."

Gut churning, throat tightening, I decide to change the subject because I'm not ready to get into this deep conversation right now. "How about we talk about something else."

Understanding, Emma returns to driving, handling the stick with precision. With a little more light in her voice, she says, "I heard you have a new nickname, sturdy tits."

"Oh my God." Softly pounding my head against the headrest, I try to escape the relentless, yet loving, teasing of my friends. Of course, Smilly would tell everyone about sturdy tits. And of course, everyone would follow suit by calling me it.

Stupid fountain training. Stupid—and slightly adorable—Adam . . . *Andrew.* It's his fault. Sturdy. Tits.

CHAPTER FIVE

ANDREW

Bouncing back and forth from one foot to the other, I hold a bag close to my chest and look around behind me, swearing someone followed me. How long does it take them to open a damn door? I pound on the wood again.

Hurry up. Hurry up.

I go to knock again just as the door flies open, Jimmy on the other side, his glasses perched on his head. I don't give him time to greet me. I burst through his door, shove the bag in his hands, close the door, and press an eye up against the peephole, looking for anyone who might have followed me from Friendly's.

"Hey, psycho, what the hell are you doing?"

"Checking to see if anyone followed me." Who invented the peephole? They did a terrible job. They should have made them significantly bigger. They should have made them for spying, not just peeping.

"Do you really think you're that important?" Jimmy asks from behind me.

Giving the parking lot to the apartment complex another once-over—or perhaps it should be called a twice-over—I declare the space clear and turn toward my brother. "Call me paranoid, but I've never stolen ice cream before."

I've never felt so nervous or scared in my entire life while I scooped up some sundaes to take to Jimmy's apartment. Everyone does it, takes a sundae home on occasion, but doing it my first week, that's just risky. I had no choice. I was *forced* to listen to Jimmy beg and plead for some ice cream, so I caved.

"You're fine," he says condescendingly, taking the stolen frozen treats into the living room where Mae is playing Super Mario on the Nintendo NES she's had since middle school. "Did you get me extra peanut butter sauce?"

"Yes." I roll my eyes and sit on one of the stools at the kitchen bar that looks over the living space. "World seven. Nice, Mae, I'm impressed."

"Don't talk to her," Jimmy says. "She knife-handed me in the throat earlier for throwing off her concentration."

Without taking her eyes off their little thirteen-inch tube TV, she says, "When you come over to the TV and start dancing naked with only a washcloth over your dick, I'm going to knife-hand you."

Chuckling, I say, "Sounds like you deserved it, man."

"Not when I was giving her some of my best moves. It's not easy dancing, your dick twerking on its own, and having to keep a washcloth from falling off your rod. She should have praised me."

"No one wants a dick twerking in their face." Mae presses pause on the game and turns toward me with a smile. "Hey Andrew, how's sturdy tits?"

"Come on," I groan, my hands scrubbing my face.

Laughing, Mae comes up to me and pats me on the shoulder. "I'm sorry, but I've been dying to ask you ever since Jimmy told me about your first day."

"Thanks, Jimmy."

A mouthful of ice cream, he answers, "Hey, I hold nothing back from my lady."

"Is this mine?" Mae asks, popping the top off a soft serve sundae with chocolate syrup and brownie bites.

"Yup, mine is the strawberry one with fudge." She hands me my cup and I dig in with the both of them.

"So, have you had any other instances with sturdy tits?" Jimmy asks.

"Her name is Sadie, and no. She was supposed to train me all week but she switched her shift somehow, so I've been working with some guy named Blaine. I'm sure he's the president of the douche committee and unfortunately, I know he's trying to recruit me."

Yeah, the switch in training partners was a bit of a surprise to me, especially since I knew Stuart was adamant about Sadie training me. The next day when I saw Blaine in the fountain area instead of Sadie, I started sweating profusely. I feared Sadie told Stuart about my little slip into her bosom, and that I'd be fired, but as the day went on, Stuart never approached me. Even after four days, he hasn't approached me. And it's not like she quit. No, I get to see her every day working the main dining area, acting all sweet and cute with her customers. Too bad I never got *that* Sadie. She's almost as cold to me as ice cream.

Instead, I get douche-canoe Blaine, who prefers to tell me endless stories about his fraternity than teach me anything about the fountain area.

And I know what you're thinking. Don't you have to make Sadie's sundaes when they come in as a ticket? You would think. But before I can even grab the slip from the printer, she's pulling the ticket herself and making her own desserts.

"Do you *miss* her?" Mae teases.

I shrug. "Not really. I would prefer her cold shoulder to

Blaine's endless high fives though." Imitating his douche voice, I hold up my hand and say, "Soft serve ice cream refill. Yeah, bro."

Laughing and shaking his head, Jimmy says, "There is no way he high-fives over soft serve ice cream."

Mouth full of soft serve, Mae adds, "Hell, I want to high five right now over this creamy delight, so I don't blame him."

I mean, if Blaine wasn't such an annoying douche, I really might have high-fived him with enthusiasm because I agree with Mae, soft serve is the shit.

"So sturdy tits isn't giving you the time of day?" Jimmy asks.

"*Sadie* is in her own little world, and honestly, I have no plans to get to know her." That could be a partial lie. I can't deny the attraction; it's there in full force every time I see her, but Jimmy and Mae don't need to know that.

"Then why have you been harping about her in text messages? All I here is Sadie this and Sadie that. Dude, you have something for her."

Did I really mention her that much? Note to self: tone down the Sadie talk around Jimmy.

"You know Dad will have an aneurism if he finds out you're getting frisky with someone—"

"I know. I don't need to be reminded, and I don't plan on dating her or getting frisky as you so immaturely put it." Sighing, I stir my ice cream carefully, making a bit of an ice cream soup. "I just don't like it when someone doesn't like me. You know that. And it's clear as day she doesn't like me."

It's true. I have some sick obsession of needing everyone to like me. It's not healthy, not even in the slightest. But I've come to realize and accept my faults. So, *twiddles fingers together* how do I get Sadie to like me?

"Why do you want to please everyone?" Jimmy wiggles his

eyebrows at me.

Rolling my eyes, I get up from my stool and toss my ice cream in the trash can, as it's melted to shit. "There is no reason for Sadie to hate me. I did nothing wrong—"

"She fell victim to your motorboating within the first few hours of meeting you," Jimmy points out, a shit-eating grin on his face.

"She hated me before that, dickhead. Falling into her was just the nail in my coffin."

"So why care?" Mae asks, licking her spoon. "I say just be done with it."

Easier said than done.

"Because," I sigh, "there is something dark in her eyes, something that has hardened her to become the person she is today. I can see the pain, and I don't know, I just want to figure out why she's so angry, why she can't genuinely smile at a stranger. And maybe, just maybe, I can help her learn to smile again."

"You do like her." Jimmy points at me.

"Christ, can't I just be a good guy?"

"With your history, there is no way you can just be friends with this girl."

"He's right," Mae adds. "I love you, Andrew, but you've never been able to be just friends with a girl. You always hand over your heart."

"That's not true. What about Stephanie? She's my friend."

"She's a lesbian," Jimmy deadpans. "She doesn't count, there is no romance blossoming there, no matter how much you think you're capable of helping her cross over."

"It's not a choice," I chastise my brother, supporting my rainbow flag for my friend. "It's what's in their heart."

"Dude, I was kidding. Step down from your soapbox. Jeeze." Tossing his ice cream in the trash as well, he wipes his mouth with a napkin. "All I'm saying is there is no chance you're not going to fall for this girl. You should see your face when we talk about her."

"Only because she's new and interesting. Just watch; not only am I going to make her smile again, but I will do it by being one of her best friends. Anything between us will be strictly platonic. Mark my words."

•••

Shit, why does she have to be so damn hot?

Friends. We are going to be friends. Do not watch her bend over. Do not stare at her ass. Do not envision her naked. Nope, not happening.

Think about computers. Computers, computers, computers . . .

Recite the seven layers of the OSI model. Go!
Physical Layer.
Datalink Layer.
Sadie's eyes are pretty.
Network Layer.
Transport Layer.
I wonder what her lips would feel like on mine.
Session Layer.
I bet her skin is soft.
Presentation Layer.
I really like those pants on her.
And of course, the Application Layer.
There, I did it.
"Did what?"

Sadie's voice breaks my thoughts. Standing in front of me, putting on a fountain apron, she studies me, looking for an answer.

"Uh, the seven layers of the OSI model."

"What?" Her brows knit together in confusion.

Really winning points here, Andrew. Get your shit together.

"It's on my nerd bucket list. It's actually on all nerds' bucket lists, to program all seven layers by yourself. What an accomplishment that would be."

Leaning forward, bringing her girly scent closer—God, she smells like a fucking dream—she sniffs me. "Are you drunk right now? I asked you what needs to be stocked, and you start stammering like you're having a stroke."

"Do you find it endearing?" I ask, for some self-deprecating reason.

Studying me for a second, an odd look on her face, she shakes her head. "Not even in the slightest."

Shit, there goes being cute. Focus on being friends.

"Uh, what are you doing over here? I thought you were working the dining room today."

"Blaine called in sick. You didn't answer me." She finishes tying her apron and is now putting her luscious locks under a hat. "Is everything stocked?"

"Uh, yup," I answer like a doof.

"Good." She huffs and looks around. "I don't know why Stuart puts me on fountain when it's this slow."

Lamely, I answer, "Me either."

Silence falls between us as we awkwardly stand in the middle of ice cream and toppings, not knowing what to say to each other. Literally, nothing is coming to my mind right now. I never have this much trouble coming up with something to say; I'm always the person who can't seem to shut up. But Sadie is so different. She doesn't follow the unspoken social etiquette that forces us all to make small talk and pretend we're enjoying it.

Sadie doesn't fuck around, as she wears her feelings on her face. You can tell when she wants nothing to do with you.

Right about now, that's the vibe I'm feeling.

I go to open my mouth to ask how her night was, because I honestly can't think of anything else, when Stuart comes into the fountain area and plops an economy-size squirt bottle of bleach on the counter. Nodding to the corner, he says, "It's slow, clean the milkshake wall."

In horror, both Sadie and I turn toward the corner where the two milkshake mixers rest against a plastic, milk-encrusted wall.

Why is there something called a milkshake wall in the restaurant, you ask?

When I first saw it, I was caught off guard—maybe dry-heaved a bit—unsure why there would be a section in the fountain area that looked like little Smurfs came and jizzed all over the area. But then I made a milkshake for the first time.

There is a certain technique to get down when making a milkshake. Not too much milk and if you have to make one with soft serve ice cream—also known as a Fribble—be prepared to be splashed. I have yet to not spray milk all over the place when making one. And when you get busy, you forget to clean up, *and* the crusting process begins. And after a few crusted overspills, you start to develop a surface that milk continues to bounce off, reaching down the length of the wall until you coat the entire thing.

"Brushes are under the counter. Get to work."

Stuart walks away and I'm about to ask Sadie how we should go about cleaning it when she puts her hand on her hip, looks at me and then down at the bleach bottle. Implying . . .

"You don't expect me to clean the wall by myself, do you?"

"Listen, I've had my fair share of days spent scrubbing that crust. You're the newbie, you have to earn your stripes."

Yup, could have guessed she was going to say something like that. Tough as nails this one.

Putting on a good smile, I snag the bottle and say, "Not a problem. Care to supervise?"

"Nope."

"Okay, care to sort the straws then? That's the only thing I haven't done yet."

Eyeing the straws, that have been mangled to no longer accompany their like sizes, she huffs out a long breath and nods. Lucky for me, the straws are right next to the milkshake wall so I can attempt a conversation with her.

"So, plan on drinking any 'cough syrup' today?" I give her a wicked smile, letting her know I'm joking around.

"Don't tempt me," she replies.

"Do you always drink at work?"

Leaning close, she says, "Can you not say that so loud?"

"I didn't shout it, but I can if you would like." I take a deep breath to let it rip when she covers my mouth. The feel of her hand over my lips is everything perfect, like I just solved Euler's identity.

"Don't you fucking dare."

And then the most marvelous thing happens. The smallest of smiles appears at the corner of her mouth, and when I say small, I mean a hobbit came along, latched a fish hook to the corner of her mouth, and barely tugged on it. It was minuscule, brief, but I caught it and it gives me hope. Maybe she doesn't hate me all that much after all.

Point for me.

Pulling away, I chuckle. "Better watch yourself, I might blow your badass cover."

"If you did, I wouldn't be surprised."

I sit on the floor to gain better access to the wall, scrunching together in the corner, trying to fit my larger body, which is proving to be quite difficult. "You sure you don't want to do this? I don't want to take away the pleasure of scrubbing soured and crusted milk away from you."

"I'm good," she answers.

"All right, but don't come crying to me when—" I pop the top to the bleach bottle and accidentally squeeze it at the same time, shooting bleach out of the bottle—like a pre-mature ejaculation—straight onto her extra black, perfectly fitting pants.

Fuck. Me.

Not even bothering to look down at me, her eyes fixed on the straws, she asks, "Did you just get that all over my pants."

Now I could say no but in a few hours, she will know it was a lie from the tie-dye creation on her black khakis.

"If I said yes, what will happen to me?" I cringe, hoping she doesn't try to take me to the freezer in the back and castrate me.

Sighing, she reaches into her pocket for her phone and starts texting someone.

Straightening up, I ask, "Calling in a hitman?"

"No, asking my friend to bring me more cough syrup."

Pocketing her phone, she turns and heads to the bathroom.

Shit.

Sadie: 1. Me: -50.

Best friends . . . not so much.

Scratch that.

Probably never.

CHAPTER SIX

SADIE

Is there something inherently wrong with me? Why can't I stop chuckling when I think of Andrew's face when he sprayed me with bleach? The utter devastation in his eyes, like he just accidentally spilled holy water on the devil. So comical. I know I've been a little hard on him, but for good reason. He's one of those guys who can easily suck you in. Just with that smile of his, he's a lifer, someone you know you'll never be able to "phase out" of your world. He sticks like superglue, never letting up.

But still . . . I chuckle some more. God, he looked so cute, absolute shock and regret in his expression.

Shaking the memory out of my head, I grab a sack of fudge and head out of the stockroom where I see Andrew talking to the guys on the grill.

"There is no way in hell Giancarlo Stanton holds a candle to Derek Jeter. Are you insane?" Andrew pleads. "First of all, they are nowhere on the same playing field. You can't compare a shortstop and a right fielder. On fielding percentage alone, Derek Jeter outweighs Giancarlo."

My eyebrows rise in interest. Andrew speaks baseball? I never would have guessed the hot nerd with tempting forearms would like baseball, let alone hold his own in a conversation.

"Baseball isn't about fielding," David says while flipping a burger on the grill. "It's about home runs, everyone knows that. It's what brings in the crowd."

Visibly shaking, Andrew responds with so much passion, I almost want to go give him a hug. *Almost.*

"Are you insane? Baseball isn't about home runs. Maybe for the guys who mask their flaws behind a bat. True baseball, the good kind of baseball, is played with intelligence, with well-thought-out moves. It's like an equation: you have to put all the pieces together to get the perfect solution, a win. You can't just stock your roster with home-run hitters and believe you're going to win every game. Every player is essential in their own way from the catchers, to the fast left-handers, to the big home-run hitters. Without every piece to the puzzle, you'll never go anywhere. I mean, look at the ninety-six Yankees. That team was full of a bunch of no-names and might arguably be one of the best rostered Yankee teams in history."

"Ninety-eight, Yankees," I say, barging in on their conversation, pulling a surprised look from Andrew. "Ninety-eight Yankees are arguably the best team in history."

"Ah, there's my girl. I knew you could smell a Yankee conversation from anywhere," David says, flipping a burger.

"You're a Yankees fan?" Andrew asks, a little perplexed.

"You're an idiot if you're not." With my fudge, I head back to the fountain area, my heart beating a little faster than normal.

So he likes the Yankees.

That doesn't change anything.

But why does it feel like it's thawing the icy wall *I* erected around me to avoid any kind of conversation with him? And why did I just think he has tempting forearms? His forearms are normal man arms. Nothing special about them.

Nothing.

Although, when he scoops ice cream, the way they flex . . .

"Are you a real Yankees fan, or a flyby fan? I mean, did you even cry when Derek Jeter retired?" Andrew asks, putting a stack of sundae glasses on the center island, which is really just a metal table.

"What kind of question is that?" I'm squirting fudge into the pumper when I answer him. "If I know about the ninety-eight Yankees, wouldn't you know I'm a real Yankees fan?" I pause for a second and then add, "And if you didn't cry then there is no hope for you in life."

"I don't know." He steps up to me, challenge in his stance, and pushes up his glasses, his sincere and beautiful whiskey-colored eyes looking down at me. God, he really is good-looking. "If I asked who your favorite player was from the ninety-eight Yankees, would you be able—"

"Bernie Williams. An understated player. Full of class, talent, and the drive to win for his team, not for himself. So easily overshadowed in his career being surrounded by the Core Four, which honestly, he should have been a part of."

Mouth agape, Andrew stares at me for a second. Ha, bet he didn't expect that answer. Don't test me on my Yankees knowledge; I will slaughter you in that department.

Clearing his throat, he says, "Bernie, huh? All right," Nodding his head, he stops and sticks up his finger and says, "I bet you don't have his CD—"

"*The Journey Within*? I have a signed copy." I smirk; I can't help it.

"Oh yeah." Hands on his hips now, he thinks for a second. "And his birthday . . ."

"September 13, 1968, which was a Friday actually, in case you were wondering."

"Well, what about Tino—"

"You mean Constantino Martinez, born December 7, 1967, the first baseman for the Yankees from 1996–2001 until he came back in 2005? What about him?"

Huffing in frustration, Andrew scratches the top of his hat, looking for any kind of fact to stump me.

"Listen, I'm going to stop you before steam starts pouring from your ears. I know everything there is to know about the Yankees. I've read every book, every autobiography, watched every film, seen almost every game since I can remember, subscribe to the YES network, and I've collected their baseball cards since I was five. I have a mind of steel, and it's full of useless baseball facts. Your challenge is just going to end up frustrating you more than anything."

He sits back against the counter and studies me, his arms crossed over his chest. A chest I can't seem to stop myself from glancing at. There is something about this guy that is a stark contradiction to the vibe he portrays. His heart and mind give off the goody-two-shoes vibe, one I don't mind, but one that doesn't mesh with my belief that the world hates me. And then he stands there and . . . smolders at me. Yes, smolder is the correct word. Thick-rimmed glasses framing his hazel eyes, right above that pronounced jawline—he's kind of devastating actually.

"Uh, not to be rude or anything, but are you okay? It almost looks like you're having a stroke. Your face isn't moving and your tongue is doing weird things with your lips. Do you need to sit down?"

What?

Oh my God, I was just staring. And what was my tongue doing?

Shaking my head, a flush of embarrassment staining my cheeks, I turn back to the fudge and tend to it. "Fine. Just thinking about something."

"What were you thinking about?" he asks, stepping up next to me and helping me with the fudge bag. Immediately my body heats up from his shoulder brushing against mine. What is happening to me?

"Nothing," I snap, bouncing off him, giving us some room.

"Whoa." He sticks his hands up in the air. "I was just helping."

"I've poured fudge in the pump before," I say, stepping up to the pump again to finish the job.

"Oh, I know, but with the whole tongue thing you were just doing I thought you might have needed a little bit of help. Are you sure you're okay?"

Squeezing from the bottom, I move the fudge carefully into the pump, focusing on the task at hand. "I'm fine, okay? Just put away the glasses."

"Okay." Turning away from me, I hear the distinct sound of him stacking glasses again. "If I had to be honest, it's kind of badass that you know so much about baseball. I don't think I've ever met anyone who knows that much."

"It's just useless facts." I don't want to accept his compliment, because if I do, the warming sensation flowing through me will turn up a notch. Am I really this pathetic? The guy says he likes the Yankees and all of a sudden I see him as a new man? A very attractive man, one who I wouldn't mind seeing with his shirt off, maybe scooping some ice cream with those forearms of his . . .

No! Oh my God, no. Get that thought out of your head right now.

But . . . Andrew's forearms scooping ice cream.

"Still, it's pretty cool. Have you been down to the stadium to see a game?"

I can't help but chuckle. Facing him now, I lean against the counter and say, "Every year on my birthday, my friends and I go watch a game. Cheap seats, of course, because who can really afford the lower seats?"

"Yeah, especially as a college student, but talk about a dream day—lounging in those executive seats, getting waited on while hobnobbing with the players. Man, that would be a fucking amazing day."

A shiver runs up my spine. Why did I like it just then when he cursed? It so easily rolled off his tongue, that it makes me wonder if just maybe there *is* a little hint of a bad boy under his exterior. Maybe.

"It would be. Have you ever—?"

"Hey, Maaa!" Smilly's voice rings through the takeout counter, shocking me out of the interesting conversation with Andrew. "Brought you your cough syrup."

Smilly slaps the drink on the counter as a small snort comes from Andrew who starts putting away sundae glasses again.

I toss the empty fudge bag in the trash and head over to Smilly who's now sitting on the counter. When I reach her, she hands me the Gatorade bottle I know isn't full of Gatorade.

"Thanks. I didn't think you were going to be able to stop by. Didn't you have to take care of the twins?"

"Sandy got home early." Looking out toward her car, she says, "Uh, you might want to go see what I have in my car. I have to hit up the bathroom."

She hops off the counter and starts walking away when I stop her. "Wait, what are you talking about?"

"Just go out to my car." With that, she takes off toward the bathroom, being beyond evasive. I've known this girl forever, so why do I still expect more from her?

Slightly annoyed, I remove my apron and put it on the metal

island, then say to Andrew, "I'll be back in a second. If Stuart asks, I'm in the bathroom."

"Taking your cough syrup with you?" he asks, a smirk on my lips.

"No, but help yourself. You're looking ill," I throw at him as I walk away.

The muggy heat of upstate New York hits me the minute I step outside. I'm convinced humidity is the devil's creation, preparing us sinners for the afterlife. Given how unbearable the summers can be, there must be a lot of sinners in New York.

Smilly parked her car right next to mine and before I can even guess what she's talking about I see him.

What the hell is he doing here?

Wearing a threadbare T-shirt, worn jeans, and a few leather bracelets, he approaches me.

Tucker.

Fuck. I'm going to kill Smilly.

Not wanting to cause a scene in front of the restaurant, I meet him by the car, which is off to the side and out of hearing range.

"Hey, beautiful," he greets me.

"Tucker, what are you doing here?"

"Good to see you too, Sadie." Without my permission, he pulls me into a hug, but I don't let him hold me for more than a second.

Straightening up, I ask again, "What are you doing here?"

"Truck is in the shop. Smilly was the only one not working who could pick me up."

"Okay, well, I don't know why she told me to come out here." Literally going to kill her.

"I asked her to send you out here. Listen," he takes a deep breath and pulls me into him by the loops of my pants, "I know our last break-up was rough. I'm working on some things, some things I should have worked on a while ago. My head hasn't been straight for a while and I can now see how that's affected my relationship with you. I want you to know I'm working on it."

"Tucker, it wasn't just you. It was me too. We're not compatible. Not long term."

"You don't know that," he says. "We haven't shown each other our best selves. Let me get my shit together, and I'll show you I can be the guy you need."

"The guy I need? How do you know the kind of guy I need when I don't even know what that is?"

Hell, I have no idea what I want these days. Apparently superb forearms are on the list though.

Pulling me in closer, his arms around my waist now, he presses a kiss against my forehead, attempting to melt my cold exterior—and possibly my heart. "Sadie, I've known you almost your entire life. I've been there for you through thick and thin, and you think I don't know what you need? I can read you better than anyone."

He used to be able to read me better than anyone, but now, I don't think he can. I'm not the same person I was in high school. Hell, I'm not the same person I was a few months ago. I really have no clue who I am, and truthfully, that's what is most terrifying.

He tries to lift my chin but I step away, needing to put distance between my past and me. "Tucker, I don't even know who I am anymore. I can't jump into another relationship with you." *I won't.*

His eyes soften as he puts his hands in his pockets. "You didn't have to drop out of Cornell, Sadie. We could have made it work."

Shit, I don't want to talk about this, but from the look in his eyes, it seems like I don't have an option.

"No, we couldn't have." I shake my head. "I was killing myself to get decent grades before I got pregnant. There was no way I would have been able to keep my grades up with a baby. And all the expenses." I shake my head, "Every last cent I had was going toward tuition."

"I told you I could have helped you. I wanted to help you. You wouldn't let me."

"Because I didn't want you to feel obligated to me," I shout, a little louder than intended. I grip the bill of my hat, because I need to do something with my hands to calm myself. *Why is he so persistent? Yes, we have known each other for years, but surely he can see we need to stop this merry-go-round.* "I don't want to have this conversation right now. I have to get back to work."

As I start to walk away, Tucker calls out, "The miscarriage wasn't your fault, Sadie."

Without turning around, I answer back, "Sure as hell felt like it."

The last thing I want to do right now is cry, but with Tucker showing up at work—and bringing up a past I very much want to forget about—my eyes are stinging, brimming with tears.

"Shit," I mutter, making my way back to the restaurant. Going through the front doors, I bypass Smilly who is talking to Andrew and go straight toward the stockroom where I try to catch my breath. Images of that horrid night flash through my mind. Waking up in a pool of blood, not knowing why, unsure of what to do, who to call. The blinding, life-altering pain coursing through me. So scared. So damn scared. *Yeah, it sure as hell felt like it.*

I grip the shelves in the stockroom for stability as I squeeze my eyes tight, trying to rid the images.

Let it go. Let it go.

Taking deep breaths, I try my best at calming my racing heart and easing the tension from my shoulders. *Why? Why did she drop by with Tucker? Why do that to me?*

Breathe in, breathe out. Just like that.

"Are you okay, Sadie?" Andrew's broad frame shows up in the doorway of the stockroom, his voice full of sweet concern.

"Fine." I turn away from him so he can't see my face. I'm on the verge of tears, and there is no way I want him to see that.

"Okay." He's silent for a second before saying, "Not to be a dick or anything but you didn't seem fine when you came charging in here. I know what fine looks like and that wasn't fine."

This guy.

"Notice the tone, Andrew. I don't want company."

"Ah, yes, you do sound like you want to be left alone. I'm going to be honest, though. I don't like seeing people upset but I can hear the tension in your voice. I don't want to piss you off anymore. Just know, it pains me having to leave you alone right now. I really don't like it." *He doesn't like it?*

Where has he come from that despite the bitch I've been toward him, he "really doesn't like" leaving me alone?

"I'll be fine. Just give me a minute." Ugh, I hate that I now want him to stay. Why does he have to be so nice? *Why would he not like seeing me upset? He's so confusing.*

"Okay. Can I just ask you one thing?"

"What?"

I hear him step forward and whisper, "Would you like me to bring your cough syrup to you? Seems like a cough syrup kind of moment."

Simultaneously, a light snort pops out of me, a tear falls down my cheek, and a laugh bubbles up my throat. Turning toward him, my hand hovering over my face where I snorted, I nod at him. "Cough syrup would be perfect right about now."

His smile stretches from ear to ear, causing a warm wave of affection to wash over me. As he winks at me and takes off toward the fountain area where my *syrup* waits, that's when it hits me.

Calm.

I feel calm.

How is it possible that one of Andrew's smiles can make me feel a little more at ease? Is it those kind, sweet eyes of his? Or the way he seems to understand what I need at the moment, even though he presses me further than I would have wished? Whatever it is, it's possible he's working his way into my world and I'm not sure I'm ready for that. *No spaces available . . . just how I need it to be. Isn't it?*

CHAPTER SEVEN

ANDREW

Yup, I'm confirming it right now. I shouldn't be here. This is a mistake.

A big mistake.

Maybe they won't notice I'm here. Maybe, I can quickly turn around and head back to my car without being noticed. Everyone seems to be busy, there is no way they will notice me quietly step back into my—

"Annnndrew!" Stumbling up to me, Smilly is wearing a giant zebra hat on her head and holding what I'm hoping is a fake sabre in one hand while the other is gripping a thirty-two ounce can of Pabst Blue Ribbon. Operation escape route is aborted. "You came."

Yes, like an idiot, I came.

Earlier when Sadie was outside, being upset—something I'm still not happy about—Smilly kept me company while playing with the straws on the counter, a favorite pastime of hers apparently. Our conversation was slightly awkward . . .

"So, you from around here?"

"Grew up in California actually. My parents moved to Albany when I graduated from high school. They are originally from *the area."*

"California, huh? Do you know any celebrities?"

"None."

"That's boring. Did you surf?"

"You know California isn't just about celebrities and surfing, right?"

"Of course I know that." She pauses for a second. "So, spend any time in the wine country?"

Laughing, I shake my head. "Wasn't twenty-one."

She sits up straight and stares me down. "How old were you when you had your first drink?"

I swallow hard. "Um, twenty-one. I had a beer with my brother. I am actually one of the older kids in my grade so it was kind of exciting that I could drink before all of my peers."

"Oh Andrew." Smilly shakes her head. "You know it's rare when someone waits until they're twenty-one to drink? I'm going to guess a percentage of your peers have been drunk for their first half of college."

"How old were you when you had your first drink?"

"Thirteen." Leaning on the counter while looking into the abyss, she reflects back on her first sip. "It was at Sadie's house. Her dad had gone to bed and instead of going to sleep, I unzipped my backpack and showed her the Bartles & Jaymes wine cooler I stole from my mom's special fridge. We shared it that night, giggling under a blanket draped over the both of us. That was the beginning of the end."

"Sounds like one hell of a night. I can practically envision the montage in my head."

Staring at me, she giggles and says, "Huh, you can be sarcastic. I like that. What are you doing tonight?"

Confused, I ask, "Don't you have a boyfriend?"

"Weird that you know that, but I'm not asking you out. We're *having a bonfire at my mom's house tonight. You should come."*

"Oh, I don't know . . ."

"I won't take no for an answer, so you have to come. Give me your phone and I'll plug in the info and my number in case you get lost. Driving in the backwoods can be confusing."

And that's how I ended up at Smilly's mom's house, regretting my decision immensely. What the hell is Sadie going to think if she sees me? Is she even going to be here? For some reason, I really hope not. The thought of seeing her on her turf freaks me the fuck out. Angry eyes wouldn't even begin to describe it.

"Hey Smilly." I stride closer to her, hands tucked in my pockets, trying not to show how nervous I am.

"Everyone is going to be so excited to meet you."

Everyone? *The fuck?*

"And I can't wait for you to meet Emma. I really think she would be perfect for you."

"Emma?" I ask. Was this a blind date setup? If so, things just got that much more uncomfortable.

"Yeah, my friend Emma. She's single, cute, and looking for a good guy. I believe you fit the good guy prerequisite, you know, since you waited to drink and all."

"You're deciding I'm a good guy by what age I first drank? You know some psycho killers never have a drink in their life but instead get drunk off slaughtering people."

Stopping in her tracks, Smilly turns toward me, her sabre raised to the sky. "Now why would you say something creepy like that? Am I going to have to watch over you all night?"

"No, I just thought you should change your way of diagnosing people. You should really consider creating a combination of a pie chart and Venn diagram for proper evaluation. With thoughtful data input and carefully chosen social standards, you could make yourself one hell of a chart. In fact, if you were interested in moving forward with this idea, I wouldn't mind helping you. I have a great program on my computer that could help us and with a little tweaking on my end, a laminator, and a three-whole punch, we could have one hell of a time getting down to the nuts and bolts of judging a human." *Why is she smiling at me?*

Patting my arm, she says, "Yeah, I have nothing to worry about. Right this way, Andrew. Or should I call you Sheldon?" Ah, *The Big Bang Theory*, such a good show, although if I had to identify with one of the characters, I would consider myself more of a Leonard.

Ignoring my rather generous offer, she guides me to the bonfire where people are milling about, talking, drinking, and playing beer pong.

"Saddlemire, get your ass over here."

A man with a very burly beard, wearing a Yankees hat and Beatles shirt, walks over. He wraps his arm around Smilly's waist and says, "Is this the guy you recruited for our threesome?" Scanning me up and down, he nods in approval. "Not bad. Hope he knows how to tweak nipples. I've been looking for a good nipple bruising from a man lately."

You know that emoji on your phone, the one with the incredibly wide eyes and blushing cheeks? Yup, that would describe me right about now.

Horrified.

Slapping his chest, she says, "Don't scare him away, he just got here. Say hello to Andrew like a normal human being."

Saddlemire reaches out his hand for a shake, but I'm a little too nervous to take it. Is he going to rub the back of my hand with his thumb, asking for me to tweak his nipples right here?

"I'm just kidding, kid. I only let people I know tweak my nipples. Maybe after a week you might get lucky."

Taking my hand, he shakes it as I say, "Just for the record, you terrify me."

Chuckling, he nods his head. "I like your honesty. Want a beer?"

"Yes," I say a little too eagerly, needing to relax.

We start walking toward the house when a man with no shirt and the letters USA painted across his chest comes up to us. "Who's this?" He's bouncing up and down, looking very excited, possibly incredibly drunk. The two go hand in hand a lot of the times.

"John, this is Andrew. He works with Sadie. Andrew meet John, our resident solider, home on leave."

"Nice to meet—"

Before I can finish, John scoops me up in a bear hug and spins me around while screaming, "Fuck yeah, America."

Not even giving me a chance to respond, he sets me back on the ground and takes off toward the fire where he picks up a branch—an actual tree branch—and starts jabbing at the fire, while making deafening warrior calls.

Straightening myself, slightly caught off guard, I say, "He seems nice."

"John is a good guy. His girlfriend, Bitch, is around here somewhere."

"Bitch?" How many of Sadie's friends have weird nicknames?

"Yeah, her real name is Jennifer but we call her Bitch."

"Does she like the name?" I sure as hell hope so.

"Oh yeah. If I call her Jennifer she thinks I'm mad at her." Interesting. Why do I suddenly want an offensive nickname?

What would my nickname be?

Penis Breath?

Scrotum Face?

Dirty Asshole . . .

Yeah, I think I'll stick with Andrew.

Passing the raging bonfire—thanks to John and his intense poking—we head up a rickety back deck and into a trailer home. The kitchen is quieter than outside with only a few people in the living room next to it. The house is outdated with shades of brown everywhere but you can feel the love inside.

"What do you drink, kid?" Saddlemire asks, leaning into the fridge.

"Whatever really."

"If you say whatever, I'm going to hand you piss."

"Well, I'm not the piss-drinking sort, so let me see what you have."

Saddlemire steps to the side and I grab a Pabst to go along with Smilly. I've never had one before but reaching for a Bud Light seemed like the easier, dorkier choice.

"And here I thought you looked like a guy who enjoys being peed on during sex." Saddlemire nods at my choice of beer.

"What kind of look is that?" I ask. "If it's something I can fix cosmetically, I'd like to know. Being the guy who looks like he enjoys a good pissing during coitus doesn't appeal to me."

I pop the can of beer and take a swig. Not bad.

I go for another sip when Saddlemire slaps me on the back, laughing. "Coitus. Oh fuck, I'm going to say that now. Smilly, want to participate in some coitus tonight?" He starts pelvic thrusting in her direction, but she holds out her sabre to stop him.

"Say coitus again, see where it gets you."

"Who's saying coitus?" A pretty brunette with blue eyes walks up, her hair dancing with her shoulders, just barely touching the straps of a red and white-checkered dress.

"Andrew likes to be peed on during coitus," Saddlemire announces, really putting a blemish on my already soiled image.

A disgusted look on her face, the brunette looks me up and down just as Smilly starts to laugh.

"He's kidding. Emma, this is Andrew."

"Andrew, why do I know . . ." she pauses and starts chuckling, "*this* is sturdy tits?"

Oh for fuck's sake.

"Yeah, Sadie's coworker," Smilly says.

Putting her hair behind her ears, Emma steps forward, and looking like the pristine lady she is, holds out her hand. "Nice to meet you, Andrew."

I take her hand in mine and give her a smile. "Nice to meet you, too, Emma."

Smiling brightly, she walks past me and reaches for a beer.

She's pretty. She also seems a little different from everyone I've met so far. A little more refined, a little more soft spoken, a little more reserved despite her use of the word tits.

"So what are we all doing in here?" she asks, looking around.

"Just grabbing a drink. Is the table up? I want to play a round," Smilly says.

"I think Tucker is about to drown another team." Turning toward me, Emma asks, "Do you play beer pong?"

I nod. "Yeah, I've played a few times."

"Do you want to be my partner? I don't have a very accurate toss but I'm good at cheering people on."

"I would love to."

"Awwww," Smilly drags out, holding onto Saddlemire's arm. "Look, they're already in love."

Oh Jesus. This is officially awkward.

As a group, we head out to the beer pong table where one guy is playing against three girls who are already too drunk to stand on their own two feet. I'm assuming that's why they're all hanging on to each other.

The guy they're playing seems intense with a beer bottle in one hand and his other hand in his pocket, occasionally catching a pong ball that is tossed his way. Barely looking, he takes one of the balls and tosses it at the last cup left on the girls' side, ending the game. The girls all cry in disappointment and topple over on each other, turning their cries into laughter.

Working her way toward the drunk girls on the ground, Smilly pokes them with her sabre and tells them to get out of the way. "Andrew, Saddlemire and I will play you and Emma. You don't mind, Tucker, do you?"

"Nah, I'm good," he answers. "Have at it."

Stepping to the side, I can feel him keep an eye on me as he sips his beer and observes the game I'm about to partake in.

"You can ask for one restack. If you make a shot, you get the ball back. We don't drink from the cups, only from our own drinks, so if you need more beer, we'll pause the game so you can grab some more. Loser chugs their drink. Got it?" Saddlmire stacks up the cups and I nod.

"We got this," Emma says with excitement.

"Rock, paper, scissors to see who starts. Em, you and me are up," Smilly calls out.

Facing off in the middle of the table, the girls go through two games of rock, paper, scissors before Emma takes the win with paper. Smart girl.

"Paper, smart," I tell her. "I read an article by the New York Post that said rock is the most chosen object while playing because it signifies the most testosterone in competition."

"Are you saying I have a dick, Andrew?" Smilly calls out, pointing her sabre in my direction.

Not even the least bit threatened, I answer, "Odds of you having a dick are kind of stacked in your favor right about now with your rock, paper, scissor choice, your penchant for erecting your sabre when you have the chance, and the fact that your boyfriend likes a good nipple tweaking from men." Casually, I take sip from my beer as everyone around me breaks out in laughter, even Smilly.

"You felt it when I hugged you, didn't you? You felt my little salami."

"Hey, don't discredit yourself, it didn't feel little against my leg. Average size at best, but don't give up, I'm sure with a little more pushing on your end you can pop it out to above average." I wink at her.

Turning to Saddlemire, she jumps up and down. "He sees so much potential in me, it's overwhelming."

"Stop acting like you have a mini wiener. Jesus, Samantha." Saddlemire shakes his head and takes a giant swig of his beer.

Samantha? Huh, never would have guessed.

"Great, now sturdy tits knows my real name. Thanks a lot, *Sebastian*."

Sebastian? If my eyes could pop out of their sockets, they just did. There is no way Saddlemire looks like a Sebastian. Not even in the slightest.

"All right, enough with this shit. Sturdy Tits, you're up," Sebastian, I mean Saddlemire calls out.

Before I toss, I say, "If we could come up with another name for me, that would be awesome. Sturdy Tits isn't settling well."

Smilly and Saddlemire both look at each other and then back at me. Together they say, "You're turn, Sturdy Tits."

Yeah, I didn't think that was going to work for me, but I gave it the old Boy Scout try.

Shaking off the ridiculous nickname, but also feeling like a part of something—something strange—I toss my first ball, sinking it immediately. Saddlemire raises an eyebrow at me in question. "Don't tell me you're good at beer pong."

"Might be." I shrug and push my glasses back on my nose.

"He's calculating the distance with the wind and his alcohol intake. Look at the gears working in his head. It's like watching a computer process. He's going to kill us," Smilly whines. She's very accurate in her assessment. What can I say? I like math. It works.

Emma is up next and tosses her ball nowhere near the general area of the cups. Cringing, she turns to me and says, "Um, looks like you'll be carrying the team."

Chuckling, I say, "Hey, you'll get it. Don't give up just yet. That was a warm-up shot."

The rest of the game unfolds between the two teams, Emma scoring one cup for us, which causes her to jump up and down in my arms until she collects herself and smooths down her dress. Smilly smacks a cup off the table with her sabre every time she misses, which she gets away with twice until Saddlemire puts her in timeout. Aka, a lawn chair with a giant beer. It comes down to one cup each and luckily I am able to sink my ball before Saddlemire, making Emma and me the winners.

"I'm impressed, Sturdy Tits. I wasn't sure if you were going to be any good," Saddlemire says.

Feeling the effects of the beer already starting to kick in—since their version of taking a drink of your beer when a ball is sunk is drinking half your drink—I saunter/waddle over to Saddlemire and shake his hand. "Good game, man. With all that nipple-tweaking talk earlier, I thought you were going to be too distracted by my masterful fingers to make any shots. But you gave me a good run."

"Don't fool yourself, I know how to block out temptation when I need to." Smirking at me, he nods his head and walks back into the house for some more beer.

"Would you like another one?" Emma asks, eyeing the beer in my hand.

I pat my stomach, wishing I ate more before I came. "No, I'm good for now. I think I should slow down a bit after that game."

Leaning forward, she says, "Thanks for taking some of those swigs for me. I'm always the designated driver at these things so I like to keep my beer intake to one."

"Always the designated driver?" I ask. "That doesn't seem like much fun."

She shrugs and shifts back and forth. Her dress reminds me of a church bell, swinging back and forth. "I don't mind. It's better than having a wicked hangover in the morning."

I point at her. "You got something there." Looking around at the festivities, I ask, "Do you guys always have parties like this?"

"During the summer, yes. Everyone is back from college, which means endless nights of one giant party."

"That's awesome. I grew up in California and when I graduated from high school, my parents moved to New York, so I really don't get to go back to my hometown. It's kind of awesome you guys all still have each other despite the different directions you've gone in."

"Yeah. I feel pretty lucky to have such a tight group of friends, but believe me, it comes with its fair share of drama."

"Oh yeah, like what?"

Emma is about to answer when she is interrupted by a deep voice from the beer pong table. "Hey, Sturdy Tits, come clean up with me."

Turning behind me, I see Tucker starting to rack up the cups along with two other guys. When I turn back to Emma, she says, "Go on. I need to go check on Kiera. Usually by now she's crying in the bathroom about how she's never going to find a man who appreciates her love for CrossFit." Laughing to herself, she gives me a brilliant smile and says, "Drama, it never ends."

"Yikes." I cringe. "Have fun and thanks for being my partner."

"Anytime." With another quick smile, she takes off toward the house. Yeah, she's cute.

"Get a good look?" Tucker asks, referring to my wandering eyes on Emma.

Clearing my throat, I walk over to Tucker and hold out my hand to him. "Andrew. If you want me to clean house with you, Sturdy Tits is off the table."

Not moving, only glancing at my hand for a second, he nods, ignoring my handshake. "Andrew, there are two beers on the grass for you, make sure you don't have to drink them. I don't like losing."

"An outgoing guy, nice to meet you," I say sarcastically, saddling up next to Tucker, who seems a little intimidating with his dark stare and man bracelets. If I tried to wear those, I'd look like a total dickhead. Glasses and bracelets on a guy equals too much accessorizing.

Across from us, standing tall, chest puffed is John, still shirtless sans six-foot tree branch, and a guy who is much shorter than him, also shirtless. But instead of USA painted on his chest, it says, *Penguins, Yay!* Not quite sure what that's about, but I'm going to go with it.

"We're up first," Tucker says. "I'll start, you follow up behind me." Barely even looking, Tucker tosses the ball and sinks it immediately in the first cup, leading the pyramid.

Okay, this guy is good.

Doing as I'm told, I shoot my ball into the cup right behind the one he just sunk. And like that, in order, back and forth, we eliminate each cup without even giving the other team a shot at trying to score.

"What the fuck?" Penguins asks. That's what I'm calling him because I didn't catch his name and for some reason, it seems fitting. "That's not fair, we didn't even get a chance to play."

"Rematch!" John yells, pulling an American flag bandanna out of his back pocket. To my surprise, he ties it around his neck like a bow tie and then claps his hands together. "Let's go."

Playfully slapping his friend's shoulder, Penguins says, "Dude, we need more beer."

Emptying out his beer, John nods. "Be right back."

Together, like a weird little bro-mance, they take off toward the house for more beer, leaving me alone with the intimidating Tucker, who is now turned toward me, beer halfway to his mouth.

"So, you work with Sadie?"

Shit, having so much fun, I forgot about the possibility of seeing Sadie here.

"Yeah. She trained me on my first day."

A knowing smile crosses Tucker's lips. "She must have loved that."

"Yeah, she was interesting in her approach."

"Let me guess, she taught you with a *don't fuck with me* vibe?"

Chuckling, I nod my head and sip my beer, feeling a little lighter with each swallow. "Yeah, you could say that. Didn't seem to mind talking about me in front of Smilly while I was only a few feet away."

"Ha!" Tucker shakes his head. "Sounds about right. Tell me, did Smilly bring Sadie her cough syrup that day?"

"I'm not sure a day goes by when Sadie is in the fountain area without her cough syrup on hand."

"Yup, so fucking accurate." Tucker takes another sip of his

drink and says, "She's a good girl who drew a bad hand."

Finally. I've wanted to get to the bottom of Sadie's frown since I first met her. *She's a good girl who drew a bad hand. What does that mean?* And that's when John and Penguins show up with an armful of beer and a bag of Fritos. By the determined look on their faces, we're hunkering down for the night.

Tucker exchanges a glance with me. *Yeah, we're a tad smug.* They're going to have to put up one hell of a fight to beat us. Let the games begin.

CHAPTER EIGHT

SADIE

"Right here is good, Dad."

"I can drive you to the house. It's okay if your friends see me dropping you off, you know. They aren't going to think you're a loser because Daddy took you to a party."

"Not my worry, Dad. The driveway is full of mud, and I don't want you getting stuck."

"You're such a liar." He chuckles, leans over, pulls my head toward him and kisses me on the forehead. "Have fun and don't get into any trouble."

"Thanks for dinner, Dad."

"Anytime, sweetie. Call me up more often. I miss you."

"Miss you, too." With a sad smile, I get out of the car, wave goodbye, and make my way up the driveway, sticking to the grass to avoid the mud.

Having dinner with my dad was nice because we got to catch up, but it just reminded me how distant we are with each other and the many lies between us. He doesn't know I dropped out of Cornell University. He doesn't know I broke up with Tucker, and that I'll never go back to him. He doesn't know about the baby, and he doesn't know that I have no intention of going back to school.

Instead of talking about our actual feelings and what's really going on in our lives, we skirt around the important stuff and talk about easy subjects like the Yankees and what current shows we've been watching. We never bring up Mom, or my sisters, or the fact that I've been floating around from couch to couch for the past few months until Smilly finally got a second full-sized bed in her one-bedroom apartment for me to sleep on. Yes, we share a bedroom. It's very classy. Half the time she's at Saddlemire's place anyway. It's not that big a deal.

My boots sink into the ground with every step forward. I welcome the smell of the burning fire ahead, and the laughter and bustle of my friends no doubt causing a ruckus at Smilly's mom's house. It's been nice hanging out with all my childhood friends this summer, especially since John is back for a short period of time. But the partying, the familiarity, and the sense of belonging, will end once summer wraps up and everyone returns to school, returning to *their* normal lives, leaving me behind.

Funny thing is, it was always assumed that I had the most potential out of everyone in my class. I was the one supposed to go places, the one supposed to prove the small-town gossip wrong, and make something of myself.

But instead of becoming the child psychologist I'd dreamed of, I'm a college dropout with a colorless waitressing job and an inconsequential future in front of me.

Even more depressed than before, I skip past Emma's Jetta parked in its normal spot and head straight into the kitchen where I snag a beer from the fridge and pop it open. Lifting it up, I start to drain the liquid when I hear a loud cheer outside. Peering past the sliding glass door, almost everyone is circled around the beer pong table cheering on the teams.

That's odd. No one in the group cares that much about the

stupid drinking game. Not ready to be bombarded by friends and what seems to be Smilly's sabre, I observe from inside the house, trying to make out who's playing. From the group of friends hanging around, it's John and Kirk playing on one team, both chests painted—I'm not surprised—and Tucker on the other team. I would know Tucker's backside easily, as I've spent my entire life with that boy. But who the hell is he playing with? Whoever it is, my friends seem to like him because every time he shoots, they cheer obnoxiously loud. And he doesn't have a bad backside to stare at either.

"Don't move, Kiera, I'll be right back." Emma's voice trails down the hall as she approaches the kitchen. When she spots me, she smiles brightly. "Hey, Sadie. Gosh, I thought you weren't going to come tonight."

"Had dinner with my dad, and he just dropped me off."

Wincing from the mention of my dad, she asks, "How did that go?"

"You know." I take a sip of my beer. "The normal conversation where we're both in denial about our real lives. Extremely healthy conversation of avoidance and omitting lies."

"Oh perfect, sounds like a splendid evening," Emma sarcastically responds as she digs into the drawers.

Looking back down the hall, seeing the light is on in the bathroom, I ask, "Another no-one-understands-CrossFit episode with Kiera?"

Emma sighs heavily, her shoulders slouching. "What else could it be with Kiera? I just don't understand why she doesn't take down the ban of dating fellow gym mates. Wouldn't that make the most sense?"

"You would think." Another roar of cheering erupts from outside. Glancing outside again, I catch a glimpse of the back of the guy next to Tucker. Tall, obviously fit, with a nice head of hair, looks shaved on the sides, heavy on top. Hmm, who is this guy?

"What's going on out there?"

Holding up a bar of chocolate, she says, "Aha. I knew Smilly's mom had chocolate somewhere." Looking at me, she says, "What did you ask?"

"Outside, what's all the commotion about?"

Taking a quick look at the beer pong party, she answers as if I should already know. "John and Kirk are trying to beat Tucker and your friend."

"My friend?" My brow scrunches. "Who's my friend?"

Just as Emma is about to answer, a chanting from outside interrupts her, drawing both of our attention.

"Andrew, Andrew, Andrew."

What in the ever-living hell!

"Why is Andrew here?" I ask as I watch Tucker cheer him on. What the fuck is happening?

"Oh, you didn't know he was coming?"

Turning toward my friend, I point at my face and ask, "Does this look like a person who knew her coworker was barging in on her territory?"

"You seem a little angry."

"Pointing out the obvious, Emma."

Setting my beer down, I head to the door when Emma calls out, "He's really nice, and everyone seems to like him."

"Great," I mutter, opening the glass sliding door. The cheering is louder once I step outside, and in the middle of it all stands Andrew, clear as day, looking . . . *Oh God.* He looks so good. Seeing him outside of work—not wearing his Friendly's uniform—is detrimental toward my ability to block him out of my mind.

God, that devastating smile. He's wearing his glasses but instead of hiding under his hat, they're framing his strong features perfectly. Then there's his chiseled jaw, his eyes full of laughter. And his hair . . . why does it make him look like Ryan Reynolds? Oh Christ, that's who he looks like, right now. Ryan Reynolds. Muscles, charm, and all. *Shit.*

Trying to stuff away the hormones partying inside me, I move past the mini crowd of friends and straight to Andrew, who is pumping his fist in the air like an idiot.

"Hey," I snap close to his ear.

Turning toward me, his face reads shock but then his smile grows even bigger. Picking me up in a giant hug, he spins me around and says, "It's Sadie. Everyone, Sadie is here."

Mortified can't even begin to describe how I feel. Not because Andrew's strong arms are wrapped around me, but because with each revolution, I see Tucker's face. It reads, *what the fuck is going on?*

"Put me down, you oof."

Not so gracefully, he stops spinning only to tip to the side and bring us both down to the ground, him toppling over me. Brushing the hair out of my face, he hovers over me, that smile still on his face, the one that's making my stomach twist in all different kinds of knots, and says, "Hey, Sadie."

He's not cute. He's not cute. You're mad. Be mad.

But that smile . . .

"What are you doing here?" I barely squeak out.

"Smilly, or should I say Samantha invited me." I'm going to kill her. Although this could have been avoided had I killed her earlier today when she threw me in Tucker's face at Friendly's. "You don't seem happy to see me, not that I should be surprised. You're never happy to see me." From the smell of beer on his breath and the glaze in his eyes, he's drunk. He doesn't seem too drunk, but drunk enough to lower his filter and speak his truth. Pouting his lower lip, he asks, "Why don't you like me,

Sadie? Everyone else here likes me." His eyes widen and then his head lowers. He's so close, his smooth and fresh cologne hitting me hard. "Oh, is this one of those elementary school things? You like me, but you pretend you don't like me so you're extra mean?"

"No," I answer quickly which makes him smile even bigger . . . if that's possible.

"Wow, you like me. I can see it in your eyes."

"You see nothing." I press my hand against his chest to push him away, but I'm caught off guard when I feel just how strong he is beneath my palm. Oh hell.

"Okay." He winks at me and hops up effortlessly before reaching down with a hand to pull me up. Addressing the crowd—shit, I forgot there was a crowd—he says, "She's okay, folks. Sadie's going to make it."

Once again, an eruption of cheers rings through the late-night air. Everyone is clinking beers together, causing a gleeful scene, except for one person. Behind a now-dancing Andrew—who surprisingly has moves like Bruno Mars—is Tucker, his arms crossed over his chest and a scowl on his face.

Oh crap.

"Come on, Sadie, dance with me," Andrew says. As "24K Magic" by Bruno Mars echoes through the country air, he takes both my hands in his. My body instantly heats from the contact, and he keeps a few feet between us as he starts moving his feet like some kind of moonwalking magician, twisting and turning, spinning around only to grab my hands together. "Put your pinky rings . . . up to . . . the moon!" Andrew sings and then starts pelvic thrusting in different directions.

I can't do anything but be a little mesmerized as he floats around me, including me every once in a while, singing away like he's putting on his own damn concert. My friends fade away, Tucker disappears in my mind, and in this moment, the one where Andrew is charming the fuck out of me, all I can do is watch as his charisma enthralls my friends. *He's mesmerizing.*

The anger that once consumed me slowly fades, replaced by a funny, tingling feeling deep in my belly, one that I know is bad news; one I know I never let myself indulge in, at least not anymore. It's not until my arm is pulled on from the side that I'm returned to the present. Andrew continues to show off his best moves while everyone cheers for him, but it seems like my dancing time is up. Gripping my hand and yanking me to the side is Tucker, with a not-so-happy look on his face.

Behind a tree, he turns me to him and asks, "What the fuck was that all about?"

Playing dumb because honestly, I have no clue what to say, I reply, "What was what about?"

"Don't fuck with me, Sadie. Were you trying to make me jealous back there?"

"Jealous?" And that deep-rooted anger is back. "Why would I want to make you jealous? I have no reason to do so, plus that's not the kind of person I am."

"I saw the way you were looking at him. Is there something going on between the two of you?"

First of all, Tucker has no right to be questioning me right now. We are not together, and when is he going to get that through his head? And second, is there something going on between Andrew and me? Is he insane?

"Why do you even think that is a question I should answer? We are not together, Tucker. I don't understand why you don't get that."

"Because we have history, Sadie. Because I love you. Because I want nothing more than to have you in my fucking arms again. So please forgive me for caring if there is another guy you might be fucking interested in."

Pain oozes with each word from his mouth. My spine stiffens from his confession, but my heart reaches out to him.

Sighing, I cut the defensive act and say, "I love you, too, Tucker, but I really think we need to give each other space."

"Space is the last thing we need. If I give you space, then you're going to forget what we have. Just give me a chance to take you out, please, Sadie. I've changed. We've both changed."

His eyes beg me, his body language beseeches me, and his hands slowly pull me closer. I don't know if my heart can take much more of this. *Years.* We've known each other for years. He has been inside me, both physically and emotionally. But our time is done. *We* are done. We *both* need to move beyond our habit of falling back into what we know. *I need to move forward.*

Sensing my hesitation, he says, "Think about it. You don't have to give me an answer right now." I nod, looking down at the ground. He lifts my chin and forces me to look him in the eye. "Just answer me one thing. Do you like him?"

Do I like Andrew? Jeeze, I would rather answer the date question than that. Instead of skirting around the truth, I say, "I don't know how I feel about Andrew." The truth pains me a little because I've been denying his ability to penetrate my walls. Faced with these thoughts, it's clear my desperate attempt to keep both my heart safe and my little world contained is slowly failing. Andrew *is* working his way in.

Nodding, Tucker pulls me into a hug and kisses the top of my head and then chuckles. "Don't let the dance moves sway you. They're flashy."

I push away from him and start laughing. "Please, I'm not that easily swayed."

Spinning on the spot, he does his own little move and then smiles at me. "I beg to differ. Uncle Tony's Halloween, 2015.

One of the best nights of sex we ever had."

Groaning, I walk away, trying not to recall that night. Before I can get out of earshot, Tucker calls out, "Be careful, Sadie, and remember, I'm still looking for an answer."

Relentless.

Andrew is now resting against the deck fence when I approach him, a beer in his hand and a cheesy smile on his face.

With my arms crossed over my chest, I ask, "How did you get here?"

"Is that a way to greet someone properly who just whipped you around the dance floor?"

I hide the smile that wants to peek past my lips. "Did you drive?"

Pushing off the fence, he closes the space between us, seeming a lot more confident than usual. It has to be the beer. "Why do you ask? You want to go home with me?"

Yup, it's the beer.

"No, it's time you say goodnight to your friends and get going."

"Kicking me out of the party?" He drains the rest of his beer and tosses the bottle in the recycling container a few feet away. Impressive. "I hope you plan on driving me." He reaches into his pocket and pulls out his keys. "Because I don't drink and drive."

Still smart when drunk, can't help but like that about a guy. Snagging the keys from his hand, I start walking toward the cars. "Which one is yours?"

"The white Ford Ranger." He follows closely behind me and stretches his arm over my shoulders. "Thanks, sugar britches."

Sugar britches?

"Don't call me that," I say, making our way to his truck. Why do I feel like this has mistake written all over it?

•••

Yup, this was a mistake.

In the passenger side of Andrew's truck, is the man of the hour, passed out, his glasses askew and mouth wide open. He fell asleep once I pulled out of the driveway, giving me no other option but to drive him back to my place since I have absolutely zero idea where he lives.

Now I'm parked in the carport, wondering what the hell I'm supposed to do. Do I leave him in his truck, maybe crack a window for him, and hope no one tries to steal him in the middle of the night? Or do I take him back into my apartment where we have two recliners and two beds? One being mine, the other being Smilly's?

A part of me wants to toss him the keys and say good night but the other part of me, the nice part of me, knows what I have to do. Looking to the sky, I take a deep breath and exit the vehicle, rounding the hood to his side. This was not how I planned to spend my night.

Opening the door, I try to decide how to wake him up. Poking him seems like the right thing to do. So, I poke him in the shoulder a few times. Nothing.

Okay, I poke his side this time, stiffening my finger so hopefully it feels like a branch coming after him.

Nothing.

Getting a little irritated now, I place both my hands on his shoulders and shake him, hoping he's a heavy sleeper and not needing medical attention.

Nothing.

"Oh come on," I huff in frustration. "Hello?" I tap his head, not sure what else to do.

Slowly, at a snail's pace, a smile starts to play on his lips as he turns his head toward me. His eyes laze, he looks at me and says in a worn-out voice, "Your bedside manner could use a little work."

"Oh my God, were you awake this entire time?"

Shifting out of the car, he says, "No. I woke up with the first jab you gave me from that bō staff you call a finger." Taking a look around, he asks, "Where are we?"

"My place."

He raises a single brow at me and from that little movement, my insides flutter again.

"Your place, huh? Well, you move fast."

"You passed out before I could get your house address. Just be thankful I didn't steal your car and leave you on the side of a road." I walk up to my apartment, unlock the door, and let myself in, Andrew following close behind.

"Leaving me on the side of the road might have been fun. Kind of a Where's Waldo drunk edition."

"Uh, no, more like Survivor drunk edition."

I shut the door behind Andrew and lock up. When I turn around, he's already searching the place. "Where's the bedroom?"

Um . . .

"I'm not sleeping with you."

"Wasn't asking to, sugar britches. I want to go to the bathroom and go to bed."

"Just so you know, you're not sleeping in my bed, but the bathroom is around the corner."

He slightly stumbles toward the bathroom and shuts the door. Trying to calm myself—my hormones are jumping everywhere—I head to my little dresser, pull out a pair of shorts and a tank, and wait for my turn in the bathroom.

For a guy who doesn't have any of his nighttime items, he's

taking quite a long time in there. Sitting cross-legged on my bed, I wonder what he could possibly be doing.

Oh God, did he pass out on the toilet? Willy out? What's a girl to do if that's the case? Do I tuck it back into his pants and push him to the side? No one wants to tuck a flaccid wiener back into underpants, especially foreign flaccid wieners.

Chewing on my lip, wondering if I should go knock on the door, I bounce my foot up and down. I need to pee. If he's passed out on the toilet, I might just have to knock him to the side because I'm not going to be able to hold this all night, nor am I one to go squat it out in the bushes. Smilly, now she just might conduct such a pee with nature, but not me. I need porcelain to sit on.

"Oh come on," I mutter, now standing from my bed and heading to the bathroom where I pace in front of the door. Leaning my head closer, I hear water running so that has to be a good sign. Then the unmistakable sound of someone spitting into the sink. Is he . . . brushing his teeth?

I'm about to knock on the door when Andrew opens it, shirtless, pants-less, wearing nothing but his glasses and black boxer briefs. He's wiping his mouth with the hand towel that rests next to the sink when he makes eye contact with me. That damn smile greets me but it's not what holds my attention. Oh. No. My eyes go for a wander down his body. I take in the very cut man, with beautiful muscles flexing under the dim light of my bathroom.

Oh.

My.

God.

Andrew, champion forearms, Mr. Sunshine, dork with the hot glasses, boy who won't quite leave me alone at work, he's . . . oh God, he's *everything* under his clothes.

"If I wasn't about to pass out from exhaustion, I would say

something witty about you staring at my body, but I'm just too tired right now." He drapes the towel back on the rack, gathers his clothes, and stops before he walks past me. With a smirk, he says, "Thanks for letting me borrow your toothbrush, I just hate beer breath."

Before I can respond, he's shutting the bathroom door, leaving me looking flushed and angry at the same time. For some reason, I can't get myself to be mad about him using my toothbrush, not after the sight he just gave me.

Damn him.

Damn him and his stupid hot-nerd appeal.

Going through the motions, I get ready for bed, debating if I should use my toothbrush or not but in the end, the brush wins out because I agree with Andrew, beer breath is the worst. Finishing up, I take one last look in the mirror and brush my hair out before exiting the bathroom.

When I turn the corner to the bedroom, I'm hit with another unexpected image. Andrew, in my bed, the only bed that has bedding on it—Smilly must be doing laundry—completely passed out, his glasses on the side table.

Fucking great.

Sagging my shoulders, I look out to the living room and eye the lumpy recliners.

He's passed out, how bad could it really be to sleep in the same bed? He probably won't wake up until I'm already up and about.

Taking a chance, I drop my clothes in the hamper and then slide into the bed, making sure to plug my phone in. The minute I settle myself on one of my pillows, I take a deep breath and sink into the mattress. *I have a hot, nerdy man in my bed.* Can't say I've ever had that before. And then I'm no longer on my side of the bed.

A well-built arm has pulled me into his strong body, spooning me to his front. *Oh shit.* God, he smells so nice. Feels *so* nice. On second thought, holy yum.

So much for staying on each other's side of the bed.

CHAPTER NINE

ANDREW

What is that?

My brain is full of fog, my mind not quite processing what I'm holding.

Is that an orange?

No, why would I be sleeping with an orange? Plus it's way too soft to be an orange. I squeeze some more, eyes closed, trying to comprehend what the hell I'm holding on to.

Wait, I feel something. Moving my palm down so my fingers can explore, I find that little nub that was poking my palm and I squeeze it between my finger and thumb. The tip of the orange? Maybe a rotten orange?

It doesn't smell citrusy . . .

Needing to figure this out in my sleep-ridden brain, I give another hard squeeze only to be startled by a female cry.

What the fresh hell?

Sitting up, my eyes a blur because my glasses aren't assisting me in my vision, I try to make out where the fuck I am. A girl—at least I hope a girl—sits up next to me, long blonde hair cascading down her shoulders.

"What the hell do you think you're doing?"

I know that voice. I reach over to the nightstand where I thankfully feel my glasses and push them on my face with my palms fumbling as Sadie's very angry face comes into view.

Oh shit.

It all comes flashing back to me. Beer pong with Tucker, too many drinks, dancing with Sadie, calling her sugar britches, passing out in her bed. I'm going to take a wild guess and say Team Andrew isn't fairing well right now.

"Um." I clear my throat, choking on how dry it is. "I didn't know I was, uh, touching you." Shrugging I ask, "Did you like it?"

"What is wrong with you?" she asks, looking me up and down.

"If I said I was still drunk would you believe me?"

"No," she answers firmly.

All right, this isn't working well for me; time to try a new tactic. Bringing the sheets up to my chest, covering my nipples, I ask, "Oh yeah, well why am I naked?"

"What?" she asks, completely confused.

"I remember wearing clothes last night and now look at me, bare for you to see. Taking advantage of a drunk man. What gives?"

"Are you psychotic? You took your clothes off last night, used my toothbrush, and then passed out in my bed all on your own."

I chuckle to myself. Sounds about right.

"What's so funny?" she asks, her face gentling a little.

Dropping the sheet now, I stretch up against the wall and tilt my head toward her. "You fell victim to Tanked Andrew. He's a bold fella, takes risks like using people's toothbrushes."

"And you're proud of this?"

I shrug my shoulders. "Eh, he's okay. He got me a comfortable place to sleep last night, next to a pretty girl who likes a good bosom massage in the morning."

I eye her from the side and see a deep-tinted blush creep up her cheeks. "I did not like your little manhandling. It was unwarranted."

"Yeah, then why did your nipple get hard?" Bold question, maybe Tanked Andrew is still hanging around.

"Because you were pinching it. It's not going to take that kind of abuse and stay flat. If I did that to your nipples they would get hard too."

"Want to try?" I puff my chest out at her.

"No!" She turns her head away from me but doesn't get out of bed. Hmm. She also didn't scoff when I called her pretty. I wonder what would happen if I tried making a move on her, like pulling her onto the mattress, throwing the covers over both of us, and kissing her in the dark.

Wait! No, I'm supposed to be making friends with this woman, not envisioning kissing her. Jimmy would be so—

She licks her lips and stares at my chest, her fingers twisting in the sheet on her lap.

Oh fuck it. I don't care what Jimmy thinks.

This girl has me by my nuts with her mysteriously beautiful eyes, her rough edges, and the small glimpses of a smile I catch every now and then. She's so goddamn beautiful that it's hard not to think of her in any other way but romantically.

Fuck my promise to my parents, I just need a taste.

Tilting my head toward her, I nod in my direction and say, "Get over here, sugar britches."

"What?" Her eyes finally snap up to mine, wide as if caught red-handed. "No."

"You know you want to." Under the covers, I move my hand closer to her.

"No, I don't."

I inch even closer. "Yes, you do. I can see it in your eyes. Now come here."

"You can see nothing." She looks down at her lap but still doesn't leave the bed. If she really wanted to be left alone, she could easily hop out. She makes no attempt to move away.

So I lean toward her and slip my hand around her waist, my eyes still connected with hers. When I start to pull her toward me, her pupils go wide. "What are you doing?"

"Giving you a hand. Now . . . come . . . here," I grunt out, dragging her across the mattress until she's right next to me, shoulder to shoulder. Straightening up, I tease, "See, that's not so bad."

"This is ridiculous. Why do I need to sit right next to you?"

"Easy, so we can do this." Under the covers, I take her hand in mine and lace our fingers together.

Her eyes remain focused on the wall in front of us as her fingers tighten around mine. It feels like she is gripping my heart. Dare I move forward? Dare I push her a little more?

God, she smells sweet. Like cherries.

I'm going with yes.

"Thank you for taking care of me last night."

"I just drove so you wouldn't crash your truck in a ditch."

I playfully shove her with my shoulder. "Something I greatly appreciate."

"It's no big deal."

Wanting more, needing to see how far she'll go, I pull on her hand so she's forced to straddle my lap. Stumbling a little, not making the smooth transfer I foresaw, she head-butts my chest but then stumbles back when she gets her bearings.

"What are you doing?" My hand lets go of hers and I grip her hips, willing myself not to get too excited and scare this woman away.

"I wanted to see your face. Figured this was the easiest way," I answer casually.

"And sitting on your lap is the best way to do that?"

"To me it is." I smirk at her and from that little smile, her shoulders drop, the tension in her brow easing.

Hmm, note to self: she seems to like my smile.

"You know you're my coworker, right?"

"I'm well aware." I move my hands slightly up her hips so my thumbs slip under her tank top where I rub them against her soft, silky skin.

"I don't get involved with coworkers."

"Really?" I ask, moving my hands up just an inch higher. "That's a shame, because I'm pro getting involved with coworkers. In fact, I was thinking about asking David out, but I've been nervous about his response." I bite my lip and look nervous. "Do you think he'll say yes?"

Sadie laughs under her breath, making my heart expand a few inches more. She's loosening up, and *that* realization makes my chest bolster with pride.

"Well, given he has two little girls and a wife, I'm going to say you might get a big, fat rejection."

"Damn." I shake my head and then peek up at her as I move my hands a little higher, now reaching her ribcage. "I do have my eyes set on another person, but that person hasn't been very welcoming since I started. Not sure if I should go for it or not."

Smirking, a little sparkle in her eyes, she says, "I'm pretty sure if you ask, Blaine will say yes."

That garners a full-on belly laugh from me. Fucking Blaine. For some reason, I believe Sadie. I think Blaine would say yes, thinking it was some kind of wingman shit where he would spend the night high-fiving me over every girl that passes us.

What a fucking nightmare that would be.

"He's option number three."

"Oh yeah, who's option number two?"

She's going to make me work for it. Fair enough. I'm still completely amazed where I am. I. Am. In. Bed. With. Sadie. She's on my lap. My hands are touching her gorgeous skin. *Holy. Shit.* I couldn't imagine a girl like Sadie just giving in easily. No, Sadie's a girl you work for, a girl you put your best suit and tie on for.

"You know the blonde with the soulful eyes, killer ass, and sassy-as-hell attitude?"

"Denise?" Sadie asks with a cute scrunch to her nose.

I move my hands up another inch, my thumbs skimming beneath her breasts. With each stroke of my thumb, her breath hitches.

"Not Denise." I make up that last inch, hoping she doesn't slap me away. The tops of my thumbs barely touch her bare breasts, and the soft graze makes us both clear our throats. "You have five seconds to decide if you don't want me to kiss you because I'm not going to be able to hold back any longer."

"Why are you holding back?" she asks, shifting on my lap.

"Hmm, I don't know, maybe because you've been hostile toward me ever since I met you. For some unknown reason, I like it. Now, are you going to just sit there, rubbing that perfect ass of yours on my lap, or are you going to let me kiss you?"

She bites on her bottom lip for a brief second before she smiles, and *that's* all the inclination I need. Instead of pouncing on her like I want to, I lift one hand from under her shirt and slowly glide it up the column of her neck, reveling in the way her skin feels against my palm. When I cup her cheek, her head leans into my hand ever so slightly. She wants this. Me. *How?* When did she change her mind about me? I'm not going to think too hard about it, I'm going to indulge myself instead.

Gently, I run my thumb over her lips, slightly pulling on the bottom one before running my hand to the back of her neck. Her hair falls like a golden blanket over the back of my hand, the soft strands adding to the thrill of holding this gorgeous woman in my arms.

One hand is still up her shirt playing with the bottom of her breast, I bring her forward with the other until our mouths are only inches apart. When she leans forward, she balances herself on my shoulders where her hands clasp behind my neck, playing with my short strands of hair. The sensation sends a tingle down my spine, awakening my body from the tips of my toes to the strands of my hair. You would think it would be the woman sitting on my lap that would fire up all my senses, but it's her touch, because that little caress of her fingers is voluntary. She's just as much into this powerful force between us as I am.

"Last chance, sugar britches." I bring her mouth so damn close that there is only a whisper of a breath between us. No protest. Green light. Closing that last bit of space, I seal our mouths together and relax into the pillow behind me, letting my mouth do all the work.

Soft, pliable lips meet mine, exploring at first, and then igniting into a lip lock of pure, unfiltered lust. The back of her neck rests in my strong grip. She's going nowhere and neither am I by the way her hands start digging into my hair, setting every last synapse on fucking fire.

She shifts on my lap again, this time rubbing against my growing erection. A moan slips from the back of my throat from the friction. Everything about this woman is hard as nails but it's as if when she's with me, in this little comfort cocoon we formed, she's soft, sweet, and playful, a completely different person than the fierce girl I work with.

I like this side of her. She's like a teddy bear.

Moving my lips across hers, I can't help but love the way she tastes, the way she smells like cherries, or the way little, soft sounds rise from the back of her throat with each press of my lips against hers. Needing more, I part her lips with my tongue, loving how easily she opens for me. Fuck, yes. Her tongue meets mine, our kiss becoming more intense in a matter of seconds. No longer is she tentative or reserved. Now her entire body is rubbing against mine, knocking my hand from her breast. I hang on to her undulating and mind-altering hip action where she's rubbing her center against my lengthening cock.

"Fuck that feels good," I mutter in between kisses.

With every thrust, the strain in my neck grows. I'm not one to blow early, but with Sadie on my lap, her hands sifting through my hair, her mouth doing wicked things to mine, I wouldn't be surprised if I turned into a two-pump chump.

Her pace starts to quicken, her breathing heavy against my mouth, her hands growing tighter around my head. Is she going to orgasm? Fuck, that would be so hot if she did. Wanting her to let loose, I glide my hand back up her shirt, this time at a quicker pace.

"Oh God," she quietly moans, her forehead resting against mine for support.

She is straight-up dry humping me right now, riding my boxer-clad cock, and I'm loving every second of it. Needing more, I match every rub of her clit against my cock with a thrust of my hips, intentionally driving it home that I want this just as much as she does and that she doesn't have to do all of the work.

"Fuck, yes," I moan.

Shit. I'm going to blow it in my briefs, but if it feels as good as I think it's going to, I don't care.

Sweat coats both of our skin, her legs sliding easily against mine from the slickness. Our breaths trying to keep up with one another and our hands now starting to roam.

God, I'm almost there.

"Oh God," she says louder this time. She's concentrating on the connection below where she's rubbing feverously against me, putting out a relentless pace that has my fucking balls tingling with anticipation.

Just a few more . . .

Reaching up to her breast, I'm seconds from finally gripping it, seconds from blowing my load, seconds from falling into a morning bliss, when the front door to her small apartment opens and then slams shut.

As if I'm fire and she just burnt her beautiful clit on me, she jumps off my lap and runs to the bedroom door where she clicks the door shut. In a panic, she turns to me and points to the window. "You have to leave, now."

"What?" I ask, because let's face it. The functioning brain isn't the one in my skull at this moment. My very hard cock, therefore, is still trying to figure out what's going on. *In his present condition, he isn't that smart.*

"Leave, now. You have to go."

Is she serious?

"What? Why?"

"No time for questions." She kicks my jeans toward me and says, "You just have to go."

"Uh." Looking down at my lap I say, "Kind of have a fucking boner right now."

"Good for you." She tosses my shirt at me. Pointing to the window—yes, the window—she says, "Go on. Get out of here."

"Sadie, are you home?" a voice calls out from the living room.

Panic rises in her eyes. Smilly.

"Do you not want Smilly to see me in here? With a boner?" This time, the smile I give her does not diffuse the situation.

Not even blinking an eye, she answers, "No, I don't. So, if you could please just leave, that would be great."

Holding my clothes over my still hard-as-fuck dick, I say, "No."

"No?" Her eyes nearly pop out of her head. "What do you mean, no?"

"Sadie, are you here?" Smilly calls out. "I want some Doritos, do we still have some?" *We were stopped seconds from coming for Doritos? What the hell?*

Calling out, Sadie says, "Uh yeah, be right out, just getting changed. Doritos are in the cupboard above the fridge. Remember you hid them from Saddlemire?"

"That's right, such a fucking pig. Hurry up. I want to watch *Rudy*. That little football geek starred in my dreams last night. I need to see the real thing."

"Okay, be right out." Turning back to me, pleading now, Sadie says, "Please, Andrew."

God, if she wasn't so fucking pretty . . .

"Only if you promise me one thing." Compromise. She wants something and I want something. I think it's fair.

"What do you want?" She eyes me suspiciously.

"A date. Tonight. Neither of us have to work. I want some one-on-one time with you."

"A date?"

The knob to the door jiggles. "Hey, why did you lock the door?" Smilly calls out from the other side, knocking on the wood.

"I'm naked." Sadie panics, her hands going to her bright red face while looking from me to the door.

"So, it wouldn't be the first time I saw your knockers. Remember I saw them when you got them pierced."

"Pierced," I mouth to her. I don't recall feeling a nipple ring when I thought her tit was an orange.

She holds up a hand to me.

"Just give me a second, I'll be right there." She bounces on her toes, obviously holding her breath, waiting for Smilly to give her a little bit of space.

"Oh God, are you jilling off?" Sadie puts her hand on her forehead in distress. "If you're looking at my collection of dick pics just keep it away from your diddling digits. Two hands, Sadie, two fucking hands."

I snort. I can't help it, causing Sadie to send daggers my way.

"I'm not . . ." She sighs. "Just give me a second." Marching her way over to the side of the bed, she pulls me off and starts shoving me toward the window. "Time to go."

"Hey, hold on a second." She's already opening the window and popping the screen. "I didn't get an answer. I'm not leaving until you agree."

"Don't be ridiculous."

"I'm being ridiculous?" I point to myself. "You're the one pushing me out the window, mostly naked, with a fucking hard-on casting a shadow over my bare feet. If you don't want to go on a date with me, I will just go say good morning to Smilly and partake in some Doritos and *Rudy*."

Huffing in frustration, Sadie says, "Fine. I'll go out with you tonight."

Smiling, I say, "See, that wasn't too hard."

"Okay, get out." She pushes me out the low window but I grip the edges before I fall out. "What are you doing?" she hisses.

"I'm going to need a kiss goodbye as well."

Exasperated, she grabs my head with such force—I'm afraid I might be a victim of whiplash—and plants a kiss on my lips.

Nothing intimate or sexy, just a kiss that an incredibly inappropriate aunt would dole out. It kind of dampens the mood actually. "There, now get out of here." With one last push, I'm out the window, my clothes scattered across the soil terrain below her window, my dick still standing at attention.

"Hey, I don't have my shoes."

"You'll live," she calls out.

"And my dick? He still wants to play with you."

Scanning my tented briefs, she smiles to herself and shakes her head. "Get the hell out of here."

With that, she shuts the window, leaving me naked, aroused, and as happy as fuck for scoring a date with her. Shoes or no shoes, I'm going to get her to smile a hell of a lot more tonight.

Not bothering to dress myself—because what's the point really?—I head toward my truck. And *that's* when I realize I'm missing one thing . . .

Keys. *Shit.*

Knowing I have no choice, I try to be as nonchalant as possible as I walk up to their front door, clothes placed in front of my dick because no one wants to be greeted at their front door by a boner; that's just some creepy shit. I take a deep breath, put on a smile, and knock.

"Got it," I hear Smilly call out. The minute she opens the door, she scans me up and down and while looking me square in the eyes, she says, "Sadie, I do believe it's for you."

"What?" Sadie walks up behind Smilly and the minute her eyes meet mine, they narrow. Fuck, I think I might be kissing that date goodbye. "What the hell are you doing?" she asks between gritted teeth.

Leaning forward, on a whisper, I say, "Uh, you still have my truck keys."

Her face pales as she realizes her mistake. While she retrieves my keys, I rock back and forth on my feet trying to avoid eye contact with Smilly. Maybe if we don't look at each other, she won't notice me. Not exactly sure where to cast my eyes, I take a quick glance at Smilly who has a knowing look on her face. With a twiddle of her finger, she waves. Not wanting to be rude, I wave to her just as Sadie returns, tossing my keys at my chest. She does not look happy.

I put my finger up and start to ask, "Pick you up tonight?" when the door is slammed on my face. "Yeah, sure, eight sounds awesome." I shrug casually. "See you then. Thanks for the dry-hump session by the way. You can bring my shoes later. Don't worry, I don't need them right now."

Slumping, I do the walk of shame to my truck. Well, it could be worse, she could have kicked me in the nuts after she threw my keys at me.

Here's to small wins.

CHAPTER TEN

SADIE

I don't want to turn around. I want to stand here in front of the door I just slammed in Andrew's face and slowly disintegrate into the floor.

"So, that was interesting," Smilly says from one of the recliners.

I squeeze my eyes shut, attempting to turn back the time to where I remembered to give the man his damn keys. I was just so flustered. I didn't expect Smilly to be home so early. Usually when she spends the night at Saddlemire's place, she's there until noon.

Expertly—at least I think it's expertly—I sidestep Smilly's comment and take a seat in the recliner next to hers. "Didn't stay long at Saddlemire's place today?"

See, perfect avoidance, doesn't get better than that.

"Oh, so we're doing that right now? Pretending you didn't just sneak a guy out of our bedroom window. That's fine." Maybe I'm not as stealth as I think. "Saddlemire had to go help his brother this morning, and staying at his place by myself gives me hives, so I came home early. If I would have known there was a special guest here last night, I would have grabbed myself a Boston Kreme donut over at Dunkin'." Slamming her fist on the arm of the recliner, she says, "Urgh! I should have gotten a donut. Now it's all I want." She tosses the Doritos to the side, licks her cheese-coated fingers, and stands from the recliner. "Come on, we're making a trip to Dunkin'. Mama needs a donut in her mouth."

Not wanting to argue with Smilly, I slip a light sweatshirt over my head, put on my sandals, and follow behind Smilly to her car. The moment she turns on the car and rolls down her window—hand rolls it down—*Alabama* starts blasting through her speakers. This girl is all country.

"I'm in a hurry to get things done," she sings, pulling out of the reserved parking spot. She turns down the music slightly so I can hear her better. "Don't you just love *Alabama*? God, they make me want to twiddle myself every time I hear their music."

"Um, I wouldn't necessary say I need to twiddle myself, but I do appreciate their music."

"You're doing it all wrong if you're not twiddling yourself to *Alabama* weekly. Saddlemire and I like to bone to "Take Me Down." There's something about that song that really gets my nipples hard. What about you?"

"Uh, yeah, not so much."

Turning on her blinker, she turns onto Front Street, a straight shot to Dunkin' Donuts and says, "I think I need a dozen donuts this morning. Do you ever just want to pig out without worrying about what it will tack onto your hips?"

So confused that she's not grilling me about Andrew, I tread carefully and say, "Wish it all the time."

"Why can't our bodies just process things like we want them to? If I want to be a veggie-nut and suck on celery my whole life, my body should be okay with that. If I want to live my life and eat Doritos for breakfast, donuts for lunch, and apple pie for dinner, my body should say, thank you for the nutrients. But no, the little fuckers go and give you love handles."

Flying into Dunkin', on two wheels I'm sure of it, she pulls into the drive-thru and asks, "Blueberry cake, Boston Kreme—obvs—strawberry frosted, and glazed?" It's our typical order.

"Sounds about right. Grab me a medium coffee, too."

Smilly places our order, rattling it off like a pro, and we both chip in a few bucks to pay. With donuts in hand, coffee in the other, Smilly doesn't take any time driving to our favorite place where we overlook the Chenango River. Parking near the bend, getting closer than allowed, she backs up and puts the car in park.

"Come on." She nods her head toward the back of the car where I meet her. Just like every other time we've looked over the river, we hop up on the trunk of her car, place the box of donuts between us, and stare out into a little piece of nature.

We both reach for a blueberry cake donut first, like always, and take a big bite. Once Smilly swallows, she says, "Want to talk about it?"

I knew it was coming. Clever girl. She just buttered me up with donuts. The problem with having a small, loyal group of friends? They know you far too well. She knows my weakness is donuts. *She knows.* And today, she made a sneak attack . . . But will I talk? Nope.

"Not really," I answer, taking another bite.

"Too bad. Spill, girl. And start from wherever your mind lost it and slept with Andrew."

"I didn't sleep with Andrew," I say quickly. Just a heads-up: Smilly has always been a big Tucker/Sadie fan. I'm not sure that will ever change.

"No?" She sips her coffee. "Could have fooled me. By the looks of it this morning, you let him dip your donut."

Rolling my eyes, I say, "We didn't have sex. We just . . ." How do I say dry humped without blushing? "You know, did some things."

"Did you touch his penis . . . with your vagina?"

"No," I answer exasperated. "All clothes remained on. We just kissed and did some, you know, frictional rubbing."

Mid-sip, Smilly eyes me over her Styrofoam coffee cup. "Did you dry hump?"

God, why is this so embarrassing? "Yes," I answer shyly.

"Seriously?" Smilly shakes her head. "What were you thinking, Sadie? Aren't you still seeing Tucker?"

"No. We're not together. You should know this. He hasn't been around the apartment for months. Did he tell you differently? I'm going to kick him in the testicles if he did."

"Hold on." Smilly pats my leg. "He just said he was trying to get you back. That's all. No need to kick his testicles just yet. So, what does this all mean? Are you moving on?"

"I don't know." I pause. "That's a lie, I know I'm moving on from Tucker. We're over. There is just too much baggage between the both of us, too much history, too many things we can't overlook or ignore. We're not right for each other, Smilly. He needs to accept that."

Tucker. How do I even explain that relationship? Destructive, that's what it was, but it wasn't always like that. It started off as a friendship, a mutual understanding of the pain we were going through as kids. My mom destroying our family, Tucker's mom neglecting the fact she had a son. We leaned on each other and after a while, that friendship blossomed into a relationship, an all-consuming relationship that became volatile at times. Both seeking the love we needed as kids, we turned into jealous, unhealthy individuals, relying too much on each other for comfort, losing ourselves in one another. Tucker is two years older than me and when I left for college, his jealousy was so smothering that I distanced myself, unable to cope with the fights. When he visited, it felt different, better, but when he left, our relationship turned toxic once again. It was unhealthy. It still is. He's a good man, I know this. But he isn't the right man for me.

Interrupting my thoughts, Smilly says, "I don't think he sees it that way. I think he still believes you two are meant for each other."

"I know. Believe me, he's made his thoughts on the subject clear. I just can't go there with him again."

"Instead you decide to fool around with some guy you work with?"

I sip my coffee and say without looking at Smilly, "Funny, I don't recall asking you to judge my personal life."

"I'm not judging you, Sadie." Smilly sighs and leans back on the car, her hands propping her up. "I'm just looking out for you. It was only a few short months ago when everything happened. You haven't been the same person lately, and it's scary. You barely laugh, you've given up on school and your goals. I understand being lost, believe me, I've been there, and I see that in you right now. I just don't want you to jump into something when you're not ready."

"I'm not jumping into anything. It was just . . . ." Hell, I don't even know what it was. This morning was so out of character for me but for some reason, I couldn't stop myself. I wanted him from the moment he started accidentally fondling me in his sleep. Call it my hormones or what have you, but my head was telling me no, whereas my body was screaming yes. Clearly my body won out. And honestly, I'm pretty sure my body will win out again tonight.

Yeah, I'll be going on a date with him tonight. I just hope he comes by after I slammed the door on his face.

"It was what?"

I shrug and dust a crumb off my leg. "It was fun. He's ... fun. Not intense like Tucker. More easygoing, happy. It's infectious, Smilly. It's good, and I think it's the kind of company I need right now." Life has been far too tense for months now, and he is like a bright light in a very dark and void-of-hope existence. He has irritated me, but he has also rejuvenated me. *Somehow.*

"I thought you couldn't stand the guy. Where did the change come from?"

Hell if I know. "I have no clue, honestly. Sometime last night I'm guessing. He's different, Smilly. I've been stuck in my past, in my hometown, in everything familiar. I need to break out of the mold, away from my history. It's eating me alive."

"I get that." Reaching into the box, she grabs us both a Boston Kreme, which means she's getting down to business. Blueberry cake donuts are warm-ups. "What about school?"

"What about it?"

"Are you ever going to go back?"

"You know I can't. The minute I dropped out I lost everything. I couldn't afford to go back to Cornell even if I wanted to."

"So you're done? You're just giving up? You're going to drop your goals, drop Tucker, drop school, and *have fun* instead? Where's the Sadie I went to school with? The Sadie who was going to marry Tucker when she graduated. The Sadie who was going to become a psychologist so she could help children who went through similar instances like her. Where is the Sadie who was valedictorian at our high school, the smart-as-a-whip Sadie?"

"Gone," I whisper. "She's gone, Smilly."

Silence falls between us. The faint sound of traffic behind us mingles with the almost silent trickling of the water rolling over rocks. It's a peaceful, serene moment, and yet I feel nothing but anguish and anxiety. *I'm so sick of feeling listless, aimless . . . alone with the lies and hopelessness.*

Leaning forward again, Smilly asks, "Will she be coming back? Because I miss her."

"I sure as hell hope so." *I miss her too.*

Pulling me into her side, Smilly cradles my shoulder with her arm and rests her head on mine. This girl is tough as nails, honest, and doesn't bullshit with you; it's one of the reasons why she's my best friend. We hold each other accountable, even if we don't necessarily agree with what we're doing.

Hopefully she'll comprehend that there is no longer a Tucker and Sadie, because if there is one thing I'm one hundred percent sure about, it's that the dreams of Tucker and me getting married are dead and buried.

•••

"Oh yeah, don't worry about me. I just plan on ordering some Chinese and binging on Netflix. *The Crown* has really caught my eye."

"Are you sure? Saddlemire said you are more than welcome to come play poker."

"I'm sure he did. I'm good with not losing my money tonight. Go on, I'll be good. It will be nice to have a quiet night."

Smilly studies me and I try not to show panic. I have no idea when Andrew is showing up and I still have to get ready. I need Smilly to get the hell out of here.

"Okay, text me if you need anything."

"Yup." I give her a little wave as I cuddle up in a recliner. "Have fun."

With a click of the door shutting, I hop out of the recliner and sprint to our shared bedroom and start rummaging through my dresser. What to wear, what to wear. Nothing too slutty, that gives the wrong impression, especially after this morning and my enthusiastic pelvis. But I also don't want to look like a nun with a turtleneck as that would also give off the wrong impression. Turtleneck equals *back the fuck off, buddy*, an image I don't want to portray.

I don't even know what he has planned. Are we going to be outside? Inside? Movie? Dinner? A punch to the face? No, not a punch to the face. God, I'm nervous. Can you tell?

Going with a safe option, I put on my dark wash skinny jeans, my black T-strap sandals, and my black floral halter-neck silk tank. It shapes me nicely and shows off my shoulders, an attribute I'm quite proud of. I'm no Kiera the CrossFit devotee, but I don't mind going to the gym.

Heading to the bathroom, I check out my outfit in the mirror and mentally give myself a thumbs up. Cute with a hint of sexy . . . just a hint. Since my hair is already blown dry, I French-braid the right front side and then bobby pin it down, creating a fresh look. Not needing too much on the makeup front, I reapply my eyeliner, lipstick, and add a bit of bronzer. Mascara is already intact, so I'm ready to go.

Looking at my phone, I check the time. Seven thirty. Hmm, I really wish I had his number because sitting here waiting, wondering if he's going to show up will be torture.

Oh God, what if he doesn't show up? What if he decides I was too much of a bitch to him this morning and stands me up? Does it qualify as being stood up when there was only a promise for a date, no real specifics?

Sweat starts to happen. I need to air out my pits. Heading to the bathroom, I grab the blow dryer and I'm about to turn it on when I hear a knock at the door. Shit, he's here. Chucking the blow dryer idea, I snag a few tissues from the box on the bathroom counter and stick them under my arms, blotting them as if trying to perfect my lipstick, but instead remove sweat from my underarms. *Classy.*

Attractive. Oh so very attractive, yet . . . effective.

Flapping my arms like wings, trying to soak up as much as possible, I look in the mirror and immediately start to hate myself. I've completely lost it. Quickly, I remove the tissues, check them for any leftover remnants and then apply some more deodorant followed by a squirt of my perfume.

With one last glance in the mirror, I head to the living room, push my hair back over my shoulders, and answer the door. Standing in front of me is Andrew, wearing hip-hugging jeans, black Vans, and a plain white T-shirt. His hair is perfectly styled to the side, and those glasses frame his kind eyes. Yup, I'm very glad I agreed to this date.

"You came," I say, letting out a breath I didn't know I was holding.

That killer smile greets me as he steps forward. "Did you think a little slamming of the door on my erect penis was going to keep me away? You have to do better than that, Sugar Britches." He cups the back of my neck and smoothly pulls me close, no hitch in his swagger at all. Lowering his head, he brings my lips to his where he gently kisses me, nibbling on my mouth a few times before pulling away.

When he puts a breath of distance between us, my eyes still hazy from his kiss, I say, "Don't call me sugar britches."

"Doubtful I'll be able to stop that but you're cute for asking." Linking our hands together, he says, "Ready?"

"Yup." I snag my purse off the hook by the door, lock up, and follow him out to his truck, which is parked right out front. "What do you have planned?"

"Do you really want to know? Or are you going to let me be dream-worthy and surprise you?"

"Dream-worthy? This better be good, you're setting the expectations pretty high."

"Hmm." He pulls out of the apartment complex and heads toward downtown. "I guess I am. But I have confidence in my idea."

"Yeah, been thinking about this for a bit?"

He squeezes my hand right before he shifts the truck to the next gear and keeps his eyes on the road. "I wish I could be smooth and say I've been thinking about our first date ever since I laid eyes on you, but we both know that would be a big, fat lie."

"Why? Because you were scared of me?"

"No. You were just a nasty she-devil. I wasn't quite sure what to do with you."

I can't help but chuckle at the name. "A nasty she-devil?"

"Yeah, you still have a little of her inside you. She pops out on occasion."

"Like when you spray bleach all over my black pants?"

"That was an accident." He laughs. "I think when you have too much of that cough syrup of yours the she-devil comes out."

"That's not true," I counter, really enjoying this idiotic conversation. "My cough syrup eases the tension in my shoulders. It's when uppity people like you, who ask question after endless question about a job I hate, encourage the she-devil to appear."

We stop at a red light and he turns toward me. "It was my first week. What did you want me to do?" His face is full of humor.

"Request a different trainer."

His head falls back as he laughs. "Yeah, and then get my dick chopped off in the back. No, thank you." He playfully nudges my leg. "Come on, admit it, you liked training me."

"I really didn't."

"But the company was nice?"

"You talked too much," I answer with mirth.

"But the package, come on, the package is a pretty one to look at."

Okay, he's got me there. From day one I noticed how hot Andrew is, how intensely buff his forearms are. You can't mistake that.

"Ahh." He laughs. "I take that silence as a yes. Ha, you wanted to jump my bones from day one."

I roll my eyes and look out the window. "You are ridiculous."

"Hey, if it makes you feel any better, I must have stared at your ass at least a dozen times when we first met. Every time you bent over to scoop ice cream, Little Andy got excited."

"Oh my God." I laugh. "Did you just call your dick, Little Andy?"

"Do you have a problem with that?"

"Just with the fact that it's creepy."

He nods his head and turns onto Chenango Street. "Hey, I never said you have to call him that. Just sharing."

"That's too much sharing."

He scoffs. "As if you're not dying to tell me what you name your tits."

"I'm really not." I chuckle.

He parks under a bridge, one I'm not familiar with, and turns toward me. "You know that laugh of yours, the one you so annoyingly keep hidden? You should really use it more often because it can brighten some of the darkest of days." Winking, he gets out of the truck, leaving me momentarily speechless. Then he opens my door. "Ready?"

I don't think I am—ready to jump in with this man—but with his hand stretched toward mine, offering me protection for this new adventure, I realize something unusual. I've started to trust him, and trust is not something I hand out very easily. *Am I ready? Should I give him my hand and my trust?*

"Yeah, I am."

Hand in hand, we walk along the gravel under the bridge until we turn the corner, past a cement pillar. Bright lights illuminate the dark, starry sky.

"You're taking me to a baseball game?" I ask, barely hiding my excitement.

"Where else would I take you on our first date?"

Binghamton, New York is known for a few things: carousels, spiedies, Nirchi's Pizza, and the Binghamton Rumble Ponies. Yes, you read that right, the Rumble Ponies. They are the New York Mets Double A minor league team. Formally known as the B-Mets, they changed their name to the Rumble Ponies a little while back. Fans had the opportunity to vote online and decide their new team name. I voted for Stud Muffins, for obvious reasons, and of course on my scale, the Timber Jockies came in a close second. But the Rumble Ponies won out, probably because of the whole carousel thing.

Side note: Binghamton declares itself to be the carousel capital of the world. Big statement right there.

Walking toward the gate, my hand in Andrew's, my heart beating wildly, I joke, "Are you going to buy me peanuts and Cracker Jacks?"

"Hell, no. We're getting spiedies." Just a heads-up, spiedies are sandwiches filled with marinated cubes of chicken. It sounds gross, but they are really good.

"You're a spiedie guy?"

"Spiedies and half-moon cookies, baby. It's what I lived on every time I came to visit Jimmy, my brother."

"You're not from the area?"

"Nah, grew up in Southern California. Moved out here with my parents when I graduated from high school and then went to school in Maine up until last year when I transferred here."

Pulling out his wallet, he hands the elderly person at the gate two tickets. His preparation for this date is cute. When we are let into the small ballpark, he grips my hand again and takes us straight to the spiedie kiosk where a line is already formed.

"You grew up around here, right?" Andrew asks.

"Yeah, a small town called Whitney Point. There were only ninety-five students in my graduating class, so to say we were all in each other's business is an understatement."

"Ninety-five people?" he asks in disbelief. "Damn, you must have known everyone's underwear size."

Glancing up at him incredulously, I shake my head. "Yes, teachers included."

He wraps his arm around my shoulder, brings me flush against his body, and kisses the side of my head, lingering a few seconds before he gently lifts away. The natural and small show of affection sends chills up and down my body, lighting up my body in a way I haven't felt in quite a long time, even with Tucker. What is it about this man that changes every thought I've ever possessed about relationships?

"Tell me, Sadie, what makes you laugh?"

Caught a little off guard, I ask, "What do you mean?"

Removing his hand from my shoulder, he links our hands back together, his fingers entangling with mine. His thumb rubs the back of my hand, the gentle touch doing all different kinds of things to my rapidly beating heart. "I want to know what makes you laugh, Sadie. I want to know how to easily elicit that amazingly beautiful and happy sound of yours. It's addictive, and I know you reserve it for truly special occasions, but help a guy out and tell me what makes you laugh."

Can I tell him what makes me swoon instead? Because this right here does. The simple act of holding my hand, taking me to a baseball game under the summer night sky, and telling me he wants to make me laugh. This is swoon-worthy. This is not what I ever expected from Andrew when I first met him, when I first shook his hand. His go-get-'em attitude initially annoyed the crap out of me. Now his assertiveness is attractive, especially when it's him asking me out, or taking charge in planning the evening, or holding my hand.

"Come on, just give me a little hint." He winks. *How the hell are his winks even sexy?*

Looking down at our clasped hands, I shrug. "I don't know, just depends. I like joking around and sarcastic humor. Oh, and I'm a sucker for slapstick humor."

"Slapstick, huh?" I really like that silly smirk on his face. "So if I walked up to the spiedie station, tripped, and fell through the wood, collapsing the entire thing, would you laugh or come to my aid?"

"That would never happen, but if it did in your little imaginary world, I would probably giggle and come to your aid at the same time."

Laughing himself, he nods his head. "I'll take it." Straightening up, he asks, "Since you like slapstick humor, did you enjoy the whole sturdy tits debacle or are you still mad about that?"

How could I forget about sturdy tits? I don't think that will ever happen.

"You want to know the truth?"

"Always." We step closer in line, only one person in front of us now, the smell of the grilled chicken is really starting to make my stomach growl with hunger.

"I laughed about it in the stockroom."

A pained look crosses his face. "I made you laugh and you

hid it from me? That's fucked up, Sadie." He tacks on a smile that hits me right in the heart. God, he is so . . . cute? Adorable? Sexy? Can someone be all of those things put together?

I squeeze his hand in mine and say, "I think you'll get over it."

"No." He shakes his head. "There is no recovering from such a devastation. Pretty sure this is the end for me."

"Dramatic much?" I ask, holding back the laugh that wants to pop out.

He sniffs the air and then looks down at me. "Yes, I can smell death in my near future. I never thought I would go in such a way. And without ever really knowing what your boobs look like, only motorboating and fondling them."

"You're ridiculous."

"Such a travesty."

Stepping up to the counter, we are greeted by a larger man with a pen behind his ear, a full goatee gracing his face, and wearing a backwards hat. "What can I get you two?"

Dramatically Andrew leans on the counter and looks up at the man. "I'm dying, dude."

Andrew must have winked at the man or they have some kind of secret guy code because instead of the man being caught off guard by Andrew's announcement, he leans forward and pats Andrew's arm. "Fuck, I'm sorry to hear that. And you look so young. Blue balls?" he asks.

Andrew shakes his head, really using the counter as his support. "See this beautiful woman next to me?"

The man looks me up and down and then back at Andrew. "She's quite the looker. Let me guess, she won't give you the time of day."

He lifts our connected hands for the man to see. "Oh, she's given me the time during the day, morning actually."

"Andrew!" I swat at him, causing the man to laugh.

Leaning a little more forward, he places his hand to the side of his mouth and whispers, "Okay, to be fair, it was a little dry humping, nothing naked."

"Oh my God," I moan in embarrassment.

"Aw, I love a good trocken buckel in the morning." As both of us look confused, the man clarifies, "It's German."

Nodding, Andrew continues, "I'm digging that term, man. If only I wasn't dying, I'd be able to use it more."

"Ah yeah, your impending death. What's sending you to the coffin early?"

"Uh, biodegradable urn actually. I would like to become a tree once I die." Interesting, never pegged Andrew as a tree-urn kind of guy. "But that's beside the point. I'm dying because this beautiful woman standing next to me, holding my hand, the one who trocken buckeled my crotch this morning, has been denying me of her laugh. And man," Andrew grabs the guy by the shirt and pulls him closer in desperation, "she has the most mind-numbing, life-altering, gorgeous-beyond-belief laugh. A kind of laugh that you swear you see angels floating out of her mouth when she thinks something is funny."

"Wow." The man steps back. "That's rough, man. I can't believe she can be so cold. You know what, two spiedies on me." Calling out behind his back, he says, "Two original spiedies." Turning back to us, he asks, "Two Cokes with that?"

"Coke Zero for me and for the lady . . ." Andrew gestures me to answer.

What the hell is going on right now? I'm so confused as to why this guy is being so nice to us, why he's put up with Andrew's dramatics with a line behind us.

"Uh, Sprite."

"We've got a Sprite girl," the man says, walking away to

grab our drinks. I glance up at Andrew who just smiles down at me. "All right, here we go, two spiedies, a Coke Zero and a Sprite. Have a good time." Looking at me, the man says, "And, sweetheart, give my boy Andrew a break. Even if his jokes are cheesy, laugh *for* him."

Gah, they know each other.

"Thanks, Hal." Andrew shakes Hal's hand, grabs our items, and walks me toward the stands.

Silent for a second, Andrew squeezes my hand. "Come on, not even a little snicker?"

"That was a bit elaborate."

"Elaborate? I was thinking more on the lines of smooth."

"Is that how you pick up girls? Talk about dry humping them in front of strangers only to score free spiedies? Does that really work?"

"You tell me, you're the one still holding my hand, batting those impossible eyelashes at me."

"I am not batting my eyelashes. It's called blinking."

"Whatever it is, it's got my butt tingling." He does a little hop in place and shivers.

I laugh out loud from his ridiculous nature. I can't hold it back. I have to give him that one.

"Fuck, yes!" He fist-pumps our clasped hands. "Damn, Sadie, you just made my night." He lifts our joint connection to his lips and gently kisses the back of my hand as he looks down at me. And what I see in his eyes is something I don't think I've seen before. He doesn't know me, but he's taking time to change that. *As if the thought of not knowing me is intolerable.* He asked what I wanted, rather than presuming. He wants to connect . . . with me. Know me.

Oh shit. My stomach just flipped itself upside down.

I really might be in trouble.

CHAPTER ELEVEN

SADIE

"I still can't believe you got a black eye." I shake my head at Andrew who's holding an ice pack to his face, trying to grip my hand as we walk out to his truck.

"Worth it, baby." Releasing my hand, he snags the game ball out of his back pocket and flips it in his hand. "Tripping over that seventy-year-old man to catch a foul ball, only to slam my face on a chair armrest? All worth it because I have this little guy. I'm just lucky my glasses fell off before I went eye first into the seat."

"You could have gotten it without tripping over that old man and spilling his Cracker Jacks."

"I purchased him a new box." He did, which was actually quite sweet. "And there was no way I could have gotten the ball before that little punk in the red polo if I hadn't climb over the old man. Did you see the trajectory and spin on that thing? The way it flew off the bat and the angle, it would have never made it up to our seats. The Cracker Jacks had to take a hit so I could get a prize."

"What a sad day for Cracker Jacks," I reply. Conversation with Andrew is so easy, so fun, so light. I've never experienced this easygoing banter with a guy before; it almost feels unnatural, but right at the same time, if that makes any sense.

Once we get to his truck, he fishes out the keys from his pocket and unlocks my door. He helps me in, like the gentleman that he is, but then turns me around in the bench seat so I'm facing him, his body between my legs.

His hand still ices his eye just under his glasses, and he asks, "Did you have a good time, Sadie?"

I did and despite my initial nerves and reservations, I'm not surprised I had a good time. That was a given. I'm learning that the man is electric in everything he does. But I am surprised about one thing. I was able to actually let an outsider into my little circle. I'm surprised I haven't pushed him away every chance I've had, and I'm incredibly amazed I want to hang out with him again.

"I did. Thank you." I hook my fingers through his belt loops and pull him closer. Dropping the ice pack on the floor of his truck, he grips the top of the doorframe, his shirt rising on his biceps, giving me a great view of his strong arms and tapered waist. Flashes of last night and this morning run through my mind: Andrew with his shirt off, Andrew with sexy morning hair, Andrew with his almighty forearms helping me rock back and forth on his erection. My body ignites. *I'm hot for the nerd.*

Trying to avoid the temptation of sticking my hand down his pants—yes, that's where my hormones are heading right now—I reach up and gently touch his face. "Is your eye okay?"

He shrugs it off. "Yeah, I'll be fine. Unless you want to play naughty nurse, then *ouch, my eye!*" He hovers his hand over his face, which makes me laugh.

"You would like that, wouldn't you? Me waiting on you hand and foot—"

"Preferably while wearing nothing would be awesome." He

wiggles his eyebrows at me.

"Not going to happen." My fingers are still hooked through the loops of his jeans as he stares down at me, the street lamp providing the only light near us.

"You're crushing a man's dream here, Sadie."

"I think you'll survive."

He leans even closer now, still holding the doorframe. "I'm not sure. With the head trauma I've sustained tonight and not having anyone to nurse me to health, I might possibly face death in the near future. My well-being uncertain for the coming morning."

"That's the second time you've mentioned dying today."

One of his hands snakes around my neck and pulls me closer. "Do you see what you do to me? I'm on the verge of death every second you're around, teetering in balance, wondering and waiting to see if you'll press those luscious lips against mine, saving me from the darkness tapping me on the shoulder."

I shake my head, and a silent chuckle is released. "What happened to the shy guy from work? I think I liked you better when you weren't so smooth with your words."

"Yeah?" He inches even closer, pulling me in. "Why's that?"

"Because," his lips are so close, I can almost taste him, "you were easier to resist."

"Hmm. Note to self: always act like an overconfident douche around Sadie."

Before I have a chance to respond, his lips descend on mine, locking me in, giving me no other option but to melt into the feeling of his lips caressing mine. Not that I would want to be doing anything else right now. He just has a way of sucking me into his little world where nothing will be able to harm me.

Demanding, more demanding than this morning, his tongue runs along the seam of my lips, begging for entrance. I don't give it to him right away; instead, I make him work for it. I make his lips work for it. Groaning ever so slightly from the back of his throat, he maneuvers his mouth over mine, making the most of my closed lips, tempting me with open-mouth kisses until I can't take it anymore. *Is there really any choice?*

When my tongue touches his, he groans even louder and releases his grip from the door so he can cup my face. His delectable body presses right against mine.

The first time I met Andrew, never in my wildest dreams would I have pegged him to be the kind of man who could bring me to my knees with one kiss. But he's proven me wrong with the delectable way he works his tongue against mine, and with the way his lips connect in the sexiest way possible.

There's no question about it; he's dangerous.

Wet, demanding, unyielding kisses wrap me up into a little Andrew cocoon, one I couldn't imagine leaving. Having Andrew wrapped around me, the way his thumbs rub my cheeks as his tongue dives around against mine, the delicious press of his lower half against mine, the sexy little moans that rumble up the back of his throat . . . it's euphoria.

I move my fingers into his waistband, and from that little touch, he shoots off me, putting at least a foot of distance between us. Visibly shaken, he runs his hand through his perfectly styled hair and stares at me through his eyelashes, a slight lift to the corner of his mouth.

"What's wrong?" I ask, a little stupefied from his abrupt movement.

"Uh, I was getting a little too excited. Popping a boner in public, under a bridge, where Joe Hobo lays his head to rest, doesn't really scream sexy to me."

Chuckling, I shake my head. "Yeah, not so much."

Coming closer again, he takes my hand and kisses the back of it sweetly. "Would you like to come back to my place?"

That question—the way he *asks* it—slays me. There is boyish hope in his eyes, as if this is the first time he's ever asked a girl back to his place, which I know can't possibly be true, not from the intimate moments I've had with him. Still, there is something so sweet and pure about him that I find myself nodding.

"Yeah?" he asks, that megawatt smile filling his face.

"Yeah, but get in the car and start driving before I change my mind."

I position my body properly in my seat as Andrew goes to shut the door but not before he slips his large frame into my portion of the cab, cups my cheek and kisses me hard, sending my heart into a tailspin of lust for this man who doesn't hesitate showing affection.

I'm left with no time to react. Just as fast as he leaned in to kiss me, he's now shutting my door and jogging around to his side. When he hops in the truck, he clicks his seatbelt in and then nods for me to come closer while patting the middle seat.

"Come on, Sugar Britches, hop on over."

"You want me to sit in the middle seat?" I ask, incredulously.

"Hell yeah, I do. Now get that perfect ass of yours over here so I can drive with you tucked under my arm." Tugging on my arm, he helps me clear the space between us. I fasten my seatbelt and allow him to scoop me closer into his chest.

Tucked right up against him, "Standing Outside The Fire" playing in the background, Andrew drives us through the streets of Binghamton to his house, singing quietly and never letting go of me.

•••

"You're kidding, right?" I ask, looking down at his bed. "That's a twin bed."

"Yup," Andrew says with a casual smile, leaning against the door of his room.

"How do you even fit in something like that? Your feet have to hang off the end."

He shrugs. "Eh, you get used to it. It's not all that bad."

Spinning around, I take in the little space of his room and look back up at him. "This room is tiny, but I appreciate that you made enough room for a life-size Derek Jeter cutout. That's dedication."

"Thank you." He bows like an idiot, but it makes me smile.

"Although, I do have to address something with you."

"Yeah?" He walks up to me and places his hands on my hips. "Does it have to do with how we're not in PJs snuggling each other in my little twin bed?"

"No." I chuckle. "But I get now why you wanted to come here, trying to get all handsy on me."

"Can't blame me. I woke up this morning thinking your boob was a playful orange, and I've become addicted. So I need to know, do they taste like an orange too?"

"No." I playfully swat him, which he takes like a champ and brings me in closer.

"Baby, I'll be the judge of that, but please tell me what you have to address."

God, the smooth timbre of his voice makes me feel so warm, his arms feel like home when I'm in them, and I'm surprised his gentle teasing doesn't bother me. *Where did he come from?*

Clearing my throat, trying not to turn into a puddle under his stare, I say, "Well, from the looks of it, you really are a nerd."

"How so?" he asks, a little pinch to his brow.

I point to his wall. "You have a poster of math equations on your wall."

He turns to look at said poster and then gives me a knowing smirk. "It's nice to have a quick reference on your wall when calculating things."

"And you also have three computers on your desk."

"Why have one when you can have three?" He shrugs casually.

"And you have four different Rubik's Cubes on your dresser."

He glances in that direction. "Ever heard about keeping your mind from turning into mush? I don't want to be that old person who doesn't remember how to wash his own dick."

"Okay, I can understand that, but can you please explain to me why you have three frames on your wall with pictures of Albert Einstein, Bill Gates, and," I lean forward to get a better look, "Steve Urkel?"

Cringing slightly, he doesn't even bother to take in the picture I'm talking about. "I would like to say someone gave that to me, but I printed those pictures myself. Three men, all geniuses, all celebrities in their own right. It's nice to model yourself after such strong, intelligent, and confident men."

In disbelief, I say, "All right, but if you start wearing cuffed jeans with suspenders, this little thing we have going on is done."

Taking pause, he thinks about my statement before nodding his head in approval. "I can agree to that. But are you opposed to red-framed glasses that almost look like goggles?" he asks, referring to Steve Urkel's horrendous glasses.

"Very much so."

Making note, he says, "Locked that one in the memory vault." He kisses me on the forehead quickly before heading to his dresser where he pulls out a T-shirt. A T-shirt that just happens to have a monkey wearing glasses holding a pen, writing out a math equation on the front. Honestly, this man. "You can have the bathroom first."

With a wink, he shoves me in the right direction where I spend a few minutes getting ready for bed using the spare toothbrush he has lying around. He takes no time at all getting ready and before I know it, we are both squeezing into this twin bed where his feet completely dangle off the end.

Facing each other now, Andrew shirtless and only wearing a pair of shorts, and me in his T-shirt that falls to the tops of my knees, we talk.

Odd at first, it's hard for me to comprehend how incredibly easy this feels, cuddling with Andrew, lying in his bed, just talking. I've only done this with one other man, Tucker, but it's never felt this easy, this comfortable . . . this *right*.

Snuggling in close, reveling in the feel of his body pressed against mine, I ask, "How did you find this place and where are your roommates?"

"Summer break. The girls are all on the women's basketball team and are from different countries: Latvia, Finland, and France. There is one American, so at least I won't be the only one lost. This was the only decent place I could find on such short notice."

"You're living with five other girls?" My mind can't fathom what that would be like.

"Yeah." His hand rides up my thigh, lifting my shirt with it where he settles on my hip, gripping me tightly. "You jealous?" His voice is playful, so I know he's joking.

"No. I'm actually worried for you. Do you know what it's going to be like living with five women? You're going to be in hell."

"I'm quite aware of the danger that rests before me, but like I said, it was last minute, and I had no other decent options."

"Last minute? You keep saying that. What made you transfer

so late? Did you not like your old school?"

His breathing starts to pick up and from his brief silence, I know I've struck a chord. Not that I really want to be talking about school at this moment, given my situation, but I'm curious why he was so late on the housing search. What detained him? What made him transfer?

"Uh," his thumb rubs along my skin as he tries to find the right words to say, "I kind of had this thing happen at my other school. Thought it would be best if I transferred rather than stayed."

Even more curious, I ask, "You kind of had this thing happen to you, what does that even mean?"

"You don't want to get into it, not worth your pretty little time."

"I really do. Come on, tell me what happened."

His hand continues to glide across my skin in a very seductive way, but he doesn't answer me, which makes me that much more intrigued.

"Was it really bad?"

He sighs. His eyes meet mine, and with his glasses on the nightstand, I get an even better view into his hazel eyes. Without the barrier of curtained glass over them, I have an unfiltered look into the gorgeous gold flecks that round his pupils. So heart-stopping. "You know how college is . . ." He lifts his head for a second and says, "Wait, you go to college, right?"

Panic snares me. From the little things I've seen around his room, to the way he's talked about different computer programming, and his nerdy references, it's obvious school and education is very important. What would he think of me, knowing I'm a dropout with nothing set in my future? Would he even want to talk to me if he knew the truth? *And it surprises me how much that bothers me.*

Swallowing hard, I nod, knowing what's about to come out of my mouth next is a blatant lie, but for the life of me, I can't tell him the truth. I can't fathom telling this intelligent man that I dropped out of college, especially because I got pregnant. "Uh, yeah. Cornell."

The sentence feels dirty coming off my tongue, and the bright look on his face does nothing for making me feel any better.

"Cornell? Damn, girl." His hand slides up higher on my body where he squeezes me. "Sexy and smart? Are you trying to kill me? Again?"

A fake chuckle pops out of my mouth, a defense mechanism I've used many times before. Wanting to change the subject, and not wanting to dig too deep on my end of education, I focus back on him. "So, what happened?"

Groaning again, he says, "I don't want to tell you."

"Why not?" I shouldn't be pressing him, especially since I just flat-out lied to his face. Jesus, I'm the biggest piece of shit ever.

He bites his bottom lip and looks me in the eyes. "My family refers to it as *the ordeal*."

"The ordeal? That seems serious."

"I wouldn't necessary say it's serious, more . . . ridiculous."

What could be so ridiculous that his family refers to it as *the ordeal* and made it necessary to transfer schools?"

Falling to his back, his hand disconnecting with my skin—I feel the loss immediately—he rubs his face. "Fuck, am I really going to tell you this story?"

Wanting to ease some of his tension, I scoot closer to him and place my hand on his bare chest where I run my fingers along the contours of his pecs. Glancing in my direction, he raises his eyebrows in question. "Are you trying to use your womanly wiles on me?"

"No." I chuckle. "Just trying to make you comfortable."

"Is that right? Because the way you're teasing your fingers across my skin, I could have sworn you were aiming for sexual torture instead."

"You are such a guy." I roll my eyes.

Smiling up at me, he says, "Thank you."

"That wasn't a compliment," I counter.

"I know, but I chose to take it as one."

I stop my wandering hand from dancing around his well-defined chest. "Are you going to tell me?"

Letting out a long breath of air, he says, "Kiss me first, just so I can taste you one last time."

"You are being so dramatic." I lean over and press my lips softly against his, loving the way his hand immediately runs up my back, under my shirt. He has no problem getting handsy, as if he can't quite get enough of the feel of my skin. I love it. "Mmm," I moan, moving my hands so they frame his face. He tries to move my body over his but I hold still. He's not about to distract me with some more trocken buckel when I want to hear his story. "Not so fast, mister."

"Ugh, fine," he complains. "But just to be clear, I warned you."

"Let it be known, this storytelling adventure was my idea."

"Okay." He takes a deep breath and says, "I've always been into three things: computers, math, and women."

"Oh my God." I laugh. "You know those three things don't mix, right?"

"I would appreciate no commentary until I'm done," he teases.

I hold up my hands in defense. "I apologize, please proceed."

"As I was saying," he clears his throat, "computers, math, and women. But I went to college with one thing in mind, and that was to become a software engineer, earning one fucking amazing internship, and working toward a master's program I could hopefully have paid for by the company I'm working for." Honestly, I couldn't imagine Andrew wanting anything less. "Studying made me restless, so I entertained the idea of going down to the free gym for students. *Entertained* became obsessed." Ah, hence the arm porn he's sporting. "I've never been a big guy, never will be, but I started to notice a difference in the fit of my shirts." Hold back the snort, hold it back, Sadie. "And the ladies began to notice as well."

"Oh Jesus," I mutter.

"Hey, what did I say about no commentary?" He tickles my side and laughs.

"I'm sorry. It's just so funny hearing you talk about the ladies admiring you. You're just not that kind of guy who speaks of all the pussy he's had."

"You act as if I have a donkey face."

That makes me tilt my head back and laugh. "Oh my God, you have the furthest thing from a donkey face. You're hot, Andrew, there is no denying that. Even if I wanted to pretend that wasn't the truth, I couldn't."

"Good to know." He puffs his chest, clearly proud of the compliments I'm tossing his way.

"You're just more humble, that's all."

"Humble, I like that." Running his hand up my back again, tracing over my thong-clad ass, he sucks in a breath and then presses his palm against my skin. "Um, back to the story. I was working out and met a guy there."

I sit up, my hand helping me as I press against his chest. "You had a gay moment." Even as I say it, I can't imagine it. Andrew is simply too smooth, too good with women.

The rumble of his laugh shakes my firmly planted hand. "No,

I did not have a gay moment. And what did I say about commentary?"

"I'm sorry. It just came out of me. Continue."

"He was in the engineering program and invited me to a party at his frat house. I thought nothing of it since the guy said his frat was full of like-minded fellas like myself. You know the ones who worship movies like *Tron* and *The Hitchhiker's Guide to the Galaxy,* and *Star Trek* remakes. All amazing movies by the way. And when I showed up at the house, I was greeted with a bunch of nerds. I'm talking pocket protectors, bowl haircuts, and button-up plaid shirts. I was kind of surprised with the amount of nerd factor that filled the house." Rubbing my back with his fingers, he continues, "It wasn't until the girls showed up that I knew I was in trouble. You see, the fraternity had a sister sorority dedicated for nerd lovers only. Before I knew it, pocket protectors were thrown to the wind and there was a lot of . . . trocken buckel if you know what I mean."

I chuckle. Where the hell is he going with this story? "Man, I can only imagine the type of heavy petting going on."

"Exactly." He cutely bops my nose. "So, of course I got drunk and started fooling around with a girl named Beth. She seemed nice and innocent, that was until we started to get a little more handsy and she pulled my pants down."

"Wow, just like that? Did she bite your dick?" I cringe from the thought.

"No," he chuckles, "and I almost feel that would have been better. She was an avid Snapchatter, had quite the following at the school. Being young and all—"

"You're still young," I point out.

"I know, but I like to believe I've matured since then." I nod, giving him the benefit of the doubt. "She thought it would be fun to Snapchat our little encounter, and being the drunk dickhead

I was, I went with it, until she started snapping a video of her practically boomeranging my dick back and forth with a caption that said Maine's very own Cannon Cock. I was mad, of course, but in the snap, you couldn't see who I was. But afterward, she posted a picture of me, claiming me as Cannon Cock."

"Are you serious?" My face heats up. Does he really have a cannon cock? Don't look down at his lap, do not look down. This is a sensitive moment, so give him the respect he wants.

DO NOT LOOK DOWN.

"You want to look at my cock, don't you?" he asks on a laugh.

"No," I reply too quickly.

"Yeah, okay, all in good time, Sugar Britches." Picking up where he left off, he continues, "So you can imagine what happened next when this popular girl posted about a cannon cock."

"I have a faint idea but who knows, I never thought this story would turn into a story about your dick."

"Not many people do. This girl ended up destroying my ability to learn. Every class I went to, someone tried to crawl on my lap to feel *the cannon* as they would call it. Some asked if they could get it to blast off, one teacher's aide actually wrote in the back of one of my papers that she screenshot Cannon Cock and has it on her cellphone wallpaper."

"What a pervert," I say in disgust. I mean, I like dick, but not enough to have to touch it every time I use my phone. Self-respect, ladies!

"Yeah, it got so bad that one day, when my parents were visiting me on campus, I brought them back to my dorm to find a line of women, caged by velvet rope, lined up next to a poster on the door where time slots were filled out to view the one and only cannon cock in his natural habitat. Some girls brought condoms, some brought magazines and lotion."

"You are so lying right now." I laugh, not able to hold back.

"I wish I was."

"College students did not bring you lotion and magazines." Reaching over to his nightstand, he snags his phone and holds it out to me. "Go ahead, call my parents. Ask them. They were there."

Laughing still, I shake my head. "No, I believe you. Oh my God, what did your mom say?"

"Ha, she was more concerned with the type of wood my dorm-room door was made of. She's kind of a wood freak. Really likes a good quality trunk."

"So do I." I wink.

Running his hand over my bare ass, he says, "Good thing you have a cannon cock in bed with you then." Yup, I'm blushing. With a playful smirk, he continues, "My dad, on the other hand, was not a happy camper. He thought I was running some kind of sex ring in my dorm. Needless to say, I was more than forced to transfer. My dad didn't want me to start school right away, let alone leave the house for the summer. He thought I had a sex addiction or that I was some unstoppable pussy fiend. He wanted to keep a close eye on me to make sure I wasn't trolling for tail."

"Because you really have that personality," I add sarcastically.

"According to my dad, I do. He had my whole summer planned out for me where I would sell fudge to little old ladies and mow his lawn with the old push mower. My parents own over an acre of land."

"That sounds like a nightmare."

He shifts and drags my body on top of his, then smoothly strokes my bare butt, curving his hands over its roundness. Almost instantly I can feel the aforementioned cannon cock starting to make an appearance.

"And there you have why I quickly got a job and moved here

for the summer. My dad put up a good fight though."

"Does he know you're rooming with five women?"

Andrew nods. "Yeah, that was a fun conversation."

My shirt is now completely lifted and up my back from Andrew's wandering hands, causing me to wiggle above him. Digging his fingers into my ass, he's casually looking up at me, but there is an inferno roaring inside me.

Resting my forehead against his, I ask, "Uh, Mr. Cannon Cock, are you trying to torture me on purpose?"

He wiggles his eyebrows at me. "Is it working?"

Good God, yes.

With just the pass of his hand over my skin, his strong chest beneath me, his growing cock pressing against my center in the most intimate of ways—reminding me of everything we did this morning—I'm wet.

Shit, was that really just this morning? It feels like forever ago.

Flipping me on my back, he hovers over me, the twin bed feeling smaller and smaller by the moment from the size of his strong body against mine. Thankfully he pushed the bed up against the wall when arranging his room, giving me zero chance of falling out of bed.

"From the way your breath keeps hitching in your throat, I'm going to say it is working."

Not able to voice my answer, I nod, waiting. *What will he do, knowing that?*

It feels so weird that only twenty-four hours ago I was staring at this man from a kitchen window, watching him easily win over my friends—even Tucker, before he found out who Andrew was. And I don't blame them. He's charismatic, but in his own way. Andrew isn't one of those men who can rip off your skirt in the middle of a parking lot only to eat you out on the hood of his souped-up Trans Am. No, he slowly chips his way into your life with his smile, his malleable personality, and his kind eyes. It's hard to be a dick to someone like Andrew, and I'm finding it out rather quickly, it's hard to forget about someone like Andrew.

Near impossible actually.

Within twenty-four hours, he's firmly placed himself in my life when I believed there were no vacancies. Not only does this man make me laugh, make me burn with excitement, and make me want *more*, he also terrifies the living fuck out of me.

Charisma, it's a death sentence for any woman, and I'm pretty sure I'm straddling condemned row from every sexy smirk and witty comment that leaves Andrew's mouth.

CHAPTER TWELVE

ANDREW

If you asked me to replay each moment before this point with Sadie, beneath me, her legs rubbing against mine, I wouldn't have an answer for you besides pure luck and drunken courage.

This is one of the first times I'm actually thanking the beer gods for coming up with the yeasty liquid, because having Sadie in my arms is the best feeling I've ever experienced. Her hardened exterior has melted, her laugh is more frequent, and those eyes, the way they look at me. Fuck, it's addicting, especially when she's waiting for me to make the next move.

Despite my growing length, I want to take this slow. This morning, I got a good taste of the kind of friction we could create, but I want to show her that I'm a very giving man, that Cannon Cock isn't the one in charge.

Slowly, I glide my fingers up to the hem of the shirt she borrowed from me and start to move it up toward her breasts, letting the cool fabric rub against her skin, until I reach the spot right below her breasts. Now supporting myself over her, I start to roll the shirt, watching the way her eyes study me with lust and the way her chest is starting to rise and fall more rapidly.

Fuck, I want to get a good look at her tits, but now is not the time for that. I have one thing in mind, and I can't get distracted by her upper half. Continuing to roll the shirt, I don't stop until it's rolled to where the shirt is barely covering her tits, the bottom half peeking out for me to see. Fuck, she's so damn hot.

Her arms are at her side, but I change that quickly, raising them above her head, which lifts her shirt a few millimeters more, tempting my fucking will. My mouth wants on those fucking beauties.

"Don't move your arms," I demand.

"If you tickle me, I'm going to kick you in the balls."

"Baby, the last thing on my mind right now is tickling. Keep them still and spread your legs."

She spreads her legs on cue. Such a good listener. *Fuck, do I want her.*

Taking my time, I lower my lips to hers. Nibbling across them, taking in how incredible she tastes—like fruity ChapStick and mint—I don't immediately notice the small movements of my hips. My cock rides along her leg until she moans, and then she's moving her hips as well. Hearing her moan, feeling her eagerness underneath me, fuck, my cock is twitching. Slow, buddy. Keep it slow.

Instead of giving in to her little incessant thrusts against me, I slow down my hips and move my lips along her jaw, where I nip at her, lick her neck very softly with the tip of my tongue, and suck gently in the crook of where her collarbone rests.

Methodically, I press my lips along her skin, never lifting up for too long while my hands gently press against her hip bones, pinning her to my bed. As if she's in sync with me, her body moves beneath mine, searching for more, *yearning* for more. It's sexy as hell, feeling her squirm. Her grip on my back intensifies with each motion of my lips. Her arms should be above her head right now, but I will let her slip go for now.

With the shirt still covering her breasts, I graze my nose over the fabric, near her hardened nipples, giving them just the lightest of scrapes until I reach her flat stomach. Her skin's so soft against my roughened jaw. The thought of my beard burn marking her skin turns me on, as does knowing I'll be claiming this woman who seemed so hard, yet is so fucking delicate. I never knew this would be in the cards with her. Yes, I admit I wanted it but really wasn't convinced I'd get the chance to be her friend, let alone granted access to her hidden beauty. She is incredible, and I want so much more.

Flicking my tongue along her skin, I revel in the way her stomach contracts with each touch, her breath hitching in unison as her hands find my hair. Pulling on the long strands, as if they are reins, she tries to direct me where she wants me, but I deny her. I'm in fucking charge, so she's going to have to learn some patience. Not everything is according to her timetable in the bedroom. *It will be in my time, in my way, but all* for *her, as I'll make her feel amazing.*

Instead of moving my head lower to the junction of her thighs, where I so desperately want to be, I move my mouth back up to where the T-shirt is folded. Wanting to tease her a little more, I run my nose along the underside of her breasts, loving how fucking soft they are. Immediately she moans from the contact, her chest jutting out, begging for more. Removing her hands from my hair, she reaches for the hem of the rolled-up shirt when I stop her.

"Hands above your head," I command.

"Take my shirt off," she answers back, a strain to her voice.

"No chance, baby. My tongue has a one-track mind right now."

Squirming under me, causing the shirt to ride up some more, almost exposing her goddamn nipples, I suck in a deep breath.

"Doesn't seem like it. Seems like your mouth just wants to fucking tease me right now."

"Ever heard of foreplay, baby? It's where I spend my fine-ass time licking, sucking, and playing with your body until you're so wet between your legs—so fucking ready—that your clit is pounding out of control. That with one flick of my tongue you'll be screaming my name at the top of your lungs."

Her eyes become hazy, her breathing more rapid than before, and her legs fall open for me. "You know," she finally replies after licking her lips seductively, "languid sexual encounters can go both ways."

I lean forward and press my mouth against hers, diving my tongue against hers, tasting every essence of her, just enough to give her a complex when I pull away. Winking at her, I say, "I look forward to our role reversal. Until then, keep your hands where I can see them and your shirt firmly in place."

"Not a boob guy?" she asks with a wicked grin.

"I'm into whatever you have to offer, but right now, I'm focusing on your pussy."

I catch a glimpse of her almost-exposed breast. I swallow hard and keep moving down her body until I'm hovering above her panty line. With my tongue, I run the length of the thin fabric. Her legs beneath me fall apart even farther, making room for my broad shoulders. *God, her scent.* She's already so wet. My teeth graze her skin, nip her, tease her, just before I snag the hem of her thong and drag it down, my nose grazing her bare pussy. Leaning back, I take the thong with my hand and quickly toss it to the ground. Not caring about any reservations she might be feeling, I grip her knees and spread her legs, pushing them up around her chest. Fuck, she's flexible.

Eyes wide, she gazes at me, wondering what I have in store for her.

"Grip your knees, Sadie, and keep them there. I have other plans for my hands that don't involve holding your legs back."

A sexy gasp pops out of her mouth before she does as she's told, giving me the perfect view of her sweet, aroused pussy.

Fuck. Me.

Licking my lips, fucking excited about tasting her, I bury my head between her legs, forgetting about the whole going-slow process, and start lapping at her clit. The moment my tongue hits her arousal my dick jolts in response. Fuck, she tastes so good, like goddamn honey.

I appreciate a well-thought-out equation, a scientific discovery, a perfectly cleaned motherboard from a computer, but holy shit do I love a tempting, sweet-tasting pussy.

The need for more overtakes my senses. My mind is focused on one thing: making this beautiful woman come on my tongue. With my fingers, I spread her lips and suck on her clit, pulling a long, appreciative moan from her. I do it again, harder, rotating from sucking and licking, adding in a few kisses here and there, but more than anything, flicking my tongue across her most sensitive area.

Beside me, her legs shake, her hands slowly lose grip on her knees, and her moans release more rapidly. Her entire body starts to quiver against my shoulders. She's close.

Glancing up, I take in her beauty. Her mouth drawn in an O, her eyes shut, her neck muscles strained, the bottom of her breasts bouncing with the shaking of her body.

Wanting to take her orgasm one step further, I remove my mouth, causing a groan to pull from her lips. "Wh-what . . . are you doing?" She's out of breath and the look of torture is eating her up.

"Lay that pretty head of yours back down and focus on holding your legs in place." When she gives in, I start to run my fingers around her hole, teasing her relentlessly, just barely skimming her skin, occasionally brushing across her clit.

"Oh God, please, Andrew," she begs, her legs shaking.

Bringing my fingers to her entrance, I ask, "How much do you want this, Sadie?"

"So much," she pants.

With the pace of a sloth, I press my fingers inside her, loving the way she tries to press her hips down, urging my entrance. She's so fucking wet, so fucking tight, it takes everything in me not to snap my will and just devour her.

My fingers now slipping deeper inside her, curving in just the right place, I bend my head back down and press my tongue against her clit once more. The pressure of my fingers and tongue pushes her over the edge.

"Oh yes," she screams. Her moans fill the small space of my bedroom while I let her ride my tongue until she's left to only tiny little trembles of pleasure.

Spent, she releases her legs and places both her arms over her face, covering her eyes in what seems like disbelief.

And holy fuck, that was the sexiest thing I've ever witnessed, watching Sadie be so exposed, so vulnerable, laying it all out there for me to take advantage of. Shit, that was . . . that was unclassifiable.

Moving up her body, my dick in so much fucking pain from Sadie's unbridled orgasm, I lay my body across hers and start peppering her jaw with little kisses.

My voice comes out husky as I ask, "Are you okay?"

"Yes," she sighs on a long breath, and then peeks at me through her arms. When she finally shows her face, a giant smile greets me. Fuck, I like her. There is no denying that feeling, not after she holds my balls in the palm of her hand after one sexual encounter.

"You surprise me, Andrew," she finally says once she catches her breath.

"Yeah, how so?" I ask, sill kissing her neck. She tilts her head to the side, giving me better access.

"Because, you give off this whole innocent vibe when in fact, you're a dirty freak in the bedroom."

I lift my head and wink at her. "The innocent ones usually are the freaks in the bedroom."

Scooting up on the bed, she maneuvers so I'm not fully lying on her. With a wicked smile, she says, "My turn."

"Oh yeah? What do you have planned?" I ask, my dick praising Jesus right now for its impending release.

"Sit up and lean against the wall." It's cute how she's trying to boss me around in the bedroom. She's not the same girl who bosses me around at work. She's more vulnerable, which makes her demands that much more adorable.

I get in position and wait, my cock begging to be released from its confines. When she looks down at my lap, her eyes go wide from the very blatant boner I'm sporting. "Don't just stare at the fella, you're going to make him think he has something in his teeth."

Glancing up at me, through her eyelashes, she says, "If your dick has teeth, what I have in mind is not going to happen."

I smirk. "Don't worry, he doesn't bite."

"I hate this conversation right now." She laughs, the sound making my cock jump even higher.

"Sadie," I groan. "You can't go and laugh while I have a raging erection, you know how much I love your laugh. Please, are you going to help a guy out here?"

Taking a second to scan me up and down, she nods and right in front of me, without skipping a beat, she lifts her shirt over her head, revealing her completely naked body to me, and holy fuck.

Her tits are just right. Not too big, not too small, with dark, rosy nipples puckered from the late-night air. By the end of the night, there is no doubt in my mind that my mouth will be all over them.

"Fuck, Sadie," I mumble, taking her all in.

She doesn't say a word. No, my girl stands before me—naked—then leans forward, her face hovering over my lap, and removes my boxers. I lift up off the bed to assist her. When her eyes return to my lap, her mouth drops open. Needing some of the tension building in my dick to ease, I stroke it a few times, leaning my head against the wall behind me. When my eyes return to hers, all I see is longing.

From the look in her face, I'm going to guess she agrees with the nickname.

I watch in fascination as her eyes turn heady with lust while her hands travel up my thighs. Bending at the waist, her breasts swaying with her movements, she lowers her head to my dick where she gently grips it in her right hand. A hiss escapes my lips from the tentative grip she has on me.

Her eyes on mine, she moves her hand to the base of my cock and squeezes like a motherfucking vise, shooting my hips off the damn bed.

"Christ." I bite down on my lip, trying to reel in my reaction.

With her hand gripping my cock tightly, she brushes her tongue along the head, circling it, flicking, fucking teasing me like I did her. The little vixen. I don't know why I expected anything less.

As she swirls her tongue around the tip of my length, flicking the underside along the sensitive vein that runs the distance, blasts of white-hot pleasure shoot through me. My hands start to clench at my sides, my balls tightening, the pressure of her hand at the base of my cock, slowly moving up, squeezing me so fucking hard that I'm pretty sure I could come any minute.

"Fuck," I breathe out heavily. "Fuck, Sadie, you have to stop."

Her tongue dances across the very tip lightly while her other hand starts to gently cup my balls, rolling them expertly along her fingers.

Oh fuck, oh fuck me. I bite down on the side of my cheek and will myself not to explode right then and there.

"Sadie." I pull her up on my lap, snapping her away from her little game of torture. "Stop, baby." My breath comes out in heavy spurts.

"Too much?" she asks, her fingers now dancing across my chest.

"Condom. Now." My voice is rough, demanding. I nod at my nightstand drawer.

Taking my direction, she leans over, pops open the drawer—a drawer I stocked when my parents were NOT around—and quickly removes the foil.

"Want me to slip it on?" she asks with a cheeky grin.

Snagging the rubber from her, I say, "No! Christ, no, I don't."

She gives me a second to sheath myself while I pray to the orgasm gods to not let me go early. If they cared about me at all, they would prevent my balls from giving in to this amazing woman.

Protection in place, she straddles my lap, my back still against the wall, and positions my cock at her entrance. Fuck, my tip rubs against her warm heat, almost exploding my mind from the friction. My hands on her hips, I lean my head against the wall. I'm momentarily stunned by the picture of beauty before me.

She leans forward, her lips barely caressing mine, her hips rotating slightly, using the tip of my dick as a tease along her arousal. She groans into my mouth as her tongue flicks my lips.

"Fucking ride me," I say, not wanting to do any more of this beating-around-the-bush bullshit—not that she has a bush to beat around actually.

Right on cue, she falls down on my dick, bottoming out all too quickly. There was no easing; there was no inch-by-inch movement on her end. No, she took me all in like a fucking boss. Her cry echoes through my head, making me feel drunk and hazy, like I was just knocked out by Captain Pleasure.

"Oh God," she moans, her head resting against my chest now, her hips slowly making circles. "Cannon cock is," she takes a deep breath, "a very accurate description."

That gets a chuckle, but it's quickly washed away when her head lifts and her eyes meet mine. Filled with desire, with a yearning I never thought I'd see from this intriguing girl, her arms wrap around my neck, and she starts to methodically move up and down on my hardened length. Her legs propelling her thrusts, they squeeze against mine for stability and in this moment, our eyes trained on each other, I don't think I've ever felt anything so intimate.

Intimate. Fuck, is that what this is? Not a quick fuck, but intimacy? Does she think of it that way? I sure as hell hope so, because for once, I will be right there with her.

Gripping her ass, I guide her up and down as well, my hips starting to thrust up when she goes down. The combination is repeated, her moan growing with each passing bout of rubbing. Her forehead presses against mine as she looks down at our connection, something I've always found incredibly sexy in a woman, wanting to experience it all.

Fuck, this is all too much. The way her tits bounce against my chest, the feel of her tight pussy squeezing me with each pass, her sweet, and sexy moans in my ear . . . I'm going to lose it.

I'm going to blow it before she even has a chance to think about visiting O-town.

Hold the fuck back. Grandma, think of Grandma. Lipstick on the teeth, curlers in her hair until noon.

Sadie's thighs slap against mine.

Grandma! Wrinkly and old, dentures in a drinking cup.

Sadie's pebbled nipples rub against my chest, and they're so fucking hard.

Grandma. Dammit! Knee-high stockings and Velcro shoes.

"Shit, Andrew. I'm going to come."

Thank, Christ. *Catch ya later, Grams.*

I assist her thrusts even more, taking control of our connection as her hands fall to my shoulders, trying her best to slam as hard as she can down on my lap. Her head falls back, her nipples pebbled in the air, her tits bouncing, and the strain in her neck . . .

"Oh God!" she cries out. Her movements are so erratic. Her pussy squeezing all around me.

That's it. Everything in me goes blank. My balls tighten and with one final thrust, white-hot pleasure envelops me. My orgasm roars through me, and my dick twitches for what seems like fucking days. I spill into her, thrusting until every last drop is drained from me, and I feel like I'll never catch my breath.

Slowing down, our bodies slide together, our sweat mixing, our breathing simply panting, and the combination is fucking aces.

Yeah, I said it. It's FUCKING ACES.

"Shit," I breathe out. "That was hot."

Chuckling, she lifts her head and kisses my lips. "That was something we *will* be doing again."

Smiling at her, I thrust up again, reminding her of our connection. "I told you he wouldn't bite."

Pushing back on my chest, she starts clapping her hands. "And there he is, the Andrew I first met, always making things awkward."

I laugh from the pit of my stomach. "Sorry, baby, I can't be suave and debonair all the time. I've got to show some faults for mankind, or how else would it be fair to men around me?"

She rolls her eyes and climbs off me, but not quick enough. I pin her to the bed beneath us and press my chest against hers.

"Say it."

"Say what?"

"Say you're into me."

Tilting her head to the side, a playful look in her eyes, she says, "Unfortunately, Andrew. I'm into you." *Unfortunately?*

"Ha!" I fist-pump the air. "I'll take it!"

CHAPTER THIRTEEN

SADIE

"Why are you walking like that?" Smilly asks while sticking her hand in a bag of Cheetos.

"Walking like what?" I ask, snagging a Gatorade from the fridge, heat chasing up my neck.

Bringing his beer to his mouth, Saddlemire adds, "Like you've been sitting on a flagpole for five hours."

Maybe because that's what it feels like. Jumping Mr. Cannon Cock wasn't the smartest idea I've ever had. I should have eased myself down. I should have taken my time and allowed myself to stretch with each inch, but no, I had to be all slutty and bang his dick like it was my own personal twenty-inch dildo.

My poor, poor vagina. *But his fabulous, fabulous dick.*

The funny thing is though, I would do it all over again because last night was . . . oh God, I'm a gushing idiot, but it was amazing. It was fun. Calming in a way. And most definitely easy. I didn't feel like I was carrying three suitcases of baggage while lying next to him. And the way he cuddles. Oh, sweet Jesus. I want to say it was the twin bed, but it wasn't, it was all him. He knew exactly where to hold me, how to faintly kiss me in the middle of the night, and how to stroke me innocently with the pad of his thumb. He could easily be one of those people you pay to cuddle you. Hell, he could be one of those people you pay to dry hump you.

"Slipped at work," I answer. I had the noon shift, which was nice because I got out early. Andrew unfortunately has the later shift, which, now that I think about it, might be a good thing, you know, because the flagpole walking and all.

"Slipped at work?" Smilly asks.

"Yeah, some dipshit spilled soup on the ground. I slipped and pulled something, but don't worry, I didn't spill out. I caught myself before I completely biffed it." I'm a little terrified with how easy these lies are flowing from my lips.

"Morons," Smilly mutters. "I would claim worker's comp, take a week off, binge-watch Netflix and day drink."

"Hell, let's all hurt ourselves at work and do that." Saddlemire tilts back the rest of his beer. "I can't remember the last time I took a week off to drink."

Turning toward her boyfriend, Smilly chucks a puff at him. "I do. When the Yankees didn't make the play-offs. You claimed to have mono when instead you almost drank yourself to a coma."

"Well, fuck. Why do they have to suck now? Get it together, Girardi!" Saddlemire says toward the Yankees' manager. "I don't think I can take another year of no play-offs. The Yankees and post-season go together like fucking peanut butter and jelly."

Smilly shakes her head. "I will never understand the passion you have for such menial things."

"Menial?" Saddlemire and I both ask at the same time.

"Babe." He sits up, a mask of seriousness on his face now. "Think about when you start humping the fridge when you make the perfect sugar cookie, transfer that passion to the Yankees. That's what we feel."

Looking between us, she pops a puff in her mouth and then says, "Not even comparable."

Outrage pours out of Saddlemire. Wanting to stay out of it, I park my ass on the beanbag chair we have—classy, I know—just as my phone vibrates with a text message.

Andrew.

My heart jumps in my chest from excitement. How quickly this man has invaded my mind.

Andrew: Denise kissed me on the cheek. Thought I would let you know you have competition.

Chuckling, I shake my head. Denise, the mother hen, is a happily married, Harley-riding old lady to an MC leader, so there is no way she would ever want anything to do with nerdy, yet sexy Andrew.

Sadie: Eh, she can have you. Not worth the fight.

It must be a slow night because he texts back immediately.

Andrew: Uh, do I need to remind you about the sexual epiphany you had last night?

Sadie: Is that what you're calling it?

Andrew: I figured that was better than an orgasmic oracle from the penis prophecy.

Oh my God.

"We are not watching The House of Steinbrenner again," Smilly complains, pulling me from my phone. "We are watching Willow, and that's that."

"Say you appreciate the Yankees," Saddlemire counters.

"Ugh. The Yankees are amazing. Rah, rah, rah, go, pinstripes," she deadpans.

"That's more like it."

If only life was that easy. Turning back to my phone, I text him back.

Sadie: It's okay to not act like a douche and brag about

your dick.

Andrew: It is? Sheesh *wipes forehead* Good. I can relax now. Want to talk about your favorite computer language? Personally, JavaScript can go to hell.

Sadie: *Rolls eyes* I'm shocked your dad even thought you could be involved in a sex ring with the kinds of things you talk about.

Andrew: What did I tell you last night? The innocent-looking ones are most likely the most freaky. You must have been so distracted by my dick last night to remember that little tidbit.

I smile to myself as I type.

Sadie: Back to the douche again?

As I press send, a slipper hits me. "Hey." I rub my head to look up at both Saddlemire and Smilly who are staring at me, a confused expression on their faces.

"Uh, what the hell are you doing?" Smilly asks.

Tucking my phone away, I answer apathetically, "Checking my email."

"No, you weren't." Saddlemire sits up in his seat now. "You were texting."

For the record, their shock isn't unwarranted; I don't really text people. I don't care for it. My friends know this, so they only text me need-to-know information. It's not something I do just for the hell of it, well, that was until Andrew sent me a text.

"Who were you texting?" Smilly asks, a pinch in her brow.

Think. Who the hell can I say I was texting? Tucker isn't an option, as he's part of the inner circle and knows not to text me. Don't text my dad or sisters for that matter, so that's pretty obvious. Telemarketer? I could be on the verge of scoring a free cruise?

No, Smilly would want in on that.

"Uh, someone from Cornell," I quickly say. "Asking about a

professor and if they should take the class. Personally, I didn't like the professor because he smelled like beets and breathed too heavily when he talked, but that's my personal opinion. Some people like heavy-breathing, beet people."

They both study me a little longer than I care for until Smilly breaks the silence and pops a puff in her mouth. "I like beets. Fucking delightful when they're pickled."

"You like anything pickled," Saddlmire replies. Damn, that was easy.

"If you can pickle it, then you can put it in my mouth."

My phone vibrates in my hand again. I so desperately want to look at it, but I hold off, knowing if I keep texting Andrew, they'll be onto me. I would prefer to keep things as casual as possible for now, especially after the little heart-to-heart I had with Smilly.

Together, we watch the opening scene of Willow, Smilly's favorite movie. At least once a month, we are subject to watching it and listening to her impersonate the characters. "Out of the way, Peck!" It's her favorite line that she says in a creepy voice, sometimes twiddling her fingers at you. You just accept this side of her and move on.

Clapping her hands at the TV, she and Saddlemire are distracted so I secretly look at my phone from the side.

Andrew: You have to admit, every girl loves a bit of a douche.

So not true, but I won't go there. Instead I read his other text messages I've been ignoring.

Andrew: Just made a Crowd Pleaser. It's official. I've made every ice cream you can order here. What kind of award do I get?

A Crowd Pleaser is the biggest sundae you can order from Friendly's. I've made a few in my time and honestly, I'm not geeking out when I say it's kind of fun to make. It's twelve scoops of ice cream, six toppings, loads of whip cream, and six cherries all on a plastic platter. Smilly, Emma, and I might have ordered a Crowd Pleaser a few times.

Andrew: Michelle doesn't understand personal space. Her boobs tried to help me restock the sundae dishes.

Michelle, that hooker. Of course she's thrusting her fake chest at Andrew. I'm surprised she didn't try it the first day of his training. Still, knowing Michelle is over there getting up in his business, it bothers me, so I respond the only way I know how to, like a catty woman.

Sadie: Next time, just poke her boob with a pin; you'll deflate them in seconds.

I'm not proud of my response, but for some reason, it feels necessary that Andrew knows Michelle isn't showing off the real stuff.

Jealous? Never. Jelly? Maybe just a little. There is a difference, you know.

Both laughing, Smilly and Saddlemire really engage in the movie, giving me an escape. Standing, I tuck my phone in my pocket and announce having to use the bathroom.

"Use the spray if you have to," Smilly calls out just as I shut the door.

I sigh, not that kind of bathroom. Jesus.

Sitting down on the toilet, because it's always a good idea to try to pee when you can, bladder infections and all, I get a text message from Andrew.

Andrew: You know, if I really wanted to look into that last text from you, I would guess you're showing a little jealousy. But I mean, who are we kidding? You would never be jealous, right?

Right. Never. Andrew is not the kind of guy that makes me swoon, that makes me rethink every rule I ever set forth to protect myself. He isn't the kind of guy that makes me forget the stagnant life I'm living in, nor is he the guy who reminds me how to laugh, how to have fun, how to just live.

Nope . . . not at all.

Sadie: What's jealousy?

I can tell you what it is. It's the feeling you have in the pit of your stomach, thinking about Michelle being within inches of Andrew. Jealousy is what's tempting you to drive to work just to pretend to get ice cream so you can catch a glimpse of him.

Jealousy is ugly.

Jealousy is screwing every inkling I had of keeping this man away from me: jealousy, and the need to forget.

•••

Do not look over at fountain again. Keep your eyes on the computer, enter the order, and then check on your customers' drinks. DO NOT LOOK AT FOUNTAIN!

Utter betrayal wins over and my eyes glance toward the fountain area where Andrew is making a milkshake while talking to a customer at the counter, exuding his outgoing personality. I haven't seen him in a few days, ever since I stayed the night at his place. Our schedules didn't match up at work, and Smilly has spent the last few nights at our apartment, giving me no other option than to rely on texting Andrew.

Seeing him today for the first time in days, he seems like a different person. Now I know him intimately, I'm more sexually aware of everything he does. Carrying dish trays, watching his back muscles flex under the pressure of the weight, how he smiles at pretty much everyone he comes across, looking so handsome it hurts, and knowing what rests underneath his apron-covered pants . . . Yup, I'm embarrassingly sexually charged.

"Are you going to finish imputing that?" Michelle asks, pulling me out of my stupor.

"Uh, yeah. Forgot where the cheddar broccoli soup was," I lie . . . terribly. *In the last few months, I've had to lie more than in my whole life.*

Michelle looks down at the screen, the cheddar broccoli button, clear as day, and then back up at where I was staring. "Ahh," she says knowingly, raising my hackles instantly. "Getting in a good look? Don't blame you. I asked him out for a drink earlier."

My head snaps to hers. "You did? What did he say?" My voice becomes higher with each question.

"Just that he has plans, but maybe another time. I think he's a tough shell to crack, but I will get there. I always do."

That's not a lie. She always does.

Clearing my throat, I say, "Well, good luck with that." I finish inputting my orders and close out one table, pulling the ticket from the printer and placing it in a black folder for my customer.

As I pass the hostess station, Stuart calls to me, "New table on twelve."

"Okay."

Twelve is right next to the fountain. I try not to get too giddy about the idea of being closer to Andrew. I have yet to say hi to him since I've started work. It's been non-stop waiting on people, and not one of them has ordered ice cream. If you come to Friendly's, you get ice cream, that's what you do. But apparently, not today.

I drop off the check to one table, pull out my order pad and go to table twelve where Tucker—*ugh what is he doing here?*—sits alone, wearing his sexy smile.

Crap.

"Hey," he says as I walk up to him.

Swallowing hard, I nod at him, hoping and praying Andrew

is too pre-occupied with ice cream to hear our conversation.

"Hey, what are you doing here?"

He leans back in his booth, putting his hand behind his neck in a mock stretch. "Can't a guy get some good old-fashion American food?"

"Not when he's you," I shoot back.

"Aw, come on, Sadie, just looking to have a little fun and check out the competition."

I knew he wasn't here to indulge in ice cream; he's never been into sweets.

"There is no competition," I hiss, trying to keep my voice low.

"Really?" His eyebrows lift in question. "My boy Andrew no longer keeping your interest? What happened after the party the other night? Puke on your shoes?"

This is not happening right now. I am not having this conversation with Tucker while Andrew is only a few feet away. Why can't he just leave me alone? From the smarmy look on his face, it seems having Andrew in the picture has only turned up his pursuit. It's evident in the way he looks at me with such determination.

"No, he did not puke on my shoes," I whisper.

"Then what is it? Not a good kisser? Likes to eat onions like an apple?" He leans closer toward me. "Likes to wear women's underwear?"

I can't help it. I chuckle, only because the image of Andrew wearing a pair of my panties comes up in my mind, for some odd reason, it works for him. Is that something I should be concerned about?

"No, none of that."

"Then what is it? Still caught up on me? That's no problem, I'm more than happy to help you with that problem."

I shake my head. "Stop, Tucker."

"Never," he says without an ounce of humor in his voice.

Sighing, I poise my pen at my pad, ready to take his order. "Can I get you anything?"

"A date," he answers without skipping a beat.

"Can I get you anything off the menu?"

"That is off the menu." He flashes the menu at me where he penciled in, "Date with Sadie."

I roll my eyes and chastise him. "You can't write on those, Tucker."

"Sure you can. It was really easy. Pretty much anything works on laminated plastic."

"That's not what I meant. Now are you going to order food? Or can I get back to my other tables?"

He's about to open his mouth when from over the half wall, connecting to the fountain, Andrew waves and says, "Hey, Tucker. Good to see you, man." Oh Andrew, so oblivious. I guess that's a good thing. "How's the old wrist doing? Mine was sore after our beer pong annihilation."

Tacking on a good smile, because that's the kind of guy Tucker is too, he says, "Ah, I've been playing far too long. My wrist is pretty used to that kind of abuse by now."

"Lucky." Andrew holds up his wrist and moves it around in a light twirl. "When I woke up, it felt like I just sprinted a masturbation marathon. Damn thing was stiff as fuck."

"Are we talking about your wrist or your dick?" Tucker jokes, baffling me. How can guys be this cool with each other? I don't get it. Michelle nods at Andrew with one of her breasts and I want to claw her eyes out, but Tucker sees Andrew as a threat and can still joke around with him. *Men are weird.*

Andrew laughs and points at Tucker in a playful way. "Stiff dicks are for the bedroom and the stockroom. Can't help but get a boner when you see all that fudge topping."

"Yeah, I've been back there. I'm getting hard just thinking about it," Tucker teases, blowing my ever-loving mind.

Fudge boners? What is happening right now?

"Purely a dick's paradise back there."

Tucker's laugh instantly annoys me. It's a throaty laugh I used to love listening to, but right now, I just want him to leave.

"Hey, I forgot to ask you," Andrew continues, "where—?"

"You have a customer," I almost shout, grateful for the four teenagers who just pushed through the fountain doors.

Andrew glances back and then with a sorrowful expression he says, "Duty calls. I'll catch you later, man. Good to see ya."

"You too." Absentmindedly, still looking over at Andrew, Tucker says, "Man, I like that guy. Good, solid bastard that one." Sighing he looks back up at me now. "Too bad he doesn't realize he's just wasting his time when it comes to you." *What the hell?*

Not wanting to put up with this anymore, I grab him by the arm and lift him out of the booth. He's not here to get food; he's here to drive me fucking insane. Tucker, laughing the entire time, allows me to guide him out the door. I don't stop until we're standing outside.

"Do not come back here," I plead, knowing he will do as he pleases; he always does.

Not replying right away, he studies me, really trying to look into the depths of my eyes. "Huh . . ." Thoughtfully, he rubs his stubbled jaw. "You like him, don't you?"

"It's none of your concern. Now please leave before I get in trouble with Stuart."

"Please, like he would ever fire you. Admit it, you like Andrew."

"I don't need to deal with this." I turn toward the door, but he snags me by the arm, halting me in my progress forward.

"Go on a date with me, Sadie."

"Tucker, I said no." Why does he keep harping on this? He's never been this relentless. Have I always been easy to him? Not worth much effort? *Any effort?* A sure thing? Maybe I've never been this relentless in my refusal.

His face grows softer while his thumb rubs across the skin on my upper lip. "Just one night, that's all I'm asking for. Strictly platonic." Ha, I snort. "I'm serious. I miss you, Sadie. I miss just spending time with you, just you and me, no one else to distract us. Give me this one night." He swallows hard, his eyes turning from soft to sad in a matter of seconds. "I, uh, I haven't been able to have a solid night alone with you since we lost the baby. I feel like we have some unfinished business. We need to find some closure."

And there it is. He brings up the baby, and I start to thaw, and quickly.

The baby I didn't want at first, but the baby I so desperately wish I had now.

How can I deny him one final night of closure if that's really all he wants?

"Just closure?" I ask, a little skeptical.

"Just a night of us, Sadie. I think it's only fair. After we lost the baby, you ripped everything I ever knew away from me. I know you were hurting, but you have to realize, I was hurting too. Fuck, I'm still hurting." He grabs the back of his neck and stares at the ground. "I lost my baby and the love of my life that day. Just give me one night to say goodbye to us."

Even though we're standing outside, it feels like imaginary walls are closing in on me, making it harder and harder to breathe with each passing second.

With one last attempt to get me to agree, he lifts his hand to my face and gently strokes it, pushing a loose strand of hair behind my ear. "Please, Sadie."

Shit, shit, shit.

I swallow hard, a lump of grief trying to make itself present in my throat. "Okay," I mutter, knowing it's the wrong thing to say, knowing deep down that if I spend a night talking with Tucker, it's just going to make everything that much more confusing.

Tucker let's out a long breath and then pulls me into his chest for one of his famous hugs I'd once relied on in the past. "Thank you, Sadie. Does Saturday work for you?"

Not able to look him in the eyes, I nod. "I have an afternoon shift, but I should be done by five."

"Perfect, I'll pick you up around seven. That should give you plenty of time to drive home and get ready."

"Sure." Pulling away, I make my way toward the restaurant, already loathing my decision.

"This means a lot to me, Sadie." I look back at him. He has his hands in his pockets, looking so freaking grateful I said yes, that once again, it tears at my heart.

No matter how hard I try, this man will always have a mark on my heart. He was the first boy to kiss me, the first boy to make love to me, and the first boy to break my heart . . . You can't just wash away those memories, because they stick with you. They're the ones that have molded me into the woman I am today—apparently a weak and very stupid woman.

When I walk into the restaurant, I don't even bother sparing a glance at Andrew. I can't, because the night I just committed to on Saturday feels an awful lot like cheating, even though I have no intention of doing anything remotely intimate with Tucker. Am I even committed to Andrew? We had one night together and a few text messages; that doesn't make us a couple, does it? Either way, Saturday still feels wrong.

Maybe it's my strong will that feels cheated. That sounds more likely. I swear I'm done with Tucker, but then he shows up, talks about the loss of our baby, and I melt into an emotional puddle, unable to stick to any of my convictions.

I don't want to say it, I don't even want to think about it, but I can't deny that Saturday is going to be one giant, massive mistake.

I can practically taste it in the air.

Good going, Sadie. Good going.

CHAPTER FOURTEEN

ANDREW

Something is off. We've been working together for the past few hours and she has yet to say anything to me, not that I need her to flee to the fountain area, tear my hat off, and run her tongue along my eyebrows. I'm a pretty outgoing guy, so a little hello would be nice, but the only time she's acknowledged me was when Tucker was here, which wasn't for very long.

I like that guy. Solid man.

But, I have noticed the glances she's been giving me. Little side-eyes. *Oh yeah, I see you, Sadie.* She tries to be subtle about it, but she is terrible at averting her eyes. Rule number one to staring at someone when you don't want to be caught: have a back-up item to focus on when you've been duped, so you can casually wander your eyes over to backup stare down.

For example, staring, staring, staring, wup! They caught me. Eyes go to old lady picking her teeth with a knitting needle. Simple. And if you pick something that is a little out of the norm, like Geriatric Janice loosening the beef tip from her teeth, you can use the old tactic where you look back at the person you were staring at and motion to the old lady where you would mouth, "Are you seeing this?" Classic aversion and inclusion.

Works every time.

As for me, I want to be caught when it comes to Sadie. I want her to know I'm thinking about her, so when she glances my way and we make eye contact, I don't avert like she does. I keep my eyes trained on her as she bustles around nervously from being caught.

It's cute, seeing her all flustered, but also frustrating. Clearly I affect her, so it wouldn't kill her to give me a little hello, maybe a slap to the ass, or even a little tap to the taint when I scoop ice cream.

All men like a gentle taint tap, key word being gentle. It reminds them that hey, you're a man with exclusively sensitive parts as well. It isn't just the women who have a magic button, you know?

A ticket passes through the printer, distracting me from trying to catch another look at Sadie. Welcoming the work on a slow day, I spy the name at the top of the ticket.

Michelle.

Christ. This woman.

Each ticket that runs through the machine clearly states which server put the order through and whenever I see Michelle's name, I inwardly cringe. She's all right, not too annoying, just very awkward and uncomfortable, because instead of busying herself while I make her ice cream, she likes to come and watch, making sure to show off her cleavage and rather pointy nipples every chance she gets.

I'm all for nipples, but these nubs intimidate me. I don't understand how they are that hard. It almost seems like someone took two pretzel rods and stuck them in her bra. Obvious exaggeration, but you get the point.

I shiver. Pretzel-rod nips, that's horrifying. The chances of poking an eye out nip style are very high in that scenario.

"Looks like I got another ice cream order," she says, stepping up to the counter and licking her teeth. Oh hey, what do you know, my balls shriveled right up into a little labia.

"Yeah, looks like it." I nod awkwardly, my lips pressed tightly together. Focus on the ice cream order and not the way she's casually thrusting her chest at me to the tune of "Sign, Sealed, Delivered" over the restaurant speakers.

This song will never be the same for me.

Stevie Wonder will never sound the same to me.

Two scoops of chocolate, a pump of fudge, and crushed Heath bar. Focus on the sundae.

"I got a new shade of lipstick that would look perfect on your cheek. We should test it out later, what do you think?"

Glancing at her, I take in the hooker red on her lips. Yikes, no, fucking thank you.

"Just kidding." She laughs. "It's LipSense. One of my favorite authors recommended it. It doesn't come off . . . even if I were to continually suck on something." She wiggles her eyebrows at me suggestively while poking the side of her cheek with her tongue.

Ohhh-KAY!

This conversation is over.

Turning toward her, I set the sundae on the counter and say, "All set," with a smile, because I'm not a total dick, no matter how uncomfortable she makes me.

"You're so good at making sundaes," she says, pressing her hand against my chest, where she squeezes my pec and does a little intake of air.

"Uh . . . thanks. I'll be sure to inform future employers when I graduate that I really have a knack with cold and creamy delights."

Leaning forward, on a whisper, she says, "I have a knack for creamy delights as well."

I slump my head forward. *Idiot.* I set myself up for that one. Swallowing hard, I nod, "Good to know, Michelle."

Winking, she snags the sundae and walks away, a sway to her hips. Once she's a good distance away, I let out a long, pent-up breath and search out Sadie. I'm going to need her assistance in washing my ears and eyes with bleach.

Since the fountain area is still slow, I remove my apron, roll it up under the cash register, and head to the back of the restaurant, past the waitress station, the grill, and into the core of it all where the dishes are washed, the stockroom is kept full, and the freezer chills everything.

Glancing around, I don't see Sadie. Did she leave early?

"What are you looking for?" Stuart asks, wandering up to me, holding a clipboard with random sheets snagged in it.

"Uh," I trip over my words, feeling like I'm being caught for something bad. "Stocking up on some fudge and candy. Man, the demand is high today." Such a lie. Shit, will he be able to tell if I'm lying by looking at the orders that have gone through today? Is that something he even does?

"Good boy." He pats me on the back. "There is a lull now, so smart thinking."

"Eh, thanks." I give him my best smile and then spin on my heel straight into the stockroom, where I find Sadie. She's holding on to one of the shelves, looking down at the ground, a load of tension in her shoulders. Wanting a little privacy, I click the stockroom door shut and lock it. She looks up in surprise. When she sees me, the look on her face doesn't necessary say, *oh yay, Cannon Cock is here.* It's more of a cringe.

A fucking cringe.

And after I licked her pussy with all the good graces of a fucking champ—not that it was a hardship, but sticking your tongue in an unknown area can be a little unnerving. Thank God it wasn't, she tasted like honey . . . Fuck, that's beside the point. I licked her pussy! You don't cringe at someone who has pressed their entire face up against the area you pee out of; it's just common courtesy.

Gesturing at her face, I say, "You seem to have forgotten how to greet the man who made you come multiple times the other night. I prefer smiles, kissy lips, huggy fingers, and I even accept lewd gestures with your tongue."

That cracks a smile from her. It isn't one of her smiles that reaches her eyes, but it will do for now.

Moving forward, I stalk her like she's my prey, closing in on her in record time. When I'm pressing her against the shelf, I ask, "So since we kissed, touched each other's unmentionables, saw each other's O faces, and have kissed each other with morning breath, does that mean we aren't allowed to talk anymore unless it's through secret modern-day Morse code, also known as texting?"

Glancing down, she says, "I've been busy today."

"Oh, I know. The amount of times I've caught you checking me out takes up a lot of that free time."

"I was not checking you out," she protests. If she added a foot stomp to that little denial train, I would have hopped on board just for fun to see where juvenile Sadie would take me.

"Okay, this is fun. We're going to start lying to each other." I rub my hands together. "Hmm, what lies can I tell? I want to make it juicy, so give me a second."

"Stop." She playfully pushes my chest and smirks at me. "Okay, I was checking you out and avoiding you all at the same time."

"Hey." I open my arms wide. "Look at you, admitting to things. I'm proud, Sadie. We should commemorate this moment by fucking each other next to the Oreos. I mean, they're used to having cream all over them."

"Wow." She shakes her head. "I'm never going to look at another Oreo the same."

"I haven't been able to since Jimmy said it was two cookies having sloppy sixty-nine sex and never cleaning up."

"I . . . can't with that." She holds up her hand.

"Hmm, ruining the mood, huh? How about this." Pressing my body against hers, I yank my shirt from its tucked position and place her hand on my skin. Then I do the same to her shirt, but instead of moving my hand up to those perfect little breasts of hers, I move down, far enough that she gasps, her eyes wide and wild when she looks at me.

"What are you doing?" she asks, her chest starting to move a lot faster with every heated breath she takes.

"Finger fucking you of course. Isn't that obvious?" I twiddle my fingers inside her thong, barely reaching her pussy.

Removing her hand from my stomach, she grips my forearm, which is currently traveling farther down her pants. "We can't do that here. Are you insane?"

"No, fully mentally stable over here." I nod at her legs. "Mind spreading a little there, sweetheart? I'm all for doing a lot of work to get you off, but the better access you give me, the easier it will be to make you scream."

"We are not doing this here," she scolds, but doesn't pull my hand out. She's dancing with the idea of going through with this.

Knowing I could give her the extra push to widening her stance, with my other hand, I brush past her *hardened* nipples—not doing this, my ass—and cup her cheek where I bring her lips to mine in a passionate, heat-filled kiss. Nipping, licking, sucking, tongues dancing, I fuck her mouth first, with every trick I have, running my tongue along her lips, diving deep until I can't go any fucking farther. And she matches every single one of my movements.

The moment she wraps her arms around my neck, I know I'm in. And since we are on borrowed time before someone tries to walk in here for some godforsaken item, I take my foot and kick her feet apart. Once I'm allotted more space, I move my fingers along her wet flesh, loving the way my fingers can so easily play around.

Thankfully, she's already fucking soaking wet, which gives me permission to press my thumb on her clit. She startles from the initial contact, but then sinks into my touch, leaning against the wire shelves and letting my mouth and fingers do all the work.

Shit, she's so soft. Touching her like this, so intimately, so dangerously, has my dick hardening to uncomfortable levels. Knowing we really don't have much time left, I curve my fingers up inside her, my thumb now rubbing against her clit.

On a breathy moan, she leans her head back and says, "Oh Andrew . . . oh God, right there." *I love how responsive she is.*

Thoughts of the outside world vanish. It's just me and her . . . and the sixty-nining Oreos having an intimate, stolen moment in this little ice cream palace. Trying to block out the image of having an orgy with confectionary toppings, I quicken my pace.

The smell of sprinkles hits me hard as I lean my head forward, kissing along her neck. So sweet. Her hands now grip my shoulders as an anchor, her hips rotating with my scooping motion.

"Oh God," she moans a little louder. I try to remind her that we're in the stockroom, but she continues to moan, my name mingled in the air. Christ, I want to hear her mutter my name when she's coming, but I also don't want to get fired.

Hurry the fuck up, man.

My fingers slide around her arousal as I pick up the pace one more time, really trying to—

"Oh, right there." Her pussy clenches my fingers and her head buries into my shoulder as she grips my shirt and moves her hips on my fingers. The feel of her coming on my fingers is just as beautiful as when she did it on my cock and tongue. *I want to taste her orgasm. So badly. Her face. Her softness.* Everything about this woman coming does it for me.

I ride out her tremors, occasionally pressing down on her clit, giving it little palpitations that shake her back up to a high until she's completely spent. Her head leans against my chest as I remove my hand from her pants. Tilting her chin up, I make her watch me as I stick my fingers in my mouth and taste her. *Fuuuuuuuuck. Tastes. So. Good.*

Yeah, that turns her on. It isn't until I step back from her that I realize how much my dick hurts from the strain my zipper is putting against it. From the shelf behind Sadie, I grab a pouch of fudge and place it in front of my crotch.

"You taste so fucking sweet, but I've got to run before someone catches us." I turn to leave but call over my shoulder, "Don't ignore me again, Sadie, or else I might have to throw you on the fountain counters and eat you out in front of everyone. Got it?"

Eyes still wide, she nods.

Satisfied, I unlock the door, pleased to see no one is around and head straight to the freezer. I rest the fudge on a counter outside of the frigid temperatures, and then welcome the cold. Finding the least requested ice cream—sugar-free vanilla, snore—I place the carton against my pants and lean against one of the shelves.

Yes, I'm using a carton of ice cream to calm my raging hardon. Judge me if you will, but everything is covered. It's not like I'm tearing open the carton, sticking my dick in the middle, and churning my own ice cream. Although, a small part of dick-churned ice cream sounds like a novelty to capitalize on. I make a mental note to run the numbers later, just for the hell of it. I have to wake up my calculators every once in a while, seeing I have a box of them.

I'm resting, trying to calm down my penis when the freezer door opens. Frozen in place, not from the cold, but from being caught, I look up to see Sadie standing in the doorway. When she catches sight of me, a snort pops out of her nose before she covers her mouth.

I can't imagine how this looks.

"Uh, are you trying to channel your inner Justin Timberlake and Andy Samberg." She nods at the carton on my cock. "Dick in the box, ice cream edition."

Glancing at my position, I chuckle. "Just thinking of new flavors. Chocolate Chip Cookie Cum, what do you think? Would you swallow?"

A devastating smirk crosses her face as she reaches up and pulls down a bag of chicken noodle soup. With a wink, she says, "I always swallow, Andrew. Always." *And that does not help my erection. At. All.*

Taking her dirty little mouth with her, she leaves me alone in the freezer, tacking on at least five more minutes of freezing time for me after that comment.

•••

"He's here," Jimmy yells to the bedroom. No greeting, no *hey bro, how are you doing?* Instead, he forcefully grabs the bag of ice cream from my hand and heads straight for the kitchen. He digs through the bag and finds his order. "Christ, it's been too long."

I follow him into his apartment, making sure to shut the door, and take a seat at the bar top of the counter. "Glad to see your addiction to the peanut butter sauce hasn't subsided."

Sticking a spoonful in his mouth, he moans, and I swear on my earlier frozen dick that his eyes roll in the back of his head. Is this what it's like to watch your own brother orgasm? If so, I'm feeling incredibly uncomfortable. Should I offer him a cigarette when he's done? It only seems like the polite thing to do after experiencing a weirdly orgasmic moment.

"You know I love you, man, but the way you're mouth fucking with your spoon is making me very uncomfortable, as if I should offer you a condom or something."

Ignoring my sarcastic jabs, he says, "I haven't had this sauce in so fucking long."

"Three days," I clarify. "It's been three days, Jimmy."

"Soft serve," Mae screeches, sliding on stockinged feet into the kitchen, knitting needles dangling from her neck, and a ball of yarn tucked under her arm. "You're my favorite." I think she's talking to me until she kisses the lid to the soft serve. Glad to see where I stand in this household.

"I'm getting a little nervous that you two have become addicts."

"Don't try to fix us, just keep bringing the treats," Jimmy snarls, giving me the old one-eye stare down.

Jesus. Message received. I'm slightly scared to see what happens when the ice cream train stops; will I even be invited back into their apartment?

Joining them, I pop open my sundae—sugar-free vanilla with chocolate syrup. I feel like we bonded today. "So anything new?"

"Not really, did Dad call you about the new fudge combo he created?"

"Key lime pie? Yeah, he told me the sourness could knock your teeth right out of your mouth. Appetizing," I joke. Although, it's definitely a little different to what I considered a creation earlier—Chocolate Chip Cookie Cum. Creativity must run in the family. *Fantastic.*

"You know people will eat it. I swear, they could shit fudge and people would still eat it."

"Please," I hold up my hand, "do not use shit and fudge in the same sentence, the color and consistencies are too damn close. You're going to confuse me."

"I'm going to have to agree with Andrew on this one," Mae chimes in. Changing the subject, she asks, "How's your friendship going with that girl from work? Crack her yet?"

Friendship? Oh yeah. Does fucking your coworker with your tongue, dick, and finger make you friends? If so we're the best of friends. The kind of friends who giggle with each other and exchange friendship necklaces.

Clearing my throat, I shrug. "I don't know, I think she's coming around."

Yeah, coming around my cock. *Or my tongue. Or my fingers. Cough.*

Wait, scratch that. Erase said tool-bag comment from your memory. That was douchebag material at its finest. Fuck, Blaine is encroaching on my brain. His douche is rubbing off on me.

Oh hell, *his douche* sounds like I'm saying his vagina cleanser is soaking into my pores. Just eliminate this whole rabbit trail from your memory. Thanks.

"Yeah? What approach have you been taking?" Why is Mae eyeing me like that, as if she knows something?

Treading lightly, I say, "You know, smiles and easy conversations. Pretty sure I'm starting to break her down with conversations about baseball."

Mae and Jimmy both look at each other, exchanging knowing glances, and then train their eyes back on mine. Why I do feel some sort of ninja attack forming?

"You totally had sex with her," Jimmy says.

"What?" I ask, completely flummoxed. Yes, flummoxed! "How, why . . . how did you know?" I twirl around in my chair, looking at my clothes. "Is there a condom attached to me that I don't see?"

Bursts of laughter come from Jimmy and Mae as they high-five each other. When their celebration dies down, Jimmy says, "Dude, we had no idea. We just asked to see what you would say." He laughs some more. "Damn, I knew you wouldn't be able to stay just friends with her, but to have already had sex with her, maybe Dad is right. Maybe you do have some sort of sex addiction."

"I do NOT have a sex addiction." My voice is rising with each passing word. Fuck, I should have known it was a trick. Jimmy and Mae are not that observant.

"Yeah? Well, then explain yourself."

I rub my hands over my face, my brow permanently pinched from having this conversation. I shouldn't have to explain to Jimmy and Mae about what happened, but they are also pretty much my only friends in the area, so I don't want to burn that bridge.

"Sadie's friend invited me to a party out in the woods. I went, got a little drunk, and she drove my truck back to her place because I passed out in the cab before I could tell her where I lived. I ended up using her toothbrush without permission, then passing out in her bed, where I woke up the next morning, feeling up her breast, thinking it was an orange at first. I thought I was done after that but apparently she liked my orange-squeezing skills, and she started dry humping me. Her friend interrupted us. I was forced to go out her window, boner waving in the air, but not before I clinched a date for that night. I wooed her with a little baseball, brought her back to my place, and we had sex. Okay, Jesus." I take a deep breath and await their questions.

They come flying at me before I can begin to start thinking how to respond.

"You used her toothbrush without asking?"

"You thought her tits were oranges? Come on, bro."

"Dry humping seems very extreme for a boob grab. What kind of morals does this girl have?"

"Did your boner get in the way of the steering wheel when you were driving home that morning?"

"Yeah, did it?"

"And what kind of sex are we talking about? Drunk, or totally cognizant?"

"Did you cuddle her at night?"

"Did you think her tits were grapefruits the next morning?"

"Yeah, did you?"

They bounce up and down, happy about their questions, not even bothering to look apologetic for their invasion on my privacy. *Or Sadie's for that matter. These two have been together for too long.*

Taking a deep breath, I answer their questions in succession. "Yes, I used her toothbrush; it was pink in case you were wondering. Yes, I thought her tits were oranges; I was hungover and had no idea where I was or what I was touching. Dry humping is never too extreme, and Sadie has good morals, at least I think she does. Driving with a boner proved to be successful. The sex was cognizant and fucking good. I cuddled the fuck out of her and when I woke up, and I did not assault her tits looking for grapefruit." Round one complete. I know these two. I know there will be a second barrage of questions. Another round. Deep breath, Andrew.

"Well that's a relief." Mae chuckles. "A girl never likes to be milked unexpectedly."

"Didn't think it was a pleasant experience for you ladies."

Jimmy turns to Mae and says, "For the record, I don't mind you milking my dick. You can do it anytime, anyplace you want."

"Why am I not surprised by that statement?" Mae rolls her eyes and throws her empty sundae cup into the trash. Coming up next to me, she pats me on the shoulder and says, "Friends was never in the cards for you, Andrew. I just hope she sees the good in you, despite your collection of pet rocks."

"Those are at my parents'," I state, wanting to make it quite clear that they didn't make the college move.

When Mae leaves, Jimmy leans over the counter with a smirk on his face. "I fucking knew you would never just be friends with this girl."

"Yeah, I should have known as well." I sigh. "She's too special just to be friends. She's a one-of-a-kind girl."

"Shit." Jimmy sits up. "You like her."

"Yeah, I fucking do," I answer, not trying to hide it from Jimmy. Besides, he has Mae, so he gets it. I like Sadie more than I think I should. Although, I'm still not sure if that is a good thing of bad thing . . .

CHAPTER FIFTEEN

SADIE

"Wow, could you have picked a more obscure place?" Andrew asks, looking around at The Spot Diner, a hidden gem in the tri-state area.

I could say I came here for their phenomenal pie selection, or for the dim lighting, or the quirky and fun waitstaff, but that would be a lie. I wanted to go somewhere with Andrew that I knew was off the beaten path of my friend group. Plus, they're open late at night.

Last time I talked to Smilly about Andrew, we were sharing a dozen donuts on her car. We left it at *he's fun*, but I never went into detail about my intentions, or about seeing him again. And I don't think I can. Every time I think about telling her the truth, my mouth turns dry, and a wave of anxiety takes over me.

As much as she *just wants me to be happy*, I know she's pulling for Tucker and me to work through things. I can't blame her. When Tucker and I were together, we did all the fun couple things we always talked about. Tucker and Saddlemire would relentlessly tease us girls, while we would make the men eat their words if they ever wanted to see our clothes on the floor again. We were the perfect little foursome. Smilly's been there during the bad times, though, so I often wonder why she can only see one side of the awesome foursome. It wasn't always *good*.

But then everything changed the moment I dropped out of school, throwing our adequate worlds for a loop. It hasn't been the same since. Even Saddlemire and Tucker's friendship has struggled.

From across the table, Andrew lifts my chin with two fingers, forcing me to look him in those sincere eyes of his. "Hey, where did you go then? Did you even hear my story about the alien?"

Err, alien?

"Uh . . ." I drag out.

Laughing, he sits back in his chair, his hands resting on the table. "I'm going to take that as a no. Would you like me to repeat it, or are you that bored with me that I should call you a cab right now so we can avoid the whole awkward phone call from Smilly saying she's been in an accident and needs your help?"

I chuckle and shake my head. "Not bored at all. Sorry, had a rabbit trail of thoughts. Tell me all about this alien."

"What can I get you?" the waitress asks, interrupting Andrew before he can even get started.

"Coffee for both us, right, Sugar Britches?" He nods at me. I do like his playful side.

"Yes, coffee," I say to the waitress. "And I would like a slice of the blueberry pie and the cherry." Andrew's eyebrows lift from my order. I shrug my shoulders in response. "You're paying," I tease back.

"Is that so? Well, in that case, I'm going to up your order with slices of the Black Forest cake, the sugar-free cheesecake, and a Boston cream pie."

"Sounds good, I'll put that in for you right now." The waitress leaves us as I stare back at Andrew, questions swarming my head about his order.

"Sugar free?" I ask.

Playing with his spoon on the table, he casually says, "I feel prone to get sugar-free things now that we've bonded in such an indescribably way. I want to support all sugar-free items."

"Isn't that noble of you," I tease, still slightly confused as to how someone could bond with something sugar free.

"Why, thank you." Leaning forward now, spoon on the table, he rubs his hands together. "Now, do you want to hear my alien story?"

"Sure," I giggle, "but I would like to state for the record that I'm not into outer space. I think it's all a joke. Wasted taxpayer money."

A very loud, and very obnoxious gasp comes out of Andrew's mouth as he sits back in his chair, hand to his chest, as if I just slapped him twice across the face . . . with a moldy tube of salami. "Blasphemy!" He shakes his head. "You have GOT to be fucking kidding me. Right? You're kidding. You're not one of those people who think the space program is a waste of money. Right? You love astronauts. You like stars and planets. You wish you could live on the moon for a day. Please tell me you're kidding, Sadie." His voice is full of desperation. It's rather cute.

I cross my arms and shrug my shoulders.

Gripping his head now, as if it's about to explode, his eyes run wild. "I think . . ." he pauses to take a breath, "yup, I think I'm having a panic attack."

He isn't. But the dramatics are spot on.

I lean across the table and pull his hands away from his head. "Oh, stop it. You're fine." Hmm, maybe I really should work on my bedside manner.

"Sadie," he pauses and gathers himself, "do you realize the amount of technology and leaps and bounds we've made because of the space program?"

"We beat the Russians to the moon. Yippee." I twirl my finger in mock excitement.

"Oh, fuck!" He scoots his chair forward, pushes the table items to the far left, really getting into this conversation. "For a girl who attends Cornell, you are poorly educated." That's a slight knife to the heart, but I can't blame him; he doesn't know the truth. "Let me ask you this, do you happen to use light-emitting diodes? Also known as LEDs?"

"Sure."

"Well, imagine your life without them."

"Okay, easy." I pause to think about it. "Pretty sure I'm living the same life."

He shakes his hands and head together to erase that example. "Okay, that was a bad example. Apparently, you don't care about LEDs like I do. How about artificial limbs? Hmm? Ear thermometers, radial tires, land-mine removal, uh, firefighter gear. And don't forget about solar panels and temper foam for all the people who need that cozy sleep at night. There is so much more." The passion in his voice is reaching new levels.

Thoughtfully looking into the air, I point my finger to the sky and say, "I do like firefighter uniforms, especially when the guy is bare chested and only wearing the pants."

"Of course you would think that, you hussy."

"Hey!" I smile.

Throwing his hands up in capitulation, he adds, "You're the one who humped the fuck out of my dick. Seeming like you put the ho in whore." He tacks on a mirthful smirk.

"Good to know." I nod. "I'll be sure to remember that when you're looking to pull my bra off with your teeth tonight."

His eyes widen and then points at the table. "Wait, this isn't dessert? Pussy is on the menu also? Well damn, I should have skipped the Black Forest cake."

Speak of the devil, the waitress arrives with a tray full of obnoxiously large desserts we'll never finish along with our coffee. We have to expertly move items around on the table to get everything to fit, but once we do, Andrew asks, "Is it just pussy, or do I get a topping of nipples too?" He unfolds his cloth napkin and tucks it into the collar of his shirt, right before he pushes his glasses back and holds up his fork.

He is the most ridiculous man I have ever met. *Adorably ridiculous.*

"You'll be lucky if I don't text Smilly right now for a distraction."

"Ouch." He dives his fork into his sugar-free cheesecake—blech—and says, "Hitting a guy where it hurts, in his ego. Can't you take it easy on a fella?"

"Just tell me your stupid alien story."

Mouth full of cheesecake, he shakes his head. "With that kind of attitude, I would rather pass."

Rolling my eyes, I pull out my phone and jokingly threaten to text Smilly when he snags it from my hand and puts it on his lap.

"Fine. I'll tell you my story."

"Thank God." I try to hide my smile, but it's no use, he gets me every time.

His mask of indignation morphs into the face of excited storyteller. "Have you ever been to Pine Bush . . . oh hey-o." Bouncing in his chair, he brings my phone into view, the vibration shaking in his hand. "That just buzzed my dick and I liked it." Glancing down at the caller ID, he shoots me a glare. "You told her to call you?"

I look too and see Smilly's name on the phone. The burst of laughter that pops out of me is unavoidable, as I shake my head no.

"Oh my God, that is so funny. I really didn't tell her to call me. I promise, but let me answer this."

"Oh yeah, sure," he says. "I should probably just say good night right now."

"Oh stop." I hold my finger up to my mouth to motion for him to be quiet as I answer. "Hey, Smilly. What's up?" His face sours for a second but then he goes back to his cake.

"Maaaa! What are you doing? I came home to a cold bag of Doritos and a dark apartment. Where are you? Mama needs a drink in her belly. Come pour some Pabst in my mouth."

Swallowing hard, I get ready for the lie about to breathe past my lips. "Uh, babysitting the boys," I say, referring to my two young cousins. "We're making papier-mâché turtles right now."

Where the hell did that come from?

Andrew's brow knits together as he confusingly mouths, "Papier-mâché turtles?"

I put my hand over my mouth to hold back my laugh.

"You're papier-mâchéing without me? That's fucking cold, Sadie. Stop what you're doing, I'm going to head up there now so I can join in."

"No!" I shout, a little too loud. Smilly showing up at my aunt and uncle's house with spare newspaper and her favorite Modge Podge brush would be a disaster especially since I'm not there. "I, uh . . ." Think, Sadie. This is what you get for lying; just think of something. "The boys are going to bed soon. We are just finishing."

"That's even better. I can come work on their creations when they're asleep and you can make me pizza bites. I know your aunt keeps them in stock."

She does. It's my weakness when I'm babysitting. *Clearly Smilly's too.*

"She's all out of bites."

"Liar!" That *was* a really bad lie. "You just want them all to yourself. Don't be a dirty whore. I'm coming up there."

"You can't," I say quickly. Across the table, Andrew has his arms crossed over his cut chest, enjoying my obvious struggle.

"And why not? The only reason I can think of is because you're being a pizza-bite-hogging whore."

"I'm not hogging the pizza bites. I can buy you pizza bites."

"No, I don't want you to buy me pizza bites. They only taste good if stolen from your aunt's fridge."

Probably the stupidest thing I've ever heard, but I continue anyway. "I would love to have you over, Smilly, but my aunt and uncle made it quite clear they wanted me to stay for a chat after. A chat about . . . responsibilities."

"Oh fuck, I don't want any part of that. Okay, I'm out." There, I knew that would steer her away.

"Yeah, didn't think you would want to be a part of such a conversation. Are you going over to Saddlemire's like you initially planned?"

"No," she sighs. "We're fighting. I told him to shave his Sasquatch foot and he refused. So, I'm going to spend the night binging on Grey's Anatomy."

"Okay, that seems fun." There goes my plans for dessert dessert—aka, pussy and nipples for Andrew. "I'll catch you when I'm done here."

"Sounds good. Eat extra bites for me."

We hang up, and I set my phone on the table just as Andrew starts shaking his head.

"I can't believe you had her call you. Was pizza bites the code word for abort the mission?"

"I did not have her call me."

"Sure," he draws out. "But it's nice that you're trying to spare my feelings."

Exasperated, I say, "Just tell me your damn alien story."

His smile is not the vibrant I-have-to-tell-you-my-story smile from before the phone call. Is it because I blatantly lied to my friend about where I was? It was a shitty thing to do in front of him, but I'm not ready to face an onslaught of questions about Andrew and me yet.

Although, did I hurt Andrew in the process, trying to safeguard my own situation? *Is he angry?* I'm about to explain when he seems to rally himself. With a small smile and shake of his head, he looks down at the assortment of desserts before him, and then, as if hunkering down, he gets back into storyteller mode again.

"It all started with the spotting of a saucer, and I'm not talking about a saucer you set your teacup on . . ."

This man . . . shit. I can't help it. I'm really starting to like him. With desserts in front of me, I listen to him speak of his great-grandma's alien encounter, loving the way his handsome features show excitement with retelling the most absurd story I've ever heard. *I do. I just like him.*

• • •

"You can drop me off here," I say as we hit the entrance of my apartment complex. Guilt consumes me from even suggesting it, especially after the amazing night we spent together. We shared stories. Andrew pulled from his childhood, and I talked about my friends, because letting him in on my family life wasn't happening. We laughed a lot, more than I have in a while, and even acted like teenagers, stealing touches of each other any chance we could get.

It was blissful . . . up until this moment.

Rather than listening to me, he drives into the complex, but instead or turning right, he turns left and finds an empty parking spot next to a dumpster. He puts his truck in park and sighs, leaning back on his seat.

Without looking at me, he says, "How's this? Far away enough?" The words come out harshly.

"You're mad," I state, wondering what he must think about my inability to lie to Smilly about whatever is going on between us.

"What? About being your dirty little secret?"

Turning to him, I press my hand against his cheek. "You're not my dirty little secret, Andrew."

"Huh, could have fooled me." He's mad, but he's not really good at being mad. Perhaps it's because he's the nicest guy I've ever met, which indicates I'm the biggest bitch in the world.

Removing my hand, I say, "I'm sorry, Andrew. Things are complicated."

"I could tell." He rubs his hand over his face and stares out the window. "You're an interesting one to calculate, Sadie. You have an almost impenetrable wall that makes it difficult as fuck to get to know you. But when I do break through that battled armor you wear, I've learned you're incredibly sweet. You show humility when you're wrong, but can also be more stubborn than a mule. You're loyal to your friends and have such a heart for them, but you refuse to let anyone else into your orbit." He turns toward me, hands in his lap. "There is something dark in your eyes, a story to your heart that you're hiding and no matter how much I open up to you, you ensure our conversations about you are light and barely skim the surface." Now resting his head against the back of his seat, I watch his throat contract as he says, "I want to know you, Sadie. Every inch of you, but you're going to have to cut me some slack somewhere. If there is something in your life that's holding you back from telling people about whatever we have, that's fine, but you're going to have to open up about something else. There are only so many secrets I can take."

Open up about something else? What would that even be? My mom and her multiple stints in jail? Maybe about how I dropped out of Cornell. Or the man Andrew thinks is amazing actually impregnated me. Or maybe I could tell him about my miscarriage. Yeah, those all seem like winning topics.

This isn't going to work. He wants something from me I can't give him. I wanted this to be light and joyful. I wanted him to distract me from the pain I've been carrying. I wanted to soak in every inch of his innocent fun, but he wants more. He wants answers, and I can't give him that.

A nauseous churning feeling starts grinding my stomach, and my hands start to shake from what I'm about to say. Glancing up at him, knowing I need to make eye contact when I say this, I give him my full attention. "I can't do that, Andrew."

He doesn't look at me, his head still leaning against the headrest. "Can't, Sadie, or won't?"

"Both." I cringe, hating myself right now.

He presses his lips together and nods. "Okay, so what do you want? A quick fuck when you're available?"

"No." Now I'm wringing my hands together. Why does this have to be so hard? "I just . . ." Tears start to prick my eyes, and I will them not to fall. Do not cry in front of this man. "I . . ." A lone drop coats my face and I immediately loathe myself. "I wanted to escape."

He must have noticed the anguish in my voice because he turns toward me. The pinch in his brow eases and is replaced by concern when he sees the determined tears now falling from my eyes.

"Christ," he mutters right before he pulls me closer so he can wrap his arms around me.

"This hasn't been the easiest year so far for me," I admit. "And then I met you. You've helped me forget. I just want to forget, Andrew."

"Forget what, Sadie? Give me something. Make this thing between us more than just sex."

Make this more than just sex? Is that how he feels? It might have started off with an attraction for one another but it already feels more than that to me. He's more than an escape from my crappy reality. I don't want to lose him, lose this joyful outlet I finally have in my life, so I offer him something . . . something small.

"My mom." My breath is heavy as I speak, my nerves spiking. I hate talking about this, but it's the less relevant issue in my life. It's stale, yet still affects me on a day-to-day basis. If I'm honest, especially in my relationships. "She is a shitty person. She destroyed our family, put a black mark on our last name, and turned us into the Scarlet Letter in our small town. I won't bore you with details about her time in jail, but I will tell you she's the reason I have such a hard time trusting people. She's the reason I don't let anyone new into my world. She's why I'm so fucked up and having a hell of a time communicating with you." I bite the side of my cheek, waiting on his response. I feel so embarrassed, but knowing Andrew, I don't think he'll judge *me* for her antics.

"Okay." He presses his lips against my head while one of his hands rubs my back. "Okay," he repeats, calming me immediately. He doesn't ask for more detail. He takes a deep breath, and somehow that gives me much-needed air as well. "You want to forget? We can do that, we can forget together."

"Really?" I feel this is too good to be true.

"Yes. I understand the need for a distraction, so let's distract each other."

"You're okay with that? You're okay with keeping things between us quiet?"

"I'm not happy about it, but I'll do it." The tense set in his jaw gives that away. "But you have to promise me something."

"What's that?" I ask, wondering what his stipulation will be. No matter what it is, I should probably grant it since he's being so understanding.

"When you're with me, you're with me and no one else. I don't share." Chuckling a little, he adds, "I know my dad thought I was some kind of male gigolo at my last school, but contrary to the cannon cock rumors, I'm a one-woman man. I require the same type of monogamy from you, even though it's your college years, and you should be exploring." He says that last bit in jest, but I can't seem to find the humor. Not only am I not a college student, but I currently have plans with Tucker on Saturday night. *Why did I say yes to that?*

It's just between friends. We're only going to talk, that's it.

"That's the only thing I ask from you, Sadie. Can you promise me that?"

Knowing I only want to be with Andrew, I nod. "I can do that."

"Good." Gently, he places a kiss on my forehead and turns back to the steering wheel. Nodding toward the door, he says, "Now get out of here. Since my second dessert has been canceled, I want to dig into my Black Forest cake and do it in the privacy of my own home, wearing nothing but my DNA pajama pants."

Tears are replaced with a small smile. That he does that so easily, changes my mood in the matter of seconds, makes me want to climb him and keep him forever.

But then I'm hit with self-doubt. *Would he still bother to make me laugh if he knew the real me?*

Probably not, but I'm not going to worry about that right now because I have Andrew, even if it's just for the summer. I have him for now.

I take a chance and lean over to his side of the cab where I place a gentle kiss on his lips. "Thank you." And I mean it. I want to show him how thankful I really am, but that's not going to happen in the cab of his truck near my apartment.

With a side smile crossing his lips, he says his goodbyes and I let myself out of the truck. I don't bother looking back, because if I did, I may run back and fling myself at him. I don't think that would be appropriate right now. I process how we ended the night after a rather heavy conversation, and in true Andrew fashion, a light kiss good night was the perfect way to say goodbye.

It takes me a few seconds to reach the apartment and when I open the door, I'm greeted by Smilly sitting in her underwear and a tank top, chowing down on a bag of Doritos and watching Grey's Anatomy, just like she said she'd do.

"You're home." She doesn't even bother looking away from the TV. "Funny how you did that."

"Did what?" I ask, setting my purse down.

"Got home from your aunt and uncle's when your car was here."

Oh fuck. I forgot about that.

Thinking quickly, I say, "My aunt swung by after work to pick me up and Uncle T just dropped me off. Convenient for him, because he's running by the ice cream shack now."

Seriously, I need to stop lying; it's becoming second nature to me.

"Oh, that makes sense." The tension in her voice eases. "So what important responsibility things did they want to talk to you about?"

Not even batting an eyelash, I say, "Going back to school."

They have talked to me about it before. They're the only ones beside my friends who know about the baby and school. They've provided a pretty stable foundation for me, so I knew they'd help me figure things out.

"Figured as much. Hey, at least you got pizza bites out of it all."

"Yeah," I sigh. "There's always a positive side of things."

But in my case, instead of getting pizza bites, I was able to snag a few more weeks with Andrew. The sad thing I'm very aware of? I really, really don't deserve him.

"I'm going to get ready for bed. I'm tired."

"Okay, want me to tuck you in when I go to bed?"

"No." I chuckle. "It's not necessary."

"Suit yourself." She pops another chip in her mouth and then says, "Take it off, McSteamy!"

Can't blame the girl. McSteamy in his prime is one impressive piece of man.

When I reach our bedroom, I sit on my bed and pull out my phone. I have this need to text Andrew, to find reassurance in the bond we've formed, and to apologize for being so evasive with him.

Sadie: Thank you so much for tonight. I think I forgot to say that in the midst of our conversation. I had an amazing time, Andrew. You always know how to put a smile on my face. P.S. I owe you dessert.

It isn't until I'm resting in bed, about to drift off to sleep that I get a text back from him.

Andrew: I'll take you any way I can get you right now. Just keep smiling and laughing, baby. Oh and yeah, you owe me a dessert for sure, pussy à la mode. I'll bring the ice cream, you bring the goods. Night, beautiful.

A burning ache takes root in my chest. *Night, beautiful.* He is way too good for me.

CHAPTER SIXTEEN

ANDREW

Ding, ding, ding, ding.
I sit ram-rod straight in bed, one hand hitting the wall next to me as I look around. Blind as a bat, I stumble while reaching for my glasses as the incessant dinging keeps sounding off.

"What the fuck?" I mumble groan, finally putting my glasses on.

I press the home button on my phone and read the time. Seven thirty. Rubbing my face, I try to understand what's happening.

Ding, ding, ding.

"Christ." I whip the covers off me and place my feet on the cold hardwood floor. Even in the summer, these floors get cold. Note to self: get slippers for winter. Reaching into my dresser, which is right next to my bed, I snag a pair of shorts and throw them on over my boxer briefs.

I take a second to gather myself and then look around. Where is that sound coming from? When I step out of my room, the sound grows stronger. The doorbell.

"Oh, for fuck's sake." Moving down the creaky stairs, I make promises to myself. "If this is a solicitor, I swear I'm going to do it. Man or woman, I'm punting the fuck out of their crotch."

Cocking my foot back, ready for the unleashing of one epic booting to the sex-junk, I unlock the deadbolt and swing the door open to find Sadie standing on the other side, finger perched at the doorbell, coffee and a pastry box in the other hand, and a wicked smile on her face. I let out a long, tortured breath and bow my head.

And here I was about to cunt-punt her to the next street over.

"Morning, sunshine." What the hell is with the cheery attitude? Did Mary Poppins crawl up her ass in the middle of the night and offer her a spoonful of sugar?

I rub my eyebrow with my palm, skewing my glasses for a second and ask, "Uh, what are you doing here?"

"I brought you breakfast. Can I come in?"

"Sure, yeah." I stumble trying to open the screen door and hold it wide for her as she walks in, giving me a once-over before stepping in.

Once inside, she turns to me and asks, "Shall we eat in your room or in the dining room?"

I glance over at the makeshift dining room, which is made up of a beer pong table and two fold-out chairs—I don't live with the most decorative girls—and think my room has got to be a better option.

"Let's go to my room. Should I grab napkins and plates?"

"Probably. I'll meet you upstairs."

We part ways, her going to the left, me going to the right, but that doesn't stop me from checking her out as she starts her way up my stairs. She's wearing denim shorts that ride high enough to make my mouth water, brown sandals, and a white lace tank top with just enough of a neckline to remind me what she has hidden underneath. No one should look that good this early in the morning, especially when visiting with pastry delights. I'm one lucky fucker.

Shaking my head, and telling my dick to crawl inside itself and not get happy just from the mere sight of her, I stock up on napkins and plates and then sprint up the stairs.

I'm actually surprised to see Sadie this morning, not because she seems like the type that would stab people in the early hour of the days if woken up too soon, but because of our conversation last night.

I was moments away from ending it all, of saying it wasn't worth it, but then I looked into those tortured eyes of hers again and couldn't let go. I grasped on to her once more. There is something somber, almost bleak in her eyes, like she has no hope left in her. And that startles me. She seems to have a lot going for her, especially since she's going to Cornell.

And then she cried. Fuck, I was destroyed after that. There was no bouncing back from there. When I pulled out of the parking lot and drove home, I had zero expectations of what was going to happen next, and then she text me. I saw the message when in bed, causing me to fall asleep with a margin of hope. Now, with her in my room, breakfast in hand, confidence in our future is blossoming. I just hope she doesn't go running scared, because from what I know so far, I like her. From what I *see* in her. I just want to get to know this woman even more. I want to know what makes her heart beat, what makes her skin tingle with excitement, what helps her make strides forward every day. I'm desperate to learn more, and I'm only hoping she'll give me the chance to find out.

When I cross the doorway of my bedroom, Sadie has made my bed—that was quick—and is sitting on it, legs crossed, coffee held out to me, and a smile on her face. And it's true. Some Disney character crawled up her ass and put her in this mood. I just hope she doesn't have to have some sort of bibbidi-bobbidi-boo to get them out. Although, a Fantasia-like crap sounds magical.

"Here you go," she says, gesturing for me to take the coffee.

Eying her skeptically, I take the lid off and look inside. "You're awfully eager for me to drink this, did you poison it? Maybe slip in some kind of sleepy-time drug so you can take advantage of cannon cock?"

She rolls her eyes. "Please, I don't need to drug you to get you to pull your pants down. One flick of my eyes at your crotch and you'll be stripping faster than a Roadrunner computer can calculate an equation."

Er . . .

What?

Computer?

Did she just reference the world's fastest computer created by IBM?

Oh, fuck me.

If I were a cartoon character, my dick would have just poked her eye out in excitement.

"Surprised?" She raises an eyebrow at me and casually sips her coffee as she leans back on my bed, one of her hands propping her up.

Garble, garble, gook. That's all my brain can process. This is what my tongue is trying to say: jakdhef, hnnnnng.

"Don't be. I know a thing or two about your precious friends you tap your fingers across on a nightly basis, I just don't flaunt my understanding like you do."

Still stunned, I try to formulate some kind of sentence. "Tron!" I shout, startling her. Good job, man.

"Excuse me?"

"What was your favorite part of Tron? Was it when he was first scooped up in the hardware, met by men in black and orange neon suits? Because, fuck, that sequence was unforgettable. If I could, I would take one day to explore a motherboard like that, being inside a computer. Think about all the things we could experience, being up close and personal with the inner workings of it all."

Her mouth is parted open in confusion, her brow knitted together, and a *what the fuck did I get myself into* thought stretching across her beautiful face.

Laughing nervously, I nod at the box. "Uh, what did you bring?"

She shakes her head. "I'm going to ignore that last part. I don't even know what Tron is."

Immediate deflation of boner. How could she not know Tron? Insert whiny emoji here. Tron is one of the greatest movies of all time right behind Star Wars, Star Trek, any Marvel Comics movie—most importantly Guardians of the Galaxy, ET—because aliens, hello—Avatar, and Titanic. Can we take a moment of silence for Jack? That rotten, horse-faced Rose could have inched to the side to make room for him. You can't tell me there wasn't enough room on that door for a scrawny Leonardo DiCaprio to hang on. And even better, they could have spooned, created body heat, and saved each other. But nooo, horse-faced whore was too damn selfish.

Focusing back on Sadie, I say, "Tron is a movie about computers."

"Sounds horrible." I'm about to kick her out of my room when she winks and pats the bed next to her. "Come sit down before your blood pressure skyrockets."

She's stroking the bed now with her palm. I can't deny such "seduction" even if she doesn't know what Tron is.

Lightening the mood, I flop on the bed next to her, push my body up against the wall, and sip my coffee. God, I love suckling from the coffee bean's teat. "What did you bring for breakfast?"

With a flick of her finger, she pops open the bakery box and says, "Cinnamon rolls from Manni's Bakery."

"Oh, fuck yes." I've never been to Manni's but I love a good cinnamon roll. I give her a plate and then grab a roll from the box; they are fucking enormous. "Damn, Sadie, you're sure winning a little spot in my heart with this special treat."

Giggling, she places a roll on her plate as well. "And here I thought it was my boobs that did that."

"Nah, if anything it would be your ass, because that's what caught my attention from afar. Yeah, your ass and your hair."

"Pig," she jokes, and takes a bite out of her roll. Joining me, she scoots back on the bed so our arms press together. "When do you go into work today?"

"Three, like always. What about you?"

"Noon. Stuart has been putting me on the lunch shift a lot lately. I'm going to have to talk to him about that especially if you're taking the later shifts."

"Yeah?" I raise my eyebrows in surprise. "You want another go around in the stock room?"

"No." She laughs and shakes her head. "That shall never be repeated. I can't believe we didn't get caught."

"If you would've sucked my dick, we would have definitely been caught because I'm pretty sure I would have cried like a little girl while you did it. Those lips on my dick? Tear-worthy."

"If you cry while we're having sex, you can count on me never coming around again." Her voice is playful, and it makes me so fucking happy to hear her joke with ease.

"I didn't say crying during sex, Sugar Britches. I said crying while getting blown, completely different things."

"Let me ask you this. When you got your first blow job, did you cry?"

A deep chuckle rips from my chest. "Does one tear count as

crying?"

"Yes." She nods while covering her mouth in humor.

"To be fair," I hold up my hand in defense, "she wore a strawberry lip gloss, so when she sucked on me, I had the pleasure of smelling strawberry fields. It was an . . . erotic experience. Hard not to cry when your dick mingles with an aggregate accessory fruit."

"That's the saddest thing I've ever heard."

"Whatever." I grin. "What about you? First time you received a tongue to the taco, did you cry?"

"What?" She shakes her head. "You're such a good guy and then you go and say things like tongue to the taco."

"Like I said, every guy has a daily douche quota to fill. I'm just starting early. So, did you cry?"

"No, I didn't cry. I was more frightened than anything."

"Frightened, why?" I pause for a second as my mind starts twisting and turning her words into something dark. "Wait, were you fucking forced?"

"No." She presses her hand against my forearm. "Nothing like that at all." The racing of my heart starts to slow down. Thank fuck, or else I was going to have to start punching everything in sight. You get a punch and you get a punch, everyone gets a fucking punch! "I was frightened because I wasn't too sure about the whole mouth to the vagina thing. You know? I was nervous if I didn't . . . prep the plate well enough."

"Prep the plate?" I barely get the words out of my mouth before I start howling with laughter. "Oh fuck." I wipe my eyes. "I've never heard anyone say that before. Prep the fucking plate." Pretending my hand is a notepad, I lick my finger and act like I'm taking a note. "Oh, I need to remember that, prep the plate."

"Stop." She playfully shoves my shoulder. "It's easy for

guys, you just have a rod that sticks out like a popsicle. Girls have crevices and valleys. We have to make sure everything is on the up and up."

"That is true." I agree with her and finish off my cinnamon roll. "But I will tell you this, you didn't need to worry. You have the nicest pussy I've ever seen."

Her face lifts quizzically. "You're saying, out of all the vaginas you've come in contact with, mine is the best-prepped plate?"

A smile pushes past my lips. "No doubt in my mind."

Setting our dishes to the side, she crawls on top of my lap and starts running her fingers along my shoulders. "And how many vaginas are we talking, here? Tens, hundreds, thousands?"

"Thousands is just obnoxious."

"So hundreds?"

She starts to slowly move on my lap and images of the morning we woke up together start to flash through my mind. This woman wants herself some friction.

"Hundreds seems more accurate," I joke.

"Ew, really?" She starts to pull away, but I lock her down in place with my hands to her hips.

"No, not really. Honestly, I haven't been with a lot of women. No more than five."

Surprised, she nods her head as if happily satisfied with my answer. "Five is a respectable number for a guy who was called Cannon Cock at his last college."

"I like to think so." Swallowing hard, knowing I really shouldn't ask, but I can't help it, I ask, "What about you? How many dicks have you seen?"

"Seen? Or been with?"

"It disturbs me that there is a difference, but I'm going to go with how many dicks have you been with?"

"Just two." She shrugs her shoulder. "You and another guy."

"Two?" Now it's my turn to be surprised. One other guy could mean two things: Sadie doesn't like to hook around and is very picky when it comes to the dong, or she was in a serious and committed relationship. Based on the way she threw herself at me the morning after I danced drunk with her, I'm going to believe the answer is the latter, which in turn makes me sweat. A serious relationship, fuck. How serious are we talking?

"Yeah." Sadie's fingers, which had been dancing playfully across my chest, pause. A somber Sadie takes root.

"Tell me, was it serious?" I'm pushing her to open up, something I know she doesn't want to do, but call me crazy, I'm actually fucking jealous.

Sighing, she nods. "Very."

Ding, ding, ding.

Did you get that, Andrew? That's the sound of your chances of being with this girl slowly evaporating.

"Cool. I like serious relationships, you know." I try to play it off like I'm not bothered at all, not one bit. "There is nothing that tickles my hiney more than watching serious relationships develop. All those emotions, those deep-rooted feelings, the promises of forever. Yes. Love the things. Don't you wish we could all be in one giant, huge, mega-serious relationship? I do. What a great orgy of commitment that would be."

Instead of agreeing with me—I mean, orgy of commitment, how can you pass that up—she presses her fingers over my lips to silence me. Looking me square in the eyes, she tamps down the fear bubbling inside me. "It's over, Andrew. Completely and utterly over. It ended badly, and there is no way to reconcile what we had. There was too much pain, and I want to move on."

Feeling a little better, I ask, "Do I need to punch him? I have a killer right hook, left hook could use a little help, but the right," I punch my palm, "I can pop one hell of a wallop."

"Why can't I actually see that happening?"

"Hey, I'm tough, baby. Don't let the glasses fool you."

"No, the glasses are hot."

"Oh, hey there, confession. Nice to fucking meet you. I don't see you around here very often," I tease.

Rolling her eyes again—something I'm becoming accustomed to—she boldly grabs the hem of her tank and lifts it over her head, tossing it to the ground.

Immediately, like the man I am, my eyes go to the gorgeous breasts encased in a teal lace bra. Fuck, that's hot. *She's hot.*

"I don't want to talk anymore."

"Fine by me." I shift a little on the bed, clearly thrilled about what she wants to do next.

In one swift movement, I remove my glasses and pin Sadie to the mattress. Her giggle shoots straight to my cock, igniting my already awakened arousal. I maneuver my way to the end of the bed where I remove her shorts and let them fall to the ground with her shirt. Lying in front of me like a fucking wet dream, Sadie smiles up at me. Her thong matches her bra; her excitement matches her eyes. This little vixen planned this. Hell, if I'm mad about it.

"You're fucking hot, you know that?"

She answers me by pulling my arm so I'm forced to fall on top of her. Her legs wrap around my waist while her hands drag my head down to hers. With a quick lick of her lips, she starts kissing me. No, scratch that; she starts tongue fucking my mouth. Talk about things escalating quickly.

Catching up to speed, I open my mouth wider and match her movements. Wet, slippery, sloppy, it's all there mixed with some light moans. It's not fucking pretty. I know it's not but it's hot, it's full of need, full of yearning, and that makes it that much sexier.

While she continues attempting to control my mouth, I start stripping her down, because with each touch of her tongue against mine, my dick throbs to an uncomfortable level.

I start to reach behind her back to unclasp her bra when she mutters, "Front clasp."

God, I love front clasps, not because they're easy to undo—which shouldn't matter; everyone should be able to unclasp a bra with one hand and eyes closed—but because I love watching a woman's breast spring free of their confines, and a front clasp turns that image in my mind to a fucking incredible reality.

I slip my right hand up the front of her and find the clasp. With ease, I flick it open and chance a glance downward to see her perfect breasts spill out of the teal lace. Fucking amazing.

Wanting a taste, I disengage our mouths and nip my way down her chest, making sure to suck and lick the entire time, loving the way her body lifts with each sensual bite. I rest my head in her cleavage just as her hands thread through my hair. Shit, there is something about a woman driving her fingers through my hair that makes me crazy with lust. *Or is it just Sadie? Her hands? Her touch?*

Loving the way her fingernails dig into my scalp, I turn to her right breast and suck in her nipple . . . hard. I show no mercy. Just like her mouth, I fuck her nipple with my tongue. Flicking it, biting it, sucking so fucking hard she lifts from the bed.

"Oh my God, yes!" she moans in satisfaction.

I release her nipple but then quickly pull on it again, this time with my teeth. Her cry is clogged with pleasure as her fingers really dig into my scalp. Fuck, I won't be able to do this for very long, so I switch to her other breast and pay it the same respect. Pinching being my favorite maneuver, it results in the sexiest reaction from her.

Lips parted, she pants as her hips really start to grind against mine. My girl is ready; I can feel how ready she is through my thin shorts.

With one last nip, I pop her nipple out of my mouth and sit back so I can shuck my shorts and boxer briefs. From below me, she watches in fascination as I maneuver around her in record speed, quickly sheathing myself with a condom from my nightstand.

I'm not fucking around, I'm getting right to the good stuff. I lift her legs and place her ankles on my shoulders. Her eyes go wide from the position but then glaze over when I move the strip of fabric covering her beautiful pussy to the side and rub the tip of my cock along her warm, wet heat.

Fuck . . . yes. She's so ready.

One swipe of my cock over her clit. Two, three, and then I thrust inside her. The moan that passes her lips only spurs me on more, the need to pound into her is too strong. I take hold of her hips and start thrusting, hard. Not removing my eyes from hers, I watch as my thrusts rock her entire body, from her heady eyes, to her parted mouth, to her slick skin, to the way her tits bounce with my movements. It's sexy as fuck, and so is the way she clenches around my cock every time I plunge forward.

I pound hard, wanting to hit that spot, but not quite getting there.

"Oh God, harder, Andrew," she cries, wanting more.

I remove her legs from my shoulders and hold them out to the side, trying to change up the position. She's spread wide for me, the sound of our bodies slapping together echoes through the room, but I still can't fucking get there.

Not wasting any time, frustration forming within me, I pull out, only to be greeted by her protest. She doesn't get a chance to make anything of it because I flip her on her stomach, stuff my pillow under her stomach, and spread her legs and ass, giving me the perfect view of that beautiful, wet pussy.

Mouth watering with excitement, I plunge forward. And if I didn't already know Sadie was the perfect partner in bed, I know right now because she raises her back end so fucking high that I have to angle down to fuck her. And that's all I need. With a rotation of my hip and a thrust, I'm bottoming out, reaching an end to her that brings her moans to an indescribable octave.

Below me she grips the sheets, her head positioned to the side so I can see the way her mouth parts every time I press into her.

"Fuck, touch yourself, baby. Press on that little clit of yours."

Letting go of the sheets, she moves one hand beneath her and starts rubbing her clit, which sets off an ignition of fire between the both of us. She screams my name, her walls around me clench, and she starts to convulse below me. Fuck if I need anything more than that.

My thighs tighten, my chest swells, and I come so fucking hard I think I might explode from the ecstasy I'm feeling.

Blasts of pleasure shoot through me, from my fucking toes, to the top of my head. My entire body tingles and I keep pounding into her until I can't feel my legs anymore.

Once my heart rate slows down, and my dick is no longer throbbing, I remove myself from Sadie, take care of my condom quickly, and then snuggle up next to her where I bury my face into her soft hair.

"You make me lose my fucking mind," I whisper.

Her fingers dance along my back. "You make me forget the world around us."

I'm not sure if I should take that as a compliment or not, but when she snuggles even closer, I realize, whatever it means, it doesn't matter. At this moment right here, I'm happy. *We're happy.*

CHAPTER SEVENTEEN

SADIE

"Catch you later, hot pants. Don't do anything stupid like burn down the place. I don't have renter's insurance," Smilly calls out while grabbing her purse.

"That seems stupid. You should probably get some."

"Eh." She shrugs. "Why would I do that when living on the edge is so much more fun? I'll see you later."

"Okay, have fun on your date."

I give her a little wave as she shuts the door to the apartment, filling the space with silence. Not sure what to do, I reach for my laptop under the side table between our two recliners and fire it up. I don't get on my computer that often anymore because all it does is remind me of what I'm NOT doing these days. I keep it around because Smilly likes to go on Pinterest and create millions of boards about vintage rickrack, elephants swinging their trunks, and recipes that include Doritos. The Dorito recipes I don't mind; she's made quite a few good meals actually. Salmon encrusted with a Dorito and dill combo was my favorite. Something about that nacho cheese flavor on the salmon really spoke to me.

It takes a few moments for my computer to come to life, but

when it does, four tabs are opened in the browser; Pinterest, Pinterest – Swinging Elephants, Pinterest – Vintage dresses, and Big, Fat cocks dot com.

"Ugh, gross." I don't even bother clicking on the tab to see what penises she was drooling over; I just exit out and then scan her newest pins. All typical for her.

Opening a new tab, I click on Facebook and sign in just as my phone rings.

Shit.

Taking a deep breath, unsure if I should answer, I press the green button and say, "Hey, Tucker, what's up?"

"Nothing much. How are you?" His raspy voice filters through the phone.

Awkward. I don't want to exchange pleasantries with Tucker. I want to get to the point and then hang up.

"Fine. What's going on?"

His deep laugh rumbles through my ear and I clench my legs tight from the sound. That laugh. It *used* to send goosebumps all along my skin, but now, it only reminds me of what we had, and what we most certainly should never have done together.

"Not much of a talker tonight, I see. How's the little boy toy at work?"

"Stop. Do not talk about Andrew. Now you can either tell me why you called, or I can hang up. I have a pack of gummy worms and some Facebook stalking scheduled in about five minutes. So spill it."

"Riveting night, sorry to have bothered it." He lets out a long breath and I can picture in my mind him grabbing on the back of his knit sock hat. "My boss pulled me into the office today. He's sending me to Pittsburg for some training for the next month. I leave tomorrow."

Tucker works in construction. When he graduated high

school, instead of going to college, he worked his way up in the company he'd been working with ever since he could be paid to work and actually makes really decent money. I assume this training will only add to his impressive résumé. The question is, why is he telling me?

"Uh, okay." I can't think why I'd need to know.

"Wow, have you already forgotten?" He chuckles again. "Man, you're making this much harder on me than I thought."

Forgot what? Before I can piece everything together, he says, "Our date for Saturday, I'm going to have to postpone it."

Oh. *Oh.*

"It wasn't a date, Tucker."

"Gathering, whatever the hell you want to call it. I won't be able to come get you. I'm hoping to be able to get a weekend off when I'm out there, but I doubt it. They have my schedule jam-packed."

Feeling a little lighter knowing I don't have to see Tucker, I say, "Well, that's exciting though. What a good opportunity for you."

"Yeah, should be making more money too."

I nod awkwardly even though he can't see me. "Okay, well, safe trip out there."

"Hey, before you hang up on me, do you think I can call when I'm there, just to talk?" The way his voice turns into this soft-spoken, broken man rips me apart. "It's going to be lonely as fuck. It would be nice to hear a familiar voice."

Say no. Just say no. Tell him I'm good with the amount of phone calls I receive and hang up.

But I can't do that.

For so many years, our lives were intertwined with one another. He'll always be my first love. He'll always be the man I gave my virginity to. He'll always be the one I whispered painful secrets to when verbalizing about my shitty home life. He'll always be the baby's father, even though our baby didn't live. Tucker will never completely disappear from my life.

Hating myself, I say, "Sure. Call me when you're lonely."

Go ahead, start throwing the pitchforks, tell me I'm the worst; curse me out for not being strong enough to let go of the man who both consumed me and broke me for so many years. It's okay to hate me, because I hate me too. Maybe we should start an *I Hate Sadie* Facebook group. Anyone want to be admin?

"Thanks, Sadie," he says into the phone. "Shit, I'm going to miss this whole summer with our friends. You're going to have to give me the play-by-play. Let me know if Kiera ever dates someone from CrossFit."

"Not going to happen." I chuckle.

"Yeah, I don't think so either. And hey, give Emma a hand every once in a while. That girl needs a break."

"I will. Have fun in Pittsburgh. I'll talk to you later."

"See ya, beautiful."

I hang up just as my chest seizes on me.

Beautiful, said in that velvety voice of his. Memories of him holding me in his truck, whispering into my ear, telling me everything was going to be okay, start flooding my brain, causing my stomach to—

Bloop.

Message request. On my computer?

What?

I click on the message button and see a request from Andrew. And just like that, he quiets those painful memories. He must have gotten off work early.

Andrew: *I found you! Facebook friend request being processed now. I'm going to creep the fuck out of your profile. Get ready to see some photos from 2013 I liked. If this is not the*

Sadie Montgomery with the best-prepped plate on earth, then please ignore this message and friend request. If you don't know what prepped plate means, then you aren't the Sadie I'm looking for, and I would appreciate it if you forget this personal encounter ever happened. Thank you.

A laugh pops out of my mouth as I type him back.

Sadie: Best-prepped plate at your service. Glad you were brave enough to search me out on Facebook. That's a big step, you know, becoming Facebook friends. Are you ready for it?

Andrew: My stalking/clicking fingers are ready. Accept my friend request already so I can start snooping on you.

Too bad for Andrew, my Facebook page is bleak and boring. I don't let people tag me in pictures because of my previous major at Cornell, and I never turned off that feature. There will probably be about five pictures for him to look at; all profile pics. They're anything but exciting. Just simple selfies. At the top, I see the friend request button lit up, so I accept his request and then type him back.

Sadie: Not much to snoop, sorry.

He takes a minute to respond, but I smile when he does.

Andrew: Well feed my dick through a meat grinder, that's shit. You have nothing discriminating on your profile at all.

Quickly I scan through his profile and can't help but smile at his many ridiculous pictures, mostly of him acting silly and over the top. I wouldn't expect anything less.

Sadie: And yet, you have a gold mine of pictures for me to use against you.

Andrew: Yeah, I'm apparently not as smart as you. But hey, you have to live a little. I have to admit, this picture of you in your bikini... I'm shocked. I thought you were a closet whore, not a public one.

Of course he would fixate on that picture. I only posted it

because I lost a bet to Tucker, who luckily, doesn't believe in Facebook.

Sadie: Public whore would be bikini and duck lips combined together. That's just a picture of a girl who lost a bet.

Andrew: That makes better sense. I see that it also says you're in a complicated relationship with Smilly. Care to explain that? Are there lesbian tendencies in your blood I need to be aware of?

Sadie: LOL, yes, Smilly and I are promised to each other. Sorry, you're just a boy toy for now.

Andrew: Why am I okay with this?

Sadie: Because you're a man, and all men are perverts when it comes to hearing about girl-on-girl action.

Andrew: Wait, so does this mean you really do have lesbian tendencies?

Sadie: NO! God, you're annoying.

Andrew: You shouldn't say things you don't mean. Annoying is harsh, but saying something like, God, I want your dick in my mouth, now that's being truthful.

Sadie: Short on your douche quota?

Andrew: Just a skootch.

Sadie: Glad I can help you make it.

Andrew: I knew there was a reason I kept you around. So what are you doing tonight? Hanging out with Smilly, maybe watching Tron?

Sadie: I'm on my own. She's going out with Saddlemire on a date tonight. She babysits twins and got a pay raise so they're celebrating by getting wasted and playing shuffleboard at the Legion.

Andrew: Whoa, do they know how to party or ahfjasfnsdfnam asfna smfn sjhenf

Huh?

Andrew: oh my akdfnao nafine a ahhh
Andrew: fuck, fufahendoa
Andrew: my hair, hafajdf help

What the hell is going on? Hoping whatever is happening to him is a joke, I reach for my phone and dial his number. He doesn't even say hello when he answers, he just starts screaming into the phone.

"Holy fucking... Fuck, get away from me." His voice sounds higher than normal as if someone is consistently yanking on his balls. Who is he talking to?

"Andrew, what is going on?" Suddenly I'm panicking.

He doesn't answer, instead there is fumbling of the phone, more curse words, and then a slam of what sounds like a door. My heart begins to race as I wait patiently to hear from him. Is he being robbed? Who else could he be talking to? Did his basketball roommates come home early? Are they trying to take advantage of him with their European ways and heavy accents?

"Andrew? Are you there? Please tell me what's going on."

"Sadie?" His voice is horse, desperate, and scared. "My life flashed before my eyes."

"What is going on, Andrew?"

"He's still out there, I can hear him trying to get in my door."

"I swear to God, if you're joking—"

"I'm not joking. Sadie, I was just attacked."

"By who?" I'm sitting on the edge of my seat now, my computer folded and on the table.

"A bat," he whispers in dismay.

A bat?

He says it with such fear in his voice that I can't do anything else but laugh, and laugh hard.

"What's so fucking funny? He was trying to wing-clip me with his rabies-infested black flappers."

"You were attacked by a bat?" I continue to laugh.

"Yes! What's so goddamn funny? You realize the probability of them carrying some life-threatening disease, don't you?" Andrew pauses for a second and then says, "He had red in his eyes, Sadie. What does that even mean? What kind of devil bird has red in his eyes?"

"Bats aren't birds, they're mammals."

He sighs heavily into the phone. "I fucking know that. Bats are the only mammals capable of sustained flight. I was being dramatic."

"Oh, how kind of you, laying the dramatics on me."

Ignoring me, he continues, "I'm seriously freaked the fuck out. Where did it come from and where the fuck did it go just now?"

"Where are you?"

"In my room. It tried to dive-bomb me twice, but I ducked under my computer and tried to type out my SOS to you. He gave me one opening by flying into the hallway and that's when I slammed my door shut. To hell if I would let that sadistic bastard fuck with my hair anymore."

Hands down, this has to be the most absurd conversation I've ever had.

"I can't take you right now."

"Sadie, I'm serious. He has to be out there still. There is no way he isn't. I mean, where would he go? I can't possibly fucking sleep tonight knowing he's out there. Maybe I should go to Jimmy's."

"Oh my God, do not go to your brother's. I'll come over to help you."

"You're going to save me?"

"No, I'm going to help you find the spot where your balls fell off. You seem to have lost them."

I hang up the phone without saying goodbye, go into the hall closet and pull out Smilly's tennis racket that she uses for drunk tennis—rather than actual tennis—and put on my shoes. Looks like I have some bat hunting to do.

•••

I don't even bother knocking on the door. I help myself into his house and walk up to his room. Everything is dark beside a small sliver of light peeking through his bedroom door. I flip on some lights and give the place a good once-over, checking the ceilings and corners. There is nothing. Although, from the time it took me to get here, the bat could be anywhere by now.

Just to be polite, I knock on his door and say, "Hello? Are you still alive, Andrew, or have you turned into Dracula yet?"

"Not funny," he calls from his bedroom. "Don't hang out there where the beast can get you."

I snort from the seriousness in his voice and open his bedroom door to find him tucked in the corner with a towel draped over his head, cinched with his hands right under his chin.

There is no use. I start laughing again. I wish I could show a little sympathy, but we're talking about a grown man—a highly intelligent grown man—terrified of a bat that is probably no bigger than his hand.

"What are you doing?" I ask him.

His brows are pinched together in irritation. "Protecting my hair. What does it look like? Bats just fucking love getting tangled in people's hair, and to hell if I will fall victim to such violence."

"You barely have any hair, so that would never happen."

"I have just enough hair for the bat to lay his larva in my follicles."

"I don't even know if that's a thing."

"Will you just get in here and shut the damn door before the beast decides to go for round two?"

Shaking my head, laughter still on the tip of my tongue, I do as he asks and then turn to him. "This is knocking a lot of points off your man card."

"I'm aware and okay with it." He eyes my tennis racket. "What are you going to do with that?"

"I'm going to swat at the bat, try to knock it out. A tennis racket is one of the best ways to do that."

"You're just going to go out there and start swinging, as if you were trying to squash mega-fly with a giant fly swatter?" He sits a little taller now, interested in my plan.

"That pretty much sums it up." I place my keys, phone, and wallet on his nightstand and then open his bedroom door again. I give the landing of the second floor a look around but don't see anything, so I start to venture out.

"Wait, where are you going?" he asks. He sounds so desperate.

"I don't see it around here. I'm going to check the downstairs."

Scooting up behind me, towel still firmly over his head, he says, "Don't fucking leave me here alone; that's what the bat wants to happen, to split us up and then go in for the kill."

"Yes, because I've heard there's been an influx on killer bats recently."

"I wouldn't be surprised," he deadpans, so certain.

Seriously, he's going to have to do something incredibly manly in order to make up for tonight. I like the kid, but seeing this side of him is almost too comical.

Together—Andrew, towering over me, looking ridiculous with his head covered in a towel—we start scouring the house.

His steps follow in line with mine, as if we're performing some kind of musical act. All we need is a jazzy little number and we'd put on one hell of a show. Our unison is on point.

"Wait." I halt quickly, causing him to bump into my back. I place my hand at my ear and say, "Do you hear that?"

"What? Hear what?" He starts ducking near my head, practically crawling on my back. Unbelievable.

"That sound, what is it?"

"I don't hear anything?" Hysteria in his voice. "Is the bat screeching?"

"Oh, I know what it is." I turn my head and look him in the eye. "It's the sound of your balls clinking around on the floor, looking for a new owner."

His once concerned face turns flat. "Real funny, Sadie. Make fun of the poor, terrified guy. I'm sure there are things you're scared of. Do you think I would rub your face in it? No." He pauses and then smiles at me. "I would try to fuck you senseless until you forgot."

I step back and look him up and down. "You're an anomaly, you know that?"

"I'll take that as a compliment," he replies smugly.

Huffing, I march around the rest of his house, searching for the killer bat as he sticks to me like glue, never letting a few inches separate us.

●●●

I drop the tennis racket on his bedroom floor before sitting on his desk where I cross my legs at my ankles. Grilling him, I ask, "Care to explain to me why you would go to such elaborate lengths to get me here when you could have easily just asked me to come over?"

"What are you talking about?" For some reason, he takes his shirt off and tosses it into his hamper. His abs flex as he stretches from side to side, his boxer briefs clinging to his waist, peeking just past his shorts. What is he up to?

"You lied about the bat. We've looked everywhere, and it's nowhere in this house."

"Maybe it flew out a window," he offers, now flopping on his bed where he places his hands behind his head, his biceps flexing beneath him. The man who was only a few seconds ago clenching a towel to his head, terrified out of his life, is now the picture of utter calm. How is that even possible?

"You don't have any open windows."

"Well, I'm not an idiot," he says, his voice an octave lower from earlier in the night. "I don't want some drunk psycho killer breaking in and stealing my computers."

"Okay, so then you made it all up. There was no bat to begin with."

He shakes his head, his chest flexing now. Is he doing that on purpose? If he is, it's working because all I want to do is lick his chest from belly button to pecs. "No way did I make up that rabid beast. He must have gone up to the attic through the crack under the door. It's the only explanation. Why do you think I just stuffed my towel in that crack?"

"Can bats get through small spaces like that?"

"Yeah. When I was tucked away in the corner, I read up on bats to see what I was dealing with and they can squeeze through tiny spaces. I bet that fucker is floating around in the attic, waiting to strike again."

"I don't know. Still seems like you made him up to get me here."

"Please," he scoffs. "If I wanted to get you here, I would not have emasculated myself like that."

"Oh yeah, what would you have done instead?"

"To get you over here? Well, besides ask nicely, if you needed more coaxing, I would have offered a good spooning while watching whatever movie you wanted to watch. Maybe a late-night ice cream run. Or a chance to lie out on the grass with you and gaze at the stars. You know, something simple, but sexy and sweet."

My heart rate starts to pick up.

"No dick pics?"

He laughs deeply. "No, I learned my lesson about pictures of my dick. I wouldn't do that again. Plus, you're not a dick-pic kind of girl. You deserve respect; you deserve to have men open doors for you, to offer you their jacket when you're cold."

The seriousness in his voice pulls me toward him. I hop off the desk and kick off my shoes. Without even giving it a second thought, I straddle him on the bed, settling myself on his lap. Smiling brightly, his hands begin to run up and down my thighs in a comforting way, not a *I'm-about-to-fuck-you* way.

"Tell me, Sadie, have you always been brave?"

I twist my lips to the side and shrug. "I learned to be brave at a young age." *It was a necessity.*

"I can tell. You have wisdom in your bravery. It's sexy as hell."

"You think so?"

"Yeah." Instead of pulling me down for a kiss, a move I thought he would make, he continues to rub my thighs. "Brothers or sisters?"

Caught a little off guard, I settle into his touch and answer, "Two sisters. I'm the middle child. What about you?"

"Two brothers. I'm the youngest."

"You would be the youngest," I tease.

"What? Do I have baby written all over me?"

"You have spoiled rotten written all over you."

"Spoiled? Oh come on, that's not true."

I scoff. "You can tell you always get what you want."

His smile turns leisurely as he looks me up and down. "Believe me, baby, I get what I want because I work for it, not because it's given to me." The way his eyes travel up to mine, I know he's talking about me. He confirms it by saying. "You weren't an easy shell to crack."

"I told you, I don't want any more friends."

"You never can have enough friends, Sugar Britches." Switching subjects, he asks, "So what are you majoring in over at the prestigious Cornell? Which, by the way, it's sexy as fuck that you're such a brain."

The compliment should make my heart stammer in my chest; instead it makes me feel uneasy, even sick to my stomach. Should I just tell him the truth, let him know I'm a dropout? It takes me two seconds to drop that idea because it's obvious how much he likes the fact that I'm smart, that I attend—technically attend*ed*—an Ivy League college.

"Psychology," I answer, not really wanting to elaborate.

"Really? Huh, I would never have guessed that." He really is surprised, it reads all over his face.

"Why not?"

Gah, Sadie. Don't elaborate on the topic, you're just asking for further in-depth conversations.

"Because you're not what some would call a people person. You know, the whole I don't need more friends than what I already have. It's hard to imagine you actually want to sit down and listen to people talk about their problems."

When he puts it that way, he's right. I don't want to sit and listen to people's problems, that doesn't interest me at all.

"Child psychology." If there is a slight chance I can give kids a chance to heal, the chance I never got at a young age, then I would feel accomplished. Although, I guess it's too late for that now.

He makes a knowing sound as his lips form an O in understanding, but then he pauses and tilts his head to the side, studying me. Normally his stare wouldn't bother me, but in this moment, it makes me feel raw and exposed, as if I'm naked in front of thousands of people and they're seeing the inner workings of my being.

I hate it.

"Sadie—"

I hold up my hand to stop him. "Don't, okay? Don't ask any more questions."

Disappointment flashes over his features. This is just as hard on him as it is on me. "Can you just tell me one thing?" He doesn't wait for me to answer. "Were you ever abused as a kid?"

I shake my head and rest my hand on his chest, feeling the heavy beat of his heart against my palm. He's worked up . . . on my behalf. "No, nothing like that."

Although, sometimes I feel like I was abused as a kid, metaphorically kicked in the heart repeatedly by my mom. She was untrustworthy, manipulative, and selfish. She put our family through hell, adopting her own way of living, selling drugs, putting our family under the spotlight, only to have our house raided many times by drug lords *and* cops. She fucked with us, split our family apart, ruined my father—turning him into a puddle of a man—and destroyed any semblance of a normal childhood.

No, I wasn't abused. I was mentally and emotionally fucked over. If there was one thing my mom taught me it was this: Never be vulnerable or give power to another human. *Because they might try to decimate my life too.*

Resigned, he pulls on my arms until I'm lying on top of him, my head against his shoulder. He holds me—tight—until we both fall asleep in each other's arms.

CHAPTER EIGHTEEN

Andrew

"What are you doing, pretty girl?" I ask just as Sadie sits down at the little two-person table across from the counter of the fountain. My workspace is small but there is just enough room past the register for two tables in case customers wanted to sit down and eat their ice cream but not sit in the dining area.

Sadie places a plate on the table as well as a drink and sits down. "I'm eating my dinner, what does it look like?"

Even though it's past five, the fountain area is slow, so I lean on the counter and talk to my girl. "Looks like you're sticking close to me. Trying to get in some flirting on your break."

She sticks a piece of broccoli in her mouth and shakes her head as she chews. "No, Michelle said there was a good show over here tonight so I thought I'd try to catch it. So far, the man candy is subpar."

My eyebrows rise in question. "Subpar?" The printer goes off, indicating an incoming ticket. "Baby, there is nothing subpar about me." I turn away, giving her the best view of my backside that I can.

Subpar, my ass. I'll give her something to remember, something to carry on through the rest of the night. I snag the ticket from the printer and stick it in the ticket holder. A classic peanut butter cup sundae; easy. Knowing my arms are porn for Sadie, especially my forearms, I roll my short sleeves over my shoulders to show off my biceps, and then seductively snap on some sanitary gloves, making sure to exaggerate my movements.

"Oh my God." Sadie giggles from the side. "What the hell are you trying to do?"

I turn my hat around so she can get a good look at my face, trying to give off bad-boy ice cream-scooper vibes and grab hold of an ice cream scoop. In the background, the classic song, "My Girl" is playing, giving me a good, slow base to work my moves with.

Really wanting to give her a show, I twist my feet together and then do a spin right in the middle of the fountain area, pulling out all the moves. When I face her again, I *Magic Mike* her ass and pelvic thrust in her direction while holding the scoop by my crotch. Her eyes grow wide with each movement, a smirk playing on her lips.

"You like that?" I ask, really feeling my groove.

"Oh yeah, you've got it going on, big boy."

"I fucking know it." I prop my arm up so she can see it over the counter and point my palm down while holding the ice cream scoop like I'm holding a weight. With the beat of the song, a little dance in my step, and a bob to my head, I start to do a reverse wrist curl, flexing every muscle in my arm with the lift. Oh yeah, this is doing the trick. Keep it up, Andrew, looking fucking good. I look over at Sadie, doing the perfect interpretation of the white man's overbite and ask, "What do you think? Hot?"

Sadie goes to answer when a booming voice startles the fuck out of me, causing me to drop my ice cream scoop and cover my ears. "Andrew, what the hell are you doing? Scoop the damn ice cream." Stuart stands angrily in the fountain area, his eyes staring me down.

Scrambling for the scoop, I pick it up and bring it to the sink to rinse. "Uh, yeah, just warming up for scooping. A proper warm-up is important, don't want to kink my wrist out," I mutter.

"Just scoop the damn ice cream," he says and then walks away.

The minute he disappears, Sadie erupts in laughter, practically falling out of her chair.

"Yeah, laugh it up." A wave of embarrassment snakes up my spine, sending my ears into what feels like a pit of fire.

"Oh . . . my . . . God." She's panting, and if I wasn't so embarrassed, I might find it kind of hot, but I was past the point of being turned on given Stuart scared my penis into the wrinkles of my scrotum. She wipes at her eyes, legit tears leaking out of her. It wasn't that fucking funny.

Making sure the coast is clear, I lean over the counter and hiss at her. "That was fucking terrifying. You could show me a little compassion."

She shakes her head. More tears streaming down her face. "The look on your face." She erupts in laughter. "Oh my God, that will forever be branded in my brain."

"Maybe you should go eat your dinner somewhere else," I suggest and then grab a sundae glass. The show is fucking over.

"Now why would I do that when I can stare at your ass for the next twenty minutes?"

I shake my head as I scoop ice cream into the glass, making sure to flare the bottom so it fits. "Don't try to score brownie points now."

Once I'm done scooping, I lean close to her and pause. "I have to know, though. That was hot, right? Seeing me flex that ice cream scoop like that?"

The smile on her face. Yep, the humiliation was all worth it. I've always been a prankster. Being the youngest son, it was my survival method with two older brothers. *But this?* Seeing Sadie smile and laugh so easily? So freely? Worth it. Might have to rein in the scoop flexing from now on though. I do want to keep my job, after all.

"I've never seen anything as sexy as you wrist curling that ice cream scoop."

"Yeah?" I lift an eyebrow at her.

"Yeah. Like a flood in my panties," she whispers, mirth in her voice.

"Hell, yeah. Sadie Tsunami Shorts, I like it."

She swats in my direction. "Don't call me that."

I hold up my hands before pumping some peanut butter sauce on the sundae. "Hey, you were the one saying you were practically coming in your panties at work. I'm just making it sound prettier than lady jizzing."

Shaking her head, she stands and grabs her plate. "Maybe you're right, maybe I should go." There is a light smirk on her face so I know she's only teasing.

I top the sundae with whipped cream and a cherry and then set it on the counter with its ticket. I then turn to Sadie and point at her. "Sit that fine ass down or I will stand on this counter and helicopter my dick for the dining area to see while saying my penis belongs to you." *Please say no. Please say no.* Cannon Cock was one thing. Helicopter Dick would ruin me. *Well, unless Sadie was doing the riding . . .*

Studying me for a second, she starts moving away from the table and says, "Now this I've got to see."

Laughing, I point at the chair and say, "Just sit down, fucking sassy woman."

•••

"Aw, you're so cute," Sadie says as she walks into my house and takes in the living room.

I shrug my shoulders and pull her in for a kiss. "Cute is okay, sexy, hot, even boulder balls with the cobblestone cock are better."

"I'm not calling you boulder balls."

I kiss the top of her head and chuckle. "So does that mean I can't call you bedrock boobies?"

She chuckles and shakes her head. "No. And what's with the rock names? Did you read an article about the earth's rubble or something?"

"Geological formations actually. National Geographic did an entire piece on it. Fascinating shit, I can send you the link if you want."

She places her hand on my chest and shakes her head. "I'm good, but you're sweet for asking." I sniff the air, yeah, that's sarcasm at its finest. She glances around again and asks, "Are those corn dogs?"

Taking in the spread below us on the coffee table, I nod. "Homemade, just for my baby."

The look of shock on her face warms my heart. "Seriously? You made homemade corn dogs?"

"No." I laugh, and she swats my chest. "But it was cute seeing your astonished face. Walmart was having a sale so I went big. Nothing is too much for my girl." I gesture to the couch and join her, pulling out the cooler by the coffee table. "Beer?"

"Please."

I dig into the cooler and pull out two beers, popping the tops off both bottles before I hand her one. "I think we've got everything." I scan her up and down, taking in her Yankees apparel.

Damn, she looks fine. The tight-fitting pinstripe jersey she has on is doing all kinds of funny things to my dick, as well as the incredibly revealing shorts she's wearing. If I weren't holding my beer right now, I would stand and slow-clap her outfit for all mankind. "You look good."

"From the way your tongue is hanging out of your mouth, I could tell you thought so." She giggles to herself which only makes my shorts grow tighter and tighter at the crotch.

Trying to distract myself from the—let's be real, erection in the room—I say, "Our first Yankees game together. Granted it's not in the stadium, but we have Derek Jeter with us," I gesture to my life-size cut-out I brought downstairs for the occasion, "we have stadium-style food, and front-row seats to the TV. Plus, if we want to make this night really memorable, we can blindfold Derek, strip down, and watch the game naked. I have a bat and balls in my pants, and you have a glove, we could play our own little game of baseball."

She twists in her seat. "Are you referring to my vagina as a glove?"

"It sucks objects in, doesn't it? Pretty sure if I could stick my hand in it like a puppet, I could get it to catch a few things. Vagina glove." The visual I'm developing in my head has me chuckling to myself. Vagina glove. All I can see are two flappy labia lips catching ball after ball. Classic.

"I suggest you say something other than vagina glove to keep me from walking out of this little date you planned."

Shit, I'm losing her. Abort vagina glove.

"Err, your hair looks nice."

Giving me a knowing side-eye look, she leans back on the sofa and takes a sip of her beer. "Decent save, but you still have some making up to do."

"Don't worry, there's plenty of time for that." I wiggle my

eyebrows at her, which grants me a genuine eye-roll. Hey, she's still sitting next to me, so I'll take it.

I lean back on the sofa with her and link my hand with hers. She smiles up at me and leans her shoulder against mine. Fuck, I like this girl.

"Thanks for having me over."

I kiss the side of her head. "Anytime, baby."

As the players are introduced and we listen to the Yankees announcer, Michael Kay, talk about the starting line-up, we enjoy each other's company, playfully feeding each other mini corn dogs and Cracker Jacks. It's nauseating how cute we are together, but fuck if I'm complaining.

By the fourth inning, food has been eaten, beers have been consumed, and the Yankees are down by two. Sadie now sits on my lap, a little off to the side so I can wrap my arm around her waist and still see the TV.

"Gah, seriously, take him out already, Girardi," Sadie yells at the TV. Is it weird that her passion turns me on? Fuck it, I don't care. It's rare I find someone as passionate about the Yankees as I am. "Mendez couldn't find the strike zone if it was a foot away and he was trying to stick his dick in it."

She's so poetic. I love it. I don't think I've ever sat and watched a baseball game with a girl before. Mae doesn't count. Sadie just seems to speak my language. Gone is the girl with the darkened, broken heart. Gone is the girl with secrets. What I feel I have is the real Sadie. A girl who is vibrant, passionate, intelligent, and astute. She's completely confident in this environment. At ease. *And I really like that.* Even though she's made it clear we are just a fun time, it's impossible to deny that kernel of desire that says, *"I want to keep her."* But I'm not really sure she is someone who can be kept.

Oh, what the fuck was that pitch?

"Why is it the best team in baseball history can't get their shit together when it comes to pitching? I swear it feels like every year we struggle on the mound. Oh sure, we have some heavy hitters, but the pitching . . . Christ."

"I know," Sadie says, snuggling in closer. "Brian Cashman should be fired. He's been the Yankees General Manager for far too long. Time for some new blood."

"You speak my language, baby." I kiss her shoulder just as Mendez walks another batter.

"Oh, for fuck's sake." She turns on my lap so we're facing each other and without notice, starts unbuttoning her jersey. Her hips begin to rock back and forth. Well, that's one way to create an erection in record time.

Her jersey hangs open as she pops the front clasp of her bra so her boobs are exposed, swaying inches from my face. Fuck, this is one awesome way to watch the game. Yep, I think it's my favorite way now.

With zero finesse, she grips my head and starts kissing me, her tongue diving right in, showing no mercy in her anger against the Yankees.

"I hate when the Yankees lose," she mutters.

I've been a Yankees fan my entire life, but if this is what happens to me when the Yankees are losing, then may they never win another fucking game ever again. If she wants to take it out on me, I'm more than happy to oblige.

I rest my hands on her hips to help her rock, loving how she has no shame in a little dry humping.

"Aren't you mad?" she asks.

Mad? Uh, she's riding my cock right now, how can I be mad . . .

Oh, the Yankees, right.

"Pissed," I answer on a short breath, buying into her little tirade.

"Me too." She kisses down my neck and starts scooting off my body until she's between my legs and unbuckling my pants. My cock presses against the zipper, begging for release. From my seat on the couch, I watch in fascination as Sadie finally undoes my zipper and pulls out my hardened length. She gives me no chance to enjoy the moment, as she shoves my dick so fast in her mouth and starts sucking that I nearly leap off the couch.

Holy. Fuck.

She works her mouth back and forth, scraping her teeth along the skin, causing me to sweat. With one hand, she pulls on my balls just enough that I'm almost about to yelp and beg for more all at the same time.

Relentless. That's what she is. Sucking so fucking hard, licking, nipping, scraping, pulling. She's doing it all, and before I know it, my hips are flexing up toward her mouth, my mind starts to go blank, and my dick is throbbing so fucking hard I'm about to explode.

With her teeth, she lightly runs them along the head of my cock just as she presses a finger in that special spot. I black out as my legs seize on me, my hips losing all control as they pound toward Sadie's face. Hot spurts spring free. Sadie pumps me until I'm completely spent. *Fuck. Fucking hell, that was so beyond hot.* I feel only two things: the light brush of Sadie's hair against my thighs and the residual throbbing of my cock.

Leisurely, Sadie licks my cock while looking up at me. She leans forward and presses a kiss against my lips. "Mmm, I feel better now." *Meanwhile, I'm still completely speechless.*

What just happened?

As if she didn't just break my world in half with that orgasm, she sits next to me on the couch and takes a sip of her beer, her top half still exposed.

Uh . . .

Pants down, dong out, I look over at her, bewildered as to what just happened, and before I can ask, she glances down at her crotch and then back at me. "Do I need to ask?" She spreads her legs, indicating what she wants to happen next and I have no problem jumping on the invitation.

Table for one at Sadie's pussy, don't mind if I fucking do.

•••

"I love it here." Sadie leans back against my chest, my arms wrapped around her, and her head resting against my shoulder.

"This was a good idea, baby. Perfect date for our day off, especially since I've never been here."

She sighs and takes in the fresh bay air whipping up from the ferry ride. "I keep forgetting you're not from around here. My friends and I came to the Thousand Islands during the summer and visited Boldt Castle. Smilly and I used to always say how amazing it would be to get married here one day."

"Married, huh? Are you fishing for a proposal?" I tease.

She elbows me from behind and laughs. "No. But you want to know me, so there's a little factoid for you."

And thank God for that. Her little factoids are few and far between, but when I'm graced with one, I absorb it.

Wanting to dive a little deeper, I ask, "Was it just you and your friends? Or did you have supervision?"

"At first we did. Emma's parents would take us, but then once we started driving, we would drive up on our own." She lifts her chin to the breeze and takes a deep breath. "Some of my best memories were made up here. Some of my favorite moments, favorite laughs."

"Yeah?" I kiss the side of her head. "Tell me one of them."

Snuggling in closer, Sadie wraps her arms around mine and stares out in front of us. There is a tour guide in the background talking about the islands but we ignore him and focus on our little world. I've had a few girlfriends, but this feels different. Is it because we're older? No idea. A large part of me hopes this day creates more *good* memories for her.

"Last year was my favorite time by far. Smilly just turned twenty-one, she has an early birthday, and we decided to celebrate. We wanted to do shots, but Emma had other plans. She put together a really nice dinner for everyone. We were asked to wear our finest and act our finest, but given the flask I had in my purse that Smilly and I kept drinking from, our finest was nowhere to be found. Once we ran out of booze, we started sneaking out to the bar across the street, acting like we had to keep going to the bathroom. After the third bathroom run in twenty minutes, Emma started catching on, and we were busted. We got pretty drunk and ended up trying to untie the apron strings on our waiter the rest of the night, a game we thought was hilarious. Unfortunately the waiter didn't share that sentiment."

I laugh, envisioning the entire thing in my head. "Why do I feel like you got kicked out of the restaurant?"

"You would be right." Sadie chuckles. "Smilly and I were asked to leave, but not before we got our meals to go. We sat on the curb of the restaurant eating out of our doggy bags while impersonating the snooty waiter. People thought we were some kind of pathetic street show and tossed money at us as they walked by. We ended up making a little over five dollars."

"Hell, that's something to be proud of."

"We were. We ended up buying souvenirs for our boy—"

She pauses.

"For who?" I ask, waiting to see if she'll keep going or if she'll shut down.

Her body stiffens. Any hope I had for her to continue sharing vanishes when she says, "Doesn't matter."

And just like that, the jovial mood fades and an awkward air surrounds us. She was going to say boyfriends. I'm not an idiot. But I wanted to actually hear her say it, to go beyond a drunk story and tell me a little bit more about her life. Who was he? Do I know him? Was he a dick to her? Did he understand the complex, yet beautiful woman Sadie is? Did he see her the way I see her? Gorgeous, complicated, the perfect combination of feisty and sexy? Or had he already been accepted into her small circle of friends, been privy to her secrets, and knew her inside out?

I sure as hell hope not, but from her stiff set posture, and her resistance to even say the word *boyfriend*, I'm going to guess he did.

Sighing, I drop the topic and revert back to the superficial where she's comfortable, hating that once again, she closed me off.

I try to tell myself in good time, she'll open up. *That she'll want to share things with me.* It's just going to take some time. I'm a patient man. Fuck, I was a patient man until I met Sadie. I just hope I can hold out a little while longer. *But does she want me to hold out? Or do I butt out completely?*

CHAPTER NINETEEN

ANDREW

The last two weeks have been fun. Yeah, that's how I would describe it, fun. Not heavy, not emotionally intimate, just . . . fun.

But hey, I enjoy fun. I like the spontaneity of fun. Who doesn't enjoy fucking in the shower, on the kitchen counter, in the backyard on a blanket under the stars? All very FUN times to give the old V a pounding from P.

And yet, I want more.

I want fucking more from Sadie, and she is set in stone on not giving it to me.

It's so fucking frustrating.

There is so much more to her than the minimal information she's given me. I know her likes and dislikes, which is great and all, but that's shallow shit. I know her mom fucked up their family's life and there was something to do with jail, but that's the extent of it. I want more. I want to know Sadie, the person. I want to know what makes her tick. For the love of God, I want to fucking know why she refuses to let me in on her life. What the fuck is she hiding?

My phone buzzes next to me.

Sadie.

I open up her text and read it.

Sadie: Getting off work in half an hour. What are you up to?

I glance down at my computer and the code I've been writing all night since I left work. I've been lost in the script for the past three hours, typing away and listening to the Harry Potter soundtrack. For the record, I'm one hundred percent Gryffindor, but if I had to be sorted into another house, I would want to go to Hufflepuff just so I could say the word Hufflepuff.

Andrew: Working on some computer stuff for a class this coming semester. I want to be ahead of things when classes start.

I lean back in my chair and ruffle my hair. In all honesty, I could use a break; my eyes feel like they're about to go cross-eyed, but for the life of me, I can't get my fingers to text her to come over. I blame it on my frustration. Not sexual frustration, but an unfamiliar frustration I haven't felt before.

What *I* think could be something great between Sadie and myself is turning out to be a glorified summer fling. *She doesn't want more.* I just need time away from only skimming the surface with her. *I want more.* It's not just that she's under my skin, but I feel more for her than I've felt for any other girl. Despite her reticence, we click and see eye to eye on so many things. I want more picnics. More of the fun interaction at work. Just . . . more. But if she doesn't, is it worth continuing to try? Am I stupid for bothering?

I let out a long breath and lean on my desk as I grab my hair. "Fuck," I mumble just as the door to the front of the house opens. My head pops up immediately from the sounds of things crashing against the wall and heavy footsteps.

I whip around to look out my door, fear prickling the back

of my neck. Eyes still trained on the door, I reach for any kind of weapon behind me and pull up a ruler. Holding it above my head, ready to stab someone with the corner, I walk toward the stairway just as I hear, "Andrew!" from down below in a very thick, Finnish accent.

"Oh Christ," I mutter and toss the ruler back on the desk, pretending I wasn't about to use the damn thing as a tool of self-defense. *When did I become so paranoid and jumpy?* That stupid bat. It's his fault.

"Andrew, you home?"

I race down the stairs to find Leena and Katja standing in the living room, suitcases scattered along the floor, both ladies wearing Finnish flag baseball hats and gym clothes. I guess they're back.

"Hey, ladies. What are you doing back here early?"

They don't answer me. Instead, they drop everything and snag me into a hug. We share the same height of six foot, but whereas my hair is a dirty, messy blond, theirs is almost white. And very long. If it wasn't for Katja's brown eyes compared to Leena's blue, I would have sworn they were twins.

"Andrew," they say together while hugging me and jumping up and down.

Friendly. I've met them once and here they are, creating their own personal Andrew sandwich.

Awkwardly, with my arms at my side, wisps of blonde getting stuck in my mouth, I say, "Uh, good to see you, too."

"We've missed you," Katja says, pulling away and gripping my face. Without any warning, she kisses me on the lips and then turns me to Leena who does the same.

"Whoa, hey there." I back away, straightening myself. "Watch it there, ladies. I'm spoken for."

"Oh, Andrew. You have boyfriend? This is exciting." Leena

claps her hands.

"What's his name?" Katja asks.

Wait. What? Boyfriend?

Uh, they think I'm gay?

"I bet he has cute butt like Andrew," Katja adds, trying to poke my behind.

"I think he dates bear." Leena holds up her hands like claws. "Grrr."

"Because Andrew is . . . what do they say, twink?"

Twink? Oh, fuck no! If I were to take a "gay personality" type I would never be labeled as a twink, more like a STUDent. Muscles, brains, and sex appeal. No arguing that.

"Wait, hold up, ladies. I'm not gay."

Katja and Leena stand tall, slightly caught off guard. "You not gay?" Katja asks.

"No. I like women. I have a girlfriend." Yikes, pulling the G-card out, pretty sure Sadie will flatline if she hears me say that.

"Oh." Leena and Katja exchange glances and I worry they might kick me out of the house since they were under the impression they'd be rooming with a gay man. I sure as hell hope not. I don't want to go live with drunk Uncle Gallom, the hairy belly-button rubber.

I need to catch them before they ask me to leave. "I hope you know I wasn't trying to mislead you when we first met." I swallow hard. "It's not my intention to impersonate a gay man, if that's what you're thinking. I'm not nearly half as cool. I barely know how to match, I really like the smell of a new box of pencils, not that that has anything to do with not being gay, I'm sure gay men like to smell boxes of pencils . . ." I pause for a second and think about what I'm saying. "Well, if you perceive pencils to be penises, then I guess they would like to smell a box of them. I know I would like to smell a box of vaginas, err . . . forget I said that. I'm not a creep." I shake my head and continue. "What I'm trying to say is that I don't want to move out. I like it here and I'm sorry if I mislead you."

Once again, Katja and Leena exchange glances, a slightly confused look on their faces until finally, Katja questions as if she doesn't understand. "Box of vagina?"

Figures.

"Eh, forget I said that. I just want you guys to know I would like to stay."

"Oh, that is fine," Leena says with a wave of her hand. "Just hope girlfriend doesn't mind."

"Nah, she's cool." I look at their suitcases and ask, "Do you ladies need help with your bags?"

"Please," Katja responds, whose room is behind the kitchen.

She points to what bags are hers and I take them back to her room, which is void of anything personal. I thought chicks dug that sort of thing. But, I have two brothers, what would I know?

When I return to the living room, Leena is typing away on her phone. As I start taking her bags to the upstairs room across from mine—three times the size of mine by the way—I ask, "Why are you ladies back so early?"

"We want to get in good training before we report back. We like the gym here."

"That's cool." Both girls follow me as I trudge up the stairs with Leena's bags and place them in her room.

"Did you decorate?" Katja asks, peeking into my room.

"Just a little."

Without being invited, both Leena and Katja walk into my room and start exploring the small space, touching my computer, and playing around with my life-size Derek Jeter cutout.

"And you say you're not gay," Leena jokes, poking Derek

Jeter in the crotch. Hmm, I could see how having him is incriminating to my manhood.

"This room is small," Katja announces, after doing a quick spin around the space, taking in everything.

"Yeah, but it works." I don't want to be ungrateful.

"Okay, I'm done in here." Both of them leave and then say something in Finnish, which immediately makes my balls shrink in self-consciousness. I want to hold my finger up and say we should always speak English, but then again, I don't want to be labeled a dick right off the bat.

"Joo," Katja says to Leena, nodding. "Andrew, we go open TV now."

"Huh? You got a new TV?"

"No. We have one. We just go open it now. We like the show Fixer Upper."

Open the TV? Do they mean . . . turn on?

"Uh, you're going to *turn on* the TV now."

"Ah yes, turn on," Leena says in her heavy accent. "We turn on TV now. We will be downstairs."

"Okay, glad you guys are back." Very awkwardly I wave as they talk to each other in Finnish all the way down the creaky stairs. I really hope they're not talking about me.

Hell, who am I kidding? They're talking about me. What else could they be saying that they don't want to say in English? See where desperation to find housing gets you?

Back at my desk, I sit down and throw my headphones on to take away some of the background noise from the TV downstairs. I need to focus on debugging this loop in my code. Focus eludes me, logic is gone, my mind is a jumble.

Sadie.

I just don't understand her. I know she's reserved and seems to operate within a very tight circle of friends, but why does she not even want to *try* and open up to me? She said the other guy was out of the picture, but what if he isn't and she's still trying to work out whether or not they are really done? No. That's not Sadie. *Did he hurt her? Is he still friends with Sadie's friends, and that's why* we *need to be a dirty secret?*

With the combination of thoughts of Sadie, my roommates talking in Finnish *and* thinking I was gay, there is no hope here. I keep reading the same code over and over again, making no progress. Seems like my studying is done for the day.

Needing a drink, I take off my headphones and make my way downstairs, still wondering if I'm an idiot trying to stick things out with Sadie. But my thoughts are completely evaporated the minute I make it to the first floor.

What the hell?

Okay . . . Can't say I've ever found this most peculiar scene in my shared living room before.

The first floor of the old New England-style home is a little awkward. The front door opens straight into the living room, which then opens up into the dining room, creating an odd space since the stairs to the second floor are right off the dining room.

So you can understand my shock when the first thing I see coming down from the stairs is two sets of breasts.

Finnish breasts.

Bare Finnish breasts.

"Uh." I quickly shield my eyes, unsure what to do. Should I sprint back upstairs and act like I never saw anything, even though I made eye contact with Katja? Should I wave and compliment said naked breasts? Give them a little fist bump and then show them my nipples. Nip for nip kind of thing? Or should I just keep moving to the kitchen that is no more than fifteen feet away?

Choosing the latter, my fucking feet have never walk-sprinted so fast in my life.

I make it to the kitchen, which thankfully blocks my view of my topless roommates, giving me a chance to breathe.

What the fuck are they doing?

Is this normal practice amongst all the people on this earth with vaginas? Do all women like to hang out in the afternoon topless? Is it some kind of boob-growing technique? Let them flap around to add extra growth? Do they even keep growing in college?

Fuck, why don't I know anything about boobs?

I'm out of my element. I have no clue what the hell I'm supposed to do. This is not normal practice; at least I don't think it is. And why the hell do I keep envisioning lifting my shirt and pressing my nipples against theirs, as if some kind of magical fucking force would spark between us all, bonding us forever, synching up our estrogen and testosterone into one magical nipple-induced rainbow?

Now that thought is fucking weird. Nipple bonding. I'm almost ninety-nine percent sure that isn't something.

At least now I'm in the kitchen, and I can get my drink. That's right, get a drink, Andrew, and then start thinking of your escape route out of the kitchen. I open the fridge and bend down to grab a Mountain Dew. If only I had a Snickers to go with it . . .

Standing up, I crack the top open just in time to come face to face with Leena and her blue eyes, blonde-white hair, and her flat but very bare chest. She can't be any bigger than a double A. I would be shocked if she was.

"Oh, can I have one too?" Leena asks, starting to bounce up and down. Okay, maybe they are As. There is some movement there.

I am not looking at them! I am using my well-honed skill of chancing a look with my peripheral vision. A skill every man has so he doesn't get caught checking out women's boobs. Because, let's be honest here. We always check out women's boobs. *They're boobs.*

"Sure," I answer, feeling like I'm living in some weird European paradox.

Side note: for the record, I don't think Europeans walk around topless. I just think my roommates do. Okay, carry on.

I hand Leena a soda and then decide to address the elephant in the room. There really isn't anything else to do but ask.

"So, Leena, I can't help but notice that you're missing your top."

"You don't like boobs?" She takes a sip of her soda so casually that it drives me crazy.

"No, I like boobs, Leena, it's just that it seems weird to me that you're topless in our house, in the shared common areas."

"It's topless Tuesday. You take your shirt off, too."

She reaches for my hem but I back up and hold up my hands, Dew in one of them.

"I'm okay. I would like to keep my shirt on, but thank you for the offer." Clearing my throat, I ask, "Do you think this is going to be something that happens every Tuesday?"

"Of course."

I nod. "Okay, that's what I figured." Taking a deep breath, I ask point-blank, "Are there any other naked days I need to worry about?"

There is a knock at the front door as Leena starts to laugh. "Oh, Andrew. You want more naked days?"

"No, no, no, no." I shake my head. "Nope. Just wanted to make sure I had all my days covered. There isn't anything like Snatch-Showing Saturdays?"

"What's snatch?" Her face contorts in confusion.

"Never mind—"

"Andrew, lady is here," Katja calls out from the living room.

Lady is here?

What does that—

The knock at the door.

Sadie was getting off work soon.

Oh fuck. *Fuck.*

Please, oh please, oh fucking please let Katja be covered up. I rush past Leena who keeps repeating snatch over and over again, probably liking the way it sounds, and run into the living room where Katja is holding the door open to no one, eyes trained on the TV, fucking boobs bouncing with her laughter as she mumbles something about Chip Gaines.

Fuck me.

Dread coiling in my stomach, I run to the screen door where I open it just in time to see Sadie driving away.

Fuck.

Fuck, fuck, fuck.

I turn to Katja and ask, "Let me guess, you answered the door like that?"

"Shhh," she waves me off, "Chip and Joanna." I turn to the TV to see two Texans talk about demolishing the inside of a house they're fixing up for a client. Great.

Leena comes into the room with her eyes trained on her phone. "The Google told me snatch is another word for vagina." Looking up from her phone, she makes eye contact with me. "You want to see vagina?"

"No! For the love of God, no!" Leaving my roommates to themselves, making a mental note to talk to them about keeping things PG, I take the steps two at a time while I reach for my phone. I cringe from the three text messages from Sadie.

Sadie: *Getting off a little early. Do you want me to bring you ice cream?*

Sadie: You're not answering. I'm bringing you ice cream anyway and it's not going to be sugar-free vanilla. You're addicted and it's getting out of hand.

It's the last text message that really has my gut churning, making me feel sick to my stomach with each word.

Sadie: Now I see why you weren't responding. One-woman man. Funny. Very funny.

She tops the text message off with a middle finger emoji.

Fuck.

CHAPTER TWENTY

SADIE

"One-woman man. Right. Blonde, tall, and topless," I mutter while I struggle to escape the small confines of my car. As I grab my purse, the strap gets caught on the gearshift. "Let go, you motherfucker." I yank on the purse, which only tears the strap. "Oh no. No," I gasp. Tears start to well in my eyes, my shoulders wilt in defeat, and I bow my head, threading the broken strap through my fingers.

I tell myself the reason I'm on the verge of crying is because I've had this handmade purse for years. It was one of the first things Smilly made for me. I'm *not* crying because I walked into the valley of boobs at Andrew's place.

Nope, it's not that at all.

A silent tear streams down my face and falls onto my black pants, the same pants that have several bleach spots.

Another tear.

It's the purse. I swear it's the purse.

I take a deep breath and focus on vacating my car. With my now-torn purse, I make my way to the apartment where a pirate's skull is hung on the front door for no particular reason. Smilly must have gone to the Thrifty Shopper again and found some treasures.

When I open the door, both Smilly and Saddlemire are sitting in the recliners, a bowl of tortilla chips and salsa sitting between them, watching a Yankees documentary. Smilly must have lost a bet.

"Hey, Ma!" she calls out just before she puts a chip in her mouth. I give her the best smile I can, but it must not work because she pauses the documentary, causing Saddlemire to grumble. "What's wrong?"

"Long day," I lie, but not good enough because tears start to fall down my cheeks—uncontrollable, fat, wet tears. Horrified expressions stare back at me. I don't cry, not in front of anyone. Including Smilly. *I've cried in front of Andrew.* No. Don't think about Andrew. Needing to come up with a reason for the crying, I hold up my purse and say, "I tore my purse strap."

Slightly frightened and definitely uneasy, Smilly slowly puts down her recliner and makes her way over to me where she takes the purse, caution in her every step. "I can fix this, Sadie. It's not a big deal."

"But it's the first thing you made me and I tore it." Cue the sobbing.

I'm a pathetic mess. The funny thing is, Smilly and Saddlemire have no idea what to do. They've never seen me as a tear-jerking emotional mess. They've seen me angry, so freaking angry that they've feared for their lives, but *sad* . . . over "a purse," this is new territory for them. Honestly, this is new territory for me. Even when I lost . . .

Why did he lie to me? He pursued me. He made me feel beautiful. *But why did he lie? Or am I just so terribly naïve? He told me he's always been into girls, and he* is *living in a house of them.* I'm so stupid.

Smilly puts her arm around me and asks, "Are you sure it's

just the purse that's bothering you?"

"Yes." I cry some more, just as there is a knock at the door.

"Pizza!" Saddlemire jumps up from the recliner. "Don't worry, Sadie, we got enough for you too, so you don't have to cry about that either."

Smilly's arm flies out and slaps Saddlemire across the chest. "Don't be an insensitive ass. If she wants to cry over pizza, she is more than welcome to."

"I don't want to cry over pizza." I shake my head, and my tears scatter to the floor.

"Don't make up your mind just yet, you haven't seen the topping we picked." Smilly pats my shoulder and guides me to the kitchen. "Let's get you something to drink."

"Uh, she might want to stick around," Saddlemire calls out as he opens the door wider.

Turning around, there he stands, Andrew in the doorway.

What's he *doing here? And why the hell must he be so handsome?* His hair is in an unruly mess; he's wearing jeans and a tight-fitting shirt. And those glasses . . .they can't help but highlight his sorrowful eyes.

A myriad of emotions hit me at once.

He came.

What is he doing here? He's blowing our cover.

Why does he have to be so freaking attractive?

There was a topless girl opening his door.

Why do I care this much? It was casual between us.

I shouldn't care.

More tears stream down my face.

"Sadie," he calls out, stepping forward only to have Saddlemire stop him with a hand to the chest.

The wiseass that he is, Saddlemire says, "I'm going to take a wild guess and say the real reason you're crying has to do with this guy and something stupid he did instead of the torn purse strap."

I shake my head, and squeak out, "I'm really upset about the purse."

"Yes, we're all upset about the purse." Smilly gives me a hug and then charges over to Andrew and stabs her finger into his chest. "What the hell did you do?"

Hands up in the air in defense, he answers, "I didn't do anything."

A sarcastic laugh rumbles from my throat. I cross my arms over my chest and stare him down. "That's funny, because it sure seemed like you did something."

Both Saddlemire and Smilly look back at me and then at Andrew again. Saddlemire pipes up, "Uh, I'm going to make an assumption here and say you two have been seeing each other in secret."

"Ugh, don't state the obvious," Smilly groans. "What I want to know is why she hasn't said anything about it to me, especially since she's capable of crying over him."

"You're crying?" Andrew asks, trying to look past Saddlemire.

"I'm not . . ." I catch my breath. "I'm upset about my purse!"

Ignoring me, Smilly asks, "What did you do to make her cry?"

"Nothing." Shaking his head, he asks, "Can I please just talk to Sadie in private?"

"No." Smilly is resolute. With her hands on her hips, she stands tall, *which would be funny if I wasn't this hurt, because Smilly is barely five foot three.* I love my friend's unswerving defense.

Concern transforms into frustration and before we can do anything, Andrew says, "Fuck this," and charges into the apartment, past Saddlemire who doesn't take kindly to being pushed to the side.

His reaction: take down Andrew, bouncer style.

Coming from behind, Saddlemire grabs Andrew in a headlock and starts to drag him back toward the door, but Andrew doesn't give in. Instead, he runs backward until Saddlemire's back hits the wall, causing a huge crash-like sound to reverberate through the apartment. Both Smilly and I screech as picture frames fall to the ground.

With his elbow, Andrew plunks Saddlemire in the stomach, which unleashes him from Saddlemire's grip. His agility and strength take me by surprise. How can he fight like *this*? Then it hits me. Two older brothers. As Saddlemire bends to take his breath, Andrew steps aside. But when Saddlemire looks up, there is rage in his eyes. I have to stop this before Saddlemire uses Andrew's face as a punching bag.

Running up between them, I block Andrew and say, "Stop it."

"Get him the fuck out of here, Sadie," Saddlemire says, spitting venom in our direction. I've seen him cross before, but not this angry.

Nervous, I take Andrew by the hand and try to bring him to the door but he doesn't budge.

"I'm not leaving," he says, his voice unwavering. "Not until I talk to you."

"This isn't the time, Andrew."

"It sure as fuck is." When I turn to look at him, he scowls at me. "I have a right to talk to you, to let you know what happened."

Sighing, I cross my arms over my chest and step back from him. "Fine. Explain."

Smilly and Saddlemire file behind me, building an audience for Andrew's "explanation."

Taking us all in, he shakes his head. He pauses for a moment and truly studies me, making me feel raw once again. He's angry. Yet he can still reach into my soul and see *me*. How he has the capability to do that I will never know.

"You know what? What's the fucking point?" he finally says. "There is no point in me talking to you about what happened." My stomach starts to churn, and anxiety rolls around in my veins. He's capitulating before he even starts? "Do you know why, Sadie?" He shakes his head, places his hands on his hips. "Because you won't believe me. Even if what I tell you is the truth, there's no point. You've been looking for a way out from the start. What we have between us has never meant anything to you, as it's always been *casual. Fun.*" He steps forward and points at his chest. "But it's meant something to me and when I said I'm a one-woman man, I fucking meant it. I gave you my word. And for you to so quickly think anything else is a fucking kick to the damn dick. You've never fully given me yourself; you've never truly wanted to be with me. You wanted fun and casual, and you got it. Fucking, fun, and casual. But I'm done. I don't want casual, Sadie. I want all of you, not just a small piece." He steps forward, getting close enough that I'm enveloped in his masculine cologne. It pulls me in, making my stomach churn even more. Tears start to well in my eyes again, and this time, I won't bother blaming the purse. "But you don't want to give yourself to me. I can only pound my head against a brick wall for so long, Sadie. Now? I'm done trying." He leans forward and grips my chin with his thumb and forefinger. "Just so you know, I really fucking liked you. I can't force you to like me. I can't force you to open up to me. So, I think it's a fucking shame you remained hidden behind your completely impenetrable walls."

He quirks his lips to the side in disappointment and heads for the door, taking the air between us with him. When he opens the front door, about to exit, he turns to me and says, "For the record, the woman who greeted you at the door was my roommate. The two girls from Finland with zero awareness about covering up came home early. I was working on my computer and had no idea what they were up to downstairs until I went to grab a drink. Sometimes everything is not as it seems, Sadie. That's something you should know pretty well by now." As he turns, I swear I hear him say, "Fuck this. Fuck."

Not even glancing back, he shuts the door, leaving the apartment in silence, and my heart in utter turmoil.

I don't say anything. I don't even look at Smilly and Saddlemire. With tears in my eyes, I go straight into the bedroom and quietly shut the door. I'm tempted to fall to the floor right there, but instead, I change into my favorite pajama bottoms with orange fish on them and put on a T-shirt. Once I'm comfortable, I slip into my bed, keeping the lights off, and rest my head against my pillow where I cry. I cry fucking hard. *"I can only pound my head against a brick wall for so long, Sadie. Now? I'm done trying. Just so you know, I really fucking liked you."*

I really fucking liked him too.

•••

Light filters into the room, stirring me from my somber-induced coma. My eyelids feel like they're glued together, and my throat is scratchy and feeling as dry as the Sahara. This is why I don't cry, because you feel like utter shit during *and* after.

"Sadie?" Smilly asks, toeing her way into the room, a plate of pizza in hand. "I thought maybe you might be hungry." From her sweatshirt pocket, she pulls out a can of orange soda and sets it on the nightstand we share.

When she sits on the bed, I sit up, propping the pillow behind me. We uncomfortably stare at each other for a second before Smilly says, "You cried."

"I know."

"Over a boy."

I can't help but smile. "I know."

"A boy who isn't Tucker."

I sigh this time and start picking at the pizza she brought in. "I know."

"Care to explain?" She snags a pepperoni from the piece and smiles at me when I give her a playful look.

"I don't even know how to explain it." I press my head against the wall, wishing I could knock some sense into myself. "I was just having fun with him, Smilly. I didn't want to make a big deal about it because I knew once school started, I would be breaking it off. But, somewhere along the way, I started to like him. I started to become addicted to his smile, to his teasing, to his nerdy quirks."

"Why didn't you say anything to me?"

"Because," I pick at the crust, "I didn't want it to get around that I was dating someone other than Tucker, especially since I knew it was only short-term."

"Is that what it was, dating?" *Was it? We did go out on dates, but were we dating?*

"I have no idea. All I know is he wanted more but I couldn't give him anything else."

"Why not?"

Her question is a little shocking. Given her love for everything Sadie and Tucker, I'm surprised she isn't delighted about Andrew's demise, trying to push me into Tucker's arms right now, and calling him to talk about the good old times.

"There is a world of difference between us, Smilly. He values education—"

"So do you," she says, snagging another pepperoni.

Annoyance filters through me. "My goals are different now. I lied to him and said I was still going to Cornell. If he knew the truth, if he knew I was a dropout, I don't think he'd look at me in the same way."

"You're not giving him enough credit. I barely know the guy, but I don't think he's a school snob. He likes you for you, not for what school you're going to. I was there, Sadie. I was there when he danced with you at the bonfire. The way he looked at you, seemed so ecstatic to see you, it wasn't school that snagged his attention." *That was weeks ago. He barely knew me. But he was looking at me?*

"I've been such an asshole to him, Smilly. From the very beginning, I've been a bitch, and yet, he still wanted to get to know me, he still wanted to hang out with me. And when I told him I didn't want to talk about anything deep with him, he took what I gave him." I shake my head in shame. *What does that say about him? About me?* "And the first moment I got a chance to break it off, I did. He was right. I didn't want to give myself over."

"Because of Tucker?" she asks, a little hope in her voice.

"No, not because of Tucker. Because I'm ashamed of who I am." I take a big, depressing bite out of my pizza and talk as I chew. "Look at me. I have a mom who preferred hanging out in jail rather than parenting, an emotionally absent father who's denied his sole-parent responsibilities since I was eight, and then I have two sisters I don't talk to. That's just my family. On top of that, I'm a college dropout with no future ahead of her. I have nothing to be proud of." *I am nothing.*

"You know I don't believe that," Smilly says. "But if you feel that way, why don't you do something about it?"

I take another bite of my pizza, waiting to talk until I finish chewing. *I can't. I can't do anything about it.* "Because, I have no fight left in me, Smilly."

And that's the God's honest truth. I've been fighting for as long as I can remember, and now there is nothing left inside me. My spirit, compassion, and will to try have been irrevocably broken. I'm exhausted and ready to throw in the towel.

Losing Andrew just falls in line with the shit journey of a life I'm living. It's done. It was casual. I just need to accept it and move on.

Except, why do I hurt *so much?*

I can't force you to like me. It's too late. I already do.

CHAPTER TWENTY-ONE

SADIE

So this is what rock bottom really feels like? I thought I hit that fucking slab when I dropped out of school and then lost the baby. Nope, this is it. It has to be it. I don't know if I can take any more.

Standing a mere fifteen feet away is Andrew, looking fine as ever, talking to Michelle and laughing up a storm. What could she possibly be saying that's so funny? I've held many conversations with her, and she's not very funny, more annoying than anything.

"If you stare a little harder, you're going to give yourself away," Denise, the mother hen, says as she comes up next to me at the soup and salad station. "Five Caesar salads; help me out."

I don't even bother to hide it from Denise, as she can see through me, and she can definitely tell when I'm lying. "Am I that easy to read?" Helping her out, I place five bowls on the counter and start filling them with her.

"No, I just know what longing looks like. Many moons ago, I once carried around that look. Tell me, did you break his heart, or did he break yours?"

"I don't think hearts were involved, not yet at least. He wanted more from me emotionally, and I wasn't ready to give him what he wanted. I assumed something horrible of him, and he decided to end things."

Denise nods. "You know I love you, right?" No, I didn't know that, but I nod. "Good, because you are being dumb right now. Look at that boy, Sadie. He's kind, sweet, handsome, smart, and has a good head on his shoulders. He's a four-leaf clover in a field of weeds; you don't let men like him slip through your fingers." She tops the salads with croutons and stacks them on a tray. "I suggest you fix what you broke, because you'll regret not jumping in feet first when it comes to him."

Spinning on her heel, she takes the salads out to her table, leaving me feeling even worse than before.

Just as I'm about to welcome another table, Stuart pats me on the shoulder and tells me to take my break. Usually I would protest, wanting to gather as many tips as possible, but today I take the much-needed time out and head straight to my car where I roll down the windows, tip back the seat, and stare at the grey ceiling of my little vehicle.

Fix things. Is that even possible? He was so angry the other day when he walked out of my apartment. This is the third day I've had to work with him, and each day it seems to get worse and worse. Seeing him smile when it's not directed at me. Watching him move flawlessly around the fountain area, it only reminds me how smooth he moved around me in bed. And hearing that laugh, the one that still rumbles through my heart? It's torture.

When did he become so ingrained in my life? Essential. When did he matter so much to me? When did this become more than a fling to me? Because I can't remember; it's like it ambushed me, leaving me no other option than to feel like utter crap when it fell apart.

Freaking wonderful.

I bang the back of my head against the headrest a few times, wishing there was an easy solution to all this.

And then my phone rings. As weird as it seems, I unconsciously sense who it is. When I look down at the caller ID, I nod. "Of course."

"Hi, Tucker."

"Sadie, what's wrong?" He's known me for a long time, so doesn't take long to notice my despondency.

"Nothing, just tired from work. What's up?"

He pauses, probably considering my lie but deciding not to acknowledge it. "Just checking on my girl. I haven't heard from you in a bit, and I wanted to make sure everything is okay."

I'm not his girl, but I'm too tired to argue. "Everything is fine. Just working, nothing new."

"You didn't sign up for any classes for the fall?"

"I told you I can't go back to Cornell, Tucker. First of all, I can't afford it, and second of all, I don't think they would take me again."

Why do people KEEP insisting I consider going back to school? It's starting to get frustrating.

"I didn't know if you were going to do some junior college credits or anything."

"No." Anger boils up in me. "What's with everyone getting on my case about going back?"

"Maybe because we know your potential, and you're not reaching it right now."

I laugh sarcastically. "Maybe you should have thought of my potential before you decided to impregnate me."

It's a low blow and if he was here in person, I know he would be grinding his teeth together, his jaw in a hard-set line. "You know I didn't do that on purpose. The condom broke, and there was nothing I could do. And if you talked to me before you dropped out, we could have made it work."

"No, we couldn't have."

"Christ," he yells into the phone. "You don't know that, Sadie. You didn't even give us a fucking chance. You didn't give me a chance to prove to you I could be the guy you needed. How was that fair to me?"

I don't answer him, because honestly, I don't know what to say. I don't know how to respond. I have so much anger, so much hurt, so much disappointment when it comes to this chapter in my life that I don't know how to let it go. But really, why should I get the chance to make something of myself when the baby I carried within me died? My mother never gave a shit about me, my sisters barely acknowledge my existence, and the man I began to see a future with, didn't think I was worth trying for either. I'm just so lost. So empty. *So alone.*

Is Tucker right? Do I not give anything or anyone a chance? Was Andrew right? Was I looking for a way out from the start?

Sighing, I rub my eye with my palm. "I don't want to fight about this, Tucker."

"That's your problem, Sadie, *you* don't want to fight. You never want to fight for what's important. You just drop it and let it stew and brew, making yourself so fucking miserable that you treat everyone around you like they're marginal, compared to you."

Ouch.

His words cut deep and even though I want to deny them, I know a part of him is right, which hurts even more.

"I can't do this right now, Tucker."

"Yeah, I'm not surprised, you never can." He lets out a long breath and then says, "I still want to meet up with you when I get back. I have a lot to say, and you owe me to listen."

"I know." Boy, do I know. It's a conversation I've been dreading ever since he asked for it.

"Listen, I'm sorry I got heated. It's just, you frustrate me so fucking much, Sadie. I'm trying, dammit. I want to make things right, and you're not letting me."

"But you want something that's dead, Tucker. We are done. I need you to understand that."

"Not until we talk," he replies, so sure of himself. "Got to go. I'll talk to you later. I love you, Sadie. That will never fucking change."

With that, he hangs up, throwing my entire world for a loop. A year ago, those words would have made my entire life brighter, but not now. My life remains dull and bland. *Empty.*

The only thing that brightened my days was Andrew. Seeing him. Laughing with him. Being touched by him. Talking with him. Now I don't even have that.

Andrew wasn't lying to me. I have no idea why his roommates were topless, but I *do* know him better than that. He wouldn't lie to me.

But he said he was done.

Done trying.

With me.

Even though Tucker's conversation hurt, there is one thing he said that's on repeat over and over in my head. *"You never want to fight."*

He's right. I can't remember the last time I actually fought for something important to me. *For someone.* And here I am, in the midst of letting a man go, a man so different—so *everything*—and I realize Denise is right. I would be incredibly stupid to throw that away.

I guess it's time to prove Tucker wrong.

He and I are done.

But I will fight for Andrew. I will fight for the man who *likes me*. I will fight for the man who looks deeply into my eyes and sees my soul. For him, I will fight.

CHAPTER TWENTY-TWO

ANDREW

Have you ever met someone who thinks they're so funny that you can't do anything but laugh at how funny they really aren't?

I'm there right now.

Michelle. Fuck, if this woman called in sick one day, I would deny her all the chicken noodle soup so she could miss another day. Dick move, I know, but fucking hell she's annoying. I wish there was a mute button that would make her shut up, or I wish I was an asshole and could tell her to get a life, but I'm not that guy.

Nope, I'm the guy who will fake laugh to spare her feelings. My wood-loving mother taught me to respect others, even if they're ridiculous.

"And then my bra popped open and everyone saw my nipples." Cue obnoxious laugh by her, followed by another one from me. I wasn't even paying attention, but "everyone saw my nipples" is her punch line ninety-five percent of the time.

This woman and her nipples. She talks about them non-stop. I kind of want to see them just to confirm they are as janky as I picture them, all bubbly and crooked.

"Can you believe it?"

"I really can't." I give her another fake smile and then turn toward the chocolate ice cream. "Hey, I have to finish scraping this carton, or else I'm never going to get out of here."

"Oh, such a hard worker." She rubs her breast against my arm and then walks away, giving me a wink.

Did she just mark me like a cat? You know how cats rub their scent glands along your leg, marking you as one of theirs? Is that what she just did? Rubbed her nipple glands on my arm, fending off any and all other female interest? I sure as hell hope not.

But it's not like it would matter. Any *wanted* female interest in this restaurant is gone. Sadie hasn't said a word to me since I walked out of her apartment. I don't even catch her looking at me like she used to. And when I have to make her sundaes, she doesn't say a word; she just takes them and leaves. Talk about a cold fucking shoulder. When I first met her, I thought she was cold to everyone, but after a few weeks of observation—and interaction—I found out that wasn't the truth. She's only cold to people she doesn't want anything to do with. And now that includes me. I fucking hate that I am back at square one, just like my first day on the job.

Not that I would want her to talk to me. I mean, yeah, would it be awesome if she actually wanted to be with me? Sure. But that's not going to happen. Something is holding her back, and I'm not sure she'll ever get over that. And I would rather not hang around, trying to get her to open up only for her to break my fucking heart later on down the road.

Because that's what she would do—break my heart, kind of like she tore at it a few days ago, without any regard to how it would make me feel.

Fuck.

Concentrating on my last task for the night, I quickly scrape down the chocolate ice cream, clean the spades and scoops, wipe down the counters, and then check with the waitstaff to see if they need any help before I leave.

When Denise dismisses me, I go to the bathroom where I change into my spare set of clothes I keep in my locker, handy since I spilled milk all over my clothes today. I stuff my smelly work uniform in a Friendly's bag because driving home smelling like milk doesn't appeal to me.

With a quick wave to everyone, I step out into the cool summer night air, enjoying the sounds of crickets chirping around me. On my way to my car, I check my phone and see three text messages from Katja. I chuckle, wondering what the hell she has to say.

Katja: *You have ton of underwear. Why so much?*

I press my lips together; good to know they're going through my things while I'm at work. Time to invest in a lock for my door.

Katja: *We need computer password. We want to watch porn.*

Once again, another reason I need a lock. With my luck, they would click on a porn site containing a virus that would infect my computer and ruin everything I ever created. I commend myself for heavily password protecting my computer.

Katja: *We ate the hot dogs. Pick up two more packs at store.*

Well, that's not going to happen, but it's cute they think it would. I'm going to have to do some serious roommate training when it comes to these ladies.

And the joke's on them, I didn't even like those hot dogs.

I push my phone in my jeans pocket and pull my keys out just as I see movement by my truck. My heart leaps into my throat when I think it's someone ready to pounce on me, ball-gag me, and take me to their lair. But when I see the slender figure of Sadie in a yellow dress step forward, my heart drops and starts pounding rapidly.

Fuck.

Under the moonlight, her skin is radiant, her hair looks so incredibly soft, and those eyes, they bore holes straight through my soul.

When I walk up to her, I remain silent. She needs to make the first move; she needs to be the one who speaks first.

After a few awkward pauses, she finally says, "Hey."

Not quite what I was hoping for, but I'll go with it.

"Hey."

Mr. Talkative has clammed up. She's on her own with this one.

"Uh, can I talk to you for a second?"

"Sure." I toss my bag of clothes in the cab of my truck and then drop the tailgate. I hop up and pat the seat next to me. She lifts herself up and takes a seat, putting a decent amount of space between us.

Even though she's trying to hide it, I can see the shake in her hands and the uncertainty in her eyes. For the first time since I met her, the confidence that first caught my attention isn't there. Instead, she almost seems weak, and that makes my heart lurch in my chest. She's always been so strong. Did I do this to her?

She fiddles with her hands on her lap and finally says, "I miss you, Andrew."

Well, fuck if I don't want to jump up and down, waving my cock around in excitement while shooting poppers into the air just for the hell of it, but I hold still. Excessive celebration could put me in the hot bed once again.

I keep quiet and let her continue.

"I have issues with trusting people, pretty sure you've gathered that. And I don't let a lot of people into my little world because of how fucked up it is. And I'm not just talking about basic daddy issues, or in my case, mommy issues. There are things about my past that make me so damn ashamed. Things that have destroyed, shamed, and humiliated my family to the point that we've been living with a black mark on our last name for years. It's not easy for me to talk about, and it's one of the biggest reasons why I avoid making new friends. I don't want to keep reliving my past as I explain it to people, so I tend to stick around people who already know me."

"I can understand that," I reply, my voice sounding more hoarse than before.

"Thank you." She takes a deep breath and continues. "And then you came along and threw my easygoing denial for a loop. You dug your way into my life and left a mark. You never even gave me a chance to deny you once you got in deep, and you made it impossible to ignore you. It was too difficult because I wanted you." As she looks up at me, those soulful eyes split me in half. "I still want you, but not just the superficial, casual relationship you think I want. You, Andrew. I want all of you and I want you to have all of me."

This is all I wanted to fucking hear her say.

"Really? All of you, Sadie?"

She nods. "All of me. But it's going to take time. I can't just spill my guts at the drop of a hat. There are some very heavy things that have happened in my life that I don't feel comfortable talking about, so you're going to have to bear with me."

I grip her cheek, her warm skin pressing against my palm, and say, "Baby, all I ask is that you talk to me. I just want to know you, the good, the bad, and the sexy." I wink at her, making that beautiful smile appear.

"I'm sorry, Andrew. I'm sorry I didn't come to you earlier. I'm sorry I accused you of something so far out of your character, and I'm sorry I've made this thing between us more difficult than it needs to be."

"This thing between us?" I ask with a raise of my eyebrow. "Baby, if we're going to continue with this 'thing,'" I use air quotes, "then we're going to be labeling it."

"What do you mean?" she asks, a scrunch to her nose.

"I mean, if you're going to be with me, you're going to be my girlfriend. No more of this 'thing.' We are dating."

Chuckling, she says, "I think I can handle that."

"Can you?" I wrap my arm around her waist and lift her up so she straddles my lap. "I'm quite the demanding boyfriend. I need attention at all times and presents, lots and lots of presents."

"Sounds a bit dramatic. But let me ask you this, when you say presents, do you mean sex?"

Her hands link behind my neck as she gets comfortable on top of me. "Sex and presents. Don't try to pass off that sweet pussy as a present. Since you're my girlfriend now, they don't go hand in hand."

"Okay, then what qualifies as a present?"

I rub my chin, feeling the scruff against my fingers. "Depends on my mood, but you can never fail with a good sugar-free vanilla sundae." I cheese it for her, which garners me an eye-roll.

"You are no longer allowed to have that ice cream. Eat the real stuff like a normal person." *And here she is. Miss Sassy Pants is back.*

"It's an addiction I can't seem to kick. It's okay to be my enabler, I won't hold it against you."

"Never." Lowering her forehead, she presses hers against mine and looks down between us. Her mood transfers from joking to serious. "I really am sorry, Andrew. I never wanted to make you feel less than you are, because you're so damn good for me. Far too good for me."

Far too good for her? What the hell? She thinks I'm too good for her? How on earth . . . Oh, my beautiful girl. She has no clue. It took strength and fortitude to apologize to me. I hadn't seen that in her, but I'm fucking glad she found it. Too damn good for me, my ass.

"Never. We equal each other out." I grip her tightly. "Please ask rather than presume, and just talk to me, that's all I want. When you doubt, or fear, or you're scared I might think differently of you—which won't happen—please just fucking talk to me rather than run away. Can you promise me that?"

"Yes," she answers, looking me square in the eyes. "I can do that."

"Good. Now, I believe we have some make-up sex to conduct. Hop in the cab, beautiful. I'm taking you home."

•••

"She's so little and pretty," Leena says, stroking Sadie's hair, no not stroking, petting. Yes, my roommate is petting my girlfriend's hair. And from the look of it, Sadie isn't very happy about the invasion of her personal bubble. Frankly, I don't mind a friendly pet. Human contact is nice for everyone, even drunk Uncle Gallum, although, I would have to be paid a hefty lump sum in cash to even raise my hand near that man. I will never know how men can grow so much hair on their stomach.

"Look at butt." Katja bends over and pokes Sadie's ass. Immediately her eyes find me and if her pupils could talk, they would first bitch-slap me, and then tell me to get these women the fuck away from her.

Hearing you loud and clear, Sugar Britches.

"Eh, I think that's enough, girls. You don't want to scare her away." I shoo their hands away and pull Sadie closely into my side, blocking her from the two blonde bombshells—fully clothed, thank God—standing in front of me.

"You shy?" Leena asks, hand on her hip.

"Yes," I answer for Sadie. "My little sugar britches is a tad shy, so please forgive her. Maybe we can all do a movie night some time." Sadie's hand snakes around my waist and pinches my side, indicating she doesn't like that idea. "Or something else." I nervously laugh, hoping her little lobster claws don't attack me again, because fuck, that hurt. There will be a bruise for sure.

"Don't be shy." Katja puffs her chest out with her hands on her hips. "We don't bite. You do topless Tuesday with us."

"That's okay." Sadie smiles. "I like to keep my top on."

"Even during the sex?" Leena asks, a little stunned.

"No, she takes her top off then," I answer without even thinking. "She shakes those titties real good behind closed doors." A searing pain shoots up my side. Lobster claws! "Son of a motherfucker." I rub my side and give her my scariest side-eye. One more pinch and I'll be playing the let's-make-Sadie-wait-a-long-time-until-she-gets-to-orgasm game.

"You do the sex tonight?" Katja asks.

"No." Sadie shakes her head. "Just sleeping. No spreading of the legs over here." Lies, all lies. This girl was rubbing me out the entire way here from the restaurant. We will be "doing the sex." I wonder . . . will Sadie be the same kind of screamer she usually is now that the girls are in the house? Only one way to find out.

"That's sad. No eating the snatch for you, Andrew," Leena adds. Even though I can hear pity in her voice, the kind of pity no man wants to hear, I have to commend her on using the American slang so well. She's learning. I'm sure her coach would be very happy to know that her heterosexual roommate with a life-size Derek Jeter cutout, formally known as Cannon Cock, taught her a slang word for vagina. That sure as fuck wasn't his intention when he asked for them to room with American-speaking students.

Oh the fuck well.

I quirk my lips to the side. "Yeah, it's all right. I'm full anyway. I wasn't even planning on munching tonight."

"You're odd man." Katja scans me up and down and then flips her hair over her shoulder. "We go to bar now. See you tomorrow."

"Okay. Do you have your house keys?" They both nod their heads. "And your Lyft app is set up on your phones?" Another nod. "And what do we do when a stranger brings you a drink?"

"Knock out of hand and say no roofie tonight."

Close enough.

"Good. Be careful and have fun."

They both wave as they walk out the front door, teetering on their high heels. I fear for the men they run into tonight.

"They are . . . interesting," Sadie says after I lock the door behind them.

"They're nice, just don't quite have filters, but that's what makes it fun. Although they did think I was gay."

"Oh, seriously? And, yes, feeling incredibly exposed and uncomfortable is really fun," she deadpans.

My eyes fixed on hers, I walk toward her until I am inches away, that's when I wrap my arms around her waist and bend her over the table. One hand holds hers down by pushing on her lower back and the other strokes her perfect, little ass.

"What are you doing?" She tries to swat me away, but I don't let her.

"I'm trying . . ." I pretend to struggle. "Damn, woman, where do you have it?"

Giggling now, she asks, "Where do I have what?"

"The stick you have up your ass. Where is it? I can't seem to locate it so I can pull it out."

She stops wiggling beneath me and instead twists her body so I'm greeted with the beautiful sight of her angry eyes. "And you want to have sex tonight? Skating on thin ice there, Andrew."

"Aw, come on." I pull her up and into my chest. "You like a good teasing . . . especially from my dick." I give her a chaste kiss and then turn her toward the stairs and smack her ass. "Now get on up there and strip down. I need to grab something so I'll meet you up there. Make-up sex commences in five, hot pants."

I leave her to do as she was told and go to the kitchen where I snag a few props and then sprint up the stairs two at a time because fuck, I'm horny and need to be deep inside my girl right now.

When I turn the corner to my bedroom, I find Sadie in her bra and thong, her back turned toward me, giving me a mouthwatering view of her backside. Fuck me, she's so hot. Her hands reach up to her bra clasp, but I stop her by saying, "Leave it on for now."

Unfazed, she slowly turns toward me, her hair dancing around her shoulders, her eyes seductive, and her body language giving me the green light in *every* way possible.

When she sees what's in my hand, she gasps but then narrows her eyes.

"Andrew . . ."

"Don't say anything, just lie on my bed."

"You're not putting that crap on me." She folds her arms over her chest.

"Sorry, babe. With make-up sex, everything goes." I point to the bed and say, "Get your pretty little ass on there now." She's about to protest again when I grab the back of my shirt and pull it over my head, tossing it to the side. She takes a moment to scan my body, and I love how lust fills her eyes. That does not get old. Just to add to the show, I make sure I flex my abs for her.

I clear my throat and nod at the bed. "Move, Sadie, I'm not a patient man right now. I need to have my tongue all over you. So, lie the fuck down." Her eyes go wide, pupils darken, and she backs up onto my bed and lies down. Yeah, my girl likes a stern voice. Fuck. Yes. I place the items on my dresser next to the bed and get rid of my shoes, socks, and pants, leaving me in only a pair of boxer briefs, which is doing nothing to restrain my already growing erection.

Leaning over her, I lightly run my finger down her body, circling her nipples over her bra, slowly drawing a line down the center of her stomach, stretching it to the top of her pubic bone where I tease her for a few strokes before moving my fingers over her slit. Her arousal is already starting to pool against her thong. This woman, so sensual, so fucking turned on for me. It's addicting.

"Sit up."

Propping herself up, she pushes her chest out and waits for my next direction. I don't give her one. I take matters into my own hands and undo the clasp of her bra. Immediately, the straps start to descend over her shoulders. The sight makes my mouth water. Itching to see her breasts, I snag the middle of her bra and yank it off her body. I'm rewarded by the subtle bounce of her breasts from my abrupt movement.

So perfect.

"Lie down," I command.

Her hair fans out around her as she gets in position. Her teeth bite down on her bottom lip, her eyes are at half-mast, and she is definitely aroused as she waits for my next direction. But I give her none. I continue to move on my own accord, sparing my attention to her thong. Why she bothers to wear anything is beyond me. The scrap of fabric covering her pussy is so small, I have no doubt it does nothing and it's only purpose is to taunt me. So, I get rid of it and toss it on the floor with the rest of our garments, leaving her completely exposed.

"Christ, Sadie. You're so beautiful," I whisper. I move my lips up her body, kissing her stomach, nipping at her ribs, licking the tips of her nipples, and sucking on the juncture between her neck and shoulder, wanting to brand her so fucking bad as mine.

She wiggles under my body, her hands going to my hair, threading through the strands, pulling when I suck hard. It's so fucking thrilling to feel her lose control, to know I'm driving her crazy with need, this woman I never thought I had a chance with. Let alone a second chance. I'm one lucky bastard.

I lift my lips off Sadie and go to my dresser where I pop the top off my favorite sugar-free vanilla ice cream and scoop a ball with a spoon.

Sadie sees what I'm doing and shakes her head. "Why sugar-free?"

"Just accept it, baby. You just need to accept it."

Not wanting her to protest anymore, I quickly put the ice cream between her breasts and smear it down the center of her body. She lifts from the cold treat hitting her skin and hisses out a long breath. Immediately her nipples go hard and I'm fascinated with how tight they get. My dick aches from the sight, so I pick up the speed and continue to move the ice cream down until it's just above her pussy.

Her chest rises and falls, her breath hitching in her throat with each press of the cold spoon against her skin. So fucking sexy.

Losing a little finesse, I trip over myself, putting the ice cream back on the dresser. I pull it together and hover over Sadie and start licking up the trail of cold cream that's starting to melt on her sweltering body.

I start high and work my way down. The feel of her heels press into my calves as she grips me with her legs. Her hands go back to my hair where she tries to direct me where to go, but I fight her. I'm in charge; she's going to have to learn that pretty damn quickly.

The sweetness of the ice cream and Sadie's skin mingle, creating an intoxicating taste that has me in a lust-filled haze. Nothing around us registers in my mind: not the sounds of the college street outside the house, not the small confines of my room. No, I can only feel and hear Sadie as I lap the ice cream off her nipples now, reveling in the way her tight nubs feel against my tongue.

Pure perfection.

Soft mews come out of her mouth when I bite down on her nipples and pull them with my teeth, making sure to apply just enough pressure to make her go crazy. My tongue is so cold, which is probably adding to the sensation for my girl.

I move down her flat stomach, sucking on her skin all the way down to her pussy where her arousal is fucking glistening, so ready for me. Knowing my tongue is cold as fuck, I spread her lips, and with one long stroke, I lick her only to press my lips against her heat and suck in her clit.

"Oh fuck." Her upper half lifts. She looks surprised from the sensation. "Oh my God, yes." Not hating the sugar-free vanilla ice cream after all.

Feeding off her reaction and the press of her hand against my head, urging for more, I eat her up. Lapping up every last bit of melted ice cream, making sure to mix my strokes with short flicks to long, languid ones. Her body tightens under mine, her grip in my hair grows stronger, and her near-silent cries grow louder with each stroke. Continuing to suck, I move my hands up her stomach to her breasts where I pluck at her nipples, pulling, pinching, and rolling them.

Her legs clamp around my head and her voice rings out through my small bedroom, reverberating against the walls, her cry of pleasure turning my dick to stone.

"Yes, oh God, yes." She convulses, her body twitching and turning in all different directions as I ride her orgasm out on my tongue.

I've never seen anything more erotic in my life, and I'm pretty sure I will never be able to top it.

Her hips start to slow down, her breath starts to grow longer, less labored, and the death grip she has on my hair loosens. Just as she's falling down from her orgasm, I'm rearing up for mine.

Protection is my number-one priority, getting inside Sadie is a close second. I snag a condom from my nightstand, chuck my boxer briefs to the side, and sheath myself. On my knees, I pump my cock, taking in the beautiful woman beneath me. I'm not going to last fucking long, as I can feel my body already tingling just from the sounds Sadie made.

Still orgasmic comatose, I flip Sadie onto her belly and prop her ass up in the air only to run the tip of my dick along her entrance. Still so fucking wet.

From over her shoulder, her head resting on my pillow, she smiles up at me, and my heart fucking stops right there. That innocent, sexy smile, the way she's so easily giving up her body to me . . . my heart stops beating. I thought I was already toast when it came to this woman, but she just broiled the shit out of me for any other woman with that one look. I'm a goner. *She's my . . . my everything? Is that even possible so soon?*

Needing to connect with her in the most intimate way possible, I plunge into her, sinking so deep that it almost seems like there is no end.

A low moan bubbles out of her throat as her entire body goes lax in my hands. Her eyes close shut and a lazy smile stamps across her face. This is her happy place. Fuck, it's my happy place. I wouldn't want to be anywhere else right now. Or in the near future. Maybe even beyond that . . .

I start to move, deliberately slow, feeling every inch of me stretch her. My teeth grind together from how tight she feels, from the small clenches she makes around my cock, and—

"Holy shit!" I cry out, my body jolting.

From beneath me, Sadie has snaked her hand to my balls where she is now lightly pulling on them, sending my mind to a fucking frenzy. Stars blind me, the world around me goes black, and only a telescopic view allows me to see Sadie's pert ass in front of me. My quads tighten, my stomach coils, and with each pull from Sadie, I moan a little louder, until I come so fucking hard, I think I might black out.

I pound one last thrust inside her, holding myself there as I empty everything out of me. Holy shit.

Holy fucking shit.

I collapse on top of her, and we lie there, catching our breath. It isn't until I hear her panting as well, and the light pulse in her heated center that I realize she came right along with me. I would have never known. I seriously almost just fucking blacked out. Every time I'm with this woman, it isn't just about the reaching for orgasm, but the connection we make, and every time she never fails to bury herself deeper and deeper into my heart, imprinting her scent, her touch, her body into mine.

I push her hair to the side and kiss the back of her neck. "Fuck, I missed you."

She sighs. "I missed you, too, Andrew."

I spend the next few minutes cleaning up, taking a warm wash cloth and running it along Sadie's body to get rid of the sticky ice cream remnants, and then put the ice cream away. When I get back, I slip into bed, naked, and spoon Sadie into my chest where I play with her hair, running my fingers through the long strands.

"Tell me one thing I don't know about you," I whisper into her ear, feeling sleepy.

"Mmm . . . I think I'm starting to feel a partial liking toward your ice cream."

I chuckle lazily. "Although, I do appreciate your admission, I want to know something about your past."

She takes a second to think about it, her fingers dancing across my abs. "I had a dog named Corky. He was a Corgi, and he was my best friend for the longest time until his hips gave out on him and we had to put him down. I always joked around that Corky and I would die together, holding hand and paw."

"Well, holding hand and paw sounds nice, but I'm glad you're still around. You'll have to show me a picture of the old guy one day."

"I will. Did you have any pets?"

"A chocolate lab named Hazel. She was the best puppy ever, loved to play, and then she grew up and turned into a seal."

"What?" Sadie snorts. "What do you mean a seal?"

"She got fat, the seal kind of fat where all they do is flop around to get places. When you tried to take a picture of her sitting, she would slowly start to tip over, her fat dragging her down."

"How did she get so fat?" The humor in Sadie's voice is filling my heart. *This.* This is what I have missed too.

I squeeze her a little tighter to my body. "We lived in the wine country back then and we had a mini orchard in our yard. We always wondered why we weren't able to harvest many grapes. Hazel was eating them all. I'm going to be honest, grape shits are disgusting. Once she became obese, it was pretty damn hard to get her to lose weight after that, despite how hard we tried."

"Poor girl, but you have to give her credit, she was comfortable in her skin." We both chuckle. If only Sadie saw a picture of Hazel, she would truly be able to appreciate the size of that dog.

"Tell me something else."

She yawns and pats my chest. "I think that's enough for tonight."

The laugh that pops out of me shakes her little body. "You answer one question and you're done for the night? That's just not going to do, Sugar Britches."

"It's either talk, or do this . . ." Her hand slips down my chest, past my stomach and straight to my cock where she expertly starts to stroke me. With two strokes I'm already hard.

"Eh, talking is overrated." I scoop her up and settle her on my legs, my growing erection between us.

Staring down at me, her hair framing her face, her breasts swaying above me, I don't think I could get any luckier than in this moment, but then she takes my cock and starts to rub the tip along her warm, already wet heat. Nope, this right here, this is luckier.

A hiss escapes my lips from the feel of my cock riding along her slick heat. Fuck me, it feels amazing.

She continues to rub against me as I say, "Don't think you distracted me from asking more questions."

"I don't believe it for a second." She starts to rub my cock against her clit faster. "But I need to ease the ache of missing you first, then we can talk."

My heart swells from her admission. "I'm good with that, ease the ache all you want, baby."

CHAPTER TWENTY-THREE

SADIE

"Do I bounce and hit it, or hit it in the air?" I ask from the other side of the net, holding a tennis racket in one hand and a ball in the other.

"Hit it in the air, like we practiced," Andrew calls from his side of the court.

Playing a little dumb, I say, "I can't remember."

My hot boyfriend, with the messy-sexy hair, and forearms for days, jogs over to me with a beautiful smile caressing his face. I watch in fascination as the rarely there sun shines down on his bronze skin, highlighting each sinew of muscle in his chest. He has the right amount of muscle.

"I thought we went over this."

"I need a refresher." Yes, I'm playing the helpless woman but how can I not? I just want him to wrap his arms around me again.

"Yeah, I'm sure." He chuckles, his chest rumbling behind me as he grips my arm and shows me how to toss the ball up and hit it once again, his breath tickling my ear as he speaks.

"Just like this, remember?" His face is pressed against mine, his lips barely caressing along my skin, the sensation of him being so close makes my entire body tingle with electricity.

Instead of answering him, I turn around in his arms and link my hands behind my neck. I press my lips against his and melt when his hands find my lower back, pulling me in closer. This man, he's so addicting, so sweet, so freaking hot, especially when he pins me up against the wall of his shower and has his way with me.

"You know, if we keep doing this," he gives me little pecks on my lips while he talks, "we're never going to get our exercise in."

"I know a better way to get in our exercise."

He spanks my behind playfully and says, "No sex until you try gnocchi tonight. We made a deal."

"I don't understand why we made that deal." I pout as he puts distance between us and adjusts himself. Satisfaction. Right there, ladies.

"Because you've refused to try it, therefore I had to make a threat to get you over your weird aversion to potato pasta."

"Why is a noodle made out of a potato? Just call it an Italian tater tot and get it over with."

He runs his hand over his face and speaks through clenched teeth, "For the hundredth time, it's not a tater tot!"

"It's made out of potato and is the shape of a little cube. Sounds an awfully lot like a tater tot."

He shakes his head and retreats back to his side of the court. "I can't handle you right now. Just you wait until tonight. I'll show you that gnocchi is not even close to being Italy's version of a tater tot."

"I'll believe it when I see it," I call out, bouncing the ball in front of me. I toss it up in the air and smack it over the net, placing it perfectly in the corner and screaming it past Andrew. The look of pure shock on his face is comical.

"What the fuck? Are you playing me?"

I hold up my fingers and say, "Just a little."

Straightening up, he looks me up and down and says, "I feel so used."

"You'll get over it." I pull another ball out of my shorts and say, "15-love. Serving up."

Quickly, he gets into position and defends my serve. We volley for a bit before he sends the ball down the line, giving me no chance to put it in play. Tricky bastard.

"Don't think because you have tits and a perfect pussy that I'm going to go easy on you."

"When have you ever gone easy on me, Cannon Cock?" I give him a pointed look.

An arrogant smile crosses his face. "That's fucking right." Feeding his douche quota for the day, he pelvic trusts in my direction, which gets a giant eye-roll from me.

"Keep that up and I won't feel bad about never eating gnocchi."

"Yeah, but that means you'll never get laid."

I pick up the ball that's stopped rolling on the green synthetic and say, "Yeah, not a problem."

"Ha!" he scoffs. "Please, baby. You're addicted to my lovin'. No way you can quit cold turkey. It's cute that you're trying to convince me otherwise."

Ugh, unfortunately he's right. I am addicted to him. As much as I wish I could say I'm not . . . I so freaking am.

•••

"Admit it. Admit it right fucking now."

Andrew stands over me, a paisley-covered apron hanging from his neck, and wooden spoon in his hand, dripping with marinara sauce. There is a knowing glint in his eyes and a smirk threatening to show.

"Come on, baby, I promise I won't rub it in. Just say the magical words. You like gnocchi." He crosses his arms over his bare chest, the one resting under the apron I made him wear, and waits for my answer.

There is no way I can lie, he'll see it in my eyes. Especially when I ask for seconds, because gnocchi is the BEST thing I've ever put in my mouth. Oh my GOD! Why have I been putting this off for so long? I am insane.

"Well . . ."

Giving in, I shove a spoonful into my mouth and answer while I chew. "It's amazing! Okay, I love it, and I want more. I want the whole pot."

Andrew has many expressions, and I have to admit, I love them all . . . except when he's angry. But that look of utter satisfaction and pride? He's just gorgeous. Even though he has just achieved something wonderful, his face shows his happiness in me. He reaches down and kisses my mouth, currently full of gnocchi. "I fucking knew you would like it. I know you, don't I know you?"

I nod. "You know me."

He fist-pumps the air and turns toward the pot on the stove. "Fuck, yeah. I know my girl. And can you admit it's nothing like a tater tot, because frankly it's insulting that you would insinuate such a thing?"

"You're being a little sensitive about gnocchi. It's slightly concerning," I joke.

"Just admit it." With a bowl in hand, he sits down next to me at the small table in the apartment I share with Smilly. He's still wearing his apron and from the side, I can just see the top of his boxer briefs poking out from his tight-fitting jeans. Mmm, the perfect dinner date. He's hot and he cooks.

Throwing him a bone, I say, "Fine, they are nothing like tater tots. Are you happy?"

Under the table, he squeezes my upper thigh and winks at me. "Completely satisfied."

Together, we enjoy our meal, helping ourselves to seconds, and talking about our second favorite Italian meals behind gnocchi, mine being spaghetti and meat logs—yes, meat logs—from Little Venice a small restaurant in downtown Binghamton, and Andrew's being eggplant parmesan.

"Let me grab that for you." Andrew stands and clears my plate for me.

"Cooks and cleans, what kind of show are you trying to put on right now?"

He starts rinsing the dishes and putting them in the dishwasher as he says, "Trying to win the best boyfriend award. Do you think I'm in the running?"

I take in his appearance and bite my bottom lip. "Most definitely."

The sound of the front door opening disturbs our little tête-à-tête, and Smilly and Saddlemire both enter the apartment, their voices carrying against the walls until they see Andrew, shirtless in the kitchen, and me sitting very closely to him. They fall silent as they take it in: the single lit candle on the table, the mood music playing from my computer, and the partially naked man in the kitchen.

"Oh, what's happening here?" Smilly asks, setting her purse down.

Better question is, what are they doing here? They were supposed to be staying at Saddlemire's place tonight. I made sure to clear it with Smilly.

"Dinner date," I answer, my throat becoming tight for some

reason.

God, it feels like I just got caught having a boy in my room.

I stand as Andrew finishes the dishes and quietly ask Smilly, "Why are you here? You were supposed to stay at Saddlemire's place."

"His roommates were having a party tonight, and he has an early morning tomorrow so we came here. I'm sorry. Can't you go to his place?"

I glance back at Andrew and shake my head. "No, his roommates are having a party as well and last time they had a party, drunks kept wandering into his room in the middle of the night to tap his life-size Derek Jeter cut-out in the crotch." It's a ritual now. Poor Derek.

"Soo . . ." Smilly looks around and then smiles. "I guess we're having a big sleepover."

"I guess so." Nerves flit over my body.

This will be the first time Smilly and Saddlemire get some real one-on-one time with Andrew. This should be interesting.

• • •

"There is no way you put that. Let me see your paper," I say, climbing over Andrew's lap to snag his board.

"I object to being used as a jungle gym." he says, playing Keep Away with his board.

"Who are you objecting to?" I ask, struggling against his strength.

"Saddlemire, of course. He's been the judge this entire game."

The bro code must be strong tonight because Saddlemire clears his throat and says, "Sadie, sit your ass back on the floor and leave the man alone."

Irritated, I find my spot on the carpet and raise my hand. Saddlemire nods at me. "I demand to see proof that he wrote 'masturbating hand' on his paper. There is no way we both wrote the same thing. If he wants to nix my points from being counted, he needs to show proof."

"That's fair reasoning." Looking more regal than I've ever seen him, Saddlemire gestures toward Andrew. "Sir, please show us 'masturbating hand' on your paper."

The biggest freaking grin stretches across Andrew's face as he turns his Scattegories board in our direction and underlines exactly where he wrote masturbating hand.

DEVIL!

"Whoa." Smilly sits back against the wall, a Twizzler hanging out of her mouth. "I'm impressed. What are the odds that you both answered masturbating hand under 'things you wouldn't touch'? I mean . . ." she glances down at her paper, "I just put measles. Masturbating hand, though, what the hell have you two been up to?"

"I was trying to be creative!"

We turn to Andrew who shrugs, not a care in the world. "I've been trying to make every answer dirty. Quite the challenge, I must say."

"Don't doubt yourself." Saddlemire points at him. "Your Milky Melons answer for 'something you bounce' was on point."

"I'm pretty proud of that one."

Even though I'm losing, terribly, because someone else blocks almost every answer I write, I can't help but feel a little giddy inside, watching Andrew get along so well with Smilly and Saddlemire. It's hard not to get along with Andrew.

Stretching my arms above my head, I yawn and then look at Andrew. "I'm tired."

He looks me up and down, a knowing glint in his eye. "You're tired? Or sick of losing?"

co-WRECKER

"I'm tired," I say with conviction.

My friends and Andrew all exchange a look and say together, "You're tired of losing."

The petulant child comes out in me as I toss my board to the center and storm off to the bathroom to brush my teeth and get ready for bed. It's all in good humor, but it proves my point: the game is over.

My toothbrush is in my mouth when Andrew comes up behind me and wraps his arms around my waist, placing a kiss on my neck. "I can go home, if you want."

"What? No," I reply with a mouth full of toothpaste.

"Sadie, you guys have one bedroom. I am not about to have a giant sleepover with Smilly and Saddlemire. It would be weird."

I spit my toothpaste in the sink, rinse my mouth, and then turn toward him. "We're going to sleep in the living room. I don't want to share a room with them either, especially since they get really handsy with each other at night."

He chuckles and kisses the top of my head. "Okay. Let me brush my teeth, and I'll help set up our bed in the living room."

Already in my pajamas, I snag my comforter off my bed and my pillows and toss them in the living room. Then I take Smilly's sleeping bags she stores in the linen closet for when friends stay over, zip them together and create a cushion for Andrew and me to sleep on so we aren't lying directly on the carpet.

"Oh good, I was wondering how this was going to work," Saddlemire says, looking at my setup while drinking his beer. "But, if you guys want to share the room, I'm all about awkward." He laughs and walks away, stepping on my pillows in the process."

"Sebastian," I yell at him, catching his and Smilly's attention. Using first names will do that.

"What happened? Why did you have to use the crab name?"

Smilly runs in place, looking around frantically.

"He stepped on my pillow with his Sasquatch foot," I complain as Andrew walks in, sans shirt.

"I didn't mean to. Chalk it up to a classic case of not watching where I'm going." Saddlemire glances in Andrew's direction and groans. "Come on, man. What the fuck? If you have abs, you wear a shirt. Got it?" Saddlemire blows by Andrew and straight into the bedroom.

Smilly slowly walks by Andrew, taking him in. "I don't mind the abs at all. New rule, if you have abs, you're not allowed to wear a shirt in this apartment." Turning to me, Smilly says, "I'll get you a new pillowcase. Who knows what kind of diseases Sasquatch foot has lingering on it. Be right back."

Andrew watches a retreating Smilly and then settles down on the makeshift bed with me. "What was that all about?"

"Stupid hairy foot stepped on one of our pillows." I shiver. "There really is so much hair on his foot, it's scary."

"Here you go." Smilly tosses a pillowcase our way and then twiddles her fingers. "Have a good night, you two." She wiggles her eyebrows suggestively and then disappears.

I situate the bedding, making sure to turn the Sasquatch pillowcase inside out and toss it near the bathroom in case anything was hatched in the process, and turn out all the lights.

Andrew is already lying down when I join him and instinctively, we both face each other. He's now down to just his boxer briefs, his jeans folded nicely on the recliner behind him. His minty breath invades me as well as that devastatingly charming smile.

"Tonight was fun, baby."

"It was." I smile . . . because he makes me happy. "I was kind of nervous at first since my last boyfriend was so well liked by them."

"Oh yeah?" He raises his eyebrow in question. "Do you think I compare?"

I stroke his jaw, scooting a little closer and answer, "Not even close. You are by far the favored one."

"That's what I like to hear."

Even as my answer echoes through my ears, I know it's the truth. Andrew doesn't compare to Tucker. Both men are amazing in their own way. Tucker is loyal, committed, intense, and very raw. He knows every last inch about my life, the good and the bad. He just wasn't right for me. Andrew, he's goofy, funny, loving, and caring. He makes me happy, whereas Tucker reminds me of everything I want to leave behind, everything I want to forget. When it comes down to it, I can see a future with Andrew.

"Thanks for letting me hang out with you guys tonight."

"You don't have to thank me, Andrew."

His hand starts to travel up the back of my thin tank top, and I welcome the feel of his strong palm pressing against me, the way his fingers expertly skip across my skin.

"I know, it was a big step for you though, so I wanted to show you I appreciate you trying for me."

"You're sweet."

"Yeah?" He pulls me in closer and moves his hand higher. "Any other attributes of mine you want to compliment me on?"

"Fishing for compliments?"

"Always." He leans forward and presses his lips softly against mine. His hand presses my back toward him assertively. His tongue flicks across my lips, but softly, with a gentle press of his lips. It's Andrew. It's sublime.

A light moan escapes my lips as I fall into his touch, into his kisses.

"God, you always feel so perfect in my arms, Sadie. Like I

was born to hold you."

I press my hand against his cheek and kiss him deeper, my hips starting to rub against his. I'm not surprised when I feel his erection, eager and ready.

No longer pulling me toward him, his hand travels to the front of my tank where he moves it up to cup my breast. He's gentle, soft in his movements, igniting a wave of goosebumps across my body, as the pad of his thumb gingerly strokes my hardened nipple.

Against his impressive body, I feel so small. I feel sexy with his firm erection eagerly waiting attention. And I feel safe, his patience holding strong, letting me go at my own pace.

Growing more intense, he deepens his kiss, his tongue searching out mine, needy with his flicks, his grip on my breast growing tighter, his thumb now pinching rather than rubbing. It's like a straight shot of pleasure to my center, setting my nerves on fire.

This quickly escalates, but that's what happens with Andrew. He can be joking one second, and the next, he has me bent over, searching to see if I'm turned on, which I always am when I'm around him. I hadn't realized how many facets to lovemaking there can be. Fun, hot, intense, blissful, hard, loud, gentle . . . *Andrew seems determined to take me every which way as if spoiling me is his only goal.* Is it normal to feel so cherished? Every time?

I move my hand from his face, down his bare chest, letting my fingers drift over the contours of his muscles, spending a little more time around his abs, loving how deliciously defined they are. My fingernails scrape down his skin, and I love feeling the heavy fall and rise of his breaths until they reach the waistline of his boxer briefs. His kissing seizes as I slip my fingers past the waistline and graze the very tip of his arousal.

"Oh fuck," he mumbles against my lips, his forehead falling to mine.

"Shh. I don't want Smilly and Saddlemire to hear us."

Whispering into my ear, he says, "You can't tell me to be quiet when you graze my dick like that."

Leaning over to his ear, I say, "If you want me to continue to graze your dick, then you're going to have to be quiet. Can you do that?"

"I don't know." His hand releases my breast and quickly works its way down to my shorts where he slips himself inside and spreads my legs. Before I can catch my breath, his fingers are sliding up and down my slick heat. "Can you stay quiet if I do this?"

"Yes," I choke on an intake of air.

"You sure?" His fingers start to move faster, testing my strength.

"One hundred percent sure." I steady my breath and pay attention to my own intention of making him squeal.

"What about this?" He removes his hand and dives down under the sheets so his legs are at his pillow. His hands snag my shorts and bring them down my legs. Since I'm not wearing any underwear, I'm bare below, and from the way Andrew's fingers are spreading me, I get the impression he's appreciating that right about now. And then he flicks his tongue out and my legs clench automatically. His chuckle vibrates along my legs. I can practically hear his cocky attitude now.

Not going to happen.

This is war.

Since he's flipped upside down, I have perfect access to his growing erection, so I do what any other competing girlfriend would do—wiggle down, release his cock from its confines, and start sucking him. His grip on me tenses, his tongue stops, and against my skin, I feel his moan of pleasure while his hips show no shame in their minimal thrusts.

Aw, the power of a woman's mouth, there's no denying—

Oh fuck. Andrew shows no mercy once he gathers himself from my attack and starts flattening his tongue along the length of my pussy, taking deep, languid strokes, so excruciatingly slow that it feels like everything is curling up and purring down there.

He's putting up a good fight, but I'm determined not to let it distract me. Instead I focus on one thing—his throbbing cock. I start licking and twisting my mouth over the head of his cock, pressing the tip of my tongue hard at the top and then sucking him all the way in while I play with his balls, pulling gently, rolling softly and then pressing the spot right behind him. He bucks against me.

I hold back my chuckle because just when I think I've got him, he presses two fingers inside me and sucks on my clit, hard. I see stars, glorious, black and white stars.

From my waist down I can't feel anything. My clit pounds, throbs so freaking hard that it's the only feeling I can concentrate on. I'm on the edge, one more curve of his fingers, one more suck that's all I need and right when I think he's going to give it to me, he pulls away.

My breath hitches and my protest is a low moan I know only we can hear, but it doesn't stop me from my eyes going wide. If he's going to play games, I'm going in for the kill. Not letting up, I continue to suck up and down his length while expertly pressing his perineum. A light sheen of sweat coats his body and below, I can sense his end nearing from the way his chest is rapidly falling against my stomach.

To keep up, he starts flicking my clit with his tongue again, and his fingers work their way deep inside me. It's a race to the finish.

There is no finesse. It's fast. It's brutal. It's sexy as fuck. It's the chase to see who can make the other orgasm first, a dangerous battle that I can feel myself losing because with each press of his tongue, my mind turns more and more blank. I'm on autopilot, my body reacting to Andrew's movements.

Pleasure builds in the pit of my stomach, coiling, stirring, burning. It's right there. I can feel it. My clit pounds against Andrew's tongue. Just one more . . .

White-hot pleasure bursts through me, rocketing my nerves into overdrive. My stomach plummets, my toes curl, and my mouth clamps around Andrew dangerously, holding in my moan. From the pressure around his cock, he pumps one, two, three times and then quickly removes himself and strokes his own cock, his orgasm hitting my exposed stomach, his moan vibrating against my swollen heat.

From beneath the covers, I can hear him mumble something, but I can't quite make it out. I'm about to ask him what he's saying when the door to the bedroom opens and Smilly walks out.

"Sorry, forgot my water. You know how I always choke on my salvia at night. Without my water I'll—" Stopping on her way to the kitchen, she looks over at me where I'm lying next to Andrew's legs. She tilts her head to the side, trying to understand what's happening. "Uh—"

"Nope not down there," Andrew says, making his way back to the head of "the bed." When he appears, his hair is slicked down from sweat and his face is flush. Oh God, it's so obvious.

Wiping his mouth—yeah, not obvious AT ALL—he smiles at Smilly and says, "She lost her socks. Couldn't find them."

"Oh yeah?" Smilly looks us up and down and then asks, "Did you search her vagina well enough? Or are you going to take a second look?"

Not even skipping a beat, Andrew says, "Might have to check

again, once my tongue gets a rest though. Didn't drink enough water today, the damn thing is cramping up on me."

I slap his arm, causing him to laugh.

Why did I even think he'd be discreet? He never is, but I think that's one of the many things I like so much about him. *That and the fact he gives me incredible orgasms. Every. Time.*

CHAPTER TWENTY-FOUR

SADIE

"Are you really not going to let me make any of your sundaes?" Andrew asks, saddling up next to me as I scoop ice cream into a sundae dish. "I don't mind, you know. I like to pay extra attention to yours, show off my sundae-making skills, impress my mentor."

"Not necessary." I chuckle. "I don't mind making mine when you're over here, gives me a chance to spend a little extra time with you."

"Whoa." He steps to the side, acting shocked. He leans over and whispers, "Are you flirting with me? The guy in the glasses?"

"Go ahead, make a big deal out of it. See where it gets you."

"Let me take a guess. Sex in the freezer finally."

"No," I scoff. Turning toward him, ice cream scoop in one hand, I prop myself against the counter. "First of all, I will never do something like that again in this establishment, we were lucky we weren't caught."

"Live on the wild side, baby." He winks.

"Second," I continue, cutting him off before he can elaborate, "the freezer is full of meat. It seems wrong to conduct sexual acts around meat."

"That seems like an odd thing to say, especially since sexual organs are referred to as meat in today's slang. You know, deli counter for the pussy, salami for the dick. It would almost make sense to fuck in a frozen square, meat-sicles dangling around us." His brows pull together in question, trying to understand my reasoning.

I have no desire to acknowledge his statement. Deli counter—blech. "Whatever. I just don't want to go fuck next to frozen beef patties and chicken fingers. It would feel like they're staring at me. Also, wouldn't you be concerned about shrinkage? I'm not about to have sex with a shriveled raisin."

"Hold up. How did cannon cock turn into a shriveled raisin? Even on his worst day, this dick beats out most dicks. Don't challenge him with shrinkage. I will stick my cock in a vat of vanilla ice cream right now and fuck you against the milkshake wall just to prove a point."

The printer goes off, sending Andrew a new order, which is good because it gives me a moment to process Andrew's *threat*. How does he always make me so horny? *Even against the gross milkshake wall.*

"Having sex against the ice cream wall with a dried-up vanilla bean dick, wow, you really know how to woo a woman. Where do I sign up?"

His head falls back as he laughs, the muscles in his throat shifting up and down in one of the sexiest dances of humor I've ever seen. Hmm, the milkshake wall isn't looking too bad right about now.

"Hey, handsome. Did you get my ticket?"

Michelle. The boob-pressing sex fiend. Every single time she puts in an order she always *visits* Andrew to make sure he got it. And in the process, she makes it clear what she wants.

She wants to fuck him. If she could, I'm pretty sure she'd work topless just to get his attention. It's annoying, even if Andrew shows no signs of being even the least bit interested.

"Yup, have it right here," Andrew answers, holding the ticket up. "Give me a few seconds and I'll have it ready."

"No rush. I'll just wait here."

Of course she will.

"Have you been working out more? You look so strong." Oh my God, does she understand how desperate she sounds? "I mean, your work shirt looks extra tight on you. Doing extra pushups?"

I take a gander at Andrew's work shirt and realize it does look tighter. *Has* he been doing extra pushups? I know he goes to the gym regularly, but has he been picking up an extra day? How come I needed Michelle to point that out to me? Shouldn't I know if my boyfriend's muscles are getting bigger?

"And your pants—are they new?—they're making your ass look like a little bubble."

My eyes go to Andrew's butt now. Huh, she's right. Are those new pants? They ride low on his hips and I know with just a little lift of his shirt, I would be able to catch a glimpse of his toned skin.

"Eh, yeah, they're new pants," Andrew answers awkwardly.

When did he get new pants? It shouldn't matter, but why is Michelle noticing? Gah, I bet she secretly takes pictures of him and puts them on her inspiration board of men she wants to fuck. I bet she calls it her fucket list. And once she gets them to fall for her boob-flopping ways, she puts them in a scrapbook and looks through that book every night, reminiscing on the penises that once stuffed her vagina. Well, not Andrew. There is no way she's getting her reconstructed nipples on my guy.

"You know, I had a dream about you—"

"Can you not, Michelle?" Irritation flows through me while my hands clamp together at my side.

"Excuse me?" Michelle asks, straightening up, as if she's ready to pluck off her fake nails and square up for a hair-pulling fight. God, she can be terrifying.

Taking a deep breath, I wrap my arm around Andrew, taking a leap of faith, and say, "This is my boyfriend, and I would really appreciate it if you didn't ask him about his workout routine and if he has new pants and telling him about some lonely lady horny dream you had about him. He is mine, therefore you need to back the fuck off."

The wind has been knocked out of Michelle's sails, because her reaction is not what I expected. She almost looks like she's gasping for air. Yikes, is she going to faint? Please God, do not let her faint. I don't need that kind of drama in my life.

Finally, Michelle points a finger at both of us and asks, "Are you saying, you two are dating . . . exclusively?"

"Yes," I say with pride. "Andrew and I are exclusive, so please, if you wouldn't mind, stop flaunting your tits at him and hitting on him. It's inappropriate, and honestly, grossly desperate. Have a little pride, Michelle."

There is no response from her, just an open mouth of shock. To break the tension, Andrew holds out the finished sundae and says, "Here you go. Hot fudge sundae is ready to go." He tacks a smile on with his sentence.

Not saying a word, she takes the sundae and walks away, still adding that damn wiggle to her hips. I guess some things will never change.

Leaning down to my ear, Andrew squeezes my hip and says, "I'm so going to fuck you for that tonight. Damn, baby. I like it when you claim me."

I turn to him and point my finger into his chest. "Next time you get new pants, you tell me. I don't want Michelle noticing before your own girlfriend. Honestly, Andrew!"

With my sundae in hand, I storm off, a small smile at my lips. His ass really does look great in those pants, and I can't wait until he *fucks me for that.*

•••

"Pass it, Andrew, pass the grapefruit."

"It's not a basketball, Katja, I eat this."

"Pass the fruit," she continues, holding her arms out.

I watch as Andrew battles it out with his roommates, trying to protect his breakfast fruit they insist upon using as a basketball. Meeting his height, they all scramble around the kitchen, trying to snag the fruit from him, as if they're on the court, trying to earn possession of the ball. They have him outnumbered.

"You not let us have Topless Tuesday, at least pass the fruit," Leena says.

Topless Tuesday was banned after the whole miscommunication between Andrew and me, and he's also made it his mission to avoid Show Me Your Snatch Saturdays as well, something Leena keeps requesting.

Now, in the dining room, stretched across the wall, are three poster boards tacked onto the wall. It's full of rules for the house. The first two are: keep your private parts private and covered. There are exceptions to the rules, of course, which are: privates are allowed to air during private bathroom time, night time, and when you're in your bedroom with the door locked. I thought that was a fair compromise. The girls can still have Topless Tuesday, but they just have to do it in their bedrooms.

Other rules are:

Knock before entering someone's room. This was established

after Katja walked in on Andrew eating me out on his desk. She did say I had a nice pussy, which I took as a wonderful compliment. *Cough.*

You're only allowed to use your own razor, and other razors are off limits. You can imagine why Andrew wrote that one up on the board.

Grabbing Andrew's crotch as a greeting is not a greeting. Handshakes and fist bumps are allowed. Leena was under the impression one night that Andrew's crotch needed a hello as well. She was wrong.

And last: no touching Andrew's girlfriend's boobs. I don't know what it is with these ladies, but they are very touchy-feely. The first boob lift caught me off guard. The second, third, fourth, and fifth . . . now those were just interesting. It got to the point that when I entered the house and didn't get a boob lift from them I felt like I'd done something wrong. That's when Andrew put an end to it. He didn't want me to be conditioned to expect my boobs to be fondled when I saw them.

With rules in place, we've been having a great time coexisting together. I love spending the night at Andrew's place because it's always fascinating—and a little scary—to see what Leena and Katja are going to get themselves into. The other three roommates are supposed to filter in during the next week since classes and practices start up soon.

"Just pass it, Andrew," Katja says with irritation, which I find funny since it really is Andrew's grapefruit.

Conceding, knowing he is never going to win when Katja and Leena have something set in their mind, he tosses Katja the grapefruit, who then does a quick pass to Leena, who fakes to the left then to the right, only to jump in the air, and slam the grapefruit through a basket Katja is holding.

In slow motion, we all watch the grapefruit push through the basket and straight onto the floor where it splatters everywhere.

Defeated, Andrew places his hands on his hips as his head slouches. "Yup, I saw that coming."

Katja bends down and looks at the squashed fruit. "Grapefruit down. Maybe you make wine now with it."

"It's not . . ." Andrew sighs and runs his hand over his face. "It's not an actual grape."

Why do I think he's so hot when he gets mad? There is something in the way anger vibrates off him that turns me on. Is that weird? Maybe a little, but, oh well. I can't help it.

"I'm not cleaning that up." Andrew nabs my hands and pulls me off the counter. "You broke it, you clean it up. And use cleaning supplies or else the floor will be sticky. I will be adding don't slam fruit on the ground to the rules."

He walks us out of the kitchen as Leena and Katja both say at the same time, "Yes, Maammo."

I snort, which doesn't make Andrew very happy because he scowls at me. Too bad for him, his scowl turns me on too. It still makes me laugh every time they call him Mom in Finnish.

He takes me upstairs and shuts his door, making sure to lock it. He leans against the wood and blows out a long breath. "Those two are going to be the death of me, I just know it. That poor grapefruit, it was attacked by Finland with no defenses. A vicious hate-crime on a forbidden fruit." He shakes his head. "I'm going to add no attacks on grapefruit or any kind of fruit to the list. Maybe this one died so it could save its successors."

I study him, listening to the nonsensical dribble coming out of him. "Are you about done?" I ask, mirth laced in my voice.

"Yes." He walks over to his desk where he sits and pats his lap for me to sit down. "Want to help me find cheap versions of the books I need this semester? I finally got the list I need and want to get a head start on everything. Can you believe school starts in two weeks? Where did the summer go?"

I swallow hard and put on a bright face. "Uh, yeah, crazy."

Guilt swallows me whole as I sit on Andrew's lap and he shows me his list of books. I don't think I've ever met someone so enthused about earning an education. It almost feels like the first day of school to him is equivalent to a beer-bellied sports man gearing up for the Super Bowl.

He's ecstatic.

"And this professor I have for Human Computer Interfaces, shit, he's great. I've been dying to get into his class ever since I heard about the engineering school at Binghamton. What about you?"

The back of my neck starts to sweat; I can feel the prickles of nerves turning up the heat in my body. "What about me?" I ask.

"Are you excited about any of your classes? I took psychology in high school, and was fascinated, albeit a little lost. It wasn't math. I'm sure you're learning some pretty sweet stuff. Do you get to conduct tests on rats? See if Pavlov's dog is a real thing?"

"It is a real thing," I answer instinctively.

"I know, I'm only teasing." He kisses the side of my head and sighs. "Hell, I haven't even thought about what we're going to do when school starts. Ithaca is about an hour away. That's not quite long distance but I know I won't be seeing you every day like I am now. Shit." He runs his hand over his face. "You're not going to find some brainiac out there in the gorges and fall in love with him while there are miles separating us, are you?"

His voice is joking, but his eyes give him away. He's nervous and it hurts my heart that he thinks there is a possibility I'd find someone better than him. Impossible. Andrew is the best guy I've ever met. He's so good for me. That's why I need to tell him the truth.

"Your silence is making me nervous, babe," he jokes. Nervously.

I press the palms of my hands against his cheeks and sensually kiss him while situating myself on his lap so I'm straddling his muscular body. Instinctively he grabs hold of my hips and locks me in place, his mouth meshing, molding, melting into mine. The kiss was meant to be innocent, but with one flick of my tongue, Andrew starts moving his hands up my shirt, his thumbs grazing my ribs, the warmth of his palms lighting me up.

I moan into his mouth and start rocking on his lap, loving how I can already feel his excitement beneath me. This is where I want to be, right here, in Andrew's arms, the world around us fading to black. It's so safe here. Nothing can get to me when he's wrapped around me. Not the lies, not the embarrassing truth, and not the messed-up, upturned situation I call my life.

I settle in, loving how he's just as greedy as I am with his kisses, with the way his hands wander my body. Matching his exploration, I glide my hands up his shirt, taking in each contour of his abs beneath my palms. Unlike other men who flaunt their body, Andrew's abs are a secret you'd never know about. He keeps them under wraps, but I'm lucky enough to get my hands on him.

"Hey, hold on," Andrew says, pulling away, his thumbs pressing against my bra.

A little out of breath, I ask, "What?"

"You know I fucking love what we're doing here, but you never answered my question, and call me crazy, but I want to know what you plan on doing when you're at school. Are we going to continue what we have? Do you have plans to fuck other guys?"

Taken back by his words, I shake my head. "Of course not, Andrew." This is it; this is where I tell him the truth. Go on, Sadie. Let it all out. *Tell him you dropped out a while ago, that you have no plans of ever returning or revisiting your education.* I feel so ashamed. Of myself. Of the truth I've hidden. Of him thinking more of me than I deserve.

He searches my eyes; I search his, gathering the courage I need to be able to say something.

I open my mouth just as there is a slam of the door downstairs and a bunch of screaming. Andrew, like the good guy he is, stands quickly, bracing me on the floor and heads to his door. He turns to me and says, "Stay here."

He runs down the stairs in his bare feet and calls out, "What the hell is—?"

"Andrew!" a bunch of women scream.

I sigh. Let me guess, the other roommates have arrived.

When I travel downstairs, three very tall, very gorgeous, and very athletically built women greet me. Yup, all the roommates are here.

Being the good boyfriend Andrew is, he wraps his arm around my shoulder, introduces me to everyone, and makes sure to include me in on their conversations. I smile, I put on a good show, even though there is a gnawing, grossly disturbing feeling in the pit of my stomach, eating me alive.

I had a chance to lay it all out on the table, and I didn't. But that's the problem with shame. Shame doesn't like company. Shame's not something that likes to be shared.

●●●

"Hand me an H," Smilly says, her hand on the iron, pressing letters onto a shirt.

"Why are you making shirts again?"

Looking at me as if I'm stupid, she shakes her head. "Sadie, are you really choosing to forget that I love a good themed party? That I go all out when it comes to getting together with our friends? And that pictures are important to me?" It's true. She will really spend her entire paycheck on a party for her friends; she's amazing like that. "This is our last party of the summer. I'm making everyone a little memento for the summer we spent together, a shirt with their nicknames on it. Who knows when we'll all be together again with John in the Army and everyone going back to college. Before you know it, people will be graduating and starting real jobs, and at that point, once you start wearing a tie, you can no longer sit at bonfires, burn your ass, and laugh about it later. No, you have to carry around a briefcase full of responsibilities."

"Is that what you think people do when they graduate? Carry around briefcases?"

"Pretty sure that's what happens," Smilly says, sounding entirely sure of herself.

"Might not be completely accurate but I don't want to get into it." I play around with the iron-on letters on the table and start spelling out random words, my gut still churning. I've felt anxious for the last week. Whenever an opportunity arose to talk to Andrew, I either couldn't get him alone, I chickened out, or we were interrupted. And, silly me, but I don't wish for an audience when it comes to telling him the truth.

Smilly tosses a pen in my direction, nailing me in the head. "Hey," I complain, rubbing on the spot that was hit.

"What's with you lately? You've been super mopey lately."

Disappointed in myself, I shyly say, "I haven't told Andrew yet."

The iron stops moving back and forth and is lifted from the shirt. With her hand on her hip, Smilly stares me down. "You're kidding me, right?" I shake my head. "Sadie, school starts in a week. What the hell do you think is going to happen when he starts at Binghamton and you continue to work at Friendly's?"

"I don't know." I rub my hands over my face. "God, I'm so ashamed. I'm embarrassed, I want nothing to do with this life I've created, and I sure as hell don't want to tell Andrew about it."

"Well, he's going to find out. You can't keep this from him, especially when he's expecting to visit you at Cornell. Hell, what a shock that would be, to drive out to Ithaca only to realize his girlfriend no longer goes to Cornell. What the hell have you been waiting for, Sadie?"

"The right moment." I cringe, knowing that's a cop-out.

"It's never the right moment. You just have to say it. Does he even know about Tucker? About the baby?"

"No. He doesn't need to know about that."

"Ahh, I see." Smilly nods her head and steps away from the ironing board, choosing to sit on the counter of the small kitchen instead. "So you're planning on building a relationship with this kind, caring, sweet man based on a bunch of lies? Am I getting this straight? You think you can just have a partnership with this man, refusing to tell him anything about your past? You know that is never going to work, right? If you're serious about him, really serious, then you need to build a foundation with him based on truth, on trust." Looking me square in the eyes, she adds, "Yeah, I said the word, trust. You have to understand that the people you grew up with, the ones who know what you've been through, they aren't the only ones you can trust. If that was the case, you would live a lonely fucking life, Sadie. People come and go, and right now, you're stagnant while everyone else is going. You will be left behind, lonely, lost, and bitter, just like your dad. Is that what you want?"

Not even in the slightest. And I hate that she's right. My dad threw away his trust in the outside world a long time ago, turning into a skeptical, bitter man who chose to live in his bubble, always focusing on the negative, and never truly living. Am I turning into him? Is *that* really what I'm doing? Closing myself off, shutting down the outside world, and becoming an island?

I shake my head, realizing I'm only a few steps away from becoming my dad, and that startles me. I've never thought of it like that.

"Shit," I mutter and then run my fingers through my hair, pulling on the strands near my scalp.

"You have to let him in, Sadie. You have to fully let him in, or else you have to cut him free, because you're doing him a disservice by keeping him in this grey area, feeding him enough information to keep him satisfied, but never truly giving yourself over. That's not fair to him, and it's not fair to you." She jumps off the counter and takes the seat across from me where she holds my hand and speaks to me from the heart. "I know you've been through a lot, and I mean a lot more than any person our age should experience. You've been hurt, you've been betrayed by your mom, and you've lost something so precious to you. You're damaged, lost, and scared, but I'm here to tell you, there is a man named Andrew who has made you smile again, who's made you light up, who's made you laugh. He's good for you, Sadie, just as you are good for him. You can't lose that over being scared about the truth. I can see it in his eyes, Sadie. He loves you, and no matter what you tell him, he will still love you. But you have to tell him, he deserves the truth."

I nod, knowing just how right Smilly is. The truth causes the cogs to start turning in my brain. *How* do I reveal the painful truths to Andrew? Just the thought of it has my nerves prickling with anxiety.

"What are you going to do? Tell him? Keep him?" Smilly asks, urging me to make a decision.

Knowing I have no choice, I nod my head. "I am. I'll tell him everything tonight." Denise was right. *Andrew's a four-leaf clover in a field of weeds, a man you don't want to slip through your fingers.* And I don't. I don't want that man to slip through my fingers.

"I think that's a smart idea. Believe me, Sadie, it will be a load off your shoulders and maybe he can help you decide what to do next."

"That's if he doesn't leave me in the cold because I've been lying to him this whole time."

"Not going to happen."

I hope.

CHAPTER TWENTY-FIVE

ANDREW

Sadie is so fucking lucky.
I look around and take it in. The smell of the bonfire, the light breeze of the chilly summer night, the sounds of crickets in the distance, flashes of fireflies off in the woods, and the feel of true friendship rounding out a perfect night.

Moving from California to New York when I graduated from high school was tough because I was pulled from my familiar environment, stuck in a foreign state, and told to make friends. Easier said than done. When I went to college in Maine, my roommates were more there for company. They weren't *friends for life* dudes.

But Sadie, she has life-long friends, people who would drop anything, and I mean they'd stop their life to help one another out. They're loyal, bonded by a small town, by the memories of growing up, and the shared experiences over the years.

I'm jealous, but grateful too, because Sadie brought me into a world I've always craved. True friendship. The real thing. These are the kind of people I want in my life.

"John, man, are you gearing up for deployment?" I ask the tall soldier who's wearing a red, white, and blue sweatband with a shirt that reads *Our Soldier*.

"Ten days and counting," he says, saluting me. "Spending the last couple of days with my girl and trying to drink as much beer as possible."

"Goals, I like them." I laugh and pat him on the back. "If I don't see you before you leave, good luck out there, man, and be safe."

"Always am." He winks just as he brings his beer to his lips and takes a sip. Looking past his bottle, he spots Bitch—still don't know her real name—his girlfriend and says, "Babe, come sit up on my lap. My dick needs to spend as much time with you as possible."

I shake my head and find Sadie, who is talking to Emma by the fire. I wrap my arm around her shoulder, lean my head down to her ear, and say, "Here's your beer, baby." I kiss her cheek before pulling away. She rewards me with a beautiful smile and I fall for her all over again.

"Ugh, you two are so sweet together, it's almost sickening. How come you can find the good guys and I keep juggling douchebags with two-tone cars? Where are the real men?"

"Maybe if you didn't spend all your time cleaning up your friends' messes, you might be able to meet someone," Sadie offers.

Emma looks out toward the party and says, "Someone has to take care of you hooligans. If it wasn't for me, every place we've had a bonfire would be burned down and half of you would be dead."

"True." Sadie chuckles. "But everyone is going back to their normal lives, maybe you can meet someone at school."

"Maybe." Emma shrugs.

"What school do you go to?"

"Binghamton. I'm in the nursing program." Why am I not

surprised? Emma would make a fantastic nurse.

"I didn't know you were going to Binghamton as well. Decker School of Nursing is such a great program to be in. Hard too."

"It is. It's actually taken me longer than I wished, but I've been taking my time, making sure I can understand everything and make the most of my classes."

"I can respect that. We should get coffee sometime on campus. It will be nice to see a familiar face in a sea of new people."

"That would be fun. I can introduce you to some of my friends. We're all in the nursing program, but it still might be nice to meet some other people."

"I would love that, especially since Sadie is going to be off at Cornell, learning how to help heal minds."

Emma exchanges a weird glance with Sadie but quickly shakes it away once her name is called from the house. She sighs and says, "Duty calls."

As Emma walks away, her little sundress sways with her. That's the hardest thing to find when you move states. Connections. Knowing someone at Binghamton, besides my crazy-ass roommates and my brother, who will have no time for me once classes start, is good.

I sit down on the ground and pull Sadie to sit between my legs so she's using my chest as a backboard. I wrap my arms around her and look over her shoulder, my head close to hers, enjoying the night off we have together. "You're lucky, you know that?"

"How's that," she asks, her voice sounding slightly off, a little more quiet. I guess it makes sense that she's subdued, given she'll be separated from her friends next week.

"Look around you. This support system you have, all these people cheering you on; it's amazing. You don't see a group of people like this very often. A group of friends devoted to each other. It's fucking awesome. I wish I'd had a close-knit group of friends like this growing up."

She leans her head against mine. "It has its up and downs. It's not all about parties and drinking together. There are times where you wish you weren't so close with everyone because everyone learns your business, things you wish you could just tuck away."

"Do you have things you want to tuck away?" I ask and then kiss her neck, loving every minute I get to spend with this woman. The reality of classes is looming over me; the end of our summer is coming closer, and the moment where I have to kiss my girl goodbye is starting to eat me alive.

"I do," Sadie answers, pulling me from my reverie. "My family life. I wish I could rewrite it, cast new parents. It would make life easier." She turns her head and looks me in the eyes, a sad smile on her lips. "But I don't want to talk about them right now. I want this to be a fun night."

"Yeah?" I wiggle my eyebrows at her. "What do you have in mind? A little romp in the woods?"

"No." She graces me with that beautiful laugh. "What has been your favorite memory this summer?"

I snuggle her closer. "Ah, my girl wants to reminisce. All right." In front of her, I rub my hands together and then place them on her propped-up knees. The fire sparks in front of us, casting an orange glow in the air, making the atmosphere almost magical. "My favorite memory this summer. Hmm, well, when you so scornfully showed me where the apples were, that was a special moment."

She chuckles and then loops her hand behind her to connect with my neck. Playfully, her fingers run through my short strands of hair. Fuck, that feels good.

"I don't know why you stuck around and tried to get to know me after that first day of training."

I press another kiss to her neck and say, "I like a good challenge, plus, I saw something in your eyes. I wanted to be the one who took that darkness away and made you laugh."

"You made me chuckle that first day," she admits. "Sturdy tits. I couldn't stop laughing in the stockroom."

"Come on, too cool to laugh with me?"

"I didn't want you getting comfortable," she jokes. "But seriously, what was your favorite moment?"

"Honestly? When we danced at the party I crashed, thanks to Smilly. Even though I was a little drunk, I remember the moment as if it's playing out in front of me right now. That smile of yours, it slayed me. It was the first time you actually loosened up around me and I got to see the real Sadie. Fucking beautiful."

Swoon away, ladies, but that's no fucking lie. I already thought Sadie was beautiful, but at that moment, I knew she was different, that she was going to push my comfort zones.

She's silent for a moment, taking in my words, and I'm nervous if I put my heart out there too much until she leans forward and kisses my forearm. "I loved that moment, too."

"Yeah?" I snuggle her closer, if that's possible. "Is that your favorite moment?"

She shakes her head. "No, I think my favorite moment was when you took me on our first date. You were nervous, but so cute, so sweet, trying to impress me. It was the first time I realized you were going to be a hard one to get out of my system."

"Still hanging in there, I hope." I might have a teasing tone in my voice, but a part of me feels insecure. She doesn't want me out of her system, right? I sure as fuck hope not.

She tilts her head back and rests it on my shoulder. Her lips graze my jaw as she says, "Permanently."

Pride surges inside me from her admission, and I actually feel hope for the future. Going to two different schools is going to be tough, but I think we can handle it. No, I know we can.

Sadie squirms in my arms and I ask, "Is everything okay?"

She sighs and says, "I have to pee, but I'm so warm and comfortable. I don't want to get up."

"I'm not going anywhere. Go to the bathroom and hurry that cute little ass back here. No one likes a person who pees their pants. It's not attractive."

"Not a pee-the-pants kind of guy?" Her laugh is contagious.

"Not so much. Hurry up." She stands and I swat her ass. "I'm not opposed to spanking."

She holds her butt in shock and turns to me. "I know that and will keep it in mind." She winks and then takes off toward the house, leaving me alone with my thoughts.

I lean back on my hands, my fingers digging into the shaggy grass, taking in my surroundings. Sadie's friends huddle around the fire, drinking, laughing, and reminiscing on their "glory days."

I wonder if we would have been friends if I'd gone to their small-town school. Would I be a part of their group? Or would I be one of the outsiders they talk about? It almost seems like they know every single person that went to school with them, in their grade, two grades older, and two grades younger. There's something to be said about growing up in a small town.

A little bored, I pull out my phone from my pocket and see I have a missed call from Jimmy. He's not much of a talker, so I call him back while Sadie is gone.

"Andrew, my man. Are you bringing ice cream tonight?" The bastard has become addicted.

"Not working tonight, sorry. Sadie and I are out at a party with her friends."

"Fuck me," he whines into the phone. "God, I need my ice cream fix."

"Then go get some. You don't have to wait for me."

He sighs into the phone, sounding irritated. "Dude, you bring *free* ice cream. I'm not about to go buy ice cream when I can get it for free; where's the logic in that?"

"You're pathetic."

"No," he replies. "I'm smart. I'm just going to have to tamp down my craving and wait for another night." I can hear him take a deep breath—he must be really desperate—before he asks, "So how are things with Sadie? Is she getting ready for Cornell?"

"Things are good," I answer, thinking back to the conversation we just had. "Things are really good. It's going to be tough not seeing each other every day like we do now, but we can work it out. I mean, hell, it's only an hour."

"Yeah, that's not bad at all. Remember when I first moved out here? Mae was still in California, trying to sell her car and get all her affairs in order. Now a country's distance, that's far."

"You're a real pioneer," I tease, looking around for Sadie. She should be done by now.

"I like to think so."

Feeling the urge, I head to the bathroom, hoping to find Sadie en route.

"Hey, I'm going to go take a leak. Beer and all."

"Break the seal now and pay for it the rest of the night," Jimmy says, offering stupid-ass advice.

"Don't be a moron. I'm not about to hold in my piss. That's just asking for a bladder infection. Remember when we were young we were taught when we feel a tingle, it's time to go to the potty?"

"Yeah, now when I feel a tingle, I'm not looking for a potty . . ."

"And I'm going now. Talk to you later, bro."

I pocket my phone and head into the house. Smilly and Saddlemire are in the kitchen, manning the keg; there are people I've never met milling about in the living room who I nod at and then head back to the bathroom. As I approach, I see that the door is partially closed with the light on. Sadie, can't still be in there, can she?

I go to press my hand on the door to open it when I hear Sadie's voice.

"Tucker, what are you doing?"

Tucker?

When I hear Tucker's voice, he sounds desperate. I've only hung with the guy once, but he seemed like a tough, short-worded man.

"I needed to see you. I need to talk to you, Sadie."

"About what?"

I shouldn't be listening to this, and yet, I can't seem to tear myself away. And hell, I shouldn't leave either, because that's my girl in there.

"About everything we talked about on the phone. About our future, about the baby, about how much I fucking love you."

Errr . . . *say that again?*

Baby?

Love?

Future?

What fucking baby?

"Tucker . . ." Sadie sighs. Fucking sighs. What does that even mean?

"I know you've been having fun with Andrew this summer, exploring your options, but what are you going to do when he goes back to school, and you're still sharing a one-bedroom with Smilly, working at Friendly's? Are you just going to pretend you're back at Cornell attending classes as well?" There is shuffling and then Tucker says, "You don't have to fucking pretend with me, Sadie. You can be real with me; you can be yourself. Go out with me Saturday, let's just fucking talk. Please."

"I don't know," Sadie answers, unsure of herself.

Wrong answer, Sadie. Can you guess what she should have said? Maybe something like, *"I have a boyfriend therefore I can't go out with you."*

And what the fuck is this pretending shit about Cornell? Does she not go to Cornell? Why would she fake something like that?

"Just give me this one night. I promise I won't bug you afterward. You owe me one night, Sadie. After everything we've been through together, you owe me that much."

"I know," she says almost on a whisper. "I'll see what I can do."

"Thanks, babe."

There is more shuffling and that's when I step to the other side of the door so when they open it, they won't see me.

Going to the bathroom has never hurt so much before in my life.

Tucker is the first one who leaves, and a part of me wants to run down the hallway, tackle the prick I don't like so much now. He's a dick. Sadie and I shared a whole hell of a lot more this summer than just fun. Or at least it was more to me. What could she possibly owe him? And he's in love with her? What the hell is going on?

The light in the bathroom goes out a few seconds later and Sadie steps out. She doesn't look in my direction, but she doesn't need to.

Leaning against the wall, arms crossed over my chest, I ask, "Have plans Saturday night?"

Her progress down the hallway immediately stops as she whips around to see me, her long blonde hair floating over her shoulders. The look of utter shock and regret crosses her features.

Busted.

"An-Andrew," she stutters. "What are you doing here?"

"Funny thing, I had to piss. Little did I know I'd hear my girlfriend talking to whom I'm going to assume is her ex-boyfriend—"

The moment the words slip from my lips, Sadie's confessions about her previous relationship and sexual encounters float through my head. Holy fuck, it was with Tucker. My stomach rolls from the realization. "Christ, Sadie. He's your ex-boyfriend, isn't he? The guy who took your virginity? The one you had an almost life-long relationship with. It was Tucker."

She bites her bottom lip but doesn't answer me.

"Fucking answer the question," I grit out.

"Yes," she squeaks. "It was Tucker."

"And there's a baby?"

"Was," she says, using past tense.

"Were you planning on telling me any of this? Did you really go to Cornell? Or did you just make all of that up to pretend to have something in common with me?" I pull on my hair and look her up and down. "Fuck, was any of it real?"

"Yes." She steps forward but I step back.

"What? What was real, Sadie? Because right about now it seems like I don't know you at all."

"I was going to tell you," she pleads, trying to get closer. "I was trying to find the right time."

"The right time." I laugh sarcastically. "When exactly is the right time to tell someone you've been lying?"

"It wasn't . . ." She chokes on a sob. I didn't realize she was even crying, probably from the blind rage enveloping me. "It wasn't like that, Andrew. I was ashamed—"

"You should be fucking ashamed," I spit back at her. "You can't build a relationship on lies, Sadie. How am I supposed to trust anything you've told me? You're all about never giving anyone a chance, never trusting anyone outside your little circle, and yet you're a contradiction to your own standards. You lie, use, and take. How the fuck am I supposed to trust *you*?"

"I didn't use you."

"No?" I raise an eyebrow at her. "According to your ex, I was just a fun summer fling to occupy your time and now that I replay our summer together, I think he's fucking right. Getting you to open up was impossible. I begged, I pleaded to get to know you better, and even though you let me in on some things about you, like you once owned a corgi, clearly you left out all the big topics." I shake my head and start walking toward her and pass her shoulder in the hallway, while mumbling, "That's fucked up, Sadie."

"Andrew, wait," Sadie calls out, following me down the hall.

I don't stop. I have a one-track mind and it's telling me to get the hell out of here. As I maneuver my way through the house, I make eye contact with Smilly who seems to know exactly why I'm walking away from Sadie right now. Fucking great. Was I the standing joke amongst all their friends? Poor Andrew, the outsider, not knowing anything about Sadie and her lying mouth. Maybe they thought I was just the summer fling until she got back together with Tucker too. Fuck.

"Andrew, please." I fish out my keys from my pocket, unlock the door of my truck, and hop in.

When I go to shut the cab door, Sadie stops me, slipping her body between the door and me. Staring straight ahead, hands on the steering wheel, I say, "Get the fuck out of the way."

"Andrew, please just listen to me."

"Why, so you can give me the runaround?" I turn to her and

ask point-blank, "Did you lie to me?"

She bites her bottom lip, her eyes wandering back and forth over mine, contemplating her answer. Finally she nods her head.

"That's all I need to know." I start my truck and say, "Get out of the fucking way, or I will back this truck up with you in my path."

Sobs wracking her body, she steps out of the way. I slam the door shut right before I push the pedal all the way down and back out of the long dirt driveway.

I told her about my past, about the humiliation. I haven't hidden things from her. I haven't lied.

Fuck.

Be nervous about your past.

Be ashamed.

Be embarrassed.

But don't ever fucking lie to me, making me feel like a fool. There is no getting around that. I've played the clown once before, and I refuse to be the laughing stock at Binghamton.

CHAPTER TWENTY-SIX

SADIE

Grass surrounds me, prickling my exposed legs as I sit in the front yard of the party house, my head in my hands, sobbing uncontrollably. And I have no one to blame but myself.

When I went to the bathroom, I had no idea I'd run into Tucker. I didn't even know he was back from his training in Pennsylvania. Meeting up with him on Saturday was going to be completely platonic. I don't want to start anything with Tucker. I just want to offer him closure, a period on the end of our very long run-on sentence.

I just want the past to be over with. I wanted to start a future with Andrew. *What have I done? How did I screw this up so badly?*

The look on his face, the anger in his eyes, his total dismissal . . . they will permanently brand my brain, forever place a stamp of regret on my heart.

I should have told him. I should have been honest.

But I was so ashamed. I was running away from it all, trying to distance myself from those chapters in my life.

Soft footsteps come up from behind me and a warm arm wraps around my shoulders. "Is he gone?" Smilly asks.

I nod into my hands, not able to vocalize it.

"Did he find out?"

I nod again, another sob slipping out of me.

"I'm sorry, Sadie." She gives me a hug but then pulls away, leaving me feeling cold and rejected. "But I'm going to throw some tough love your way. I told you this was going to happen. I love you, but you handled your relationship with Andrew badly. It was only a matter of time before this was all going to explode in your face."

"I . . . was going to t-tell him tonight," I reply through broken cries.

"You should have told him weeks ago, Sadie."

I want to be mad at her. I want to yell and scream at her, but she's right. I should have told him weeks ago. I should have been open and honest, I should have never deterred him from the truth. It is a mistake I have to live with.

"I fucked everything up."

"What's going on here?" Tucker's voice trails out over the now frigid night. "Are you crying?" He kneels down and lifts my chin to be greeted by my tears. "What the fuck? Did that shithead say something to you?"

"No." I cry some more. "He overheard us in the bathroom."

"The dickhead can't handle a little conversation? If that's the case, he's not good enough for you, Sadie. It's for—"

"Stop!" Smilly stands, her voice taking on a different kind of tone, one I've never heard before. "Don't say another word, Tucker. You've done enough damage tonight."

"Stay out of it, Samantha," Tucker says, his voice threatening. "I know you like to be in your friend's business, but maybe you should keep your mouth shut this time."

"I stuck up for you." Smilly gets in Tucker's face. "I was Team Tucker, thinking you would always be together. But seeing her with Andrew, it became clear. You brought her down. *You* weren't good for Sadie."

"She brought herself down! I love her," Tucker yells, his arms flying out to the side. "I was ready to offer her everything she fucking needed and she didn't listen. Don't you fucking put this on me. Do you really think I wanted to see her drop out, give up everything? I wanted to be there for her, support her, help her reach her dreams."

Smilly and Tucker continue to argue, their words filtering through one ear and out the other, nothing really registering. All I can focus on is the look in Andrew's eyes. The pain. I'm so freaking overwhelmed that I don't realize what I'm doing until I'm jogging to the house and begging Emma for her car keys.

She doesn't ask me any questions. She digs through her purse, pulls them out, and hands them to me with a lift of her chin. She has to know, everyone has to know what happened. I never cry, and seeing me *beg* for Andrew to stay is a new sight for my friends. It was a new feeling for me too, an agony I've only felt once before. The night I miscarried.

Genuine, all-encompassing heartbreak. There is no denying it.

I give Emma a quick hug and then jog out to her car, Tucker and Smilly chasing after me.

"Where are you going?" Smilly asks, her voice still grated from her fight with Tucker.

"I have to see him. I have to talk to him. I can't continue on with this night, knowing how much pain I caused him."

"Sadie . . ." Tucker calls out.

I shake my head. "No, Tucker." I'll deal with him later.

I slam the door to Emma's Jetta and start the car with only one destination in mind: Andrew.

•••

The lights are all on, there are multiple vehicles in the driveway—including Andrew's—and the pleasant, thick ambience of regret and sorrow hover over me as I ring the doorbell. I shift on my feet, my palms sweating uncontrollably, my breath caught in my throat. Please answer, please answer.

Heavy footsteps pad across the wood floors I've become so familiar with over the summer and the telltale sound of the squeaky door opening sounds through the quiet night on Chestnut Street.

Katja answers the door wearing basketball shorts, a tank top, and hair tied up in a tight bun. She's tall, fierce, and intimidating as fuck with her sharp eyebrows and *don't eff with me* attitude. I'm almost positive she could rip my limbs off and eat them as an appetizer.

"You," she says, her voice full of disdain. "What you want?" So, Andrew has already told them.

Pulling together my inner strength, I take a deep breath and say, "I would like to talk to Andrew."

"Too bad I don't want you to. Good night." She slams the door in my face, leaving my mouth hanging open, my mind running a mile a minute trying to work out what just happened.

She shut me down, without even giving me a chance to explain. How dare she?

A little voice in the back of my head keeps telling me to fight, to not give up. I puff out my chest and ring the doorbell again. After no one answers, I ring again, and again, and again until I hold my finger down, making the bell go on a loop. I can do this all freaking night.

After a minute of torture, the door finally opens. I expect to be greeted by Katja again but instead Andrew's angry eyes meet mine. All five girls stand behind him with their arms—ahem, their beefy arms—crossed over their chests. *They are extremely intimidating, but I can't leave. I just want Andrew back.*

"Press that bell one more time and these girls are going to tear your fingers off and use them as soup spoons," Andrew says. From behind him, Katja pretends to eat soup from a bowl, her eyes trained on mine. Oh sweet Jesus.

Clearing my throat, I ask, "Can I please talk to you, Andrew?" I look over his shoulder one more time and add, "Alone."

"Push her down stairs," Katja calls out.

"Whack the snatch," Leena adds.

Madeline—the French girl—stands tall and says, "Poke her in the eye."

"In the nipple," Katja adds.

"No." Leena hits Katja in the arm. "Snatch probably like nipple poke."

Katja nods and says, "Don't poke her nipple."

My eyes plead with Andrew. "Please."

He lets out a long breath and grips the back of his neck, shutting the door behind him. The sound of his roommates' disapproval doesn't go unnoticed. I'm not going to worry about them though because I have Andrew's attention and I have him alone.

"What do you want, Sadie?" He sounds exhausted, weathered, as if he just fought five battles and is ready to crash.

"I need to explain."

He leans up against the side of the house, his arms crossed over his chest in a defensive pose. "Little late for that, don't you think?"

I deserve that.

"I understand that you're mad—"

"Do you? Do you understand, Sadie? Do you actually get what I'm feeling right now?" I go to answer, but he stops me. "Because I don't think you do. You see," he pushes himself off the wall and stands directly in front of me, invading my space,

"I spent my entire summer with this girl I met, my coworker, a girl I fell for and fell for hard despite her reservations. I gave her the benefit of the doubt because I could see pain in her eyes, the kind of pain I wanted to wash away." Tears well up in my eyes and easily spill over onto my cheeks as he continues to speak. "I gave her everything. I told her about my life, about my mistakes, about my embarrassing moments, and in return, she gave me her laugh, her smile, but never her fucking heart. But you know what? I thought, *she will*. She will slowly break down that wall and meet me in the middle. Open up. Let me in. Become mine."

Andrew pulls on his hair in frustration, the veins in his neck starting to pulse from anger.

"But she never did." He looks me right in the eyes. "You never fucking did."

"I was going to." I step closer. "Tonight, I was going to tell you everything."

A sardonic laugh escapes those soft lips of his. "Yeah? You were going to tell me everything? You were going to tell me about Tucker being your fucking life-long boyfriend? That apparently you were pregnant with his baby? That you were planning to meet up with him behind my back? That you never really went to Cornell?"

"That's not true." I shake my head. I don't bother trying to catch the tears of sorrow scattering over the porch. "I did go to Cornell and was majoring in Psychology. I dropped out because of the pregnancy. I lost everything: my scholarship, my future, and a few weeks later, I lost the baby." I place my hands over my face and cry . . . hard. "I was too ashamed to tell you. You were so into school, I just . . ." I sigh. "I thought you would think differently of me."

I look up to see him nodding his head. "Glad you thought so highly of me."

He turns to walk away, but I grab his arm. "It wasn't like that, Andrew. You came out of nowhere, swept me up into your world, a world I so desperately wanted to be a part of, a world that made me forget about the baby, about the miscarriage, about everything I gave up for nothing. For the first time in so long, you showed me how to smile again. How to feel."

He glances down at me, and in that small moment, I see the understanding in his eyes as the anger softens. Turning back toward me, he loops his arm around my shoulder and presses me into his chest. Tears fall from my eyes. His warm comfort surrounds me. He lets out a long breath of air and speaks, his deep voice rumbling across my ears. "I'm sorry you had to experience something so traumatic as losing a baby, Sadie. I can't imagine what that must have been like, especially after you turned your life upside down and left college." *This. This is what I've needed. Why did I hold back, deny his comfort and reassurance?*

Just as I settle into his embrace, he pulls away and drags one of his hands over his face. "But that doesn't change anything." *What?*

"What do you mean?" I ask, my voice wavering.

Tortured eyes meet mine as he replies, "I fell for you, Sadie. I fell for you so fucking hard, but I fell for a girl who doesn't know who she is. I fell for a girl who is lost and clinging to anything that will help her forget the woman she once was. I don't want to be the person who morphs you into someone else. I want to be the person who embraces the incredible human you are."

I step forward to hold his hand, but he pulls away and inches to the door. With each move he makes away from me, my vision tunnels. "Andrew, please."

He shakes his head. "No, Sadie. As much as it kills me to say this, I can't be with you. I don't want to be with you. You need to find yourself, again, and clinging to me, looking for someone to shield you from the real world, that's not what I want. I don't want to be that man. I want to be the man who raises you up, who helps you accomplish your goals. Not the man who hides you." He pushes out a large breath and looks to the sky. "You lied to me, Sadie, and I think you did it to hide. Up until tonight, I thought you had your goals, your future planned out, and I had hoped it included me. You're smart. But, it's as if you're content to . . . to just give up. I'm just another wall *enabling* that." Looking me square in the eyes, finality in his voice, he adds, "And to fuck if I'm going to be the wall that blocks you from your future."

Before I can answer, he opens the door to his house, goes inside, and closes it behind him. On me, on our relationship.

And then I know. It's hopeless.

He's done.

We're done.

He's closed the door to me, to us, to the future I so desperately wanted with him. The ache in my heart intensifies, and excruciating pain envelops me.

He's done. With me.

That night, I bury my head in my pillow, dreaming of Andrew's beautiful face and the words he so thoughtfully and critically spoke.

Fuck if I'm going to be the wall that blocks you from your future.

What future?

My future? Right now, I have none.

CHAPTER TWENTY-SEVEN

ANDREW

Here is a bit of advice for you, free of charge, because I'm a good guy like that. If you ever have the urge or inkling to start a workplace romance . . . DON'T!

I don't care if he has bulgy muscles that you can see through three layers of shirts, or a smile that makes you want to pull out your stapler and start sitting on it, or hair that is blown in Fabio mode when he's under an air vent. Stay the fuck away. Close up shop, button up your shirt, point your head forward, and stay far, far away.

Why, do you ask?

Because, isn't it obvious? When the shit hits the fan—gross term—and the orgasmic relationship you thought you had crumbles at the tips of your naughty little fingers, you're left with nothing but the most tension-filled, awkward, and incredibly uncomfortable workplace environment.

Imagine this, you don't heed my advice and you succumb to Bulging Blaine's advances and you decide this is it, you've found the one. You go out with him, he woos you, seduces you, shows you that his muscles aren't the only thing bulging, and you fall in love. Collective sigh. Aw, Bulging Blaine. What a ruggedly handsome man with a schlong that tickles your intestines. You can't believe the sheer luck and smart decision you made in allowing this giant cock of a man with the abs that you motorboat at least twice a night into your life. Great job. High five. Thumbs up. Nipple-to-nipple kiss.

You're at work, doodling hearts on a Post-it Note, his name in bold, your name in cursive with a heart surrounding them. You're high, not on the hashish brownies Always-High Helen brings in to work and leaves in the secret cupboard in the break room, but from the man who sits three cubicles away. He's EVERYTHING. You're so happy that when you walk down the hallways of your office building, you cry cupcakes for your co-workers, you sneeze sprinkles, and when you flip your hair to the side, hearts sporadically fall to the floor, making it look like Cupid himself had an all-night bender and he's paying for it now.

Happiness.

It consumes you. You eat, sleep, breathe, and wax that cactus for the one and only Bulging Blaine. The way he kisses you, pressing his body into yours, the way he looks at you from over his cube, sexual suggestions waggling in those seductive eyebrows, or the way he secretly lifts your skirt up in the break room, only to run a finger near your aroused "sex." Heaven, right? Coitus has never been so good on a copy machine, right? Instant messenger has never been so naughty . . . Can I get an amen, ladies?

But then, the lust-filled bubble of cotton candy and condoms starts to fade and the truth comes out. Bulging Blaine has been lying to you. No, he doesn't have a secret life; no, he hasn't been fucking steals-all-the-tape Tanya with the hooker heels. It's worse; he hasn't been telling you the truth about himself. The man with the cock ring that sends vibrations to your larynx has been telling you this entire time that he is the proud owner of his Mustang Convertible and the stylish, yet modern townhome you've been using as a fucking surface, when in actuality, he's been housesitting for his parents who are gallivanting over in Europe, knocking fists with the Queen and eating crumpets off her crown. GASP! (Lame example, I know, but I'm so mad, I couldn't come up with a better one. Pretend it's devastating and go with it.) Gah, the horror!

Your world turns bleak, you have tunnel vision, you can't seem to breathe. The townhome you thought you were going to one day chase your child around in instead will be occupied by Bigger, Badder, Bulging Blaine Senior and his botox-filled wife, Glinda. Bulging Blaine tries to tell you he had plans of telling you the quartz counters he ate you out on five times really belonged to his parents, but he was just looking for the right time. But it's no use, the deed has been done, he lied, he betrayed you, and you can no longer see yourself taking a shower in the five-piece shower stall that blasts your clit and ass at the same time, taking you on an H20 sexual enlightenment you'll never forget.

The worst happens, you break up. You tell that lying piece of billowing bastard that you're done and you slam the door on his face because let's be honest, you're a strong, confident, and proud woman. You don't take crap from anyone, even if you spent three hundred dollars on a Photoshop artist to see what your children might look like.

You're back at work, dread and unease setting in. You sit in your cube, waiting for the moment you see him, waiting to see if he looks like the pile of rotted-out cucumbers you hoped and prayed he would turn into overnight, but no such luck. When he walks past your desk, his cologne hits your nose, reminding you of the time you let him plow you in the emergency fire escape stairwell while everyone else was following protocol during the practice fire drill. When you get coffee, you run into him, seeing that the butt you fell in love with didn't deflate overnight and for some reason looks better than ever. And when you go to the bathroom, hoping for a piece of solace, you run into him while he's retrieving his mail, his eyes looking regretful, pleading with you to have a conversation.

You want to cry, you want to plow your fist through the cube wall in hopes that your force will also take out Breathes-Too-Loud Lonny on the other side.

Everywhere you go, you see him. Every time you breathe, you smell him. Every time you try to focus on the work in front of you, his face pops up in your head. It's a living nightmare.

Can you feel it? Can you see where I'm coming from? Do you understand why I'm seconds away from storming into Stuart's office and throwing my apron in his face while demanding my last paycheck?

The clearing of a throat pulls me from my thoughts. I turn to see Sadie standing next to the counter, her hands twisting in front of her, her eyes rimmed with red, and total defeat in the set of her shoulders. In a weak voice, she asks, "Did you get a chance to make my sundae?"

I look up at the ticket machine and notice a few tickets waiting to be made. I must have completely zoned out, trying to forget the girl standing next to me.

"I can make it." Moving into the fountain area, I stop her, my hand accidentally landing on hers. Quickly I remove it and clear my throat.

"I can do it. Just give me a second." I tear down the slip and start reading it but the letters and numbers are all jumbled together. I have no clue what the order is.

"I don't mind."

"I can do it, just give me a second."

I place my hands on the counter and try to take deep breaths.

She's too close, her perfume is eating me alive, her eyes boring holes into my back. Focus, Andrew, fucking focus. It's just a sundae for God's sake.

"It's just a vanilla sundae with fudge." Her voice shakes with each word. When I turn to look at her, those crystal blue eyes of hers are filling with tears. All I see is her agony.

Fuck.

Fuck me.

See what I'm talking about? Don't engage in workplace romances. I repeat, do not engage in workplace romances.

If you engage, be warned: coworker turns into co-WRECKER pretty damn quickly.

CHAPTER TWENTY-EIGHT

SADIE

I toss my patched-up purse on the floor and fall into one of the pink recliners in my small one-bedroom apartment. What a long fucking day.

School started, and it's been three weeks since I've seen Andrew. He quit shortly after we broke up. I heard through the grapevine that he told Stuart he needed to focus on school, but really? He couldn't stand to be around me any longer. I don't blame him; I can barely stand to be around myself.

Pity party, admission for one.

I lean my head back on the recliner and close my eyes, trying to will back the tears that threaten to spill anytime I have downtime, anytime I have a moment to think.

"Sadie?" Smilly pokes her head out of the bedroom door and looks around the corner to where I'm sitting. "I didn't know you were going to be home so early."

"Slow day. Stuart asked for volunteers to go home, and I took the chance. I couldn't be there any longer than I had to be." And that's the truth. Every time I look over at the fountain area, my heart aches, my entire body pounds with misery. It's been unbearable.

"Oh, that's . . . nice." Smilly swallows hard and looks around. "Why are you being weird?"

Letting out a long breath of air, she steps out into the living room wearing a pair of leather ass-less chaps, a black leather bra, and a pink frilly bib. "I was expecting my man to come home any minute now."

I take in her appearance and even though I probably don't want to know the answer, I ask anyway, "What's with the bib?"

She strokes it, in awe of the garment draped over her chest. "Mama has quite the appetite tonight, and she knows it's going to be sloppy." Her sly smile gives it all way. I vomit in my mouth.

I wave my hand in the air, trying to erase the last few seconds. "That . . ." I shake my head. "Nope, for the love of God, never say anything like that again."

She giggles and takes the seat next to me, not caring that I can see her bare ass. If Saddlemire is going to be home soon, there is no way I'm going to be here when he arrives.

"Spoke to Emma today," Smilly says while picking at her nails. "She met up with Andrew at the coffee kiosk. Apparently they talked for quite some time."

"Information I don't need to know." The clench in my jaw almost makes it impossible to respond, my teeth on the verge of cracking. I trust Emma, and I know Andrew wouldn't meet up with her to hurt me. But Emma is probably everything he wants. She's nice. She's not screwed up. She doesn't lie.

Dramatically, Smilly flops to the side, leaning over her chair so she's draping across mine. "Come on, what is taking you so long? Go get him back."

"He doesn't want anything to do with me. He made that quite clear when I went to his house."

"No." Smilly holds up her finger with authority. "He said he didn't want to hold you back. He didn't want to be the one you hid behind. Completely different. He wants you to find yourself. Everybody does, Sadie."

"What, are you holding conventions about me now?"

"Yeah." Smilly leans back in her chair. "Charging ten dollars per entry. I'm banking a shit ton of money with the amount of people who want to see you succeed." She shrugs her shoulder and continues, "So you hit a road block, don't let it stop you from ever moving forward. It's just a speed bump, Sadie. When you were learning to drive, you were blowing over those things, flying in the air without a freaking worry about what might happen. You were fearless."

"More like stupid," I mutter just as Saddlemire busts through the door, whip in hand and smacks his palm with it.

"I'm here, baby." He takes in Smilly and then glances at me. His face falls flat. "I thought she was still at work? We really need to work out a schedule." He then eyes Smilly's bib and says, "Nice bib, babe. I hope it doesn't get too dirty." *I know when I'm not wanted.*

I stand from the recliner and say, "That's enough of that. I'm going to change and get the hell out of here."

It takes me no more than five minutes to change out of work clothes and into a pair of yoga pants and a tight-fitting hoodie sweater. I throw my hair up into a high bun and walk toward the door to grab my purse. I know where I want to go. It's the one place I know I can clear my mind.

"Text me when you're done," I call out, digging in my purse for my keys.

There is giggling behind me, and I don't bother to stick around for a reply. I need to get the hell out of there before the bib is used. Please God, let the bib be burned by the time I get back.

The drive takes me twenty minutes, but once I arrive, I shoot off a quick text and then head to my favorite spot, a broken log next to the shore of Dorchester Lake. I take a seat and tuck my feet under me so my arms can rest on my knees. I lower my chin so it's propped up on my arms and stare out into the calm ripples of the water. The sun is starting to set, but I'm struggling to see the beauty.

There is a certain comfort I seek in this lake. It was there for me when I was a little girl, learning how to splash in the water. It was there when I wore my first two-piece in front of my friends. It was there when I had my first alcoholic beverage, and when I threw up that first alcoholic beverage—sorry, lake. And it was there the day after I miscarried. This lake, this water, it's been the one constant, reliable thing in my life that I've truly counted on. Never judging me, never pushing me, never trying to make me someone I don't want to be. Instead, it has helped me reflect upon the person I truly am.

Leaning forward, I look into the water and see my reflection, the truth right in front of me. I'm not the person I wish I was. I'm tired, depressed, angry, and frustrated with the curveballs I keep getting handed.

A twig snaps behind me. I would be alarmed if I thought someone was trying to sneak up on me, but that's not the case.

He takes a seat right next to me and I don't have to look over to know who it is. His presence. It's unmistakable.

"Quiet night," Tucker says, his voice low. I haven't seen or talked to him since the party, and given our history, I knew if I texted him he would come. That's the kind of relationship we have.

"Yeah. Very quiet. I would have expected to see some teenagers out here, but it's pretty dead."

From the corner of my eye, I see him lean back on the log.

"Remember the time we came here and smoked our first joint together? I stole it from my older brother and we thought it was the greatest thing ever, that was until he caught us and beat me up for taking from his stash."

"And you were laughing the whole time because you were high." I smile at the memory. "After the first two punches, he gave up and left."

"I've never been more grateful for being high." He sighs and says, "We were supposed to go fishing."

"Yeah, and you showed up with no gear and a joint. Fishing was pretty much tossed out the window after that."

"Last thing I wanted to do with you was fish." He nudges my shoulder with his. At the time, the last thing I wanted to do was fish as well. Back then, Tucker was my everything. He was the hometown heartbreaker. The guy every girl wished they could have a chance with, but he never even glanced at them. He only had eyes for me. Apparently nothing has changed.

"We had some good times," I say, starting to feel the tension between us.

He shifts on the log and leans forward, his forearms propped on his thighs as he looks over at me. "We could still have those fun times, but in a more adult manner," he says, but I can sense the serious tone in his voice.

I shake my head. "It would never work out between us."

"Why do you think that?" He sounds insulted. Why doesn't he get this?

I turn to him, my legs still pulled in close to my chest. I see him for the first time and can't help but take him all in from his rugged jeans, to his plain white T-shirt, to his sock hat that hangs loosely off the back of his head. It's his signature look, and the reason every girl in his vicinity wants him.

I don't answer him; instead, I ask a question. "What do you

think would have happened between us if I never got pregnant? Do you think we would have stayed together? We were already starting to drift apart, things weren't steady between us."

"Only because I was working over fifty hours a week while you were at school. I was trying to make something of myself so when you got out of school, you could rely on me while you found your feet. We could make anything work, Sadie."

"But there was so much tension between us, so much anger, didn't you feel it? And be honest, Tucker."

He turns away from me and looks out to the water. When he speaks, his voice is full of heartache. "I always felt like I was losing you, Sadie. No matter what I did, I felt like each kiss pushed me farther away, each phone call, put another mile between us. It's why I stopped trying so damn hard and started working. I figured if I worked, at least I could show you I was planning for our future, that just because I wasn't at college, I could still provide for you."

My heart sinks from his admission. "You never had to prove anything to me, Tucker. I knew from the moment I met you, you were going to do great things. You don't have to go to college to make something of yourself. I hope I never made you feel that way."

"You didn't. But it was intimidating as fuck dating a girl smart enough to go to Cornell. I always felt a little inadequate for you, like you were too good." He glances in my direction, his eyes soft. "You still are."

"That's where you're wrong, Tucker; we've always been equal, always will be. Don't sell yourself short."

"Hard not to when the woman you love won't give you a second chance. There has to be something fucking wrong with me that stops you from revisiting what we had between us."

How do I even explain my feelings toward him without hurting his feelings? Before I can think of a way, he says, "Can I please show you something?"

"Now?"

He nods his head and grabs my hand. "Now."

Not waiting for an answer, he guides me to his monstrous truck and helps me into the passenger side. When he slides behind the wheel, he wastes no time pulling out of the parking spot and getting on the highway, heading south toward Binghamton.

Once off the highway, we weave through Front Street, over the bridge going toward Chenango Valley High School, straight into a residential zone. What on earth does he want to show me? We pass house after house, colonials to Cape Cods flanking the side of the roads until we turn down a dead-end road. He drives to the third house on the right and pulls into the driveway. When he parks, he holds the steering wheel tightly, looking at the little Cape Cod with the gingerbread front and the tiny little garage off to the side.

Looking around, I ask, "Where are we?"

Avoiding all eye contact, he says, "Our house, Sadie."

Our WHAT?

"I bought it when I found out you were pregnant. I wanted a place we could live comfortably as a family, in a secure neighborhood. It was supposed to be a surprise but I never got a chance to show you. The place needed some work. I started working on it so it would be ready by the time you were due, but then we lost the baby and everything came to a halt."

He bought us a house? I can't . . . I don't even know how to process that.

Swallowing hard, he asks, "Do you want to see it?"

I really don't because I know I'll break down, but I also know Tucker really wants to show it to me, so I nod while a lump starts to form in my throat.

Together, hand in hand, he unlocks the front door and guides me inside. I'm immediately greeted by a living room, a white brick fireplace to the right, beautiful oak hardwood floors, and a quaint archway leading into a dining room. Sitting in the corner, a pretty built-in corner shelf, ready for a beautiful set of dishes to be placed in it. Tucker continues to take me through the house, not saying much, just showing me, letting me take it all in. The galley kitchen is perfect. Off-white with vintage-blue glass knobs, a color so vivid it bounces off the white of the cabinets. To the left, off the dining room, there are two equal-sized rooms, one door shut, the other open with a small bathroom in between.

"What's in there?" I ask, pointing to the closed door.

"Nothing," he mumbles and then takes me up the stairs that lead into a finished attic space, which is a master bedroom with multiple closets, lower ceilings, and cute built-in shelves. It's a beautiful space.

He leads me back downstairs and turns to me. "What do you think?"

I speak from the heart. "It's so beautiful, Tucker. I can't believe you bought this for us." Still curious, I walk toward the door that's shut and say, "Why won't you show me what's in here?"

Pain crosses his face. He doesn't say anything, he just opens the door and lets it swing open, revealing a little white crib in the middle of a yellow painted room.

A nursery.

Immediately my throat clogs, and my strength starts to disintegrate with each step forward I take into the room.

It's simple. He hasn't done much besides paint. But the crib—white, vintage with knobby spindles—it's everything I would ever want for a baby. It's so sweet.

My vision starts to blur, and tears cascade down my cheeks. Before the crib, I fall to the ground where I bury my head in my hands. Silent sobs wrack my body.

Tucker wraps his body around mine, holding me closely to his chest.

We sit there, on the floor of our baby's room, crying together for the loss we both suffered. It's not that we lost our baby. It's the relationship we once shared. *All gone. Vanished.* That's what we're grieving.

We had the opportunity to bring something so precious into this world, something so innocent, but we lost it against our will. Sorrow fills the room with each tear that falls from our eyes.

I look up to him, his eyes bloodshot, his cheeks wet, his skin blotchy. He cups my face and very gently brings my lips to his where he lightly kisses me. It isn't sexual; there is no heat behind the kiss. It's for our much-needed comfort. I let my lips linger for a few seconds before I pull away. His hand still cupping my face, I search his eyes.

"You don't love me anymore, do you?" he asks, catching me off guard.

The churning in my stomach kicks up a notch, my anxiety starting to make my body shake. Andrew's words run through my head.

You need to find yourself again.

He's right. I'm in a rut. If I ever want to be happy again—feel whole—I need to get out of it, and it starts right now.

I lace my fingers with Tucker's and look him in the eyes. "I never stopped loving you, Tucker."

His face doesn't fill with hope. Instead he asks, "But you're not in love with me."

There is a difference. Loving someone and being in love with someone. You can love anyone that touches your soul in a way you'll never replace. Never forget. But being in love with someone, that is reserved for a special person, someone who you see yourself spending the rest of your life with. Once upon a time, that was with the man in front of me. A man with a good heart. A man who has loved me for many years. But now? Unfortunately, he's not the man I'll spend the rest of my life with.

Hating that I'm about to cut Tucker deep, I shake my head no.

He nods and lets out a long breath. "You're in love with sturdy tits, aren't you?"

The use of Andrew's nickname causes me to snort, bringing back a flood of memories from the beginning of the summer, when everything seemed less complicated.

Am I in love with sturdy tits? The boy who came out of nowhere, disrupted my life, made me break my rules, made me laugh, made me step outside my comfort zone, and who introduced me to the one and only cannon cock?

Am I in love with him and his penchant for calculators, his knowledge about movies featuring computers, and his incessant love for sugar-free vanilla ice cream?

There's no doubt in my mind.

Yes.

I'm so in love with that man. The man who shed some light on the dark life I merely existed in. The man who, despite my bitchiness, my awful attitude, and my inability to be polite, still wanted to make me smile . . . because *he saw something dark in my eyes.* How could I not be in love with him?

Meeting Tucker's eyes, I nod. "I'm in love with Andrew."

He leans back, a sigh coming from his chest. "Is it the glasses? Because I'm not opposed to wearing glasses."

Laughing, I shake my head. "It's not the glasses."

He nods and stares at the crib, a serious tone again in his voice. "When did I lose you, Sadie?"

"I'm not sure," I say honestly. "I wish I could tell you, but I really don't know."

We sit in silence, both looking around the room, thinking about what could have been, how different our lives would be.

Finally, after what seems like hours, Tucker stands and helps me to my feet. In the dim light of the room, he pushes a flyaway hair behind my ear, his handsome face close enough to kiss. In a soft voice, he says, "I will never stop loving you, Sadie."

I wrap my arms around him and press my cheek against his chest. "I will never stop loving you either, Tucker. It's time, though. It's time we let go of us before we hurt each other more."

He goes stiff in my arms, his breath hitching in his throat. I'm not sure if Tucker will ever truly move on from us, but all I can do is hope and pray he does. From this point moving forward, I am no longer hiding behind anyone. I'm moving forward into my future.

Step number one: closing the door to the past.

I press my palms against Tucker's chest and tell him the one thing I've neglected to say to him for so long. "Thank you, Tucker. I don't think I can say it enough. Thank you for being one of my best friends, for giving me a happy place when my innocent childhood was stripped away from me. Thank you for loving me for who I am, tarnished pieces and all. Thank you for sticking by my side, being my support, being my rock, being *my* man when I needed you. You've been everything to me for so long, but at some point, I know I can't continue to hide behind you and use you as a shield. I have to step out into this world on my own." I press my lips against the palm of his hand, trying to reassure him that no matter what happens, he'll never leave my heart. "We had good times together, Tucker. There is no denying that. But we also had some really tough, hurtful times. I think the hard things that brought us together—pain, betrayal, lies—

ultimately tore us apart. We grew into adults without learning how to *be* adults. We hid behind our past without facing reality. Our relationship became unhealthy, toxic, because we hadn't learned how to behave differently. And then the loss of our baby . . . I think the universe brought us together for a reason, during some of the toughest times of our lives, but I also think it's time to go our separate ways, it's time to grow up, push beyond what we had *and didn't have*, and search out what we're supposed to be. *Who* we're supposed to be."

His jaw clenches, his neck and shoulder muscles tighten. Just from his reaction, I can tell he doesn't agree and it may take him longer to achieve the sense of calm I've found today. But if he is mad, he doesn't let it be known in his words. Hugging me to his chest, he says, "I truly hope you find happiness, Sadie. That's all I want for you." *That's all I want for him too, but it hurts too much to say that yet.*

He kisses the top of my head and then leads me out of the house, making sure to shut off all the lights.

When we're in the car, he says, "It's time you go home. Smilly can help you get your car tomorrow."

With those last words, he drives me home, kisses me on the cheek goodbye, and takes off. It feels as though he is leaving my life forever.

That night, in bed, I go over my action plan for putting my life back together. Tucker is in the back of my mind the entire time.

Please let him find peace. That's all I want for him, peace and happiness.

And please help me through these next couple days. Knowing I have to speak to the one person I have the hardest time talking to, I'm going to need the extra courage. I'm going to need to find the strength within me.

CHAPTER TWENTY-NINE

SADIE

Fall in New York can either go two ways: it can be crisp, sunny, and refreshing, or is can be a haze of cold, casting a grey darkness over your day.

Today, I can barely see the house I grew up in through my front windshield as I sit parked in the driveway. Nerves sting my body, rolling my anxiety to an all-time high. It's taken me a week to gain the courage to come here and even as I sit in my car, staring out the window, I can't seem to make the final few steps.

The strength I need to keep moving forward is non-existent and the one person who I know could get me out of this car is no longer in my life. Pulling out my phone, I go to my contacts and read through some of the last text messages we sent to each other. A smile pulls at my lips from the way he so easily and casually joked around, how he could, with one sentence, put a smile on my face. I miss him, terribly. No, that isn't quite it. I feel like I'm missing a limb. But I now know it isn't him who can make me whole. That is my job. And if I'm incredibly lucky, he might wait for me.

My finger hovers over the keyboard. Should I text him? See

how he's doing? Would he respond? Or would he immediately delete my text message?

With every second that goes by that I don't hear from him, it feels like an ice pick poking at my heart, chipping parts away into bitter crumbles.

The need to reach out is overwhelming, and before I can stop myself, I send him a text message.

Sadie: Hey Andrew. I hope you're doing well and enjoying school.

The minute I send the message, I immediately regret it. *I hope you're doing well and enjoying school?* What am I, his grandma?

"Ughhh." I slouch in my chair wishing Apple would really come up with a way to retract text messages. We have self-driving vehicles, but we can't retract a text message? What is that about, Silicon Valley?

See where desperation gets you? Alone, in your car, outside your childhood home, looking like a pathetic mess of a person with nothing but—

Ding.

A text message. My heart starts beating faster like it's about to burst out of my chest, my palms turn into clammy-ville, and it feels impossible to breathe as I look down at my phone.

The name that registers across the preview screen deflates my entire body, like a helium balloon on the loose.

Dad.

"Shit." Disappointment is the only thing I feel as I read his text message.

Dad: Are you just going to hang out in your car, or are you actually going to come inside?

I text him back, not quite ready to make the move forward after the blow I just suffered.

Sadie: Finishing up some things, be in soon.

I rest my arm on the side of my car door and grip my forehead. What a cruel, cruel joke. The one time my dad decides to text me comes at the most inopportune time.

Taking a deep breath, I gather my purse, snag my keys from the ignition, and stuff everything in my purse. It's time to face the music.

I make my way toward the back door where my dad greets me, opening the screen door for me. We aren't the affectionate father-daughter duo, so he simply greets me with a hello.

Like always, I hang my purse on the coat rack and head into the dining room where I take a seat at the table. My dad joins me, two cups of coffee in his hand, visibly tired. The wrinkles around his eyes show his age and the previously visible laugh lines that framed his mouth seem like they haven't been touched in years. A defeated, lifeless man.

"What has brought upon this surprise visit?" he asks, sitting across from me.

I wrap both my hands around my cup and look up at my dad. "I have something I need to tell you. A few things."

He leans back in his chair, an interested look on his face. "Okay. Are you going to get right to it, or are you going to beat around the bush a bit, lighten the mood?"

"Get right to it." I take a deep breath and look down at my coffee, unable to make eye contact with my dad. "I, uh . . ." I swallow hard. "I dropped out of Cornell, Dad."

He doesn't say anything; he just waits for me to continue. I shift in my seat and glance up at him. His jaw is shifting from side to side, his eyes stern as he looks down at me. Fuck, and I thought that was hard.

I wish Andrew was here right now. How I wish he held my small hand in his large one, lending me his strength.

Taking another deep breath, I continue. "I dropped out because Tucker and I . . . I was . . . pregnant." The words feel like chalk coming off my tongue. I struggle with each word, worried and scared what my dad might say. "We had all the intentions of raising the baby, but a few weeks later, I miscarried. It was the end for Tucker and me."

Silence stretches between us. I fidget, wondering what else I should say. I really don't have any other confessions. I was pretty quick and to the point. And now I just have to wait for my dad to say something.

The drumming of his fingers on the table are the first indication he's about to yell at me. Then it's the clearing of his throat and the shift in his seat.

"Are you not in school now?" I shake my head, no. He slams the table with his hand, startling me almost out of my seat. "Damn it, Sadie. What are you doing then? Just sleeping through your days in a one-bedroom apartment with Samantha? Partying? Wasting your life away? A life I worked damn hard at providing for you?"

"I'm working at Friendly's, Dad." It's a pathetic response, but I have nothing else. *Yet.*

"I see." He nods, his pointer finger steadily tapping on the table. "So, that's it? You're going to be a waitress for the rest of your life? The valedictorian, smartest girl in the tri-state area is going to just give up and be a waitress." He stands and leans over the table. "That's fine, Sadie. Thanks for sharing. Rinse your mug when you're done."

Stunned, I watch him walk away but not before I stand from my seat and call out to him. "That's all you're going to say? That's fine? You're not going to yell at me? You're not to try to knock some sense into me?"

He shakes his head. "You're in your twenties, Sadie. You

should be able to tell right from wrong by now. If you're looking for someone to light a fire under your ass, you're looking at the wrong person."

Furious with my father, with his lack of caring, his own lack of fire, I let loose. "What happened to you?" I shout. "You used to care. You used to push us. Did Mom really take away all of *your* fight?"

Stepping back into the room, his eyes furious now, he says, "You have no fucking clue what I went through with your mother."

"Oh, you don't think so?" I ask. "Because I remember in pristine detail everything that happened, do you know why? Because you told me. You told me everything, Dad. Things I never should have heard when I was that young."

He runs his hand over his face. "You were the only one . . ." He pauses and lets out a long breath. "You were the only one I could talk to." My heart falls from his confession.

"Dad, I didn't—"

"It's in the past, Sadie." He looks up at me, an unspoken apology floating between us. "You want some fire? Fine. Be the person I raised you to be, the accomplished woman with a world of potential at her fingertips. Don't let one setback deter you from the path we set forth for you." Tears start to well up in my eyes. What is with this crying jag lately?

"I can't go back to Cornell, Dad. I lost my scholarship."

He slips his hands in his jean pockets and says, "Luckily for you, Cornell isn't the only school on this planet. Looks like you should start applying."

Nothing else is spoken between us. He walks over, kisses me on the forehead, and then goes to his room where he quietly shuts the door.

Cornell had been my dream ever since I can remember. I had

lived and breathed that future. Funny thing about dreams, they often change.

Like my dad asked, I rinse my mug before I leave. I grab my purse, and head out to my car where I check my phone, hoping and praying. When I see I have no messages, I look down, trying to swallow my grief.

Be the person I raised you to be, the accomplished woman with a world of potential at her fingertips. Don't let one setback deter you from the path we set forth for you.

Dad is right to be angry with me. And it wasn't about the pregnancy, either. It was about who I had become, despite his years of hard work to make a difference in my life. *For my life.*

I need to be my own fire. I need to believe in me again, and be the woman my dad believes I can be. Be the woman *I know* I can be. I'm still broken-hearted. I still ache and burn for the man I love.

But this time, I'm not going to let it hold me back.

I have some work to do.

CHAPTER THIRTY

ANDREW

"How many times are you going to stare at that message?" Jimmy asks, coming up from behind me, looking over my shoulder.

I quickly tuck my phone away even though I know he's already seen what was on my screen. Sadie has sent me a text message every day for the last two weeks. The LAST TWO WEEKS. They are always asking how I am, what I've been up to, and telling me about the weird things Smilly has been doing in their apartment.

And I never answer them. But this last one, it has me itching.

Sadie: Saddlemire just showed me a ring. He's going to propose to Smilly. I'm in cahoots. It's going to be a big surprise with trickery and everything. I can't wait. Wish you could be a part of it.

Her texts have gotten bolder as the days go on. Yesterday she told me how much she misses me.

Well, fuck, I miss her, too, but I meant what I said. She needs to find herself. She needs to stop hiding behind people and face the world for what it's worth. Be what she's worth. If she hid behind me forever, she'd resent me. She'd resent herself for not becoming all she was capable of. I love her, and I want her to be the woman she wants to be. I want that for her. *Even if that is going to be without me.*

Ignoring Jimmy's question, I turn around to face him in the stool I'm sitting on and ask, "Are you ready?"

Speaking of engagements . . .

"Fuck, I'm sweating," he answers, pulling on his tie. "She's going to say yes, right? I mean, she has to say yes, she moved out here for me. She's going to say yes. Fuck." He puts his hands on his head. "What if she says no?"

I chuckle, loving how insecure and nervous my brother is right now. Sounds like a dick thing to say, but trust me, Jimmy could use a little sweating every once in awhile.

"I don't know, man," I say a little uneasy. "I did see her checking out the pizza delivery man the other night."

"Because he had a mole on his face she was concerned about," Jimmy counters. "She's very much into melanoma."

"That's what she wants you to believe."

Jimmy turns, anger on his face. "What's your problem, man? Trying to fuck with me?"

Laughter bubbles out of me as I hold my stomach. Shit, he's too easy right now.

"This isn't funny. I'm really fucking nervous."

Standing from my stool, I grip his shoulders and look him in the eye. "She's going to say yes, bro. You have nothing to worry about. I promise."

"I hope so."

The bedroom door opens and Mae walks out in a purple flowy dress that falls just above her ankles. Her hair is curled and she's wearing the butterfly necklace Jimmy gave her one year ago.

Jimmy and I stand side by side as she approaches. She does a little spin and asks, "How do I look?"

"P-perfect," Jimmy stutters, sweating more than I've ever seen before. It's almost repulsive. I don't know if I should get a towel for him or try to hydrate him as quickly as possible.

"Are you okay?" Mae asks, stepping forward.

"Yeah." He pulls on his collar and swallows hard. I swear, he looks like he's about to—

Before I can finish my thought, Jimmy's eyes roll in the back of his head and he falls to the ground, his body slamming against the carpeted floor. When he hits the ground, the ring box flies out of his pocket right between him and Mae.

Well, that's one way to do it.

Stunned, Mae just stands there, unsure what to do. So being the good brother I am, I kneel down to Jimmy, lift his head and hold out the ring box to Mae.

In a Jimmy-like voice, I say, "Mae, Jimmy wants to know if you'll marry him."

Her hands go to her mouth as she squats down and starts kissing unconscious Jimmy. "Of course, I will. Oh my God, I can't believe it."

I open the box for her and she takes the ring out and places it on her finger. Staring brightly at the diamond, she snuggles into Jimmy's limp body, squeezing him tightly. "Was he that worried about asking me?" She turns back to my lifeless brother and swats him across the shoulder. "Stupid man. Of course I'd say yes."

Feeling like I've done my job here, I give Mae best wishes and ask her to text me when Jimmy wakes up so I know he's okay. He was supposed to propose at dinner, but maybe they'll just stay in now, given his rather untimely fall.

I head to my car and pull out my phone. I have a need to tell someone and the one person I can't seem to get out of my head is the one person I want to tell. Taking a leap like my brother—

or rather a fall—I text Sadie back.

Andrew: Congratulations to Saddlemire for manning up. :) My brother actually just proposed to his girlfriend. He passed out while doing it, but when he wakes up, he'll see he's engaged so all in all, a good day.

Feeling a little lighter, I drive back to my house. The girls are all at practice so I take a quick shower and sign into my computer to start studying. I stare at my screen for a few seconds and then like every other college student, I jump onto Facebook to procrastinate. It's hard to just start studying. I have to warm up first, build up some procrastination guilt before I really dive in. I study better when I feel guilty for wasting so much time.

I scroll through my feed, liking pictures of most of my friends posing with beer cans, as a message pops up in the corner.

Sadie.

My heart skips a beat as I see her picture in the corner, her blonde hair floating over her shoulders and her bright, beautiful smile filling the screen. Fuck, I miss her. I miss her so goddamn much.

Sadie: Hey there. Just got your text. Congratulations to your brother.

Should I write her back? Fuck, who am I kidding? I've already clicked on the text box. I can't hold back. I'm giving in. Just a little friendly conversation, that's all.

Andrew: Thanks. I'm sure when he wakes up, he'll be stoked.

Sadie: He really passed out?

Andrew: Yup, barely got two words out about how nice his fiancée looked before his eyes rolled in the back of his head and he tipped right over, the ring box popping out of his pocket.

Sadie: OMG, I don't mean to laugh, but that's kind of fun-

ny.

Andrew: Don't worry, I was laughing the whole time. Well, that's after I asked Mae for her hand in marriage for my brother.

Sadie: Such a commendable man, you are.

Andrew: I try. (Snaps invisible suspenders)

Sadie: LOL. You would look pretty damn good in suspenders.

I sit back and run my hand over my mouth. Fuck, I'm getting in dangerous territory here, but she's right, I would look good in suspenders. She's just paying me a compliment, that's all.

Andrew: I do believe you're right, but whenever I see them on guys, I always notice how it looks like they have a constant wedgie. Doesn't seem too comfortable.

Sadie: Looking at guys' butts? Has it really been that long since I've seen you, you're checking out men now? I've never turned a guy gay before. I don't know if I should be happy to have my first or nervous. I mean, you were always a little metrosexual anyway, so I can see it.

Say what? Oh, fuck no. What is it with women and thinking I'm gay? If it's the glasses, I'll stomp on them right now.

Andrew: Please, Cannon Cock only likes the pussy.

Sadie: Filling in your douche quota again?

Andrew: Can't let it go unfulfilled. The repercussions are catastrophic.

Sadie: Yeah? What happens?

Settling in, I no longer hold back my smile as I write back.

Andrew: Once your douche quota is revoked, then you have no excuse to make when you act like a douche. Basically ... it makes you a douche.

Sadie: Ah, I see. You realize that makes no sense, right?

Andrew: Made sense in my head.

Sadie: And I guess that's all that matters, right?
Andrew: Damn straight.

●●●

After another long day of lectures, I toss my backpack on the floor of my room, wake my computer up, and log into Facebook. While everything is loading, I unpeel the banana I snagged from the kitchen on my way up and take a giant bite.

My eyes light up when I see the message box from Sadie blinking at me. For some reason, we've resorted to Messenger to keep in touch. I refuse to download the app on my phone, knowing it will be a huge time suck in class, but hell if I don't check when I get home.

Sadie: Stuart really misses you. He says you were the best fountain worker he's had since me.

Laughing, I set my banana down on my desk and type her back.

Andrew: Since you? Doubtful. I take the fucking cake when it comes to scooping ice cream.

Sadie: I could beat you any day. Don't forget who showed you the way.

Andrew: Yeah, while scowling the whole time.

Sadie: Only because I caught you staring at my ass multiple times that day. Sorry for not wanting to be objectified at work.

Andrew: You weren't complaining when I finger-fucked you in the storage closet.

I press send and then cringe. Christ, crossing the line there, Andrew. You're not supposed to be flirting; you're supposed to be . . .

Hell, what am I supposed to be doing? Staying away? Blocking her out? Not talking to her at all?

Yeah, that's not going to happen. I can't. I'm drawn to her. Just because we're talking doesn't mean anything has changed. We're just talking. That's it.

The little bubble pops up to indicate she's typing and when I read her message, I tilt my head back and laugh out loud.

Sadie: That reminds me, the sugar-free vanilla has been very lonely lately. I've tried to tell the old gal that you've moved on but she still has hope.

Andrew: Ah, sugar-free vanilla, my first love. Tell her I miss her.

Sadie: She misses you, too . . .

It doesn't feel like we're talking about ice cream. I miss Sadie like I'm missing my breath.

•••

Sadie: Smilly thinks Saddlemire is cheating on her. She's convinced of it actually and has threatened to cut his face out of all their pictures.

The sound of the message from Sadie pulls me away from my books. Welcoming the much-needed distraction, I type back.

Andrew: I didn't know people still printed pictures.

Needing to get a little more comfortable, I detach my laptop from my docking station and sit on my bed. I position my pillows just right so I'm leaning against the wall, my back supported.

Sadie: Smilly is old school like that. She has actual physical photo albums.

Andrew: That is old school. I don't even think my parents have photo albums anymore. Did you try to calm her down?

Sadie: Yeah. I gave her a bag of Doritos and turned on The Crown. She seems to have settled down.

Andrew: When does he propose?

Sadie: Not for another two weeks. He's basing it around his parents' wedding anniversary. He's pretending to throw a party for them, when in fact, he's going to propose on the Washington Street Bridge.

Andrew: Man, that's a long time. He better hold her off. Getting your head cut out of pictures seems painful.

Sadie: He's aware of her insanity.

Andrew: Good.

I pause and bite the inside of my cheek as I type out my next sentence.

Andrew: How have you been?

I see Emma every week. We meet up for coffee between one of our classes, but we never talk about Sadie. We keep it friendly, mostly about school. I've been tempted many times to ask her what Sadie has been up to, but I've held off. I've held strong up until this point, but I'm weakening with these messages. She's breaking me down. I have to fucking know.

Sadie: Good. I've been good.

I stare at her answer. No elaboration? No update on her life? I was kind of hoping she would tack on a little more information than just telling me she's been good. Fuck, this is frustrating. It is what it is though. She wasn't willing to let me into her life when we were seeing each other. Why the fuck do I think she'll do things differently now? We're still at that forlorn place, it seems.

Andrew: I'm glad.

It's official; things just got awkward.

Sadie: Smilly is trying to cut the photos again. I have to go. Have a good night.

Before I can answer, her little green bubble in the corner of the messenger box goes grey, indicating she's logged out. Damn it. I guess some things will never change.

I don't know why I thought they would. *Hope is a bastard.*

CHAPTER THIRTY-ONE

SADIE

"This was a stupid idea. Like really stupid." I say, pacing back and forth, a knot of dread filling my stomach.

"Just calm down." Emma pats my hand. "Everything will be okay."

"No. I'm not ready. He's not ready. This isn't the right time." I shake my head and try to stand from the bench we're sitting at.

"You told me yesterday how it's time, and I couldn't agree more. It's time, Sadie."

"What if he doesn't want to see me? What if he walks right past me? I will literally be crushed."

"He's not going to walk right by you. He might be shocked to see you, but you said so yourself the other day how you two have been talking non-stop. You need to capitalize on that. It's time."

"But—"

"There he is." Emma points toward the back exit of the lecture hall where a group of students are exiting doors. You would think with the amount of students leaving the building, it would be hard to spot Andrew, but it's not.

He's taller than most of the students, his hair coiffed to the side, his thick-rimmed glasses giving him that sexy-nerd vibe, and the cardigan he's wearing over a T-shirt . . . Christ, my heart is rapidly pounding out of my chest.

"Oh my God, he looks so good."

"Girl, I know. If you weren't in love with him, I would have made a move by now."

"In love?" I ask, a question in my voice.

Emma gives me a pointed look. "Please, don't even try to deny it."

I swallow hard and watch him stare down at his phone as he walks. "I won't."

"Good. Now, when he gets over here, I'm going to bolt to give you two some room."

"No, stay. I need you as a buffer." I hold on to her arm in desperation.

She shakes me off and stands from the bench, as Andrew draws in closer. "You don't need me. Just be yourself and tell him the *truth*." She emphasizes the word truth. Noted. I learned my lesson the first time.

We both watch Andrew approach. When he pockets his phone and looks up, my breath catches in my throat. His eyebrows shoot up for a second in surprise, until a bright smile appears on his face, melting me right there in front of the nursing school coffee kiosk.

"Oh God, that smile. Sadie, you are one lucky girl."

"I'm not yet."

"No, you are." Emma quickly squeezes my hand. "That smile is all for you."

Andrew covers the distance between us in no time. He holds on to the straps of his backpack as he says, "Hey Emma, who's your hot friend?"

A wave of giddiness falls over me.

"Sadie. She's going to be attending classes this coming spring here at Binghamton. Thought I would show her around campus." Emma looks at her pretend watch and then snaps her finger. "Oh darn, I forgot I have professor hours to attend. Do you think you could show her around for me?"

Andrew scans me up and down, the sexiest look ever on his face as he bites his bottom lip and nods. "I think I could show her a thing or two."

Fuck. Me.

"Okay, I'll leave you two alone then." Emma gives me a hug, pats Andrew on the arm, and then takes off, leaving us alone.

Fidgeting in place, I lamely say, "Hey."

His face softens and he doesn't say a word as he pulls me into a hug. His strong arms wrap around me, enveloping me, spreading warmth through my limbs. I breathe in his cologne, committing this moment to memory. *This is where I've wanted to be. This is where I want to stay.*

He presses his cheek to my head and says, "I missed you, Sadie."

I promised myself I wouldn't cry, but with those four little words, tears are starting to fall from my cheeks.

"I missed you so much," I mutter into his chest.

When he pulls away, he cups my face and wipes away my tears with his thumbs. "Want to sit down?"

I nod, but when I think we're going to sit on the bench Emma and I were just sitting on, he leads me away, his hand in mine, and guides me to the library, where he takes me into a private studying room.

He shuts the door, tosses his backpack on the table, and then turns toward me. "So you're a bearcat now?" I unzip my jacket and show him the Binghamton University shirt I purchased at the student union. He smiles and takes a seat, guiding me to the chair next to him. He turns me so we're facing each other and says, "Tell me everything."

This is the moment, the one *he's* been waiting for, the one he asked for all summer.

"Earlier this year, I dropped out of Cornell because I was pregnant with my boyfriend's baby. Tucker and I had been dating off and on for quite some time and when we found out I was pregnant, Tucker thought it was going to be the glue we needed to finally stay together. I wasn't convinced a baby could fix the problems we were having, so when I miscarried, I took it as a sign. We weren't supposed to be together. I ended it with him. I then collapsed into a dark hole where I ate, slept, worked, and partied with my friends. It was familiar, easy, just what I needed. And then I met you." I lace my fingers with his. "You changed everything. You showed me how to smile again, how to laugh, how to forget, and I became addicted. I became so damn addicted, Andrew, that I didn't want to bring my past into what we had, so I hid it. I wanted to maintain our high, the happiness surrounding us. I was too damn scared to tell you the truth in fear that you would leave me, or think differently of me. I realized quickly that I couldn't lose you." I take a deep breath and look him in the eyes. "But I did anyway, because I wasn't honest and I don't blame you for being mad. I only blame myself. I was terrible to you, and I can understand if you don't want to be with me again, but I have to tell you . . ." scooting a little closer, I take a leap and say, "I love you, Andrew. I love you so much."

I look down at our connected hands, too afraid to see his reaction, but when he lifts my chin and his warm eyes meet mine, I struggle to hold in more tears. *This man.*

"Why the fuck did it take you so long to come back to me?" he asks, pulling me onto his lap now as tears fall from my eyes onto his cardigan.

"I had to fix some things in my life. I wanted to become a woman you'd feel proud of, not someone you had to shield."

His hand wraps around my neck as he presses his forehead against mine. "I never hid you, baby. You hid yourself."

I sigh, loving the way he feels against me. "I'm not hiding anymore, I promise."

"Good." He presses his lips against mine, softly, exploring, revisiting. He feels so good, tastes like heaven, smells like home. When he pulls away, he looks me in the eyes and says, "I'm so in love with you, Sadie, so fucking hard."

He grips the back of my neck tightly and kisses me with all the pent-up passion I've missed so much and yearned for. I match his intensity, thanking whoever wants to listen for a second chance with this brilliant and incredibly giving man. This man who swept me off my feet with one smile, one look through those glasses, one cheery attitude, and let's not forget one cannon cock.

He's not my everything, because I don't need him to be. I am whole and complete on my own. But I know in my heart that we're better together. *I* am better with him. He holds my heart, and will hopefully want to hold it forever.

EPILOGUE

ANDREW

"SURPRISE!" we shout at the top of our lungs as Sadie walks into the house holding a stack of books against her chest.

Startling, she jumps in place, psychology books toppling to the floor, and a screech of shock pops out of that gorgeous little mouth of hers.

"Happy Birthday!" Katja fist-pumps the air and blows a birthday horn, the other girls on the basketball team joining her.

Holding her chest, Sadie looks around at the mishmash of friends in the living room/dining room combo of my college house. Friends from her childhood, from school, and Binghamton's women's and men's basketball teams scatter around the small space, holding drinks in their hands, cheering her on.

I walk up to her and put my arm around her waist, pulling her in close to my chest. I kiss the side of her head and whisper, "Happy birthday, baby."

"I had no idea." Continuing to look around, she asks, "How did you even plan this?"

"How do you think?" I look over at Smilly, who is refilling drinks from a Gatorade cooler we borrowed, thanks to Leena's sticky fingers. We filled it with a concoction of vodka and rum, as well as juice to make our own special Sadie cocktail.

Sadie scans the room. People have returned to their conversations, games, and eating. Homemade decorations scatter throughout the space as well as Christmas lights, providing more light to the room. "This has Smilly written all over it."

"You got that right." I kiss her again on the forehead and then bend down to pick up her books. "But don't be fooled, this was all my idea, Smilly just helped make it happen."

"Trying to win brownie points?" she asks, smiling up at me.

I pull her toward the stairs as people shout happy birthday to her when we walk by and I whisper in her ear. "I'm always trying to win brownie points, baby."

Music starts to play and the party is underway as Sadie and I go upstairs to drop off her books. When we reach the top of the stairs, instead of turning to the left, we turn to the right and enter the biggest room in the house where Sadie and I reside. After having Sadie over almost every night once we made up, the girls decided to make her a permanent fixture of the house. Leena gave up her room for us but demanded one thing: once a month she was allowed to have Topless Tuesday while watching Fixer Upper. Needless to say, those are the days I'm locked up in my room, having my own Topless Tuesday party with Sadie.

It's a win-win for everyone. It's been four months of brilliance, and a whole lot of orgasms courtesy of cannon cock. I love waking up with my girl. I did ask her if she had considered re-piercing her nipples, as from the moment Smilly mentioned it, what feels like so long ago, I've had a half chub. The girl has great nips. What can I say? What I won't say is what she wanted me to pierce if she had hers redone. Fucking. Hot.

I shut the door behind us and toss her books on the futon—yes, our bedroom has a futon in it, that's how much extra space we have. Sadie turns to me and wraps her arms around my neck. "I can't believe you did this. I told you we didn't have to do anything."

"Yeah, that was never going to happen. This was your first birthday as my girlfriend, and I wasn't going to fuck that up."

I reach behind me and grip the box I expertly wrapped earlier, and when I say expertly, I mean crinkled paper on top of each other and held it down with tape.

"Here, open this." I scoot the box between us so she's forced to open it.

"You got me something too? I thought the three orgasms you gave me this morning along with the donuts was my present."

I shrug casually. "What can I say, I like to spoil my girl." I nod at the package. "Go ahead, open it."

Giddy with excitement, she rips open the box, tears away the tissue paper and . . . pauses. She raises an eyebrow at me as she pulls out her gift. She lifts it into the air and asks, "Are you kidding me?"

Containing the laugh that wants to bubble out of me, I say, "I saw it in the store window and knew you just had to have it."

"What kind of fucked-up store window were you looking through?"

"Macy's," I answer without pause. "They have a new department."

She shoves my shoulder and laughs. "You are such a liar." She looks down at the gift again and says, "Where did you find a dick on an ice cream cone dildo?"

"You would be surprised what someone can find on the Internet."

"I'm afraid to ask. Did you search this out?" The look of horror on her face is priceless.

I loop my arm around her waist, take the penis-cone dildo

and stroke it along her cheek. Immediately she swats it away, laughing and pinching my side. Need to trim those lobster claws. "Don't touch me with that thing."

"What? You don't want a penis cone?"

She lightly pushes me away and goes to our shared closet where she starts rifling through her clothes. "I don't want the penis cone coming anywhere near me."

"Aw, come on." I step closer as she starts undressing down to her underwear. "I had an entire evening planned with penis cone and fudge."

Standing in just a bra and her thong, she puts her hand on her hip. "Fudge can stay, penis cone has to go."

Once again, I loop my arm around her waist and move my hand over her bare ass, loving the way it feels in my palm. "You're going to be missing out. Penis cone was really excited about meeting your vagina tonight." The teasing in my voice pulls that beautiful smile out of her.

"Maybe penis cone is more interested in meeting what you have to offer?" She suggestively lifts her eyebrows.

Err . . . is she referring to . . . that?

Her laugh breaks through the pause in my thoughts, and she distances herself to put a dress on right before the door to our bedroom flies open.

"You're naked!" Smilly screams, taking in the scene in front of her. When she realizes we are in fact fully clothed, her shoulders slouch. "Jesus, if you two aren't naked, what the hell are you doing?"

I turn to Smilly and hold up penis cone and say, "I'm trying to convince Sadie to play with me tonight."

Stepping forward, awe in her eyes, hands extended, Smilly asks, "Is that a penis on an ice cream cone?"

Peeking past me, Sadie adds, "And it's a dildo."

"Sweet mammary glands, that's the best thing I've ever seen." She snags it from my grip and examines it. "God, I want to stick it in every orifice of my body." She goes to put it in her mouth when I stop her.

"Stop, it's not a popsicle. That's for Sadie's vagina."

"It's okay. We can share."

"No, we can't," Sadie protests. "Don't make it seem like we've shared dildos before."

Smilly rolls her eyes. "Such a prude. Are you two going to come down to the party? There are a lot of people waiting to get Sadie twisted." She looks me up and down. "Might be in your best interest if you want to use penis cone tonight."

Smilly does have a point . . .

I clap my hands and say, "She's right, we should really get down there."

Sadie chuckles, grips my arm, and speaks to Smilly. "We'll be down in a second."

"Don't dawdle." Smilly walks out of the bedroom and just before she shuts the door, she adds, "I made blueberry buckle, your favorite, and those basketball Amazons are doing a number on it."

The door slams shut, leaving me alone with Sadie once again. Turning me toward her, she cups my face, a sweet smile caressing her lips. "Thank you for tonight, Andrew. You're such a good man."

I push her hair behind her ears, loving how that look of complete and utter love in her face is meant for me and only me. "Anything for Sturdy Tits." I wink and then press a kiss against her mouth. When I pull away, I sincerely say, "I love you, baby."

"I love you, too." Instead of kissing me again, she pulls me into a hug and presses her cheek against my chest.

It almost seems unreal, that a year ago I was in the midst of transferring to another school, wondering if I would ever be able to jump the confines of my parents and the confines of "cannon cock." And then I got a job, a job where never in a million years did I think I would meet the love of my life, a girl who wanted nothing to do with me, who was so closed off, she wouldn't even welcome in new friends. And yet, here I am with Sadie in my arms, the girl of my dreams going to school with me, living in my house, and every day handing more and more of herself over to me. I know about her past, the humiliation she suffered at the hands of her family, the friendship and love she had with Tucker, which was so invaluable at the time. When we talked about the baby, and the room Tucker had prepared, she cried. But I didn't see the dark agony in her expression. It was as if she'd accepted it as part of her history, but could see it didn't have to determine her future. Even though she hasn't said much about her dad that makes me want to know the guy well, I am sincerely grateful he told her to chase her future. Realize her potential. He was right. He'd raised an incredible, accomplished woman who did indeed have the world at her fingertips. And I've gained the trust of her heart, which grows with each passing day. Fuck, I'm a lucky bastard.

It wasn't easy, but hell, whoever said the best things in life are easy? Sadie Montgomery was once my coworker whose façade sometimes matched the chilly environment we worked in. I then got to know sturdy tits, and yes, they were the best bosoms I'd ever motorboated. No. Lie. Then my heart broke when she became the co-WRECKER, and I thought I'd lost my heart and her forever. Now? She's the fucking love of my life—a title she will never lose.

Although, we have played around with the names Cannon Tits and Sturdy Cock . . .

THE END

Made in United States
Troutdale, OR
03/30/2024

18844350R00206